Sugar and Spice

Other Black Lace anthologies:

PANDORA'S BOX
PANDORA'S BOX 2
MODERN LOVE
PAST PASSIONS

Sugar and Spice

A Black Lace short story collection

Black Lace novels are sexual fantasies.
In real life, make sure you practise safe sex.

First published in 1997 by
Black Lace
332 Ladbroke Grove
London W10 5AH

Typeset by SetSystems Ltd, Saffron Walden, Essex
Printed and bound by Cox & Wyman Ltd, Reading

ISBN 0 352 33227 1

Contents

Introduction

✧ ✧

The Black Lace imprint has been known, since its inception in 1993, for its pioneering erotic novels – all of them written by women, with women in mind.

Our anthologies of extracts from Black Lace novels – the two *Pandora's Box* collections, along with *Modern Love* and *Past Passions*, have included a number of original short stories, and these have been greeted enthusiastically by our readers.

I am therefore very pleased to be able to introduce *Sugar and Spice*, the very first Black Lace anthology consisting entirely of original short stories. As ever, they are written by women, and they have all been written specifically for this collection.

The stories are as diverse, imaginative and arousing as women's sexual fantasies. And as we know, women's sexual fantasies are very diverse, imaginative and arousing.

Read and enjoy.

Kerri Sharp
August 1997

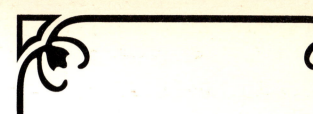

*Closely-Related
Strangers*

Larissa Hartley

Closely-Related Strangers

✢ ✢

*A*nna had spent the last four hours scouring the whole damn city for a copy of her brother-in-law's latest book. She remembered David speaking on the phone to his brother nearly six months ago, refusing to accept a gift of the book and insisting that he would buy a copy ('No, hell, make it ten') to support his little brother where it counts – financially. Typical David: bombastic, extravagant and never making time to get around to doing it himself. So here she was, the day before David's brother arrived, walking around the whole city on a miserably wet and grey day. Obviously the publication was not going to shoot its author to stardom, as most of the sales staff she asked had no idea what she was talking about, or else had heard of it, but had not bothered to order any more than the one or two already sold. There was no time to order it and she had been to all the bookstores she knew. Most of the lifeless salespeople were so indifferent to her plight that she was starting to doubt she would ever find it. In the last store she went into, the woman directed her to a small bookshop on Grey Street, in an inner-city suburb about fifteen minutes' tram ride away. Finally, spurred on by this tiny ray of hope, she went on a renewed effort to find the elusive book.

As soon as Anna walked into the bookstore she knew she liked it. It was the sort of store that reflected the owner's interests rather than the accommodation of best-sellers and conventional favourites. She would have to come back and explore this place in her own time. Right now, she just wanted to find this book and go home. The woman behind the desk knew the work and went to the rear shelf to collect it. Anna was surprised at the size of the book, a hardcover coffee-table book. She had known it was a collection of photographs and text, but she hadn't realised that it was of such a professional standard. She also hadn't expected it to cost so much and had to pay with plastic. She certainly wasn't going to start wandering around in search of a bank now.

On the tram trip home Anna felt relieved to be able to sit down for a few moments with her mission completed. The rain had diminished to a light drizzle and the sun was starting to break its way through the clouds. The general mood of the crowds always seemed to change according to the weather. Anna felt a buzz from being surrounded by people who appeared positive and energetic. Even the two women sitting opposite her seemed livelier in their conversation: they kept touching each other's hand or leg. One of them caught her eye – she realised she must have been staring for some time and quickly averted her gaze. God, that was a bad habit. She felt her face burn as she realised both women were aware of receiving her attentions. Anna busily made a point of concentrating on opening her package and decided to take a look at her brother-in-law's 'masterpiece' so as to avoid any similar confrontation.

The front cover was a simple black and white image of a naked young male. The photo was constructed to give the illusion of a framed painting. There was a large, carved wooden frame within the photo that also acted as the edge of the picture plane itself. The young man was standing in a pose that suggested he was about to step out of the portrait and right into Anna's appreciative gaze. His long, smooth fingers were actually holding firmly on to the frame and his left foot was raised as if to step out and forward. His body was not that of a statuesque demi-god, but he had a smooth definition and a confident approach that was much more carnal. His eyes were staring directly into Anna's and the corners of his mouth were upturned, not offering his audience a full smile, but suggesting a wickedly humorous edge to his personality. She let her gaze fall downwards to fully inspect this extremely pleasing vision. The young man's penis was hanging down between his legs in a semi-erect state, giving a sense of heaviness and pliability. To Anna it seemed like an invitation to touch, as if prompting her to tease it to its full potential. She could imagine herself tracing the edge of his penis with her

4

fingers, clasping them around the thick girth and pulling upwards, feeling the skin of his cock gliding over his stiffening muscle. Anna suddenly stopped. She realised she had been gliding her finger over the cover of the book, and started to smile to herself. The idea of touching someone purely in sexual intent always excited her, but she had not met anyone who could really offer such undiluted physical pleasure without at least a few (and, more often than not, a lot more) human complications in tow. But Anna had been known to be a little harsh in certain assessments. Certainly no one had been able to offer themselves as frankly as the image before her now. The thought of running her hands over his smooth thighs, and then behind him to squeeze the round cheeks of his arse, brought a self-satisfied grin to Anna's face. She wondered how such a young man would react to her tongue lapping at his nipples, to her catching one in her teeth and tugging on it like a pliable plaything. Would his cock start to rise then? If she cupped his balls in her hand and gently pressed them together, playing with the hairs that covered them, would he open his mouth with a slight moan and offer up his soft lips for her to kiss, suck, bite and lick? Would she be able to hear his breathing become more rapid, would she see his desire in his surrendering face; could she control his response from one action to the next? Ah yes, Anna definitely thought she could – now that would be pleasure.

She was so engrossed in her thoughts, and the tingling sensation of her skin that they created, that she hadn't realised the somewhat excited attention she was receiving from the two women opposite her. Anna looked over the edge of her book at the couple only to be confronted by their pointed stares and unabashed smiles. They started to collect their things together to get off the tram. One woman, with dark hair and red lips, leant across to say something in her partner's ear. The pair stood up, laughing at their shared secret, which for some bizarre reason Anna seemed to be a part of. The brunette again looked directly at Anna, raised her eyebrows slightly and gave her the broadest and most deliciously wicked grin Anna had earned for some time. After jumping from the steps of the tram, they both looked back at her before proceeding down the footpath arm in arm.

Anna was slightly bemused: she had always thought her appearance was fairly straight-looking, especially with the tell-tale wedding band branded on her finger. Certainly, she had never been singled out with such overt sexual playfulness before. She was surprised, a little embarrassed, and certainly flattered. However, as she was returning to her exploration of the book cover she noticed that the couple who had been sitting in the seat adjacent to her admirers were staring at her as well. The middle-aged woman looked at Anna with great disdain, and with pursed lips pointedly moved her attention elsewhere. The woman nudged her male partner in the side as an instigation to follow her lead, but not before Anna had caught his sheepish glance directed straight at her book. With an inward groan of horror, realisation came flooding over Anna. In her submission to social decorum she had, of course, been looking at her portrait of naked male flesh with the book upright so as to hide the view from those around her. Now blindingly clear to her was the fact that an even more interesting photo must be accompanying the blurb on the back cover. She quickly flipped the book over and was accosted by a powerfully sexual image of three amazing women with mouths, tongues, cunts and fingers locking each figure to the others. The women's bodies were, like the cover photo, overpoweringly close to the viewer. The image created a mass of flesh out of their strong, rounded thighs and buttocks. One woman's derrière was pushing itself out toward the viewer, as if to force itself into Anna's space, demanding to be touched, licked, pleasured. The very image of such beautifully rounded flesh made her skin start to flush, but instead of being appalled at her social transgression, she was amused and pleased. She liked the photo, it made her feel bold that people had associated this image with her. Anna was getting turned-on. She got up from her seat and pulled the cord signalling the next stop. As she was stepping down from the tram she looked back up towards the couple still seated there, and this time it was her turn to throw someone a large smile.

It was still only about five o'clock by the time Anna had walked into the house, poured herself a glass of chilled white, and sat down on the over-large couch in the lounge. She put on one of her more soulful CDs, kicked off her shoes and decided to really have a good look at this book. She was beginning to wonder just what sort of man David's brother was. She had only met him a few times before (David wasn't big on family get-togethers) and knew that physically he was a lot like David. David was average in height, but had nice broad shoulders with a strong chest and arms. Unlike the picture of the man she was admiring on the bookcover, David was a lot more solid.

She opened the book for the first time. She began to read the introduction and was surprised to learn that the publication was actually a collaborative effort. David's brother was the photographer, but the writer was a woman and, even more intriguingly, she was also one of the models who appeared in the book. Anna liked this twist, it added to her pleasure. With every picture she beheld she would be compelled to study each woman individually and wonder: did she write this? Is it her?

There was a picture of a woman with a stubble of dark hair on her head and no hair whatsoever between her legs. She was seated on a black settee in a large, open room. The wall behind her was a large window looking out to a smooth, sloping hillscape. The left wall was flat and tinted a scarlet red, in the corner a door was slightly ajar. The woman had one leg up on the settee and her elbow resting on her knee. She was caught in the act of lightly brushing her open palm back and forth, against the bristles of hair on her scalp. Beside her foot, resting on the settee, lay an open book. The woman was completely absorbed in her reading, the expression on her face was one of real concentration. Her dark eyebrows were raised and wide, and her mouth a little open in an ever-so-slight sneer, as if to suggest her criticism of something just read. Her left arm was resting in her lap, her fingers toying with her smooth mound: her fingers reached within her lips and delicately exposed her delight to Anna. Anna felt a great desire to be near this woman, just to let her easy sensuality affect her own. The thought of touching her made her conscious of her own body: the heaviness of her breasts, the strength of her arms, the smoothness of her belly and the tautness of her limbs. The woman inspired Anna to explore her own self rather than disturb the woman's solitary contentment.

By this time, Anna was beginning to relish every sensation of her body, and the need for fleshly satisfaction required her to put aside Paul's book and concentrate solely upon herself. She placed herself on the lounge floor, practically centre-stage within the room. Her legs faced the closed doorway, on the opposite wall the uncovered window gaped upon the scene. She sat cross-legged on the soft carpet and listened to the sound of the music, letting the noise of traffic fade into the background. She squeezed and released her breasts, savouring the feeling of the soft, round flesh. Through the cloth of her shirt the warmth of her flesh intensified the movement of her hands. With the centre of her palms she rubbed the tip of her erect nipples, moving her hands up and down then side to side. Her actions became quicker and more frenzied.

She quickly lifted her shirt up and over her head. The points of her nipples felt as hot as fire from the friction between the delicate flesh and the coarseness of her palm. She lifted her left breast and caught her nipple in her mouth, sucking on it like a baby. Her other hand plunged downwards and she began to rub herself up and down, along the inside of her lips; long, gliding motions from her clit to the entrance of her vagina. As she licked her own nipple, flicking the edge with her warm, wet tongue, she forced her legs to open even wider and began to tickle her clitoris with the tip of her finger, then moving down lower to lightly finger her portal.

Anna always suffered from impatience, and her desire for release had to be overcome by extreme self-control. Nothing would have pleased her more than a vigorous finger mastur-bation, or what she called the 'clit offensive', whereby she violently pulled and rubbed herself with pointer and index, sometimes catching her button between them, pushing it aside again and nearly beating it senseless until she groaned from the very depths of her body and shivered to the very tip of every nerve. Indeed, nothing would have pleased her more than that, except of course the extra delight that comes from extending her teasing and making her lust grow to barbaric proportions, increasing to a moment of release to absolute liberation. She was also desperate to feel the warmth of another's flesh, knowing that at any moment her husband was going to walk into his home and, Anna had determined, was going to fuck her senseless.

She heard the key in the front door. She knew David would come directly into this room to dump his things and she could not wait to see the look on his face. She opened her legs wider and rubbed her swollen lips with her wet fingers. She knew the light of the hallway would fall directly on to her pussy, and could imagine that the glistening sight would create quite a pretty picture. Anna was eager with anticipation: her little plan gave her an arrogant pleasure, she liked being in control. She felt akin to the woman in her wonderful book – she of course now thought of it as her own, the fruit of her labours so to speak. She loved her body, she loved being in this exposing position and was eager for her audience. Even more eager for a vigorously responsive audience.

She leant her head back on to the carpet when she heard the door opening. Each hand was on either side of her cunt, spreading her lips wider, then pushing them back together again. Her arms were forcing the sides of her breasts upward, so they were pressed together and her nipples were jutting straight up into the air. She knew exactly what David would be witnessing and she knew exactly what she wanted him to do. Anna, deciding to vocalise her intentions, moaned softly, 'Come inside, baby, closer so I can taste you.'

Confused by the delay of her lover's response, Anna lifted her head to look at him. Her jaw dropped and a horrified squeak was all that she could manage to welcome her brother-in-law. Instinctively she closed her palms over her gaping sex: a delicately modest act that made her previous lascivious behaviour only more appealing by contrast. A few feet in front of her, Paul was standing transfixed to the spot at which he had entered, his hands clutching each side of the open doorway. He could not believe the sight laid out before him, but he would never let embarrassment deprive him of the intense pleasure of being greeted in such a unique manner. A pleasure made all too visible to Anna by his unusual expression, that could only be described as akin to an adolescent, glazed bliss, and the fact that at the crotch of his jeans there was a substantial bulge rising. Anna could not help but also notice Paul's very broad chest covered by a tight white T-shirt. His nipples were standing up hard and straight, like two young and eager cadet soldiers. His dark eyes were glued to Anna's sumptuous body. Any semblance of rational, mind-over-matter self-control was rapidly vanishing.

Within this short time of studying her masculine apparition, Anna marvelled at the frantic and uncohesive collection of thoughts bombarding her mind and, later, could only attribute it to the panic of the situation. After her initial horror had dissipated, she began to feel the stirrings of illicit enjoyment at having this man as her captive audience. She wondered what sort of person could take photographs that made her drool with lust and greed. She thought of her beautiful young man on the cover, the fleshy thighs of the women, the lips of the shaven reader, the mesh of swollen breasts and mouths. It crossed her mind that she could now feel what it would be like to let herself be photographed, to be viewed. She thought of the women on the train, the red-lipped smiles, the wicked eyes, and the disapproval of the others. She began to realise, with great amusement and a touch of relief, that she was indeed what many people would consider perverse.

Despite the transfixtion of the two people, the music was still smoothly dancing its way around the room and the sunlight softly caressing Anna's skin, falling along the curves of her thighs and flickering across her breasts and stomach. It was one of those moments when everyone holds their breath in suspense and no one is really in control of what comes next. A lot of people just let things happen, wash over them like a wave: call it fate, destiny, karma, or even indecisiveness, weakness, fear. Anna was one of these. How often had she claimed the excuse, 'Well, it just happened'? In this instance, it was just a little movement that caused one action to roll into the next. Anna, in her new state of delectation, closed her eyes once more and rested her head back on the floor. This movement was, not directly and not indirectly, an invitation, or perhaps a resignation – whatever happens, happens.

Paul walked towards her and knelt down in front of her. He rested his heavy, large hands on her knees and slowly progressed their way up her thighs. They kneaded her flesh with a savouring touch. He lightly brushed the insides of her thighs with his fingers, then cupping the pockets of flesh just below her hips, worked his way under her buttocks, which were so round and soft to the touch. Paul was a man who adored a woman's body: the way it looked, smelt, felt, and the always astounding things it could accomplish and provoke. The whole time he was touching Anna's legs, his eyes were consuming every inch of her. His stroking relaxed her body; his tickling excited her and caused her to make little, short intakes of breath. Her hips raised to ease his hands underneath her and he forced her body further toward him, enclosing her cleft with his lips as if drinking from a glass spilling over with rich, dark red wine. He kissed her, pressing his mouth hard against her sex and then slowly releasing the pressure, but letting his lips linger, and finally relinquishing his repast with the solitary lapping of his tongue. Again he would kiss Anna in this manner, repeat it, and repeat it until she was at the fervent pitch that she had reached herself only a few moments earlier. But he refused to relent, despite the pleading edge to her sighs, moans and groans (not to mention the somewhat unsubtle grunts that escaped her dainty mouth, and the repeated thrust of her hips). Paul paused for a moment, he lifted his head and his own saliva, mixed with Anna's more intimate emission glistening around his mouth and down his chin, was quickly wiped off as he pulled his white T-shirt over his head. He quickly undid his buckle, pulled open the buttons of his jeans in one swinging motion, and frantically pulled them off (including his underwear), all the while not taking his eyes off Anna's exposed body. Naked, muscles straining within his skin, his lovely penis standing to attention, Paul quickly dived back in.

Anna loved to be indulged, and there was no greater feeling than this physical, sexual, solicitous experience that was making her feel alive from head to foot. Lifting her neck, she watched the head of this young man, like some burrowing animal, devouring her cunt. When he glided his tongue up along her lips, reaching its way to tease and suck on her clitoris, she looked into his face and thought he was the most beautiful man she had ever seen. However, in Anna's opinion a man always looked his most radiant, most exquisitely perfect when he was between her thighs; how often had she thought herself to be in love when looking upon her lover from this elevated position? She kept muttering to herself, 'Heaven', because, surely, she was very nearly there. She wanted to grab this man's head and grind herself right into his face, she wanted to suffocate him with her pussy. She wanted him hard and she wanted him inside her body. She writhed on the floor, grabbing her breasts and playing with her nipples. She pulled on them and squeezed them until they were red raw and tingling, and felt so erect and hard she could use them as some outrageously dangerous, inviolable military weapon. She rubbed her hands down the length of her torso, delighting in the lines and curves of her own body, but stopping before she reached the top of his head. She concentrated on her own pleasure, she was getting frantic, bucking her hips, arching her back. When Paul starting sucking on her clit, hard and long, like it was a miniature penis, Anna started grimacing in sweet pain. His arms moved from underneath her to glide along her body, reaching for her breasts. He found one globe for each large hand and started to milk them with firm squeezing motions. His shoulders were pushing up against her, forcing her legs above them where they were left stranded, waving obscenely in the air. How he continued to breathe, with her muff stuck in his face the whole time, was a wondering notion niggling in the back of Anna's mind.

Paul lifted his right hand to rifle through his jeans pockets. Lifting a small packet from one of them he quickly tore it open with his teeth, and began to place the sheath upon his muscle which had grown to an astonishing size during the course of events. Anna was on the verge of violent release when he had momentarily paused. When he plunged his prick into her, forcing her skin to pull back tightly, crushing and stretching her clitoris with the motion, squashing his heavy, tight balls against her cheeks, she felt the prickling sensation which she considered her signalling bell ('don't worry, lie back, enjoy the ride, here it comes . . .'). Paul's outstretched arms were holding on to the floor, bracing his upper body. He looked down into Anna's face – it was lightly covered in sweat, her lips were red, and her dark straight hair was clinging to her face at the fringe and around her neck. He eased his body down on her, still gliding his cock in and out of her pussy with deep, strong motions. He was a heavy weight for Anna, and she loved his mass, the feeling of being nearly crushed underneath living muscle. She opened her mouth, almost biting the air, as he started sucking her neck, clutching his arms around her and forcing his body into hers. Her body convulsed as a violent orgasm coursed its way through her, reaching every nerve, making her legs feel like tiny pins were playing along her skin. Her vagina clutched at her guest with fierce suction, her deep short moans rasped against his ear, her thighs holding on like a clamp.

Paul continued to thrust his pelvis into hers – their pubic hair a mass of dark, glistening curls. Anna reached her arms behind him and grabbed his arse, grinding him into her. As her body was easing its way back down to earth, she stretched her arm between Paul's legs and rubbed the underside of his balls. Soft flesh was everywhere: his cock was buried deep within the clenching grasp of her tight pussy; her rounded belly and thighs rubbed against him; and her fingers played against his hairy balls. Then he came, and came, and his face was a picture of ecstasy as the delicious sensations of orgasm took hold of his body.

Dusk's soft light was perhaps a godsend for these two closely-related strangers. With delicate smiles (and a touch of melancholy) they disentangled themselves and Anna, relieved by her guest's tidy nature, watched him as he collected his things. She stood up, changed the CD and grabbed her new book. Seated on the floor, once again she opened her book. From the doorway Paul looked back, beamed at her and waved goodnight.

Anna was happy to be alone. On each page was another startling image of strong women or lustful men. She jokingly thought herself to be more closely connected with these people now – now that she had been a living picture for the artist himself. She again fell into concentrated silence, knees tucked underneath her, book splayed out in front of her. She wore an expression not dissimilar to the photographed reader she admired so much. Anna was calm and happy, enjoying that interim moment between delightful sex and the real world. At that moment the door opened again. She looked up into the face of her husband.

Completely naked, seated on the floor, straight black bob, some strands of hair clinging to her forehead, subtle glints of sweat between her breasts and around her face, pink-flushed skin, rosy nipples, eyes glistening and the sweet smell that would have been so delightful, in different circumstances. David, being no fool, thought that this scene made the most startling erotic image that he, or his brother, could ever have seen. Not one that he could capture with a camera, but one that he would never forget. Anna, being Anna, would not have married a fool.

She closed her book, and placed it on the shelf with many others. Anna had not met anyone who could really offer absolute physical pleasure without at least a few (and, more often than not, a lot more) human complications in tow. But perhaps she had been a little harsh in certain assessments. She walked past David and stood at the foot of the stairs waiting for him. David walked across the room and closed the curtains to the window, turned off the CD, walked to the door and paused. Re-entering the room, he grabbed his brother's book off the shelf and closed the door behind him. Walking up the stairs just behind his wife, he gently rested his hand on the small of her back.

Wolf Games

Delia Shannon

Wolf Games

❖ ❖

A century ago, those exiled to Siberia were said to have been 'sent to count the birches': a reference to the millions of birch trees in the endless forests of the Taiga.

Lying on a snow-capped hilltop overlooking this same territory whose name once struck terror into every Russian's heart, Donna Brogan saw not a place of punishment, but Paradise. The eternal trees abided, dark frost-patched evergreen, as numerous and densely packed as the hairs on her head. They stretched from horizon to horizon, with irregular pauses for rivers, lakes and oil and logging camps, out to the wintry western peaks of the Urals. The distant peaks were delicate, ephemeral, more dreamlike than actual, beneath the patchwork grey of a sky of unwashed clouds.

The snow crunched beneath her blanket as she shifted her position. The crunch resounded in the solemn silence of the Taiga, as loud as the dull drumming of a woodpecker, or a snapping twig beneath a bolting sable. She had no wish to disturb the clearing below – or the wolf pack who commanded it.

There were eight adults, led by the dominant male and female (whom she nicknamed Rocket and Ash), and their cubs. They were magnificent: sharp-eared, sharp-faced, coated in a range of tawny greys and blacks, copper eyes pinpointed with ebony, and animated bushy tails. Donna had watched that afternoon as the dominant pair led four of the adults out to hunt, leaving the remaining two to mind the cubs; now they'd returned, with jawfuls of elk for those who'd remained. As she observed their

17

snaps and cringes, their games of dominance and submission, and the obvious co-operation and consent among them, Donna wondered how such intelligent, social creatures could have become objects of fear and persecution.

'*Devushka*?'

It was a cautious whisper which reached her ears, and a welcome one. She set aside her camera, twisting to watch the black-clad man approach, his size undiminished by half-crawling up the hill, unnoticed by the pack on the other side. As he reached the blanket he practically slithered to her side, putting his arm around her as if it had always belonged there.

'There's bad weather ahead.'

'This is Siberia, Valentin Alexseiovich; some things can't be avoided.' She glanced at the clearing again. 'He should be here any minute. There!'

Both went silent as another wolf appeared in the clearing, bold as brass. Donna lifted her camera again and zoomed in on Stranger: he, too, had brought food. Rocket and Silver circled him twice, acknowledging his immediate posture of abasement, then padded away.

'Looks like he's been adopted,' Val noted.

It was his typical Russian nonchalance, but Donna knew he shared her astonishment. Lone wolves like Stranger normally avoided contact with all packs, and it was this unusual behaviour below which had snared her attention for much of the last fortnight (which was no mean feat, considering how much else the Taiga offered visitors).

Val gave her a squeeze. 'We should go.'

Donna looked up at him. There was something about Valentin Alexseiovich Lavrov that seemed too massive for chairs, or even rooms, something beyond his muscular frame, beyond the worldly lines in his face and the strands of white in his neatly-trimmed beard. Even when he smiled, the smile seemed too big for just his lips.

'Maybe you love my land too much to return to England, *Devushka*?'

She always smiled at his nickname for her – 'Young Girl' – when he was only 38 to her 26. Her breath whitened between them.

'Defecting *to* Siberia? What would Wildworld say?'

Val grinned like a Cheshire cat. 'Nothing, because when you

send them your photographs, your report, you'll be joined by hundreds, thousands more, all in love with the beauty and majesty of the Taiga Reserves. Then, perhaps my government will stop the loggers and riggers despoiling my land further.'

Donna smiled, warmed as much by the man's love for 'his' land – she could not picture a more devoted Reserves warden – as by the man himself. She snuggled up closer, trying again. 'Siberian winter nights are long; I'll need something to keep me warm.'

He leaned closer, and with a sly grin offered, 'I have just the thing: the recipe for my special coffee.'

A playful kick to his booted shins initiated an impromptu wrestling match, making Donna squeal and the wolf pack retreat into the forest.

The way-station consisted of several log cabins, linked by nocturnal guide ropes and wooden planks regularly swept clean of blowing snow, and set in a tiny forest clearing. The satellite dish, protected in a heated aluminium dome, was the only visible concession to the twentieth century. But it sufficed as the warden's station, as well as an emergency medical and communications outpost for the area's loggers, riggers, and even the odd Evenk nomad.

It was comfortably warm inside the main house, particularly in the living room with its great stone hearth dominating one wall, its heat and light mocking the feeble efforts from the ceiling bulbs. Mismatched chairs and couches filled the centre, an entertainment unit sat in one corner, and maps and paintings adorned the walls between the narrow, treble-glazed windows. Recorded classical guitar music complemented the pendulum clock and the fire's crackle.

Donna listened abstractedly, curled up in the recliner, legs tucked beneath her, mesmerized by the dancing flames. She nursed her *medivka*, a honey- and herb-flavoured beer; she wasn't in a drinking mood tonight.

Nearby, Val relaxed on the couch, boots removed, warming his feet by the fire. He glanced sideways at Donna occasionally, exchanging a smile with her, but had hardly spoken since dinner. His drink was cradled in his huge hands, virtually untouched; he didn't seem in a drinking mood, either.

His colleague, however, compensated for them both. She was

constantly on the prowl, an animal on a restless, mindless pace inside its cage, her drink a lifeline. She stopped behind Donna's recliner, who forced herself not to look up when the Russian woman finally spoke, her voice dry.

'You two are quiet tonight. Hiding secrets, perhaps?'

Val glanced at Donna, more embarrassed for her than for himself, it seemed. 'We have no secrets from you, Zofia.'

'I know, Valentin Alexseiovich; you're as open as the forests you love.'

Donna wanted to speak up, to defend her friend, but held her tongue and finished her drink, knowing the futility of arguing with her other host when she was in one of her moods again. Then Zofia stepped on to the bearskin rug between Val and Donna. 'Would you be just as open with me, my dear?'

Donna knew she could be hanging herself, but, 'Sure,' she said.

The older woman stared at her, challenging. 'Do you think I'm pretty?'

Dr Zofia Davidovna Tegal was a large woman who looked older than her 36 years. Her preferred expression may have been glacial, but Donna had seen it rapidly shift from permafrost to a spring breeze – or a summer storm. Her eyes were grey bullets, her hair a pepper swirl, and her breasts and hips ample within her sweater and jeans.

She *was* attractive, Donna decided; at least, in her less morose moods. In fact, there were times when she saw Zofia as a kindred spirit: intelligent, with a wicked sense of humour and a liberal outlook on life. Thus, she was sincere when she answered, 'I think you're beautiful, Zofia Davidovna.'

The woman in question seemed taken aback by the response. So much so that, for a moment, it appeared as if the spell of Byronic gloom which usually held sway would evaporate. But it resolidified, with a wry smile and a mock curtsey.

'*Spasee'ba*, my dear. I should do well at the local nightclub then, *da*? Shall we go?'

Donna had had enough, and setting her glass aside, slipped into her boots. 'I'm tired.'

He nodded, rising as well. 'I'll walk you over.'

Zofia waited until they reached the door. 'Don't get lost, Valentin.'

*

It was a chill, starless night, the wind stirring the surrounding trees was a precursor to an oncoming storm, while in the distance the wolves howled, marking their territory.

They were barely outside before he announced, 'I'm sorry about that.'

'It's all right.'

He stopped in his tracks, shaking his head. 'No, it's not, not for her. She never realised what living out here would be like when she signed on as the way-station doctor. She misses Novosibirsk, working in a hospital, going out, meeting people. I feel sorry for her.'

Donna was less sympathetic, though she understood, even liked Zofia. She circled an arm around his, as if to keep on the path in the near-total darkness. 'She's an adult; you can't take responsibility for her bouts of cabin fever.' Or when her hackles get raised by another female, she added to herself.

They stopped outside the guest-house door.

'You're an uncommonly kind man, Valentin Alexseiovich.'

He didn't respond at first, just stood before her, his hands now on her waist. Then, finally, he kissed her. She relished the smooth brush of his beard on her cold skin. There could be more. She wanted more.

'Stay with me tonight.'

For a moment, he looked like he would accept. Then he shook his head sadly. 'No, *Devushka*.'

He turned to go, but she wouldn't release him.

'Are you two lovers?'

She was surprised at her boldness; but then, her time here was nearly over, and she was too old to be beating around the proverbial bush. She wanted Valentin, and her instincts told her the feelings were reciprocated. It was as simple and as undeniable as any other force of nature. She had no childish romantic illusions about either of them giving up their careers, their lives, to be with the other: they were from different packs. But he was handsome, intelligent, kind, powerful – she couldn't resist him.

He remained a silhouette in the lights from the main house. 'Sometimes. As you said today, Siberian winter nights can be long.'

'But if you two aren't really a couple –'

'When humans are isolated for long periods, baser instincts dominate. They fight over chocolate bars, milk rations, anything.

Thus, you become acutely aware of the hurt one can feel when another has something that one doesn't.' His head bowed, once. 'I'm sorry, Donna; I won't hurt her like that.'

She watched him return to Zofia, quickening his pace as if in fear of the distant wolves.

Fingers of light danced from her small fireplace as Donna shed her clothes, running her hands over her nude body, enjoying the freedom, then stretched in all directions, studying her reflection in the wardrobe mirror. At 26, she could appreciate the image which returned her scrutiny: chestnut hair cut short in a pageboy style brushing slim shoulders, almond eyes, small, round white breasts, a slight curve around the waist, a dark trimmed triangle crowning firm thighs.

If only her career had been as notable. After nearly two years with Wildworld Tours, she'd finally earned a coveted field assignment to evaluate the tourist potential of the Siberian Taiga, for adventure holidays and naturalist excursions. She was to have been assisting the more experienced, more respected David Cannon, but he'd contracted food poisoning on the flight, and though the company had promised a replacement, none had been forthcoming. Not that Donna was complaining: this assignment – with Val's help – would be her passport to greater things.

Donna sighed with pleasure as she slipped into her thick terry caftan and climbed beneath the covers. The bed was lovely. There was room for two.

She had once been lucky in sex and not career, now the reverse was true. But she could still fantasise. Her hand took a familiar path beneath her caftan towards her vulva, full, expectant. She pictured Val entering the room, his desires overpowering his reservations, undressing and climbing in beside her. The wolves howled outside.

'There they go again!'

It was an uncannily warm day for March, melting much of the snow on the ground into dirty slush. Val insisted it was literally the calm before the storm, and seeing the eastern black clouds, she concurred. Donna lay atop a slope overlooking a wide river cutting a crooked path through the forest. From here, she watched Ash and Stranger playing, snapping at each other's tails, then mating again. Their lovemaking was fierce, brief, but intense, passionate: not what she'd expected of any animals other than humans. But wolves mated for life, or so popular thinking went. Donna wondered at this new development.

Beside Donna, Val lay on his back, eyes shut, content to bask in the relative warmth. He would be so easy to kiss now, she gauged.

'Aren't you enjoying this weather, *Devushka*?'

'I'm busy.'

She tried to keep her mind on her work. But he wouldn't let her, setting a hand on the small of her back, stroking lightly; Donna fought back the shiver that ran through her like a wire.

'There's a lot here to enjoy, Val.'

'*Da.*' His caress became a playful smack on her bum as he sat up. 'Like swimming.'

Donna watched with both disbelief and expectation as he removed his top, revealing a hirsute, perfectly muscled chest, and biceps that confirmed the way-station exercise machines' effectiveness.

She almost declared her lack of costume, settling for the more valid comment, 'The water will be freezing!'

'The river's fed by a hot spring. Zofia and I swim here often.' He grinned as he removed his boots and socks. 'Of course, if you haven't her courage . . .'

'What about the wolves?'

'They'll ignore us, or run off. Trust me.'

She did; it was a question of trusting herself. She could have refused, made excuses. Instead, she copied him, pulling her shirt over her head as he disappeared. Donna stripped off quickly. This was just a harmless bit of fun, she reminded herself as she heard him yelp when he splashed into the river, not a prelude to sex. Then, naked herself, she swallowed hard, rising and following him, cursing the cold mud and sharp stones beneath her steps, certain her face was beetroot.

He was waist-deep in the river, his back to her. Ash and Stranger had vanished. As first suspected, the water was glacial, making her gasp aloud and her nipples scowl as she rushed deeper into it, unwilling to prolong the initial shock and provoke more teasing. As Donna neared, she saw the scratches on his back: fresh confirmation that Zofia and he did have sex – and ferociously, too. She was nearly up to her breasts when he finally turned around, as if having waited for her benefit.

It seemed so natural to Val, playfully splashing her, making her squeal and splash back. The riverbed was a ticklish silt carpet, and the water a constant pull downstream. She kept moving, invigorated, accustomed now to Val seeing her breasts, or other parts of her, as she swam about.

After a time, he made a show of pursuing her, and she half-stumbled to escape his clutches, shrieking and giggling as he chased her out of the water and on to the bank, both of them collapsing, rolling over each other, muddying themselves.

Then she felt his erection against her thigh.

Donna's eyes widened as their wrestling ceased, both of them aware of how the circumstances had suddenly changed, with that simple, undeniable physical reaction on Val's part. Then, she found her own desire present, calling, as if it had been there all along, awaiting the ideal moment.

When they kissed, not as friends but as imminent lovers, a warmth coursed through her, sending her belly into somersaults. Zofia or not, Donna needed what Val could provide. Their bodies fitted together, tongues dancing, his erection pressing into her mound with wild anticipation.

He parted from her, the breath leaving his body in a shudder, and she looked between them at the firm stem of his cock, long and thick, its damask head collared by darker skin, and rearing up from a clump of black curls over his balls. Boldly, she reached down and grasped it, easily drawing the foreskin back and forth, confirming that this was real, not some fantasy. Then he gently eased her on to her stomach, her breasts pressing into the mud, saying nothing, having no time or need for courtship. She acknowledged how he wanted her; she wanted it, too, rising on to all fours. Warm fluid seeped from between her thighs, and she desperately craved to be stretched to capacity, literal fulfilment.

With something like a growl Val parted Donna's thighs and lifted her up, before mounting her. The lips of her sex swallowed the cooler head of his cock, then almost the full stem; as he pressed into her, she enveloped him totally. She felt his balls slap against her with every thrust, while his hands gripped her sides, unwilling to release her. They found a mutual rhythm, each giving, each gaining. Her mind and body were awash with the sensations invoked.

But soon Val coaxed their rhythm into a more urgent gallop; a rhythm Donna agreed upon. She pictured how they might look to the wolves: naked, muddied animals caught in their own heat. This image, and an extra deep thrust on Val's part, made her climax with a strangled cry; wave after wave of pleasure ran through her, making her dig her nails into the mud.

Val came too, grunting, his body spasming behind hers. After a time he withdrew, leaving her feeling empty but immensely satisfied, and they lay together, facing each other, their pulses still rapid.

Relishing her dying post-coital embers, the warmth of spent lust seeping from between her clenched thighs, Donna stroked Val's mud-stained beard. They kissed as she appreciated the weight of his arms and legs upon hers. It had been an inexcusably long time since she had last felt this way. But it was worth it now.

She nuzzled into his ear. 'What about what you said last night?'

She could feel his smile against her. 'I saw what was on offer today.' The smile evaporated. 'We should wash and return.'

The reminder spoiled her bliss. Return. To Zofia. Perhaps if the woman were less possessive, especially of a man she had no real claim over, Donna might have felt some guilt. Then again, Val didn't appear too contrite either, not like she expected.

A yelp in the distance made them glance up. Across the river, Rocket had happened upon Ash and Stranger, and was now snarling and snapping at the lone wolf; it could come down to a fight to the death, a rare but not unknown occurrence. But then Stranger prostrated himself, on his back, legs in the air, throat bared: the lupine posture of utter submission to a superior.

Donna clutched Val's arm, holding her breath. What would Rocket do now? If he were human . . .

But instead, Rocket chose to take Stranger's place with Ash. Stranger, seeing this, rose again, staying near – a voyeur. More games. How very civilised. If only human problems were as easily solvable.

She turned to Val, her nipples lightly grazing against his skin, her gaze fixed, serious. 'Val, do you want to do this again?'

He smiled, stroking her arm gently, sending shivers through her. 'That depends.'

She nodded. 'On Zofia. I know, I've not forgotten.'

'Neither have I. We're rather selfish, aren't we?'

25

'Yes.'

Each looked ready to speak, sparks of inspiration in their eyes. But then the heavens interrupted with a thunderous clap, and a subsequent outpouring of cold rain. Hands linked, they rose and dove back into the river to quickly wash themselves and return to the way-station. Donna waited until they were dressed and in the jeep, before revealing the bud of an idea. To her surprise, Val was thinking along the same lines.

The storm was at its peak by evening, mercilessly buffeting the forest and the way-station with lashings of sleet. Not that the trio inside the main house took notice. Dinner was finished, and now they sat or stood in the living room, watching the fire rising with every backdraft of wind from the chimney.

Donna was in her black party mini-dress, a sleeveless, strapless favourite of her own and many admirers. Knowing she was coming to the wilderness, she wondered why she'd even bothered packing it, or her high heels; now she was glad.

Val, too, was well dressed, looking noble and powerful in an old-fashioned white shirt with billowy sleeves, and black dress trousers. He was silent, casual, drinking cautiously.

Zofia, in contrast, remained in her chequered, red work shirt and jeans, planted beside Val on the couch, never questioning the reason for their evening clothes. But the looks Donna was receiving told her the plan had a good start. Now for the next step . . .

She found a raunchy dance number on the radio, and began to slowly sway and sidle around the room, letting her body move with the beat, knowing both Russians were watching (for different reasons). Finally she cavorted on to the bearskin rug before them, slowly gyrating.

'So, who's for a dance?'

Zofia smirked confidently. 'Neither of us dance –'

'I'd love to.' Val set his drink aside and joined Donna, planting his hands on her waist and easily moving in step with her.

As Zofia watched, dumbstruck, the couple began a deliberate, leisurely duet, Donna's arms brazenly descending to his waistline, then his buttocks, as Val copied her movements.

Their bodies pressed closer, Donna felt her nipples harden beneath her dress, even as Val's erection poked at her in reply. And when Donna's back was to Zofia, Val clasped the hem of her dress between thumbs and forefingers, lifting it up to reveal Donna's black silk panties, pulled tight against her cheeks. When she could, Donna stole glances at the Russian woman, worried her initial instincts might be incorrect, and Zofia might wrongly react to this bold intrusion into 'her' territory.

Finally the dance ended, Val planting an open kiss on Donna's lips, his tongue probing, a prelude to what else might follow, if all worked out.

Zofia flung her glass aside, springing to her feet. 'Get away from him, bitch!'

Donna parted from Val's lips, but still clutched his waist, her face a defiant, theatrical dare. 'He's mine now, Sweetie. What are you going to do about it?'

Zofia stormed towards her, crossing the distance between them so quickly that Donna barely had time to sink to her hands and knees and prostrate herself on to the polished wooden floor, head bowed, arms forward, back arched. Her pussy, tight within her knickers and alarmingly moist, tingled; was it just the novelty of striking such a submissive pose, particularly for another woman, that made her feel like this?

Donna couldn't look up, could only listen excitedly to the creaking floorboards and the rustling of clothes, could only imagine Zofia's expression now. Was she aghast, offended, still angry? Or did she grasp what was being offered her?

When she finally spoke, it was with cruel satisfaction. 'So, at last the little bitch acknowledges her proper place here, *da*?'

Face still to the floor, Donna smiled to herself, knowing their scheme was working, and hoping she sounded suitably nervous. '*Da.*'

'I didn't say you could speak!' Zofia barked. 'Look at you, in that tart's dress! Remove it immediately!'

Donna rose to her knees, hesitating at the sight of Zofia, her trousers, socks and boots now removed, revealing long, pale legs disappearing into her shirt, while Val stood behind, kneading her breasts. Then Donna obeyed, casting off her dress and just leaving her knickers and shoes, as two sets of eyes feasted on her. Zofia squirmed in place, more animated than Donna had ever seen before: the dominant female retaining her supremacy, even if only on a symbolic level. Then Donna saw the look in Val's eyes: desire, yes, but also, strangely enough, gratitude, for tonight, for Zofia's sake. Donna smiled back, feeling more aroused, more in control in her submissive role than she had expected; this was hardly turning out to be a great sacrifice on her part.

Then Zofia fell back into character, removing Val's hands and nearing Donna. 'Is that a challenge I see in your eyes, my dear?'

Donna feigned nervousness. 'No, no, Mistress –'

'We'll see.' She marched towards the firewood, quickly snapping off a thin length of birch, slicing the air as she tested it against her own palm. She glared at Donna. 'Crawl over here, bitch, and kneel before me.'

For a heartbeat, Donna paused; yes, she had wanted to appease Zofia, however little the woman actually deserved it, but she hadn't planned on being switched for her troubles. Still, neither had she planned on being so highly charged by the scenario, nor on the thought of further humiliation striking a hitherto unheard chord within her libido. Knowing she could stop the proceedings at any stage, she nodded her assent quickly, then started crawling towards the bearskin rug before she had time to think twice.

When she arrived, Zofia lifted the front of her shirt, revealing a neatly trimmed black triangle. 'Kiss it.'

It should have ended before now, with Donna and Val leaving for his bedroom. But it was as if they were on an irreversible course, a stomach-churning rollercoaster – with Donna loving every minute of it. She couldn't tear her eyes away from Zofia's bush: she could smell the familiar musk, so like her own; there was the glint of silver in the strands, the division of her sex beneath. She pursed her lips and kissed, tasting honey.

'Now, back on all fours.'

Donna's face felt flushed by more than the fire, but the excitement was greater than the embarrassment, and she wriggled slightly, positioning herself so that her bum was nice and round and impatient.

Zofia didn't keep her waiting: the birch soon made sharp bursts of contact on Donna's cheeks. It wasn't painful; indeed, Donna felt a warm glow spreading from her backside, bridging and heightening the points of arousal in the rest of her body. She yelped with each switch, more because it was expected than from the actual stings, keeping her bum high, well displayed, and aching for more.

'Enjoying yourself, *Devushka*?' Val whispered.

Donna nodded, unable to deny it.

'You're not meant to enjoy it, bitch,' Zofia informed her with relish. 'Pull down your knickers!'

Donna rose to her knees and obeyed, drawing them from the moist heat of her sex to her trembling knees, noting the damp gusset, and the aroma of her own bush. She willingly, eagerly, resumed her position, feeling so close to climax. Waves of bliss were rushing through her trembling body as each switch landed on her bared bum. The strokes quickened even after she cried out, burying her face and fingertips into the fur of the rug, feeling like the fire had spread from the hearth to encompass the whole room.

Someone – Val – knelt and removed her shoes and knickers. Zofia knelt also and looked into Donna's near-tearful eyes, wiping her cheeks gently before kissing her. Her tongue was hot, zealous, so like her own. The breath caught in Donna's throat as Zofia's fingers lightly stroked her breast, revealing the excitement that she, too, felt. Games of dominance and submission over, Donna fulfilled a lifetime's fantasies as she reached up and squeezed Zofia's breast through her shirt, appreciating its size, its firmness.

Feeling powerless to resist, Donna allowed herself to be led to a bedroom – Zofia's, from the scents she detected – dominated by a thankfully large bed, flickering in firelight. She was tempted to conclude that she was dreaming and was about to wake in her own bed, or even back in London. But when Zofia held her, reaching around to tease her burning, tingling backside while Val stripped, the sensations couldn't be more real. When Val was naked, he pulled Donna on to the bed, offering his cock to her; she sucked greedily on its length, tasting his excitement, feeling him tighten further within her mouth as she darted her tongue along its underside.

Donna started when she felt Zofia's long fingers and hot breath crossing her thighs, unceremoniously parting her moist, aching lips and fastening around her stiff clitoris, spurring Donna on to provide similar pleasure to Val; his moans complemented her performance.

Then Zofia parted from her. 'I want to see Val fuck you.'

Val wasted no time, drawing Donna's head up to the pillows and parting her thighs. With her knees high up, her pussy pulsated from Zofia's ministrations as if shivering from the cool air. She was eager for Val to fill her up. He didn't wait long; the crown of his cock impatiently nudged against her moist sex momentarily before plunging in. She squealed aloud, reaching up and adding scratches to his shoulders.

Zofia explored with Val every exposed inch of Donna's glowing skin: with fingers, with tongues, a total caress greater than any one lover could manage, until Donna cried out, her pussy aching with sweet torment. Even as she was pushed over the edge it continued relentlessly until she begged for relief.

But it didn't stop, not until later, when she was near-insensible and rapidly sinking into a well-deserved sleep. Thus, snuggled up beneath the covers, between her two lovers, she couldn't be sure that she had really heard Val whispering to her, 'Devushka, we must confess: Zofia and I had this arranged all along: her moods, our swim, the sex afterwards, our plan. All a game, to get you in the proper frame of mind. And you were wonderful!'

All she could recall vividly was the howling in the distance, breaking the dominance of the storm.

Nereus

Lyn Wood

Nereus

❖ ❖

*I*t was so hot that even the fish were gasping. Andrea took off her white linen jacket, kicked off her shoes and peeled off her tights. Even that wasn't enough, so she slipped off her silk blouse, stepped out of her skirt and stretched out on the lounger beside the pond in just her bra and pants. It was a secluded garden: no one could see. Even if they could, she knew she was wearing a classy set of lingerie. She opened the can of lager she had taken from the fridge. It hadn't been a very pleasant morning: the meeting had left her with a nasty taste in her mouth that even the lager wouldn't entirely eliminate.

When she'd first taken the job ten years earlier she'd been naïvely enthusiastic – she was getting a chance to make a difference, a chance to do something positive about the environment. But slowly and surely she had begun to realise that it was all cosmetic: what really affected the environment was money, and money alone. By then she was earning a large enough salary to make her keep her mouth shut about the small atrocities she witnessed every day, and after a while she stopped thinking about it and just got on with it.

She lay on the lounger, feeling the sun soak through her to the bone; the heat was cleansing, therapeutic, it massaged the soul. A real massage would have been even better. A real massage with a gorgeous masseur, someone oriental maybe, with a golden skin and smouldering eyes and arms like a Greek god's. He'd be wearing a little white loincloth, and it would have a noticeable bulge. He'd talk to her in broken English and rub her all over with fragrant oils and she'd catch hold of the loincloth and give it a gentle tug, just hard enough to unravel it. And then he'd pounce.

She seemed to come to with a jolt. Perhaps something had startled her; she listened, but nothing stirred. Her mind drifted back to the meeting she had attended that morning: the grey suits and the bulging midriffs and the sweaty faces. The faint sensation of nausea she had felt returned as well. Over the years she had seen ancient trees felled to make way for offices, and said nothing. She had turned a blind eye to streams polluted by people who made contributions to party funds. But she had never been asked to gloss over the destruction of seven acres of ancient woodland, unspoilt woodland with rare plants. Someone had even told her there was a dragon or a wizard or something living near the lake. It was that sort of wood.

Andrea finished her drink and flopped back to the horizontal, debating whether or not to go inside and get another can. It really was astoundingly hot. She could have been in the tropics: the nape of her neck was damp from perspiration. And then something splashed, close by. It sounded rather large for a frog. She opened her eyes. Nothing. She closed them again, and wished someone else had been landed with the Coronation Wood project.

Another splash, louder.

She opened her eyes once more and sat up, blinking in the sunlight. Still nothing. Odd. Then she noticed that there weren't any frogs lurking amongst the weed, and the fish seemed to have gone into hiding. She glanced round the garden, wondering whether a heron or a cat or something was waiting in the shadows. There was a faint shimmer above the rockery as the stones heated the air to rippling-point. Nothing else moved, even the trees seemed to be prostrated by the heat.

And then she saw them. Four fingers, dusky green fingers, gripped the stone overhang at the edge of the pond.

She rubbed her eyes. It was completely impossible. How could there be someone in her pond, someone who had been invisible – underwater – for the last half an hour? Unless the someone had been there for a lot longer than half an hour . . . her hand shot up to her mouth, stifling the scream before she made it. As she stared, one of the green fingers moved slightly and she knew that the owner was alive. She swallowed, trying to pluck up the courage to stand up and investigate further.

The hand at the edge of the pond was joined by another. Eight mossy fingers, delicately shaped; the nails pale emerald and elegantly oval. She must have fallen asleep. She had heard about lucid dreams, rare dreams where you were in control, directing the action. Like most people she had wanted one, but she had hardly expected to have one in her own back garden at two o'clock in the afternoon. Most of all, she didn't want it to turn into a nightmare. She stood up and caught a fleeting glimpse of her reflection in the water, a slim dark-haired figure in what could have been taken for a black bikini. She thought in passing that she looked rather chic, and then she felt pleased that she wasn't panicking.

From her changed eye-level she could see further into the pond; she could see where the green fingers joined green hands, where the hands joined slender but masculine arms, where the arms joined well-muscled shoulders. She could see the top of his head. Her pond wasn't very deep: how could a grown man be submerged in it up to his armpits? She was dreaming. She had to be. She might as well enjoy it.

'Hello,' she said, 'who are you?'

The head turned upwards, and she saw his face for the first time. He was beautiful, there was no other word for it; very green but very beautiful, with long hair the colour of an empty wine-bottle, slanting eyes like chips of malachite, high cheek-bones and a wide sensuous mouth.

'Very self-possessed,' he said, his voice liquid, sexy. 'I'd expected more fear.' He hauled himself out of the water in one easy movement and sat on the stone surrounding the pond. He was quite naked and totally unembarrassed about it. 'I'm a naiad,' he said. 'Know what that is?'

She shook her head. She thought she probably did know, somewhere in the recesses of her mind, but she wasn't thinking terribly clearly and she didn't want to risk making a fool of herself. Water spirit, tree spirit, woodland spirit – some sort of spirit, anyway. Talking of which, a whisky was beginning to seem like a better idea than another can of lager. 'Can I get you a drink?' she said.

He laughed. 'Wow,' he said, 'you really are supercool, aren't you. Yeah, why not. Whisky. With ice.'

Supercool. Andrea rather liked that image. She drifted indoors, wondering whether she would be able to fly if she knew the right set of instructions, or screw Keanu Reeves, or go scuba-diving in the Red Sea. What to choose, when the choices were infinite? She found a couple of glasses and then she noticed her dictionary lying on her desk. On the spur of the moment, she looked up naiad. It said 'water nymph'. Surely a water nymph was female? She fixed a couple of drinks and glanced at herself in the mirror. She looked perfectly normal so she pinched herself – and it hurt. She smiled, and carried the glasses into the hall. Then she thought, I've got some smoked salmon and cold asparagus in the fridge. She pictured him eating the asparagus, sliding each spear into his mouth and savouring it before he bit into it. She went into the kitchen and did the job properly: thin slices of salmon on the Portmeirion plates, some Italian bread, some stuffed olives – and the asparagus. She put the plates and the glasses on a brass tray, picked up a bottle of suntan oil and carried everything outside, aware that she hadn't made any choices about what she was going to do next at all. She was just going along with the action, and her brain was, very considerately, fooling her into thinking it was reality.

He was sitting on the grass now with his legs crossed pixie-style, which was a mercy. His feet looked a little odd, and then she realised that they were webbed.

'Thanks,' he said, taking the drink. Then he saw the plates of food and said, 'How thoughtful. Fish.'

She laughed out loud, put the tray on the grass and sat down on the lounger. He rolled a piece of smoked salmon between his fingers like a cigar and lifted it to his mouth. It looked especially pink against his mossy lips and he took his time, slipping it slowly into his mouth and biting off the end. Then he fed her the remainder, sliding it in out and out of her mouth the way you'd tease a kitten with a strand of wool, until she caught hold of it with her teeth. She became all too aware of its textural similarity to intimate organs, and when she swallowed it she felt faintly cannibalistic.

'Naiads are water nymphs,' she announced, 'and you don't look very feminine to me.'

He didn't, at all. Even though he was slightly built and smooth skinned he was all muscle, with slim hips and sinewy thighs. He could have been the model for the Discus Thrower, that Roman statue of athletic marble perfection.

'Nubile young women belong to a male mythology,' he said. 'Narrated by men, painted by men, sculpted by men – for men. There's a female version too, Andrea. It has just been suppressed. The mysteries were passed on by word of mouth from woman to woman and from generation to generation. They had their erotica as well.' He took a piece of asparagus.

'How do you know my name?' she asked him, watching him bite into the purple-green flesh and suck at the stem. She rather liked the way she still seemed to be able to think logically; she wouldn't have expected that. And the Scotch definitely tasted like Scotch: cold and faintly metallic.

'Oh,' he said airily, 'I know a lot about you.'

She grinned. 'Prove it.'

He reeled off a description of her character that would have shocked her if she hadn't seen him as a manifestation of her subconscious: avaricious, slyly ambitious, unprincipled, promiscuous when it suited her. She smiled at her own deviousness.

He smiled back. His teeth were very white against the soft jade of his lips. He reminded her of Puck: boyish, mischievous, unpredictable. She finished her drink in one go; she needed it after that nasty little character sketch.

He sipped his drink with rather more panache and said appreciatively, 'Glenfiddich. Nice.'

He picked up another piece of asparagus and fed it to her this time. She decided to give as good as she got. She ran her tongue round the bulbous purple tip, then she took it all the way into her mouth and fellated it. After that, she ate it. He smiled, and put the chewed end of the stem back on the plate.

'What's your name?' she said.

'Nereus.'

'Oh.' She couldn't think of anything else to say. Nor could she think of any of the things she had always wanted to do in a dream, which was intensely annoying. She took an olive.

'Well,' said Nereus, 'you're an odd one. I move into your pond without so much as a by-your-leave and you just accept it.'

'It's a dream,' said Andrea.

'Oh sure. Check the level of the whisky bottle tomorrow.'

'It has to be a dream,' said Andrea.

Nereus smiled. Then he leant over and ran his hand along her thigh, and his fingers felt like real fingers. She felt a shiver of arousal, so on impulse she took hold of his hand, raised it to her lips and kissed it. The webbed fingers were joined at the knuckles by a thin fold of skin and she touched it with her tongue, wondering if he had any feeling there. It was like kissing a bat. She wanted to laugh, but there was something strangely erotic about webbing. A wicked glint appeared in his eyes. They were incredible eyes: the whites a pale, milky green, the irises an iridescent emerald. His lashes were long and thick and the same wine-bottle shade as his hair.

'That's more like it,' he said.

'More like what?'

He grinned. 'The usual reaction.'

She let go of his hand. 'You've done this before then.'

'I think Alma Mahler, the composer's wife, was the last one. Catherine Howard was the first.'

How surreal, she thought. History had never before interested her in the slightest. 'I'm in exalted company then,' she said, liking the idea.

His other hand travelled further up her leg, and a finger lifted the elastic of her pants and explored underneath. 'Take them off,' he said, 'that elastic stuff is perfectly dreadful. I like hooks and eyes, buttons and bows, strings and laces. Little fiddly things to undo, one by one. The Victorians knew what sex was about – the slow, secret unveiling of the forbidden.'

She hesitated. Then she thought, why the hell not? This has to be the safest sex you could ever have. This is my fantasy, created by me. I can do whatever I like. She clambered off the lounger and took off her pants, aware there was a damp patch on the crotch. She tried not to be embarrassed about it.

Nereus stood up, reached round behind her and unfastened her bra, one hook at a time. He slid the shoulder straps slowly down over her arms, allowing the satin to trail across her skin. Then he stepped back, surveyed her from top to toe and whistled appreciatively. She could see his genitals for the first time: as green as the rest of him. Either he had a slight erection or the female water nymphs had a whale of a time.

She laughed. 'Oh,' she said, 'this is totally ridiculous. But it's fun. I don't want to wake up.'

He tossed back his wild green hair and she wondered if his lovemaking was equally uninhibited. There was something of a cat about him: the loose easy confidence of a creature at ease with its physique and its appetites.

'Don't you want to know anything about me?' he said, sitting down again and taking another sip of his whisky.

Not really, she thought. You have the most desirable body I've ever seen, and that's all I want. But she didn't say that. 'All right,' she conceded reluctantly, 'tell me how old you are, what you do all day, and where you lived before you moved here.'

He patted the grass beside him, and she sat down next to him. 'I'm a water spirit,' he said. 'I'm very old by your standards and just a slip of a thing by mine. An apprentice I suppose you'd call it. We've been around for aeons, we nature spirits. We remember a time when you lot paid some attention to us, when you were hunters and gatherers, when you were part of the world, not separate from it. I watch over things. In the old days I watched over drunken farmers nearly drowning themselves on their way back from the Coach and Horses. These days it's more technical: pesticides and pH levels. I used to live in the lake on the edge of Coronation Wood.'

Coronation Wood? She felt a sudden chill move across her even though the sun was as hot as ever.

'I can't live there any longer,' he said. 'Not if they're going to fill it in. You can't be a water spirit without any water. So I thought – why not move in with the woman who's causing all the trouble? So here I am. It's a bit cramped, your pond, but it'll do for the moment.'

'You've moved in with me because I'm going to give the go-ahead to fill in your lake?'

'That's right. Unless I can persuade you to behave in a responsible manner for once.'

'I'm none too happy with the way this conversation's going,' said Andrea. 'I thought I was meant to be able to direct a lucid dream the way I wanted it to go.'

One side of his beautiful mouth lifted in a half-smile. 'And which way do you want it to go?'

She looked at him sitting there next to her and imagined him putting his arms round her. Imagined stroking his damp, mossy skin, running her fingers through his long wet hair. Imagined him making love to her, right there on the lawn in her own back garden.

'I . . . er . . . haven't quite decided,' she lied.

'Right,' he said sarcastically, glancing at her discarded pants.

She blushed and he smiled, a faintly lecherous smile that flattered far more than it offended. There was something so exotic about him. The chlorophyll effect was just a small part of it. A touch of Thai, a hint of Sudanese, a trace of Polynesian. She knew she had never seen his face before but he was an amalgamation of everything she found most attractive, and she delighted in her own ingenuity. She felt as though she had invented her own personal myth from odds and ends, and done rather a good job. Clever old Andrea.

'I want you to do something for me first,' he said, tracing a line across her midriff with his index finger.

She felt the muscles tense, and the hairs on the back of her neck lifted. 'Anything.'

'Anything?' He raised an olive-green eyebrow.

'Why not?' she said. 'I can be generous in my sleep, even if I can't quite manage it when I'm awake.'

He laughed, and ran the finger up to her nipple which hardened immediately. 'It can wait a little while,' he said. Then he put his whole hand against her chest and pushed her backwards, so that she toppled on to the grass. He looked at her for a moment, then he rolled her on to her stomach and picked up the bottle of suntan oil.

She lay there, her head turned on one side, watching him. He tried to remove the cap but he didn't seem to quite know what to do: twisting it and pulling it until she took the plastic bottle from his fingers, squeezed it and made the lid flip up like a jack-in-the-box. He jumped. She shivered with delight at his strangeness, and then at the sensual way he proceeded to trickle the oil on to his palm.

He started with her back, kneading it with his fingers, and then her shoulders, her neck. She felt the relaxation seep through her like ink through damp paper. No one had ever massaged her like this before. He moved his attention to her feet, tiny expert movements of his fingers producing wave upon wave of pleasure. Then her calves, her thighs, her buttocks. He sat astride her to get more leverage; she felt his testicles settle between her legs. They felt cool and damp, and a sudden rush of arousal went through her. The massage became more intimate. His wet hair draped across her like a fishing net as he bent over her neck. The weight of him felt good, she could feel his hand between her thighs, feel his fingers exploring her. He knew what he was doing: he had had four centuries of experience to draw on. She felt a flush of exhilaration. He was going to make her writhe with pleasure, beg for it, plead for it, scream for it, and the longer he kept her on the edge the more intense the final release would be. She turned and clawed at him, pulling him closer, wondering what would happen if she drew blood. Would that be green, too?

Suddenly he sat back and looked at her. 'There's a price,' he said, 'but you're used to that aren't you? Everything has a price in your world.'

She sighed. What a pity. 'Tell me what you want of me,' she said, 'and I'll do it.'

'I want you to write some letters. And I want you to fax them. And after that I'm going to fuck you senseless.'

'I see,' she said. Then – 'OK. Let's do it.'

He stood up. She got to her feet as well, and they both walked into the house. She was slightly surprised that he knew about fax machines, but then, he knew about Glenfiddich and the plans for Coronation Wood. Maybe he had magical powers. He left some very unmagical wedge-shaped footprints on the carpet, however; he didn't seem to like the texture very much: he lifted each foot sharply and seemed relieved when they reached the parquet flooring of the study. She took him inside and switched on her computer. She didn't expect it to work, electrical gadgets always played up in dreams, but this time everything behaved itself. There was something very erotic about sitting naked on an office chair and tapping things in on the keyboard. She could feel the leather against her body like skin, soft and smooth and faintly reptilian.

Nereus stood there, looking ill at ease in the hi tech surroundings of her office, running his fingers through his hair. He picked out a strand of pondweed and examined it, frowning, then he glanced at himself in the mirror on the wall. 'Zeus!' he said. 'Can I borrow your hairbrush? I look like a sewage farm.'

She rummaged in her bag and gave it to him. He went over to the mirror and, merman-fashion, used the tortoiseshell brush in long, slow, regular strokes. The suggestiveness of it wasn't lost on her; she watched him out of the corner of her eye and was consumed with desire. Then she saw him glance at the poster on the wall. It said, 'How many men does it take to carpet a room?

One, if you slice him very thinly.' He didn't smile. He didn't react at all, and she wondered whether perhaps he couldn't read. There was a glass paperweight on the shelves by the window and he picked it up and looked at it, turning it this way and that like a child. As he put it back he noticed the stapler, and before she could stop him he had put his finger between its jaws.

'No!' she yelped.

He dropped it in surprise.

'It's for fastening papers together, not fingers,' she said.

He picked it up carefully and put it back; then he held up his hand to the light. She could see fine veins in the webbing as the sunlight shone through the delicate skin, turning it a vivid lime green.

'Mine are fastened already,' he said, smiling.

He walked back to the desk, sat on the edge of it, and started to dictate. She typed in exactly what he said. Now and again he stopped and asked her a question. His phraseology was flawless and his prose was passionate and compelling.

She noticed that his pubic hair was the most beautiful deep-sea green. She wondered how it felt: soft and feathery or coarse and vigorous. She remembered that there were no rules in dreamland, so she reached out and touched it lightly with one finger. He caught his breath. It was the first spontaneous reaction she'd had from him, and her typing went haywire.

'Whoops,' she said, laughing and correcting it.

He laughed too, fizzing like champagne. But he was laughing at her amusement, not the words on the screen. At that moment she wanted to keep him there forever with her: he was so exciting, so seductive, so different. His occasional displays of innocence, combined with his blatant sexuality and his obvious intelligence, was a very powerful turn-on, and she was finding it harder and harder to concentrate.

She wrote three letters, all to national newspapers, giving details of the carnage about to be loosed upon Coronation Wood. She named names, quoted figures, listed endangered species. She used the word 'corruption'. They were the sort of letters she might have written ten years previously, but ones she would never have sent now. It was professional suicide. She printed them out, and then she faxed them. Nereus slid off the desk and stood there looking at her, appraising her. She felt as though he saw right through her skin, like an X-ray.

'Now I'm going to make love to you,' he said, 'because I want to see you let go of thousands of years of civilisation. That's what you really want, isn't it?'

She smiled. 'You know me so well,' she said, 'but then, you are me, aren't you?'

'Can we go back in the garden?' said Nereus. 'I don't like being too far away from water. Not for any length of time, anyway.'

They went outside again and lay down together on the grass beside the pond, fitting together like blocks of crazy paving.

'I want you more than I've ever wanted anyone,' said Andrea.

He smoothed her forehead with the palm of his hand and murmured, 'Lord, what fools these mortals are.'

She laughed, and then he started to kiss her. It was an odd sensation: one moment he seemed to taste of pond water, brackish and pungent; then a slightly fishy flavour, subtle, sexual, unexpected but not unpleasant. His erection brushed her thigh and the damp velvet touch of his skin made her press herself against him, hard, intensifying the thrill. She kissed him back, pressure for pressure, softness for softness. She left his mouth and worked round to his ear, and again there was a faint suggestion of pondweed. His eyes were closed now, although his fingers were thoroughly occupied, and she began to explore his ear with her tongue. She heard him sigh but it had a bubbly quality to it, as though he was responding to her underwater. Her tongue had nearly completed its roundabout journey from lobe to orifice when she realised that his ear was actually a very strange shape: elfin, Vulcan, non-human. There was a point at the top, a real point. She smoothed back the wonderful green hair and looked at it, feeling pleased that she had created something so exquisite.

He opened his eyes and smiled at her. 'It's all procedure with you, isn't it,' he said. 'I bet your partners could predict exactly what you were going to do when.'

She felt herself bridle. What sort of a woman was she, when she could insult herself in the middle of a fantasy? But it was the truth behind it that hurt. She had used sex like a letter of recommendation: used it to procure positions, set up alliances, improve her chances – and she had used it as a weapon, too. She got pleasure from it, certainly, but it was calculated, formulaic. He was right, she had never really let herself go.

'Come on,' he said, 'surprise me. What is it with you, fear?'

'No,' she said, annoyed.

He turned her over on to her front and spread her legs with his hands and rubbed the tip of his penis against her; she felt her hips move in response.

'I'm not suggesting you're frightened of the act itself,' said Nereus, sliding back and forth and running his fingers lightly across her skin, 'just that you're frightened of what you might find.'

'And what's that?' she said, twisting back to face him and daring to separate his buttocks with her fingers. She ran her thumb quickly from back to front – he shuddered and she did it again, developing it into a sequence, faster and faster. She felt his penis jerk against her and it was a small victory.

'You're frightened you might find another human being underneath,' he said, his voice low and slightly rougher than before.

She looked at his ears, his skin, his hair. He smelt dank, organic; he tasted of pond water. He was her creation and he was a nymph, not a human being. 'A human being?' she said. 'No chance, not this time.'

'Perhaps you're frightened you might find yourself then,' he whispered, rolling on top of her and entering her. The sensation was incredible; he was moist and warm and muscular, all at the same time. A hundred images flitted through her mind: sea cucumbers, octopuses, eels. Wet things that thrust and retreated, thrust and retreated, waves, tides, whirlpools. Sex had never been like this before. She put her hands on his hips, pulling him harder against her; she was tingling from belly to knees as the sensation grew stronger and stronger and she fought to contain it, then to increase it, then to extend it. She wanted to be at the point of orgasm forever, suspended there, always on the brink of annihilation. The sun beat down upon them the way it must have done from time immemorial, before buildings and rooms and religions isolated the act and imbued it with sin and impropriety.

She rolled him on to his side, then on to his back. She rode him like a demon, her hair flying, her eyes alight. He gripped her tightly, and they rolled again. They left the grass and she felt the stone paving slabs against her skin; they burnt her where they had been baked by the sun, and the pain was short-lived but exquisite. Then the contrast of the bog where the stones ended and became wetland. She felt her thigh sink into the cool, sensual mud; she felt the gentle caress of marsh marigold and lobelia, then a quick touch of something slimy, primitive and basic. All her preconceptions about what was right and proper had gone: she had become a human animal, at one with its environment. She could hear the water like music as they rolled into it and it enfolded her, enclosed her, overwhelmed her. The rhythm of his body was the rhythm of life itself. And then the orgasm, on and on for eternity as the water closed above her head.

An open verdict was recorded at the inquest. Initially, suicide seemed to be the most likely conclusion, after the letters to the papers. But there were a few anomalies that suggested Andrea Fisher hadn't been alone: two empty whisky glasses, some chewed asparagus stems and a long strand of theatrical green hair in a hairbrush.

Night's Kiss

Astrid Cooper

Night's Kiss

❧ ❧

'*O*nce done, it cannot be undone,' he whispered against her neck.

He playfully nibbled along the length of her artery. His tongue followed, licking the places where his teeth had grazed. Though he made it a game, she knew it was not. His teasing concealed his fear. Fear that at last she would reject him: reject his offer of immortality.

Hers was a bittersweet choice: should she leave behind all she knew, witnessing friends pass from youth to old age, while she lived on, eternally young? A lifetime of thousands of years, with her lover at her side, was within her grasp.

She drew his head away from her neck and studied his face, cupping it in her hands. His exotic beauty still astonished her: the cinnamon-coloured skin, the high cheekbones, the eyelids slanting ever so slightly upwards over amber eyes dark with passion, the sensuous mouth now drawn in a tight line, the thick raven hair in tangled disarray around his neck and naked shoulders. As beautiful now as when she had first seen him.

At her photographic exhibition he had been surrounded by a circle of women, each vying for his attention.

As she had wondered why he held himself so aloof from his admirers, their eyes had met across the crowded room. A cliché, if ever there was one. But, for her, the world had ceased to exist as his sultry gaze locked with hers. It was a gaze that probed through to her soul. Her heart had laboured as it tried to pump blood as thick as molasses around her veins. Her breath had caught in her throat and a throbbing heat weighed heavily between her legs. Tension and desire had spiralled upwards, constricting her stomach, rushing to her nipples. Her body had thrilled as he strode towards her, all feline grace and predatory maleness, in his black silk suit.

He had stood before her, his eyes impaling her. Unspoken thoughts and promises had flowed between them, searing, caressing. His musky scent, tinged with the spice of ginger, had washed over her.

Silently, he had taken her hand and led her out on to the verandah, into the garden, leaving behind the noise; the world.

His arms had enfolded her as her body snuggled into his. A perfect fit, she had thought, as if they were two halves of the same mould. He had laughed then, a rich, deep laugh, and her legs had gone to jelly. His mouth upon hers breathed life into her. She had drunk deeply from him, again and again.

Breaking apart, they had introduced themselves.

Jocelyne Munroe, fashion photographer.

Jalan. Just Jalan. His smile was enigmatic.

A man of mystery and contradictions. There was delicacy and vulnerability in his strong features. Although slender he was all whipcord muscles. She had wondered what he would look like naked. He had grinned and pulled her to him. Her hands, snaking in under his jacket had ineffectually tried to span the width of his shoulders. As he moved, muscles ruched beneath her fingers.

She had groaned. And in response he had cupped her buttocks, drawn her to him, so that one muscle in particular lay against her flat belly. A heavy arousal, a promise of something special to come. His scent of spice had filled her all the way to her core. Again her breath had caught in her throat.

He had looked at her, his eyes asking, almost pleading. As she nodded, he had raised her skirt. His warm fingers had slid into the top of her panties and drawn them down her legs. He had knelt momentarily at her feet, gazing up at her. Standing again, his hand had travelled up her inner thigh. His smile had been one of triumph as he had felt the sticky heat of her sex. He had lifted her to him, wrapped her legs around his waist. At the sound of his descending zipper her body had pulsed in expectation. Moments later she felt his rigid member nestle against her.

She had groaned, and so had he, as their hips thrust simultaneously forward. United at last.

Never before had she allowed a stranger to have sex with her, but she let Jalan do it to her in the garden, up against a wall: a hasty coupling driven by insane, burning need that had satisfied her. For all of two minutes.

He had suggested that they leave. With her excuses made, she had gone with him in his black Porsche to his beach-house. They had made love throughout the night and over the next day, stopping only to eat and drink, to catch a few moments of rest, before their mutual need had spiralled out of control and they writhed and panted, again, in each other's arms.

What had started out as lust and mutual fascination quickly developed into much more. Three weeks passed. The only darkness on her horizon was Jalan's mysteriousness: he skilfully turned aside her questions, distracting her with his now familiar lips, tongue and body.

They made love on the sand, in the sea, on the floor, on the stairs, his positions as inexhaustible as his desire for her – her desire for him.

One day as he lay sprawled, like a naked Adonis, in satiated sleep on the rumpled bed, she had taken his photo. But when she had developed it in her darkroom, he was not in the picture. She had bided her time to take another photograph, but Jalan had proven to be an elusive subject. He had an aversion to cameras, he had said, despite the fact that she made a living from photography. They both laughed at the contradiction.

Though their loving was beyond satisfying, she always sensed his frustration. He wanted more. And when she had asked what more he wanted, he turned away, sorrow and loneliness etching harsh planes into his face.

After that, he stayed away. One week. Two. And every minute Jocelyne burned with a fire that only Jalan could quench. He had captured her soul, her love, her body, until only he mattered. She could neither eat, nor sleep, nor work.

When he next came to her, he had lost weight. The dark smudges under his eyes bespoke sleepless nights. Jalan told her he had to leave. She had anticipated this moment, but the pain of his announcement was like a knife slicing her in two.

One last time, they made love. A desperate joining. He plunged again and again into her hot body, possessing her with a fierceness that frightened her. A uniting of bodies and souls: something to remember in the empty days ahead. He tasted every inch of her while she wept.

'I cannot do it!' Jalan had cried. 'Heaven forgive me, I cannot leave you!' Tears flowed down his cheeks and she smoothed them tenderly away.

'I don't want you to leave,' she had whispered. 'Stay with me forever.'

He had drawn back from her a fraction and smiled down at her. A sad and bitter smile.

'Forever is a long time, my love,' Jalan had said. 'But you ask it of me without knowing what it is you say.'

'Then tell me.'

'I'm afraid to. We've known each other less than a month.'

'What are you afraid of?'

'Your fear and loathing. Your rejection.'

'I love you, Jalan. How can I be afraid of you?'

He had flung himself away from her and sat at the edge of the bed, his head in his hands. His trembling fingers had torn through his hair.

She had looked at his back, seen the shivering of his body. A sudden fear quenched the fire within her. She had crawled across the bed and placed her hands on his shoulders.

'Tell me, Jalan. Please.'

The minutes had stretched to eternity and only the hammer of her heart, the blood racing in her ears, broke the silence between them.

'Jalan!'

She had reached for him. Deliberately, she had run her fingers slowly across his belly, down to his thick, hot, pulsing shaft. His hand had stilled her questing fingers.

'If you touch me like that I cannot think. Cannot breathe. They said it would be like this.'

The last words were ground out between clenched teeth.

'Who is "they"?'

'My brothers.'

'You have brothers?'

'Many.'

'And what did they tell you?'

'That when you meet your woman it is heaven, and the worst kind of hell.'

'Am *I* your woman?' her husky voice had asked.

He had glanced back at her, smiling, a mischievous light in his eyes. 'Do you doubt it, after all we have shared?'

'You are the one to have doubts, not me.'

'For your sake.'

'Oh, please! I'm a big girl. I can look after myself.'

He had laughed.

'Anyway, Jalan, it's not just you who feels this heaven and hell . . .'

Her voice had trailed away as his dark eyes locked with hers.

'You feel it too?' his breathless whisper had asked.

'Yes.'

'Then I have touched you deeper than I intended, without explaining first what I am!'

Even as she had reached out to him, he had hurled himself from the bed, to stride around the room. Naked, he paced back and forth like a wild animal. Caged. Cornered. Dry-mouthed with desire she had watched the muscles ripple along his long, lean torso. His arousal always preceded him, jutting outwards, like a silent sentinel.

Her body had constricted and flooded, hot and ready, just looking at him.

His frantic pacing had ceased as he glanced at her over his shoulder. 'When you are aroused your scent is like jasmine; it reminds me of my homeland.' His eyes had narrowed then, taking in her every detail. 'Did you like the photograph you took of me?'

'How did you know? You were asleep!'

'A part of me remains awake, ever vigilant. It is a survival mechanism.'

'You're an undercover cop? A spy?'

Each time, he had shaken his head and chuckled. Striding to the wardrobe door, he had opened it. The mirror reflected the room: her own naked self, sitting on her heels upon the bed, her blonde hair tufted and standing on end, where he had stroked and teased it with his fingers. But that was all. Only a curious rippling where Jalan might have stood – if he had had a reflection.

She had looked back and forth between Jalan and the mirror. A chill had swept down her spine. Not exactly fear.

'Who . . . who are you?'

'A man who loves you, Jocelyne. Never doubt that. When I first saw you, I knew you were my heart and soul. My body knew it too. I could not help but seduce you.'

'I'm not sure you did the seducing.'

His smile was sad. 'Until me, you were not in the habit of having sex with a stranger.'

'I don't regret it.' She had entered into their relationship with her eyes wide open, and her legs wide open too.

Jalan laughed. 'I enjoy your legs wide open, Jocelyne, provided it is me, only me, always between them.'

'How did you know what I was thinking?'

'We are linked. Given time, our psychic link would grow. It is the way.'

'Why can't I see your reflection in the mirror or take your photograph? And all this psychic stuff! Jalan, are you an alien?'

He had thrown back his head and laughed. 'No, I am human, but different.'

'I can see that!' Jocelyne had said as she stared at his rigid penis.

Jalan had followed her gaze. 'More than obvious male–female differences. I am . . . I am a vampire!'

His gaze had captured hers. Before she could speak again, had minutes or hours passed?

'Come on, Jalan. Where are your fangs? You eat and drink, and walk in the sunlight.' Her laughter had died on her lips, as his gaze pierced her.

'I am a vampire, of a brotherhood of vampires. I have fangs, but they only emerge when I am ready to drink.'

'Vampires don't exist.'

'Oh, but they do. Ten thousand years ago, in Egypt, a High Priest of Osiris followed a secret, sacred tradition. He succeeded in extending his life. He cheated death for himself and a few followers. My brothers and I are his descendants. The gift of immortality is passed between father and son.'

'No women?'

'There are a few women in our clan, but no woman can bequeath the blood-gift to another. Some of my brothers have brought their lovers into the clan to share their immortality.'

'How many vampires are there in this clan of yours?'

'Three hundred.'

'And you're immortal?'

Jalan had smiled bitterly. 'We live for perhaps two thousand years.'

She had shaken her head, but she had known that he had spoken the truth. It was strange how calmly she could accept it.

'And the blood sucking? The walking dead?'

'Myths. We need blood to survive, yes. Never, though, do we take it from an unwilling partner. If I could love you fully, as I desire, I would take of your blood, and when you were ready, I would return it so that your blood would begin to change. In that way you would become like me.'

'I know you've always wanted more. You hold back, even when –'

'What I need, you must give to me by choice, and I will only accept it when you understand what it is you give. Only then. The joining between a vampire and his woman is indescribable.'

He had closed his eyes, and for a moment Jocelyne had caught a faint vibration, an emanation from him of what might occur. The sensation had shot straight to her core, flooding her, tightening secret muscles. The pain of longing had torn through her: pain amid delight, amid desire.

Jocelyne had swallowed against the tight knot in her throat. 'And after this joining, I'd become a vampire? The blood ... I couldn't kill –'

'A woman does not need to take the blood of another. As in all things, I will be the one to quench your thirst. But for a man, while the blood-lust is all-powerful, it can be controlled. Those from whom I have taken nourishment have not died of my caress. So, now you know. I am a vampire. Would you give up your life for me, Jocelyne? To become one with me, you must suffer the kiss of night. You must die, in order to be reborn, to become blood of my blood, to live with me for the centuries.'

'I would have to die?' Panic had gripped her. Death had always been her fear, but perhaps she had always feared growing old more. 'How would I die?'

'In my arms. I would drink from you and, at the point of death, return a part of your blood, synthesised, to act as a catalyst to irrevocably change the rest of your blood.'

'I love you, Jalan. But this ... I just don't know. It's so unbelievable!'

He had spread his hands. 'I cannot lie to you. Our bond precludes it.'

Jocelyne had looked from him to the mirror, to his ripple-outline.

'We could be lovers until . . .'

'Until you die?' Jalan's voice was harsh, as chill as ice, as cold as the grave. 'I could not bear to see you wither, and know that we were forever sundered by death. Even if I agreed, that path is denied me.'

'How?'

'I am one with you, Jocelyne. Rightly or wrongly, I went against our tradition and touched your soul with mine, before you knew what I had done. So I pay the price. If you die, so will I. Without our soul mate, our kind will die of loneliness, or sorrow. Our existence is a bittersweet thing. I did not understand my brothers' warnings. Until now.'

'I need time,' Jocelyne had said.

'Yes. When you have decided, call me.' He had scooped up his clothes and left the room without a backward glance.

A month later, she had left a message on his answering machine: 'Come to me tonight'.

He had come. How long he had been standing there, Jocelyne did not know. She had been sitting at her dressing table, brushing her hair, thinking, dreaming, imagining. Gradually, she had become aware of the ripple-reflection next to hers.

With a shaking hand, she had set the brush down and turned to him. Dressed in black, he resembled a shadow as he stepped from the balcony into her bedroom.

On weak legs, she had gone to him. His fingers had cupped her cheek. Holding her out at arm's length, his eyes had taken her in from head to toe and back again. His smile, slow and languid, had turned her body inside out.

She had chosen the black silk négligé with care, certain that it would seductively highlight her curves. The robe had cost a fortune, but if one was to die, one should go out in style. She had prepared herself and her bed – their bed – for this night of endings and beginnings.

He had drawn her into his arms, and rested his cheek on her head. Beneath her hands she had felt the trembling of his body. The spice and musk scent of him had aroused her empty sex.

'You're doing it to me, again, Jalan,' she had said.

'I cannot control it any more. You said to come. I am here. I will not hold back. But are you certain? Once done, it cannot be undone.'

The words echoed in Jocelyne's mind. Blinking, she drew her thoughts back to the present.

'Welcome back,' Jalan said. 'You were gone a long time.'

'I was remembering everything.'

'I know, I shared it with you. But that was the past, Josie. This is the present. I am here.'

She lifted her eyes to his, and drew his head down to her mouth. 'Stay with me, Jalan. For ever.'

His sigh came from the depths of his being. She felt his body tense, and moments later he lifted her into his arms. Still carrying her, he laid her gently on the bed and stared down at her.

'You are so beautiful. You have gone to much trouble to prepare this place, the place of our beginning.' He glanced at the bed, bedecked in red rose petals, like drops of blood against the black silk sheets.

'Come to me, Jalan. I can't wait.'

Laughing, he shrugged himself out of his jacket and let it fall to the floor. With a lazy grin, slowly, teasingly, he unbuttoned his shirt. His fingers rested on the buckle of his trousers.

Jocelyne strangled back her cry of frustration. 'Jalan, please.' The silk rustled beneath her as she writhed impatiently on the bed.

Smiling a secret man's smile that sent a thrill to her sex, he unfastened his belt and zip and stepped out of his trousers. Red silk boxer shorts slid to his ankles. She took in the sight of his cinnamon-skinned erection, now red and painfully engorged. He knelt beside her on the bed. She reached out to stroke his thighs, up to his rock-hard sacs at the base of his shaft. He leaned over her. She felt his searing heat on her skin.

Knotting her fingers in his hair, Jocelyne drew his head to hers, opening her mouth, inviting him inside her. His tongue coiled against hers, entwining, stroking her length, in and out.

His lips whispered across her cheek, down her neck. She shivered as he playfully nipped the length of her carotid artery.

'Relax, Josie. You're not ready yet. And neither am I.'

Lazy kisses trailed down her neck, to her shoulder, down her arm, to her hand, to her fingers, back up again. His palm rested against her breast, kneading gently, his fingers curled around her, while his other hand cupped her between the legs. Through the silk négligé, her warmth spilled out on to his hand.

'You're hot for me, sweetheart,' he said.

'I've been hot for you from the moment I saw you.'

'I know.' He grinned.

'I'm going to curb your conceit!'

Laughing, he lowered his lips and sucked her breast, drawing flesh and silk into his mouth. He moved to her other breast and brought the nipple to a throbbing peak. The tension spiralled down her length and thrummed at the apex of her thighs. Slowly, slowly, Jalan inched the négligé up her body. The silk teased over her flesh, tormenting, igniting.

Finally, he tugged the négligé up over her head and flung it aside. Straddling her body, he bent forward. He shook his head slowly back and forth. His hair swished across her breasts. Lower, back and forth, he teased her with his hair. She captured him, pulled him down, forcing his body to cover hers. She parted her thighs and he came to rest against her, his arousal pressed to her belly. He smothered her frustration with his mouth.

Jalan's kisses engulfed her, while his hands cupped and caressed every inch of her. His mouth worshipped the smooth, flat plain of her belly, then down to her thighs, to the blonde curls shielding her hidden valley.

He plunged his tongue into her cleft, lapping her woman's honey like a starving man. 'Hot and spicy like home,' he whispered against her mound. 'I am home, Josie. Finally.'

She clutched his hair to anchor her as the bed, the room, spun about her. He worked at her pleasure nub, tongue scrolling and teeth nipping. He kept his fingers from her centre, though she cried out for him to test her depth. She moved her hips, inviting his entry, but he held one of her thighs while his other hand kept her petals open to his questing tongue.

She watched him until she could watch no more, until her world exploded in a burst of heat and light that permeated her every cell. Her climax lifted her from the bed. She was only dimly aware of Jalan drawing her across his body, so she lay on top of him. His legs wrapped around her waist.

Where before he had explored her body, now it was her turn. After his month of absence, she reacquainted herself with his every contour. She lapped and sucked, kissed and kneaded, until it was he who writhed beneath her like a wild thing, groaning and moaning in pleasure. As she moved to take his length into her mouth, his fingers knotted in her hair, gently drawing her upwards.

'For later, Josie,' he whispered harshly.

'But –'

'Later.'

His kiss silenced her protests. He turned her gently, so that she lay face down on the bed. From behind, she felt the tip of his shaft against her. He drew her hips up to his groin, probing, finding her woman's channel, immersing himself with one swift, sure stroke. Skin whispered against skin, a deeper and deeper entry and acceptance until they both went rigid as the first wave of ecstasy shivered through them. On and on they carried each other, again and again until at last they collapsed as one on to the bed.

Lying side by side, Jalan drew her back against him. Again, she thought how well they fitted together, like two halves of a mould.

'Like two peas in a pod,' he whispered against her ear.

'When will I be able to share your thoughts?'

'After the change, we shall be as one.'

'Please, Jalan. I've waited long enough. Now. Do it, now!'

His hands ceased their fevered wandering over her skin. She felt the quiver of his fingers.

'Do it, Jalan.'

'Yes,' he said.

He raised himself on an elbow. Slowly, gently, he lowered his face to her neck. She arched herself, inviting his mouth to her artery. But he did not stop there.

'Jalan!'

He laughed gently, and turned her in his arms. 'The neck is considered an erotic zone by some, but for this, our beginning, a sweeter place exists.'

His languid lapping of her flesh extended from her breasts to her inner thigh. Bending forward, he cupped her hips and raised her woman's mound to his mouth. As before, tongue and teeth caressed and lathered her.

She cried out as wave upon wave of pleasure crested from her pulsing canal to engulf her body.

'Josie!' his husky voice commanded. 'Look at me!'

His eyes held hers as he lowered his mouth to her secret flesh. She gasped at the gentlest of bites between her petals.

As his vampire's kiss deepened, so did the pressure build within her. A drawing from her to him. Not exactly pain. She was in a place she had never experienced, a place between heaven and hell. On and on, the demand grew until she trembled and hung limp in his hands. Her climaxes came and went and still he continued, inexhaustible, inexorable, relentlessly taking her beyond fulfilment.

After one last cry of pleasure, she felt him lower her gently to the bed. His body blanketed her; his shaft nestled in her cleft. He lay unmoving within her, his breath as fast and as ragged as her own.

'Don't stop, Jalan!'

'Save your strength.'

'But I want to feel you move inside me. What about you? You're as hard and as hot for me –'

'This time is for you. Only you. Now, sleep!'

He brushed her temple with his hand, smoothed back her hair. Jocelyne closed her eyes and, with him still deeply united with her, she slept.

Just before dawn, Jocelyne awoke. Her heart shuddered against her ribs. Her throat constricted as if she were choking. Her body felt on fire, every inch of her as taut as a bowstring. Her woman's mound throbbed, not with pain, but with longing. Opening her eyelids she saw Jalan beside her, propped up on an elbow, gazing down at her. His midnight eyes, in a face all harsh places and angles, were red-tinged.

'It is time for night's kiss,' Jalan whispered. 'I'll be with you, darling, all the way. Do not be afraid.'

'What must I do?'

'Accept my gift, that is all.'

'Drink your blood?'

'Taste my life, Josie.'

'How?'

He sat before her. Taking her head between his hands, he threaded his fingers in her hair. Tenderly, he guided her to his burnished manhood. Larger than ever, his shaft, engorged with blood, with life, pulsed and glistened. She laid her head in his lap, and took his penis into her mouth. At Jalan's triumphant cry, her own body spasmed. His fingers crept to her love-canal, in and out, mimicking the action of her mouth. She drank in his hot life, a bitterness amid the sweetness.

Time stood still.

Then he lifted her away. Tucking her beneath him, he entered her with one powerful stroke that branded her forever his. With his tongue stroking hers, he seared her mouth with a deep kiss.

As he rocked against her, she felt the stinging pressure in her neck. It spiralled outwards to her breasts, across her stomach to the secret garden that Jalan filled so entirely. Mouth and phallus probed and lunged, loving her until the final explosion, until she clung to him, and he to her.

A few minutes later her first convulsion cramped her from head to toe. With a cry of pain, she tore away from Jalan. With seeming ease, he returned her to his arms. She fought him: desperate, afraid, disoriented. Her nails raked against his shoulders, drawing blood, as he had drawn blood from her.

He took her chin; his eyes, red-glowing, held hers. Love, coupled with soothing, calming thoughts washed through her.

'It begins, Josie. My blood, my life to you.'

Shivering, Jocelyne pressed back against Jalan. His arms crushed her fiercely close.

'The gift is never accepted easily. Do not fight it. Welcome it.' His hands soothed her, while his manhood rested within her, unmoving, anchoring her.

For hours they lay like that, bodies intimately enjoined, arms and hands straining to hold and be held.

Afraid, she wanted to cry, to run. Run where? She was in Jalan's arms. The only place she wanted to be. She had to endure this. Had to. But she had not expected that it would be so awful. Beneath the soft, certain strokes of Jalan's hands, she felt his trembling, sensed his sorrow and fear, his anguish: for the kiss of night was a taste of hell.

Her heart laboured with every beat. Her blood rebelled through her veins. Her body tried to reject the invasion. Every breath was an effort in the sudden suffocating heat that gripped her. She struggled to live.

'Do not fight it, sweetheart. Give in,' Jalan whispered against her ear.

She tried. But some survival instinct, some primeval urge, made her claw for every moment of what remained of her human life. Jalan's once seductive scent of musk and spice was now so thick, so rich, it was cloying, almost choking her. She was burning up. A weight pressed down upon her. Too hot. Too heavy. Could not breathe. The darkness laced with red swirled around her, through her. Jalan's whispers grew distant and then indecipherable.

She ran into the darkness, on and on, seeking him, crying out in the silent wilderness. Alone. Alone for ever.

'Not alone!' his feather-soft voice caressed.

She felt Jalan's presence around her. Hurrying forward, she saw him ahead, in her dream-place, opening his arms in welcome.

'Jalan!' She hurled herself into his embrace, and raised her face for his kiss. His dream-image faded.

The world twisted inside out and with a cry she flung herself away.

Something warm held her, steadied her.

Jocelyne opened her eyes. Her vision swam before clearing. She saw Jalan above her, smiling down, his triumphant eyes still tinged red with the blood-lust. With the kiss of night. Life sang in her veins. Her body felt light and content. At peace.

'Welcome, darling,' Jalan whispered.

'I . . . It's over?'

'Your old life, yes. Your new life has only just begun. In the future we shall share many kisses. But none like that last. From now on, I will only give you love, and never pain or sickness, in my embrace. I promise.'

'You promise?'

'Yes.' He nuzzled her ear. 'And I never lie.'

'Prove it!' Jocelyne ordered.

'As you command, so I obey. How shall I begin?'

'At the top of my head and finish at my toes. Don't miss any place in between.'

'Gladly,' Jalan said. Dutifully, he bent to his task.

Paradise Garden

Kate O'Neill

Paradise Garden

⟡ ⟡

Soft shadows of dusk were starting to spread across the garden path as Clio brushed past the yellow rambling roses and began to make her way down the stone-flagged steps towards the herb garden. She would gather some fennel, she decided, for the Provençal *pot-au-feu* she was making for her guests tonight. And she would pick a sprig of lavender, for herself, just for the sheer indulgence of rubbing the grey leaves between her fingers and letting the aromatic scent bring back memories.

She stopped. Down below, in the soft shadows of a recessed arbour that was covered with white-starred clematis, she could see two figures moving, twining together like the flowers on the vine. A young man and a girl, making love; the man was cradling the girl to his body, covering her face with kisses, his hands moving tenderly over her pink-tipped breasts. The girl's long, slender legs were spread apart, her flimsy cotton dress rumpled round her waist as the man arched his hips and thrust powerfully, passionately into her. Clio could see his penis, dark and strong as he held himself poised above her then drove himself in; the girl clung desperately to his shoulders, moving her slack head from side to side in bliss, her eyes closed, her mouth murmuring words of love as he kissed her cheek, her throat, her breasts.

Clio smiled softly to herself and turned to go back towards the house. She would postpone dinner a little. Her guests had more important things on their minds.

*

After the meal, which was suitably delicious – no one noticed the absence of the fennel – Clio sat on the terrace in a wicker chair, and Sally knelt on a cushion at her side. Clio breathed in the heady scent of the nearby floribundas that filled the evening air.

'The roses are better than ever this year,' she said softly. 'I fell in love with this garden the first time I saw it. I never, ever dreamed that one day it would be mine.'

'Do tell, Aunt Clio!' pleaded the leggy, lovely girl at her side. 'I somehow imagined you'd lived in this gorgeous place all your life. Tell me how you first came here, please! Ben's inside, phoning home – he won't be joining us for a while.' She blushed as she said his name.

Sally was Clio's god-daughter, and this was the first time she'd brought Ben to stay. They were obviously very much in love. Sally was becoming beautiful, thought Clio, with her long, soft tendrils of dark hair and her windflower-blue eyes. Her body was suntanned and slender beneath her thin cotton frock. She was nineteen, just as she, Clio, had been when she first arrived here 25 years ago.

The haunting notes of a nightingale's song drifted from the woods.

'I didn't want to come here,' Clio said thoughtfully. 'I'd just finished school, and was due to start university in the autumn. My mother was ill, in hospital, and my father was desperately worried about her.'

'So your father sent you here? To your friend's house?'

Clio gave a rueful laugh. 'They thought Felicity was my friend; we were in the same form at boarding school, and Felicity's mother knew mine. But Felicity didn't like me. Oh, she pretended to be my friend. But she was rich, popular, spoilt. I was shy and thin and clever, with parents who were nothing by Fliss's standards. I dreaded coming here, but I had no choice.'

'So you hated that first summer here?'

'Not exactly.' Absently Clio brushed a little shrub of cotton lavender with her fingers, releasing its bruised, heady aroma into the sultry air. 'I didn't hate all of it. The garden, you see, was exquisite, just as it is now. Warm, drowsy, secretive, filled with scents.'

'And her brothers? Felicity had two older brothers, didn't she? Tell me about them. Were they good-looking?'

'Impossibly so.' Clio laughed. 'Their names were Miles and Ewan. They were both arrogant and beautiful. All Fliss's girl-friends worshipped them, but they despised me. At first, anyway.'

'But you still had a wonderful time?'

'Oh, yes . . .'

Sally grinned. 'You look all dreamy and lovely, Aunt Clio. I bet you fell in love that summer. Was it Miles, or Ewan? Look, I'll go and see what Ben's up to, and leave you in peace for a while. Then, over drinks, you must tell me more, much more. OK?'

Clio smiled and closed her eyes. To Sally, 25 years ago must seem like history. But to her, it was like yesterday.

She'd arrived on the first day of the summer holidays, feeling alone and unhappy and worried about her mother. Fliss was chatting to a friend on the phone, clearly resenting having Clio foisted on her. Miles and Ewan had just come in from playing cricket for the village team. They were gloriously handsome, with brown, rangy bodies and thick dark hair swept back from their arrogant faces. Their eyes flickered briefly over the pale, shy Clio, who had just that minute dropped her one cheap suitcase which had burst and spilt out its meagre contents. Her face burned brick red. Miles and Ewan moved on dismissively.

Things didn't improve. Clio, awkward and miserable, felt painfully alone. Fliss's mother had been kind, but busy with her main occupation of social climbing; Fliss's father, who was tall and handsome like his sons, was hardly ever there, due, Clio realised later, to a new affair.

Even the naïve Clio soon realised that they were all preoccu-pied with sex that summer. It was something to do with the heat, perhaps. People were restless, aroused, predatory. No one had time for the quiet, unhappy visitor.

Then one day, about a couple of weeks after she'd arrived, Fliss found a use for her.

Fliss was sprawled out on a sunbed beside the outdoor pool, oiling her voluptuous brown body. Her long blonde hair was pulled back in a ribbon, and her bikini top was carelessly discarded. Clio, who was reading a book, felt painfully thin: all long white legs and no bust, compared to the gorgeous, bosomy Fliss.

'Clio,' Fliss said conspiratorially, smoothing yet more oil into her ripe brown breasts, 'you must cover for me this afternoon. Go into town, go for a long walk or something, and tell mother I'm going with you.'

'Why?'

'Because I'm meeting a man from the village, silly. He works in the pub. Mother'd go spare. He's not in our social sphere, you see.' She stretched her silken body voluptuously, admiring her own full breasts. Her dark red nipples had gone hard beneath the oil. 'Oh, Clio, he's got the most heavenly body, and the most enormous cock. He loves me to play with it. Though, of course, we haven't done it yet. Not properly, you know.'

No, Clio didn't know. At least, she knew the biological rudiments, but little else. She was silent, shocked and aroused. Lucky, glamorous Fliss had always had boys after her. Clio, an only child incarcerated in a strict girls' school, hardly even knew any.

Fliss drew herself up, carefully easing on her bikini top. 'He adores my breasts. Pity you've not got any, Clio. Miles calls you the white stick insect.'

That hurt. Clio secretly thought Miles the most heavenly, unattainable creature; she fantasized at night about him gathering her into his arms and kissing her and saying in his husky, upper-class drawl, 'God, Clio, but I've just realised how gorgeous you are.'

Fliss was pressing on petulantly, 'So you'll clear off this afternoon? Get the bus or something, and for God's sake tell mother I'm going with you.' Then she gathered together her towel and lotion and was gone.

Instead of getting the bus, Clio went for a walk. There were acres of lovely, well-tended gardens spreading around the house, blending gradually into leafy woodland. Clio loved the rambling old house and its gardens; they were the only compensation for being here. Her father had been on the phone last night to tell her about her mother's operation. 'You're all right there for another week or two, Clio?'

Her heart went out to him, he sounded so tired. 'Yes, of course,' she lied. 'I'm fine.'

She wandered down past the immaculate tennis courts, and heard the click of racquets meeting the ball in the still, hot air. Miles and Ewan were playing doubles with two girls. They all looked exquisitely fit and brown in their tennis whites. Miles glimpsed Clio on the path.

She heard him say, 'Look, it's the stick insect. Wish she wouldn't creep around like that. Puts me off my stroke.'

'And it takes something to do that, Miles, doesn't it?' grinned one of the girls, sidling up to him and kissing him on the mouth, just as Clio did in her dreams.

She went on quickly, a lump in her throat. The coolness, the privacy of the ancient beech woods calmed her somehow. The air in there was full of fresh, invigorating scents after the blazing heat of the sun.

There was a small lake, once used for the mill race. Its surface looked clear and inviting; quickly she stripped off her clinging dress and dusty espadrilles and waded in, just in her skimpy bra and pants. The water felt wonderful against her hot skin. She swam slowly, feeling the coldness against her nipples and between her legs.

She turned over to float on her back, and thought of Fliss and her village boy. She remembered Fliss's words: 'He's got the most enormous cock . . .' She felt a strange, aching tug at the pit of her stomach, where the water lapped over it. She knew, vaguely, what people did, but tried not to think about it. Her nipples were hard and aching as the little waves caressed them. They used to go like that when she thought about Miles. But she hated Miles now.

She turned over to start swimming again but, as her feet brushed the bottom, she felt a sudden sharp pain slicing through her toe. 'Oh . . .'

She swam blindly to the edge of the lake and pulled herself out, the water dripping from her bra and pants. She shivered when she saw the blood on her foot. Then she heard someone pushing through the bushes behind her.

'Are you all right?' It was a man's voice, gentle and concerned.

She turned round to face him. 'I think so. But I seem to have cut my foot or something.'

Afterwards, she remembered how she had instinctively trusted him, even though she had never seen him before. He had thick, sun-streaked blond hair and was dressed in cut-off denim shorts and a loose white T-shirt; he was perhaps two or three years older than she was. His blue-grey eyes were full of concern as he bent quickly to examine her foot. She saw, with a little lurch at her stomach, that his sinewed brown forearms were deliciously covered with soft blond hairs.

'It's all right,' he said quickly. 'Only seems to be a shallow cut – should stop bleeding soon. Those stupid kids should be horsewhipped for this.'

'Who do you mean?' she said, wonderingly, through her shivers.

'Miles and Ewan,' he said scornfully. 'They had their friends up here for a barbecue the other day. All drunk, the lot of them. Some of them threw empty bottles into the lake. I must see to getting it cleared. No one else will.'

She frowned, puzzled. 'Who are you, please?'

'I'm Jon,' he grinned. 'Got a job here for the summer – gardener, if you like. Look, you're freezing. Have you got anything else to put on?'

She pointed to her short cotton dress. He dismissed it with one glance, then pulled off his white T-shirt and offered it to her. She pulled it over her head, rather unsteadily aware of the warm, clean, male smell that lingered on the soft fabric. And, once she'd pushed her head through, she tried not to stare at him because her heart had done another unsettling flip at the sight of the hard, ridged muscle of his tanned chest, the silken tautness of his stomach. Seemingly unaware of her consternation, he was pulling a clean handkerchief from his pocket as he knelt to tend her toe. She saw how his long brown thighs stretched the frayed denim of his shorts; his fingers were gentle as they worked over her foot.

'Just checking it's clean,' he said, matter-of-factly. 'Then I'll bandage it up.'

Before Clio had realised what he intended, he'd lifted her toe to his mouth and was sucking gently. She leaned quickly for support against a nearby tree as his tongue worked over her sensitive flesh. A little pulse throbbed tremulously in her groin, and her nipples hardened acutely under the wet scrap of her bra, thrusting achingly at his borrowed T-shirt. Oh, God, didn't he realise what he was doing to her?

Then he'd finished, and was pulling himself back up, and gazing at her with those incredible blue-grey eyes that crinkled in the sunlight. 'OK,' he said. 'No glass splinters, no grit. I'll help you home, and if I see Miles or Ewan, I'll tell them what I think of them.'

'No!' she said. 'I can't go back yet. I'm supposed to be out all afternoon with Fliss – I'm her alibi.'

His brows gathered in thought. Then he said, 'You like that family? They're friends of yours?'

'No,' she said, honestly. 'And they don't like me.'

'Be thankful for small mercies. Look, I'm supposed to be fencing some saplings in the south wood this afternoon. Come with me if you like. Sit in the sun, and we can chat.'

Afterwards, Clio couldn't really remember what they talked about. But she remembered his husky, warm voice, and the dappled sunlight dancing through the young trees, and the lovely play of the powerful muscles of his back as he fenced the young trees skilfully, caringly.

'They'll have grown another few feet by next summer,' he said.

'You'll be here next summer?'

He turned and grinned, his teeth even and white in his tanned face. 'Hope so, yes. I need the money. I'm doing medicine at Cambridge – another two poverty-stricken years to go.'

He pushed his thick fair hair back off his forehead, and Clio felt herself melt with desire. No doubt he had a beautiful, glamorous girlfriend already. She sat watching him with her arms hugged around her knees and wished she had a bigger bosom and curvy brown legs like Fliss.

At last, it was time for her to go back.

'See you around,' he said. She nodded, quivering with longing.

'You must have your T-shirt back,' she said.

He shrugged. 'Keep it. I'll see you again, won't I?'

'Oh, please,' she prayed silently.

She walked slowly back through the silent woods, the late-afternoon heat thrumming through her body. She decided to keep away from the path that led past the tennis courts and find her way through the dark shrubbery instead, because she didn't want Miles and Ewan to see her and spoil her happiness. She hugged Jon's T-shirt to her body, feeling a kind of dazed euphoria as she remembered the magical afternoon.

Suddenly, she stopped. There were strange, subdued noises coming from just beyond the laurel bushes to her left. She turned, and saw Miles and one of the girls, Suzie, lying on the ground. Miles, still in his white tennis gear, was stretched out on his back, laughing lazily.

71

'Dear God, Suze – no, don't stop – Christ, you're wicked . . .'

Suzie was bent over him, her long hair cascading over his groin, and she was deftly unfastening his zip. Clio, somehow rooted to the spot, saw his penis spring out, thick and dusky and already erect. Suzie grinned and licked her lips, then bent down to take it in her mouth. Clio felt the colour rushing to her face as the girl swirled her pointed pink tongue over the swollen glans, then sank her mouth down over the long, rigid shaft. Up and down her eager head bobbed. Miles had gone quite tense, his eyes shut tight, his mouth slack with bliss. Now Suzie was gripping the base of his cock with tight fingers, and stroking his testicles. Clio could see the heavy twin globes that were wrinkled and covered with soft dark hairs. And then Suzie bent to lick at his balls with her dancing tongue, and was rubbing his hard cock with her fingers. Clio, scarcely able to breathe, saw Miles jerk his whole body, and saw the milky semen start to spurt slowly, rapturously from his throbbing penis.

'Oh, God, Suze,' he was muttering. 'Oh, God. Game, set and match to you.'

They rolled over together then on the grass, kissing. Suzie's tennis skirt was up round her slim brown thighs as Miles' hand found its way to the warm mound beneath her white knickers; and Clio turned and hurried back to the house.

That night, as she lay in her bed with the windows open to catch the cool, scent-laden air, Fliss sought her out, pushing open her bedroom door in the darkness.

'Oh, Clio. Thanks! It worked. We did it. Clio, I must tell you, or I'll burst!'

She perched on the edge of Clio's bed, her face flushed with excitement. Clio listened.

'You know I said I'd played with his cock? Well, I was frightened, because he seemed so big. But this afternoon, in his little room over the pub, I let him take all my clothes off. He was panting for it, Clio, desperate! He was licking my breasts, taking them in his mouth, while his fingers rubbed me slowly down there – you know? Until I was all, all wet . . . Then he took it out, his penis, and it was so long, and throbbing so angrily, and I thought, Christ, how do I get that great stick of a thing inside me? But he told me it would be all right, and he put a condom on, and guided it into me – and, my God, Clio, it was gorgeous! It felt so huge as he pushed it into me – I was so tight, so wet –

and he kissed me, and played with my tits while he was doing it. I was bouncing around the bed, squealing, I tell you! Can't wait to do it again . . .' She sighed dreamily. 'I'd better go. You'll cover for me again, tomorrow? Say yes!'

'All right,' said Clio. 'Same time?'

'Same time. Bless you!' She scampered off.

Clio lay there in her little bed. A sultry breath of air stealing through the open window did nothing to cool her heated skin; she'd got sunburnt today, and her body was throbbing. Slowly her fingers slipped between her thighs, and she felt her secret flesh there, swollen and glistening. She thought of Jon's lovely brown, silken body, and somehow it got mixed up with Miles, and what Fliss had just told her. She imagined herself pulling down Jon's frayed shorts from his narrow hips, and easing out his penis, and doing to him what Suzie had done.

She rubbed herself quickly with her fingers, lifting her hips and moaning softly with longing as the pleasure flooded through her. Then she lay back, and reached for Jon's T-shirt, which she'd hidden under her pillow when Fliss came in. Tomorrow, she'd find him again.

She did find him the next day, and every day after that. She helped him in whatever he was doing, and learned from him about the trees, and woodland birds, and the secret haunts of animals. He showed her a badger set, and she watched the young ones at play, enthralled. She grew brown and lithe in the sun, and laughed with him, and loved him desperately. He always seemed pleased to see her, but how could she make him actually *want* her? Fliss would just flash her breasts and seduce him. Suzie would unzip his shorts with a wicked giggle. But her? The shy stick insect? Gloom descended.

Then, one day, Fliss burst in on her. 'Mother and Daddy are going away for the weekend. Bliss! Party!'

All Saturday afternoon, the phone was frantic. Miles pinched his mother's car and drove out to pick up wine and food.

'Come on, Clio,' he said, seeing her in the hall. 'Help me.'

'OK,' she'd said obediently, quite unfazed. At one time, she would have fainted with delight at the thought of being alone with him.

On the way home, he tried to kiss her. 'Come on, Clio. You're really quite pretty.'

He touched her slender brown leg, exposed by the very short

denim skirt she was wearing, then took her hand and planted it on his thigh, sliding it up so she could feel the hard bulk of his genitals. She pulled away quickly.

'Come on,' pleaded Miles, fondling her shoulder.

'No,' she said. 'I don't fancy you.'

Miles sulked, but Clio's heart was thumping. Perhaps she *was* getting prettier. But what was the point? No way was Jon going to be there tonight. He hated Miles and Ewan and their friends.

That evening, as Clio was pulling on a clinging ribbed top and floaty long skirt in preparation for the party, Fliss knocked and came in.

'Clio, I'm in love!'

'I know,' Clio said patiently as she tried to buckle the thin suede anklestraps of her shoes.

'No, not him – somebody else! Oh, Clio, he is so gorgeous. Tonight I'll get him into bed – God, I can't wait!'

'Who is he?' Clio asked, but she was now more interested in trying to get her long dark hair to respond to the attentions of her hairbrush.

'His name's Jon. He's working here, just for the summer, and he's the most beautiful guy – I've been slavering over him for days now. Suzie told me about him – she's had him several times, and he's incredible in bed, she says. A medical student, would you believe, so he's brainy as well! And Suze has gone to the south of France with her family, so I'm moving in on him!'

Clio felt as if her heart was clenching in agony. Gazing at herself in the mirror, she saw that the make up she'd put on, and the long silver earrings, looked stupid and tawdry.

Oh, Jon.

That night, she drank lots of cheap wine and let Ewan dance with her. Dozens of people had arrived in their cars, braying and drinking and giggling and openly fondling one another as the wine took effect. Ewan groped her as they danced.

'You're lovely, Clio,' he muttered drunkenly over the blaring music.

While she was extricating herself from his wandering hands, she saw Fliss coming in, with Jon. He looked achingly handsome in a pale linen shirt and sun-bleached Levis that clung to his long, muscular legs. All the girls were gazing at him with lust in their eyes. He went off to get Fliss a drink, and Clio watched his

mane of sun-streaked hair disappear into the crowd with a stab
of despair. Fliss came up to her, gloating.

'Isn't he gorgeous? Suze said he's got a divine cock, and knows
just what to do with it. We'll be up till dawn . . .'

Clio ran off to her room, ignoring Ewan. She couldn't bear any
more.

There were two people she didn't know in her room, on her
bed. The air was filled with the musky reek of sex, and she could
see the man's white bottom thrusting dementedly away. She ran
downstairs and out through the french windows on to the
flagged terrace. She wanted to cry. Suzie, and Fliss. She'd
thought Jon was different.

The night air was warm and sultry; a pale moon hung in the
velvety sky. She found herself wandering through the garden,
and into the woods where the badgers were. She watched them
playing in the moonlight. She still ached, still felt terrible, but at
least she'd learnt not to trust anyone, ever.

Suddenly she heard footsteps coming slowly up behind her,
and a quiet, familiar voice saying, 'Aren't they wonderful?'

She spun round, her eyes wet with tears. Jon. He was watching
the badgers.

'Where's Fliss? She let you go?'

He gazed at her, frowning slightly at her tears. 'What do you
mean? She doesn't own me. She invited me to the party, that's
all.'

'But she said – she said you'd been seeing Suzie, sleeping with
Suzie, and now it was her turn . . .'

'You believe everything you hear? Suzie tried it on one night in
the village pub, but I turned her down. She's really not my type.'

'But Fliss? Fliss said –'

'Oh, Clio. Lovely Clio. I only accepted Fliss's invitation
because I just had to see you again before I go.'

Fresh misery smote her, stopping her absorbing properly what
he'd just said. 'You're going?'

'Yes, tomorrow. Got some extra reading to catch up on before
term starts.'

Tomorrow. She couldn't bear it. 'Oh, Jon.' If she wasn't careful,
she'd start crying again.

He caught her in his arms.

'Hey, Clio,' he murmured. 'Don't cry, please. Clio, I'm mad
about you. Don't you realise that?'

'Nobody's mad about me,' she gulped. 'I'm thin, and plain, and they all prefer stupid people like Suzie and Fliss.'

'I don't,' he said. 'You're beautiful. You've got class. Believe me, they all want you.' His blue-grey eyes darkened suddenly. 'Earlier this evening, at the party, when Miles was boasting about what you'd done to him in the car, I wanted to strangle him.'

She stopped breathing. 'What did he say?'

'He said you'd given him a hand job in the car.'

She shook her head. 'No. Oh, no.'

This time his eyes were dark with relief. 'You didn't? Thank God. I should have strangled him after all, for lying about you. Oh, Clio . . .'

He kissed her. His teeth tasted clean and fresh, his tongue was enticingly warm inside her mouth. She clung to him, kissing him passionately back. She felt the hard bulge of his groin pressing against her filmy long skirt, and she felt weak. He deepened his kiss, thrusting and caressing with his tongue as his hands gently stroked her breasts, bringing the nipples up like aching little fruits of delight.

Carefully, he laid her down on the soft turf and eased up her clinging top. Then he pushed aside the lacy little cups of her bra, and gazed at her. 'Oh, Clio. You're so lovely.'

He bent his head to kiss her breasts; she squirmed at the hot, moist touch of him, feeling fire tugging at her loins, wanting her whole body to melt in the furnace. Oh, she wanted him, so much.

He was still kissing her as his hand moved up inside her slender thighs, stroking gently at her tiny panties. She was wet there already. He was pushing them to one side, caressing her hot, furred mound, slipping between the plump folds of flesh with his index finger. Glorious starbursts of pleasure shot through her.

'Please, Jon. Oh, please.'

Gently he eased off her panties, murmuring, 'It's OK, Clio. We have all night.' Then he was rubbing at her rhythmically with his knuckle, just catching the little hard ridge where all her pleasure seemed to concentrate. She squirmed beneath him, her thighs falling apart in melting delight. Oh, God, she thought rather weakly, he knows what he's doing. And it was paradise, though still she was stirring, clenching her loins restlessly, longing for something more.

Then she heard him unbuttoning his faded Levis. Glancing down, she saw his long, thrilling cock, already straight and thick. She touched it, and as it quivered she felt an answering tremor run through her own body.

His face was dark with passion as he knelt between her legs and gently cupped her bottom with one hand while guiding his penis with the other. She watched raptly as he eased himself into her, and her eyes widened with shock as she felt the swollen, blunt head pushing against her throbbing sex. But then he stroked her clitoris tenderly, so that her whole body leapt and opened. He slipped his shaft inside her, gliding in her silvery juices.

'Oh,' she gasped, frightened to move in case the wonderful feeling should stop.

But it didn't stop. He rocked himself slowly into her, his face intent over hers, his beautiful male body arched devastatingly over her as he gradually penetrated her with his lovely hard penis. She lifted her hips to him, felt herself clench almost unbearably in tension around the long thick shaft; and then she was rushing headlong into a blissful vortex of sensation, quivering beneath him as his finger rubbed gently at her clitoris and his mouth suckled her swollen nipples. She cried out his name as the dark ecstasy engulfed her, and she felt his cock quivering deep inside her as he thrust hard towards his own powerful release. She lay sheened with sweat in his strong arms as the lingering afterwaves of delight washed through her.

They made love all night. She explored his lovely brown, hard body, kissing him everywhere, raking him with her fingernails and taking his lovely cock in her mouth. He taught her how to ride him; she gazed at his face below her as she rose and sank on his pulsing shaft and took him steadily to the extremity of pleasure.

Then she lay back and gazed at the sparkling night sky, shivering with renewed bliss as his hard tongue lapped at her lushly unfurling sex and penetrated her warmly, wickedly, until he'd brought her to yet another exquisitely sensuous peak of delight. Overhead, the stars seemed to explode, dazzling her.

She must have dozed in her chair on the terrace, because she could hear Sally's voice, offering her a glass of wine.

'Here you are, Aunt Clio. Ben's helped Uncle light the fire in the sitting room. Uncle likes Ben, doesn't he? I do hope so. You looked as if you were dreaming just now. Nice dreams, I hope?'

Clio stretched like a cat in the warm evening air, smiling at her. Her body was still slender and lithe. 'Oh, yes.'

'You were going to tell me how you got this lovely house.'

'I worked hard, was left some money, was lucky with some investments. Unfortunately Fliss's father lost heavily on Lloyds, though the children had all left home by then. So I was able to buy this place.'

'And Uncle Jon? Where did you meet him? He must have been quite a catch.'

Sally smiled fondly as a tall, distinguished looking man with fair hair and clear blue-grey eyes came out on to the terrace to join them.

'Oh,' said Clio, smiling mischievously as she moved towards her husband, 'he was once the gardener. You could say, I suppose, that he came with the house.'

*The Man Across
the Street*

Zoe le Verdier

The Man Across the Street

⁙ ⁙

The first time was an accident.

Juggling ambitiously with steering wheel, mobile phone and take-away coffee, it was the sudden braking of the car in front that started it all. I looked down in dismay: Boss shirt and tie streaked with brown, Paul Smith trousers with a damp patch in a most embarrassing place. I would have to go home and change.

Luckily, my flat was on the way. As the lift whirred me efficiently to the third floor, I dabbed tentatively at the stains with my handkerchief, soaking up the worst of it as Madeleine had instructed, the day the waiter at the Ritz had tripped and spilt tea down my linen suit. Maddie always knew what to do.

It wasn't until I put the key in the door that I remembered she wasn't there. Expecting to return home to the rich sounds of her cello, the silence shocked me. She was still inside my mind, playing incessantly in my head like an unfinished symphony.

Standing in front of the bedroom window in my clean suit, the now familiar mid-life worries clutched coldly at my neck and I shivered despite the flood of summer sun pouring through the glass. I wasn't special, I knew that. Most men of my age go through a year or two of self-doubt, of questioning their existence, mourning the loss of the bright bloom of youth. I knew that, and yet I couldn't help wallowing in despair. Was this it? I had everything – except the things I really needed.

'There's more to life than your sodding computers!' Maddie had screamed as she had whirled like a tornado out of my flat, out of my life. 'Passion, fun – remember that? You'd better start enjoying life, Philip, or you'll spend the rest of it alone.'

I stared vacantly at the sprawling urban view, the distant, grey haze settling over the sun-baked city like an itchy blanket, and I wondered whether the world would end if I cancelled my afternoon meeting. Perhaps, I thought, I should go back to the office and flirt with my young secretary in an attempt to revive my flagging ego.

Then something caught my eye in the building opposite, and there she was. Standing with her back to me. Naked. The sight was so shocking, so wonderfully natural and so wrong that I flinched guiltily; but I couldn't look away.

Everything about her was beautiful. The long, golden-brown waves of her hair. The curve of her waist, the gentle flare of her hips. The air of self-absorption with which she smoothed body lotion into her skin. In a trance, I stepped closer to the window, raising my face to the soft breeze in the vain hope that a quirk of fate would bring the scent of her body wafting across the street to my nostrils. I wanted to rest in the shelter of her elegant neck, to breathe her in. I was intoxicated.

She turned, and I gasped. Not at the sight of her breasts, although they were full and high, and her nipples were dark and wide. It was the way she looked directly at me that stole my breath away. For an interminable moment, our bodies were frozen, trapped by the shock of discovery. Then, with a slight smile, she walked out of sight.

I toyed with that smile all afternoon. It faded and appeared throughout my meeting, making me lose the thread of conversation more than once. Like a stubbornly disobedient child, my mind kept wandering to her. I typed a two-word memo into my electronic personal organiser: 'Buy binoculars.'

I arrived home at seven. As I put the key in the door, I remembered that Maddie wasn't there. And I realised, for the first time in a month, that I didn't mind.

Standing back from my bedroom window so that I wouldn't be seen, I focused my new binoculars on the flat opposite. Suddenly, the road between the two buildings was gone and I was free to pry, unimpeded by the distance between my life and hers. My gaze wandered around her bedroom, savouring the details:

crumpled white sheets on the unmade bed; tasteful line drawings of nudes, both male and female, on the walls; small piles of clothes littering the floor at irregular intervals, like the droppings of some strange prehistoric bird. The bra hanging from the iron bedstead, a delicate cage of white satin and lace, felt so close that I reached out to touch it.

Carried on a wave of guilty excitement, I strode in and out of the rooms adjoining my bedroom. As I had suspected, the two buildings were identical inside as well as out; on either side of the bedroom my living room looked into her kitchen, and vice versa. But the similarity ended with the architecture; her flat was full of colour and life. Her kitchen, a mess of empty wine bottles and bright crockery, was more than a place to make coffee and toast. Suddenly, I looked at my clinical, minimalist décor with disappointment, and found myself wondering what she would think of it.

I broke all the rules and ate my Chinese take-away from a tray in the living room, binoculars ready at my side. But she didn't appear. Darkness enveloped the flat, and I sat in the gloom with the curtains open, waiting eagerly for a light from across the street. At nine o'clock, I grew frustrated. I turned on the evening news, but the newsreader seemed to be smirking at me, and I switched over to an impossibly dire TV movie. At midnight I went for a bath, lying dazed for so long that the water went cold. On my way to bed I caught sight of myself in the hall mirror. Grey was creeping into my dark brown hair, showing my age, but my blue eyes were possessed with the unwavering hopefulness of a teenager. It was ridiculous. Feeling deflated and slightly foolish, I went back into the living room to pour myself a large, whisky-flavoured sleeping pill.

As I turned the light out, she turned hers on. Anticipation gripped tightly at my stomach as I moved to the window, the binoculars unsteady in my fingers. In the kitchen, she shrugged her jacket on to a chair and poured a glass of red wine. My heart stopped and I held my breath as she opened the wide sash window. She stood there, sipping her wine, a long curl of hair waving at me in the faint breeze, and she looked directly at me. I closed my eyes, a desperate sweat oozing from my pores as I imagined the light catching on the lenses of my binoculars, imagined her disgust and indignation, imagined her lifting the phone, calling the police.

I opened my eyes, and my dread at being discovered dissolved into the night. There was that smile again, and this time I realised what it meant. Almost imperceptibly, my penis began to thicken.

Raising a hand, she began to trace abstract patterns on her neck. It was as if her fingers belonged to someone else: she tilted her head away from them, and her eyes half-closed in ecstasy. Her touch slipped to the collar of her dark-red blouse, then to her cleavage. Undoing two buttons there, her fingers disappeared beneath the material and on to the luscious slope of her breast. Setting her glass down, her other hand smoothed down her leg, then up again, pulling at the soft fabric of her skirt. Stunned, I watched as she revealed first her black stockings, and then the sweet, pale cream of her upper thighs. In the distance, I heard a muffled, indistinguishable sound; it was me, struggling to sigh as her finger disappeared into the dark silk between her legs.

Over the weeks that followed, a strange friendship developed between us. We became more open with each other: I would masturbate in front of her, she would wave and blow kisses. I found her honesty irresistible. Even the mundane parts of her existence began to fascinate and arouse me. I would watch her making pasta, half-heartedly tidying up, crying at a sentimental movie, and a strange warmth would envelop my heart. The night she didn't come home, I realised I was in love with her.

Whoever he was, she didn't see him often – three times during the first month – but it was enough to make me jealous. She monopolised my thoughts, and I found it increasingly hard to accept that I didn't dominate hers. Don't get me wrong, I wasn't obsessed. At least, not in an unhealthy way. I just wanted to be more than the man across the street.

'What's up with you, then? That's the first time I've trounced you, Philip.'

I poked my head out from beneath the towel. Ben was glowing with sweat and pride. Several club members had been watching us play, admiring Ben's muscular black body, resplendent in his Lacoste tennis whites. Now he had removed his shirt, much to the delight of the four women waiting for the court. I watched him pick the prettiest and wink at her, and I smiled to myself. Ben's ego was just another muscle, to be pumped up like his biceps; it was what made him such a good salesman. It was the reason I had employed him.

'I haven't been sleeping very well.'

'Still pining for Madeleine?'

I shook my head. 'Actually . . . I've met someone else.'

'What's her name?'

'I don't know.'

Ben grinned wickedly. 'You dirty dog. You didn't even ask her name?'

'I haven't slept with her.' I zipped my tennis bag and stood up. 'I haven't even spoken to her, yet.'

Ben ran his thick fingers through his close-cropped black hair, as he always did when confused. 'I don't understand.'

'You wouldn't believe it, if I told you.'

He was intrigued. 'Try me.'

'Wow. You can see everything through these.' Ben put the binoculars down and turned his back to the window.

I passed him another glass of wine.

'And you're sure she can see you?'

'Positive. She waves at me.'

Ben whistled and slowly shook his head. 'I can't believe how many kinky women there are out there.'

'And what would you know? You're a married man.'

Ben's dark eyes assumed an expression I recognised – the one he always used when about to announce the clinching of another lucrative deal for the firm. 'I'm having an affair.'

My mouth fell open. 'I can't believe it. But you love Debbie, and she's –'

'Yeah, yeah. She's beautiful, clever, successful . . .' Ben took a large gulp of wine. 'But Lauren's different. She knows what I want.'

'How did you meet her?'

'Debbie was away on business. I went to this new wine bar for dinner – Lauren's the manager there. I couldn't take my eyes off her. She came to ask if everything was all right with my meal, and we got talking.' Ben stared into the bottom of his glass and swilled his wine around. His wide mouth leered uncontrollably. 'I knew I had to have her, Philip.'

'So?' I prompted.

'So, when she came to take my dessert order, I asked for her, in a light coating of baby oil.'

I snorted, spraying wine into the air. 'Did she slap you?'

'She just laughed. She wasn't phased at all, as if customers make suggestive comments to her all the time, which they probably do. She said, "I'm sorry sir, but I'm not on the menu." And I said, "I've got to fuck you tonight, or I'll go insane."'

'Jesus, Ben! What did she say to that?'

'She said, "I finish at one o'clock. You can fuck me then, if you like."'

I shook my head in disbelief. If Ben hadn't been so much younger than I was, I would have asked him for lessons. 'You've got some balls. Is she good-looking?'

'She's . . . hang on, your woman's home.'

I jumped as she appeared at her living room window. 'I'll turn the light out,' I whispered, then I remembered there was no need to whisper. 'I don't want her to think I've invited my friends round to leer.'

'Which is exactly what you have done,' Ben said, smirking. 'She doesn't waste any time, does she?'

The familiar warmth slid over my skin as she undressed, and I began to regret letting Ben talk me into this. Too late, I realised that I didn't want to share my view with anyone.

'Give us a look,' Ben urged impatiently. Reluctantly, I relinquished my grip on the binoculars. 'Oh . . . my . . . God.'

'I told you she was beautiful.'

'Oh my God,' Ben repeated. 'I don't believe this.' Slowly, he lowered the binoculars and turned to face me. 'That's her.'

'What?'

'That's Lauren. The woman I'm having an affair with.' Ben dived towards his jacket, fumbled in his pockets and triumphantly produced his computerised little black book. 'I think, Philip, it's time you met the woman you've been slavering over.'

'Hello?' Her voice was soft and low: just as I had imagined.

'Hello.'

'Who is it?'

'It's me.'

'I know quite a few people called "me". Which one are you?'

'Come to the window.'

She appeared in my view. Fresh from the bath, she was

wrapped in a towel. Her hair was twisted messily on top of her head. 'Christ!' There was a long pause. 'How did you get my number?'

'I work in computers. I hacked into the phone records.'

'I see.' There was uncertainty in her voice.

'I hope you don't mind,' I said, sure I could hear alarm bells ringing in her head.

'I don't think so,' she admitted hesitantly. 'After all, we know each other pretty well.'

'I'd like to know you better.'

Even without the aid of the binoculars, I could see her smile.

'That's a rather well-worn cliché.'

'It's just a polite way of saying I want to fuck you.' I heard her breath catch. 'I've got a bottle of wine open. Why don't you come over?'

She moved closer to the window. 'How do I know you're not a weirdo?'

'How do I know you're not? You like to take your clothes off in front of strangers.'

'And you like to watch.'

'I'm a man.'

She laughed softly. 'I'll just get dressed.'

'Wear something nice.'

I buzzed her into the building and opened the door to my flat, then returned to the living room. I sat down opposite Ben and waited, my heart pounding furiously.

Outside on the landing, I heard the lift whirr and then clunk to a halt. Heels tapped along the corridor, my front door clicked shut. Then she was there, in my living room, standing a few feet in front of me.

I looked her up and down. It was strange to be so close to her, to be able to see without the aid of magnification, and I lingered over the details. Her golden hair shone, curling softly over her shoulders. She wore a rich mink-brown shirt, made from a soft velour which clung tenaciously to her curves and stopped at the flare of her hips. Just covering her thighs was a straight black skirt, beneath which her stocking-clad legs seemed to stretch forever. Black high heels showed off the sensuous curve of her insteps; the thin straps around her ankles inexplicably made my mouth turn dry. As I drank her in, the long fingers of her left hand moved to her neck, and she began to trace gentle patterns on her skin, as I had seen her do so many times before. Her nails were painted with a dark reddish purple, the colour of sex. Slowly, she began to smile.

'Hello again,' she said.

'Hello, Lauren.'

Her smile disintegrated and she turned towards the voice. 'Ben! What...?' She looked at me, then back again. 'What's going on, Ben? What are you doing here?'

'I could ask you the same question, but I already know the answer.' I could see that Ben was enjoying himself. 'Lauren, I'd like you to meet Philip Rothwell, my boss.'

Her pretty lips fell open, her eyes widened with surprise. For a split second she looked so vulnerable, I longed to hold her. I handed her a glass of wine, which she shakily accepted.

'Philip's been enjoying your performances,' Ben smirked. 'Why haven't you ever performed for me?'

She turned her back on him. 'You never asked.'

'I'm asking now.'

'No.'

She looked up at me as she sipped her wine. I had been unsure as to the exact colour of her eyes; I realised now that they didn't have one. They were green and brown, with flecks of amber and rims of smoky grey. They were smiling secretively.

'You'll do what I say, Lauren. You always do. Now come here.'

'No!' she insisted.

'Come here!' Ben shouted, with a false show of anger.

Lauren and I turned to find him sitting, legs astride, black cock rearing angrily from his trousers. Lauren passed her wine back to me. As she walked away I sat down, my own penis straining in anticipation.

'Kneel down,' Ben commanded. He leaned forward in his seat and grabbed her chin. 'Now suck my cock,' he hissed.

She lowered her face to his groin. I watched as her head rose and fell, and Ben's dark fingers clutched at her hair. Through the split in her skirt I could see the tops of her stockings, her creamy inner thighs, the taut strip of black satin that covered her pussy. I struggled to breathe, desperate to touch her, smell her, taste her. I had never wanted a woman so badly.

Ben shuddered and groaned. He opened his eyes and smiled

when he found my gaze on Lauren's behind. 'Your turn, Philip,' he said. 'Tell her what you want.'

She stood up slowly and turned to face me, brushing her hair away from her face. Her cheeks and neck were flushed with arousal, her lips parted expectantly.

I held out a hand. 'Come closer,' I said. 'I want to touch you.'

She stood in the gap between my knees. I put one hand in the small of her back, the other on her leg. Her thigh muscle tensed beneath my palm as I smoothed my hand upwards. Tentatively, my fingers brushed over her mound.

'Open your legs,' I whispered. My gasp brought Ben to the edge of his seat.

'What?' he urged, eagerness in his low voice. 'What is it, Philip?'

'She's so wet,' I said, looking up into her eyes. 'Her panties are soaking.' I slipped a finger beneath the elastic, and into her soft, damp curls. Easing her labia apart, I slid inside her.

'Oh,' she said.

'Oh God,' I agreed. 'She's so warm, and wet, and tight,' I added, to no one in particular. Removing my shining finger, I lifted it to my face, my head spinning as her faint musk reached my nostrils.

'Let her smell herself.' Ben stood up and moved towards us. 'She likes that.'

I raised my hand to her face. With eyes half-closed, she inhaled, then tilted her head back slightly until my finger moved over her top lip and into her mouth. I felt her teeth and the tip of her tongue, warm on my skin, and I lost control.

As Ben sat down beside me on the sofa, I pushed her skirt up over her thighs. Grabbing the thin strip of fabric at her hips, I ripped hard until it tore, and flung her damp panties aside. A low sigh escaped from the back of my throat as my eyes feasted on the narrow triangle of hair, on the black frame of her stockings and suspenders. Hooking an arm underneath her thigh, I lifted her leg on to my shoulder, and pressed my eager lips to hers.

Ripples of pleasure shuddered up her body and out of her mouth as my tongue lapped and dipped inside her. There was an ache at my neck with the force of her leg gripping me, a dig in my back as she pressed me further inside her with a sharp heel. For a moment I resisted, teasing her. My penis grew unbearably hard as I watched her squirm, blindly searching for the source of her pleasure.

'Please,' she whispered desperately.

I pursed my lips around the pink swollen nub of her clitoris, sucked and nibbled, holding her hips as she rode the wave of a tumultuous orgasm.

She lifted her thigh from my shoulder and with trembling legs, she knelt before me. I looked deep inside her. I tangled myself in the complex, violent beauty of her eyes.

'Lick him clean,' Ben demanded. She put her hands to my face and began to wash her juices from my chin. She moved up to my lips, lapping with long strokes, and I caught at her and kissed her deeply. I was falling further in love with every heartbeat. Worried that Ben would sense it, I tried to inject my voice with an edge of hardness.

'Show us your tits, Lauren.'

Unflinching, she stood, and without taking her eyes from mine, she unbuttoned her shirt. A strip of pale skin was gradually revealed, then the gentle curves of her cleavage, then her shirt was discarded. As she reached behind herself to unfasten her bra, arching her back, I savoured the view. The length of her neck, the smoothness of her shoulders, the half moons of tender brown flesh around her nipples, peeking provocatively above the low lace edge of her black bra; then that, too, was dropped to the floor.

Her breasts were incredible. Their gentle slope and luscious swell, the almost intolerable softness of her wide areolae. I pulled her closer and discovered every detail, first with gentle fingertips, then with lips and teeth. She cried out as I bit the tips of her breasts into stiff peaks.

'Sorry,' I whispered, 'I can't control myself.'

'Don't even try,' she breathed.

'There's no need to apologise, Philip,' Ben snapped. 'You can do what you want with her.'

'I want to tie her up,' I admitted, gently pinching a nipple. 'I want to fuck her.'

'Then do it,' Ben urged.

I stood and shrugged off my clothes, holding my stomach in as her eyes roved from the curls on my chest to the hardness at my groin. I moved my body into hers and, grabbing her legs, raised her up. Clinging strongly to me, she straddled my waist as I carried her to the bedroom. My insistent lips on her neck made her head fall back in abandon. My penis strained at the pouting flesh between her legs.

I threw her on to the bed, reverently unbuckled the straps of her shoes, pulled off her skirt and gently rolled down her stockings. Kneeling astride her waist, I tied her wrists to the bedstead with the stockings, while Ben muttered his approval from his seat on the edge of the mattress. With urgent lips, I caressed her throat, her cheeks and eyelids, then my mouth sank on to hers, and our tongues entwined. I pressed my hands to the curves of her breasts and sucked at her nipples again, turning them a deeper crimson, before moving down her body. Smoothing my palms into the interminable softness of her inner thighs, I spread her legs wide. I raised my body over hers. Balancing on one arm, I reached between her quivering legs and slid two fingers deep inside her.

'Oh God,' I sighed. 'You want me, don't you? You want me inside you.'

'Yes.' Imploringly, she looked up into my eyes. 'Fuck me,' she breathed. The words sounded so deliciously dirty coming from her mouth. 'Fuck me, fuck me . . . please.'

I plunged my body into hers. The world stopped turning, and we were marooned on the bed, alone in the whirling, chaotic centre of the universe. She engulfed my senses; I was unaware of anything except her. The warmth and tightness of her beautiful cunt as it clutched at my long penis with every thrust. The curve of her throat as she pressed her head into the pillow. The sight of her breasts, jiggling with the force of my fucking, nipples engorged with desire. Her swollen labia, dragging against my cock. The sounds of pleasure fluttering from her lips. The pungent smell of sex. The writhing of her body beneath mine, the grinding of her hips, the helplessness of her fettered hands. The way she kept her eyes open, looking up at me as I plundered her. Relief shook the bed as we came.

I collapsed on top of her, pressed my face to her neck and breathed her in deeply. She smelled of summer, of trees and white beaches, of dark earth and life itself. The scent of her went to my head.

Later, I touched her hair while she sucked my cock and Ben took her from behind. Then we bathed her, soaping her breasts until they glistened, dark nipples poking stiffly through the soft lather. I manoeuvred her pliant body on to all fours in the bath and, sitting behind her, washed between her legs, rubbing her pouting labia until they swelled, gently circling the puckered rim of her anus until I could resist no longer. As my finger disappeared inside her tiny hole, I saw the shock waves skid along her spine and the purple head of my penis loomed above the bath water. I knelt behind her, and the sight of her anus slowly swallowing my cock made me forget about the hardness of the bath on my knees. My fingers twitched between her legs, rubbing at the tender nub of her clit. The anguished sounds of her pleasure made my coming violent and quick.

I had been awake for some time when she opened her eyes. I welcomed her into the day with a smile.

'Good morning.'

She blinked sleepily. 'What are you doing?'

'Watching you.'

She stretched languidly and rolled on to her side to face me. 'Where's Ben?'

'He had to go to work.'

'Don't you have to go?'

'I'm the boss,' I said, winking. 'No one's going to tell me off for being late.'

I slid the sheet from her shoulder, tugged it away from her body. With my fingertips, I brushed over her cheek, neck and shoulder, around the scoop of her waist and on to the ripe curve of her buttock. Her skin was warm in the morning sunshine, and so soft it made me ache.

'I had to talk to you.'

'What about?'

'I want to see you again. And again. And again.'

She arched an eyebrow, mocking me, and nodded towards the window. 'You can see me anytime.'

'I don't mean that, Lauren. I want to be with you. I . . . I'm falling in love with you.'

She touched my mouth lightly with her fingertips. 'You hardly know me,' she whispered.

'I know that you go to bed early in the morning, and get up early in the afternoon. You drink red wine, never white, and rarely do any housework. You play your music loud, your favourite foods are pasta and ice-cream, and you love sad films.'

A smile began to form at the corners of her lip and eyes, making my heart flutter.

'I know that I wanted you from the first moment I saw you. I know you're not like any woman I've ever met. Last night was the most incredible night of my life.' I sighed resignedly. 'I also know you've already got an extremely handsome boyfriend.'

'He's not my boyfriend. And you're not so bad yourself.'

'I'm ten years older than Ben.'

'You're forty?' She pursed her lips and drew in a breath. 'You should have said something last night, Philip. We could have had a rest for some cocoa.'

I slapped her buttock. 'I'm being serious, Lauren. Ben's young and fit, and intelligent –'

'Ben's married,' she said, running her fingers through my dishevelled hair. 'I only get to see him when his wife's away. I'm under no illusions. He's using me to relieve his frustrations.'

'What do you mean?'

'He likes being in charge – you probably noticed that – but he's too embarrassed to ask his wife. He loves her, but he can't tell her what turns him on. It's so sad.' Her eyes twinkled. 'She'd probably like being told what to do.'

'You like it, don't you?'

She hooked her leg over my thigh. 'I like lots of things, Philip.'

'How about this?'

She followed my eyes downwards. My long penis pointed angrily at her open sex, its tiny eye weeping in frustration. 'It's not bad,' she mused, 'for a man of your age.'

Roughly, I pushed her on to her back. Pinning her arms down, I opened her thighs with my knee. 'You make comments like that, young lady, and you will have to be punished.'

'Is that a threat?' she asked breathlessly.

The head of my penis nudged between the fleshy lips of her pussy. Slowly, I eased inside her until, with a long, quiet sigh, her body surrendered to mine.

'It's a promise.'

The Dragon Bridle

Jan Smith

The Dragon Bridle

⁂

Night slipped over the land like a velvet glove, diamonds scattered in its palm. Murasaki Shikoku watched the servant boys lighting the paper lanterns that were looped between the almond trees, as deaf to their laughter as she was to the fluting of the wind in feathers as the palace swallows flew over her head to their roosts.

'The ivory seller is here, my lady.' Wu Yan, her serving maid, had come on to the veranda and was looking at her with anxious eyes. 'Do you wish to see him? I can always send him away again.'

'No. I asked him to come.' She rose from her cushion, her limbs stiff under her loose white robe from sitting so long in one position. Ignoring her maid's worried frown, Murasaki followed her into her chamber. Wu Yan bustled around the room, lighting the oil lamps and incense burners, filling the air with the scent of sweet pine and camphor, and spilling light on to the man who was waiting there.

The ivory seller was well known in the royal city. His body was as crooked as a *bonsai*, with a face wrinkled like a monkey, and skin as yellow as the ivory he sold. Murasaki's satin slippers whispered across the floor towards him. He bowed, and placed something in the palm of her hand. It was smooth, hard, and as warm as flesh. She signalled to Wu Yan to bring a lamp closer so she could see what it was. It was a *netsuke* toggle, exquisitely carved in the shape of a pair of nesting ducks – the traditional symbol of marital fidelity. The two holes for the cord of the *inro*, the box that hangs at the waist of a kimono, were cunningly concealed beneath the wings of the birds, and their eyes were turquoise chips that glinted in the light.

'A most suitable wedding gift, my lady.' The old man's voice rattled in his throat like bamboo canes, and his words stabbed at her heart. What gift could be suitable for the man Murasaki loved, who would be marrying another in the morning? She blinked back the tears that blurred her eyes: a common concubine had no right to such thoughts. She stroked one of the bird's wings with the tip of her finger.

'You are right. It is lovely. I will take it. Send me your bill tomorrow.' She placed the toggle carefully in the *inro* box that hung from her own waist.

'As you wish, my lady.' The old man bowed and backed away.

Suddenly, they heard a vigorous knocking coming from the outer hall.

A voice, low and urgent, called: 'It is I. Open the door!'

Murasaki's heart thumped, and her blood sang in her veins with joy: he had come! But her exultation swiftly turned to alarm.

'Quickly!' She pushed the ivory seller towards the gold lacquer screen that hid the washing alcove from the rest of the room. 'My lord must not see you here or he will guess my gift. Hide.' She turned to the maid. 'Quick, Wu Yan, let him in, before he suspects something is amiss.'

The old man had barely arranged his creaking limbs behind the screen, when the doors to the inner chamber were thrown open. Ohara Hokusai was dressed in a long-sleeved scarlet court cloak, with a gorgeous underdress of saffron silk embroidered with *shi shi* lion dogs. His high cheekbones and olive skin spoke of his Mongolian ancestry, as did his thick, ink-black hair, that had been oiled and plaited specially for that evening's banquet. Eyes the colour of jade swept over Murasaki as he loosed his sword and placed it on the sword stand. The sword was Ohara's most precious possession, with guards decorated with tigers in gold, silver and *shakudo* – a gift from the Emperor to his most celebrated *samurai*. Wu Yan bowed and left the room, not daring to meet her mistress's eyes, her face as expressionless as a theatre mask.

'I had not expected you tonight,' said Murasaki. Her own

cheeks had gone as white as cockleshells under their layer of rice powder.

'I managed to slip away, but they are sure to miss me if I stay too long.'

Ohara shrugged off his cloak, then dropped heavily on to a cushion. Murasaki hurried to pick up the cloak where it had settled like a spreading pool of blood on the floor, and hung it up, smoothing the creases with her fingers. Then, when she was sure she had mastered her expression, she turned to let her eyes devour her lover, following the curve of his lips, the droop of his eyelids, the circumference of thigh beneath his embroidered *kimono*. Seeing her scrutiny, he laughed low in his throat.

'It does me good to see you, my love,' he said. 'And it is even better to see you looking at me like that.'

He beckoned her to him, and she knelt on the floor by his side. For once, she did not move to kiss the lips that so tempted her, but waited for him to make the first move. He stared into her eyes, then caught the nape of her neck in his hand and brought her face gently to his. His lips moved over hers, spicing them with the taste of the rice wine he had been drinking. Conscious of the old man hidden behind the screen, the girl was unable to respond with her usual fervour. Ohara released her, and frowned.

'You are as prickly as a sea urchin tonight. Is it because I am to marry?'

When Murasaki did not reply, he let himself fall back wearily against the cushions.

'You know that the Lady Shonagon is the Emperor's choice for my bride. Her father is one of the most powerful nobles, and her marriage to me will help to cement his loyalty.'

'I know that,' said Murasaki. 'But I cannot help but wish it otherwise.'

Ohara sighed, then took her hand and drew her towards him again. 'If it was my choice, you would be the one to stand beside me tomorrow. See how I burn for you.'

He groaned and pressed her hand to his groin, where she could feel his manhood, long and hard in her palm. Blushing, she pulled her hand away – she did not want to put on a show for the old ivory seller. Once more, Ohara mistook her reluctance, and laughed.

'Fastidious as ever.' He made a show of sniffing at his

undergown. 'You're right. I stink of court intrigue. Come, help me to bathe.'

He gave her a roguish grin as he got to his feet and moved towards the washing alcove, but Murasaki's look of horror stopped him.

'Whatever is the matter?'

She struggled to control her expression. 'Nothing. It's just . . .'

Of their own accord, her eyes flew back to the screen. Ohara's gaze followed hers, and his grin melted like snow in summer. In one fluid motion he seized his sword off its stand, and slid it from its sheath.

'Don't!' shrieked Murasaki.

But Ohara shouldered the screen aside with a crash. To Murasaki's astonishment, the alcove was empty. The only movements within were the snowy petals of almond blossom that were drifting in from the veranda outside, through a broken shutter. She sagged with relief: Wu Yan must have succeeded in smuggling the old man out. But the splintered shutter told its story, even so.

'*Hannya*! Female devil!' Ohara smashed an incense burner with the hilt of his sword and swung round to face her. His expression was ashen, and hurt burned deep in his eyes. 'Is this your way of paying me back for my marriage? You know it grieves me as much as it does you.'

Murasaki realised she would have to admit the truth. 'It was not a lover behind the screen, but the ivory seller. I was buying you a wedding gift.'

She reached into her *inro* box, and handed the *netsuke* toggle to Ohara. He looked at it a moment, holding it up to the lamplight to admire the skilful carving of the feathers.

'I wanted it to be a surprise,' she admitted.

Ohara looked at her, and she saw the gleam of amusement in his eyes. 'I am not sure whether to believe you. Are you sure it wasn't a lover?' He smiled as a thought occurred to him. 'Perhaps the ivory seller is your lover!'

Thinking of the old man with his skinny legs and arms, Murasaki couldn't repress a giggle.

'My Lord! What is happening, *Hokusai-san*?' It was the soldiers of Ohara's bodyguard, who, hearing the clatter of the incense burner, had broken into Murasaki's chamber and run in with their own swords unsheathed. The men looked at their master, then at Murasaki, and then back at their master again. Wu Yan, standing behind them, was shaking.

'Bring me the Bridle,' said Ohara. His face was turned away so that no one could read his expression.

'The Dragon Bridle, my lord?' The leader of the guard licked his lips and darted a sly, salacious glance at Murasaki.

Ohara nodded, and the soldiers ran to do his bidding. His face was still turned from Murasaki, and she stood motionless. Wu Yan was horrified.

'I beg you, don't do this, my Lord. Not the Dragon Bridle.' The old woman threw herself at his feet. 'My lady is devoted to you. I swear it.'

Ohara silenced her with a look. When the soldiers returned, she had withdrawn to a corner, her kimono pulled over her head, weeping. The men carried a wooden collar, decorated with a mother of pearl and lacquer inlay of fighting dragons. It was the traditional way of punishing a disobedient woman, and was polished with use. Murasaki stood very straight while they locked her into it and then bound her wrists to the collar with the silver alloy cuffs. Knowing that Ohara's anger was feigned, she was not alarmed: her mind was suffused instead with the anticipation of pleasure to come.

'Now leave us! All of you,' snapped Ohara.

When they were alone once more, he approached the fettered girl. 'What should I do with you now, Murasaki? Should I punish you?' he whispered. He was standing so close behind her that she could feel the heat of his body and smell the cloves he used to scent his hair.

She nodded, with some difficulty because of the grip the bridle had on her throat. 'It is your duty, my Lord.'

Ohara pushed her on to her knees. 'If you had taken another lover, I would break you, like a lotus blossom on a rock.'

As he shook her, the tortoiseshell combs tumbled from her hair, and her hair uncoiled like a sinuous black python on the floor. But she had heard the catch in his voice that betrayed his arousal. In spite of the Dragon Bridle that clasped her in its harsh embrace, it was she who wielded the greatest power. She became aware of a warm scent, rising in waves off her skin through her gown. As a concubine she had adopted the courtesan's tradition of eating food flavoured with musk so that, when she was aroused, she gave off the heady fragrance of coupling. Her awareness of her vulnerable position sent a dark thrill through her limbs. Ohara was not unaffected by her scent. His hands began to rove over the arch of her back and buttocks through the silk of her gown.

'How could you betray me so?' he whispered, his voice roughened with desire.

'I have not betrayed you, my Lord,' she said, warming to their game.

'Then who was hidden here? Don't tell me no one, for I can smell his hair oil.'

Murasaki said nothing, her lips drawn into a stubborn line with the hint of a smile. She was beginning to grow hot under the caress of his hands, when he pulled her to her feet.

Ohara tossed the *obi* sash of her gown to the floor, and a wave of musk from her warm skin washed over them both as he parted her gown. Beneath the barbaric wooden collar, Murasaki's breasts were as ripe as pomegranates, with delicate coral tips that were already hard. Ohara pinched them with his fingers, making them tighten even further. His face was dark with desire as he looked down at her. He was so beautiful, with his slanting cheeks and eyes, that she felt her breath catch in her throat. Abruptly, he bent her backwards over his arm. Pinned in the Dragon Bridle, she was utterly at his mercy, unable to push him away even when he grazed her nipples with his teeth. She gave a little cry, and her cheeks flushed the colour of peonies under her powder. In the year since Ohara had chosen her as a bedmate, they had learned to enjoy darker pleasures than straightforward lovemaking. All her natural curiosity and sensual training were aflame to find out what would happen next. Under the cover of her drawers, her sex began to ache and moisten.

Ohara groaned, the sound sending a flash of fire along Murasaki's limbs that turned them white-hot. His hands dropped to her open-gusseted underdrawers and parted the material to find the smooth, hairless mound of her sex beneath. He ran a thumb over the plump lips. Murasaki moaned and opened her thighs to his questing fingers, even though her neck and shoulders were aching unbearably from the weight of the Dragon Bridle. The delicate folds of her sex spread like curled chrysanthemum petals around Ohara's fingers, and then, as he penetrated further, a tiny pearl of dew trickled down to burst on his hand.

'Wanton!' he whispered. 'Are you like this with your ancient lover?'

He nipped the bud that was at the centre of her pleasure between his fingers so that it was caught, pulsing in his grip. His fingers tightened, the tingle turned to fire, and he gave a grin. Then he frowned.

'I have not forgotten I am supposed to be punishing you.'

He pushed her on to her knees once more and unwound his sash, pressing her face into the floor, so that she was forced to raise her buttocks to keep her balance under the weight of the bridle. There was a pause as he unwound his sash and moistened his fingertips with almond oil from a bowl on the *tatami* mat nearby. While he anointed the tight, still-virgin entrance to her backside with one hand, the fingers of the other delved between the lips of her sex, not with the aim of giving her pleasure, but merely to see if she was wet. She was. She wriggled beneath him, her senses fired by the unfamiliar touch on her anus, to such an extent that she felt as if the very centre of her being had melted to trickle down between her legs. Then he withdrew his fingers from both orifices.

Murasaki lay perfectly still, hardly daring to breathe, listening to the rustle of silk as he released his manhood from his gown and anointed it too with the almond oil. He nudged the slickened entrance between her buttocks, then thrust hard, burying himself to the hilt inside her. Murasaki squealed and squirmed beneath him, as if trying to escape, but she was pinned as surely as a butterfly, her whole body flooded with sensation. When he started to move inside her, she moaned and bucked, driven half mad with pleasure, desperate to feel his fingers in her sex once more. But Ohara was resolutely selfish, concentrating only on his own sensations as he made his deep thrusts between her buttocks, his whole body rigid with anticipation. Murasaki twisted and groaned, fervently wishing her hands were free so that she could bring herself to fulfilment. But the cuffs of the bridle were biting into the tender flesh of her wrists, and with every thrust Ohara made, her cheek was driven against the floor.

All at once, her mind seemed to float free, and she was suddenly struck by a mental image of herself: subdued, fastened in the wooden collar, her buttocks raised and pierced by her lover's manhood. At the image, she was seized with a tremor so powerful, so violent, that it communicated itself to Ohara. He sobbed aloud and increased the speed of his thrusts. Every inch of Murasaki's body was flooded with sensation, and as she bent beneath his onslaught she was forced to draw breath in great shuddering gasps like the great *coi* that swam in the palace pools. Then, suddenly, he grasped her hip with one hand, and buried his other fist in her hair, pulling her head back towards him. He gave a shout that was almost one of pain, then slumped on top of her.

They lay like that for some time, the room growing darker around them as the oil lamps burnt lower. Then at last she felt him move off her. He turned her towards him and brushed her long black hair away from her cheeks, where it had been glued by her sweat and tears. He kissed her gently, tasting the salt on her lips, and then turned his attention to the Dragon Bridle, hacking off the locks with his *shibayama aigushi*. As the bridle fell to the floor under the ministrations of the dagger, Murasaki gave a moan of relief. Ohara's eyes flashed up at her, and he took her wrists to examine them.

'You should not have struggled so,' he said, rubbing the reddened flesh with his thumbs. Once more he was the gentle lover she had fallen in love with.

Murasaki watched him as he stooped to pick up the Dragon Bridle and toss it away from them both and, as she did, she was engulfed by a wave of sadness that swiftly crested into anger. Her soul burned. How could she bear for him to marry the Lady Shonagon? Driven by pride and despair, she snatched up the dagger from where it lay on the floor, and lunged towards Ohara on her knees, pressing the point of the dagger into his throat.

'What are you doing?' His voice was sharp with surprise.

'I am going to kill you, and then myself,' she hissed.

'But why?'

'You will go to your new wife's bed and forget me.'

He shook his head slowly: it was as much movement as the dagger permitted him. 'You know I would never do that.'

'Do I?' The only thing that Murasaki was sure of at that moment was that Ohara took her threat seriously. A single tear slid down her lovely cheek. She was pressing the dagger so hard that her knuckles and the skin around the point were white.

'Please, put the dagger down,' he urged, his face ashen in the dim light. 'I would never abandon you. In your heart you know it.' He grasped her free hand with his own, and she could feel that it was trembling slightly. 'Kill me if you must, Murasaki, my love. Kill us both. But you know I have to obey the Emperor.'

She closed her eyes and swallowed. When she opened her eyes again, he met them without flinching. She realised he was telling the truth. She moaned, low in her throat. The dagger fell from her fingers to clatter on the floor, and she let Ohara take her in his arms. As he kissed her, murmuring words of love into her throat and hair, she could feel that his cheeks were wet.

Later, when the oil lamps had burnt down and the only light was the moon shining through the parchment shutters, his lips found hers in the darkness like a bee seeking nectar. He was gentle with her at first, hesitant, as if he might scare her off. But Murasaki was impatient with his reluctance. She helped him off with his gown and then removed her own clothes. When they were both completely naked, she sat astride Ohara's thighs and placed his hands on her breasts, throwing back her head at the sensation of skin on skin. She ran her own hands over the sculptured flesh of his chest, criss-crossed with scars and hard with years of martial training, and was surprised to find that he was shivering with his need for her. Without warning, the urge to punish him welled up inside her again, and she dug her sharp nails into his chest.

He gasped at the unexpected pain, and then gasped again as she seized his swollen manhood and as she slid herself on to him, pushing down hard until she could feel him at the very neck of her womb. Murasaki's fingers found the oily cleft between her own thighs. She groaned her pleasure aloud, losing herself in the flooding sensations. She began to move, with small strokes at first and then more urgently, using her thighs to raise and lower herself on the man underneath her, grinding her pelvis against his, forcing satisfaction on herself like a punishment. Again and again, she slammed against him, then gave one last urgent thrust before her whole body went rigid and her face contorted as if in pain. Suddenly, she went limp. Her hands dropped to her sides and, as they did so, brushed against something cold. It was Ohara's dagger, still in its hard lacquer sheath.

Unsatisfied, Ohara was bucking beneath her, frustrated by her lack of motion. A thought occurred to Murasaki. She moistened the dagger sheath carefully in her sex, coating it in the viscous juice there, gasping at the chill of the lacquer on her throbbing flesh. Then she dropped it down behind her, to the cleft of Ohara's buttocks below his scrotum. Slowly, she pushed it up against the snug crevice. Ohara shuddered and arched himself up under her, his head thrown back, his neck muscles straining. She clenched the muscles of her vagina tighter, as she rose and fell like the tide on top of him, tormenting him all the while with the sheathed dagger, running it lightly up and down the sensitive puckered skin. She rode him hard, until he was gasping broken words of love and desire, and the sweat ran off his skin. She wanted him to shatter with the force of his pleasure, wanted him to dissolve beneath her so that his wife would never have joy of him, wanted to suck out his life-force with his sperm, into her womb. Glad of the shadows that hid her face, she allowed her frenzy to take hold of her and sluice through her veins, transforming her until she felt as if she had indeed become a *hannya* demon. She twisted and clutched at him and spat, raising welts on his skin with her fingernails, driving him harder and harder with the muscles of her sex and the dagger. Then, at the moment he was on the very verge of his climax and his manhood had stiffened to iron inside her, she gave one deft twist of her wrist, and thrust the slickened sheath of the dagger deep inside him. He screamed, and his seed exploded into her with the force of a volcano spewing lava into the air.

Afterwards, they slept.

The palace cockerels woke them at dawn. When he realised how late he had slept, Ohara leapt up to collect his clothes.

'I must go. There is no time even to bathe.'

'Will you have been missed last night?' whispered Murasaki.

'Without doubt.' He smiled at her. 'But I cannot regret spending it in your arms.'

She watched him as he dressed, and then as he felt through the silk of his kimono for his own *inro*.

'I have a gift for you too,' he said.

She took it, and gasped with surprise. It was a *netsuke*, almost identical to the one she had given to him, only the birds' eyes were mother of pearl, rather than turquoise.

'But this is a wedding gift,' she said, confused, 'a token of long life and happiness between man and wife.'

Ohara took her hand. 'I may be marrying the Lady Shonagon today, Murasaki, but in my heart I am bound to you.' He placed her palm on the smooth skin of his breast beneath his undergown. 'Nothing will change between us, I swear it.' He kissed her deeply. Then, aware once more of the lateness of the hour, he hurried to join his wedding party.

When his footsteps had died away, she stepped over the collar with its broken locks, and looked at the gift. The birds seemed to wink at her in the morning light. With a half smile, she tucked it into the bottom drawer of the box of treasures that stood in the corner of her chamber.

In the years that followed, Murasaki bore Ohara Hokusai two daughters and the son who eventually became his heir. The Dragon Bridle was repaired and regularly sent for – but never in anger.

*Be Careful What
You Wish For*

Sylvie Ouellette

Be Careful What You Wish For

❖ ❖

*H*e stands behind me. At times he leans forward, coming so close I feel his breath comb through my hair, brush my ear and die on my cheek. I shiver under the sweet, moist assault.

He does not know the passion he stirs in me. He is so near I could touch him. Yet, in many ways, he is so far away my dreams of ever being his are only a cruel illusion. He steps back, unaware that the magnetic field between our bodies is still very much present. He has no idea of the fire burning within me.

At night I lie awake, wondering how I should make my desire known. Wondering how much longer I can stand this. The wait only increases my yearning to be with him.

It has been weeks since he first triggered that feeling in me – long work days spent hoping he will come near again, longer weekends wasted in his absence, impatient for Monday to come round again.

Just thinking of him as I lie in bed is enough to send bolts of arousal down my abdomen, a series of sparks along this familiar path connecting the tip of my nipples to the core of my female flesh. I run my hands over my body as I wish he would.

I am eager for him to seduce me. How, where and when he does are unimportant: mere details. All that matters is that he comes to me, and that his intentions are unmistakable. I not only surrender but encourage him to go further, to take me now. I am so impatient to finally be his that I am unwilling to tolerate any hesitation from him.

I take his hand and guide his fingers over my lace-covered

nipples, making him graze them with his nails, toying with them until they become so stiff they practically pierce the delicate fabric. He guesses they are much more sensitive when teased through the lace and he becomes bolder, torturing them deliciously. Then his fingertips slide inside my bra to caress the underside of my breasts, cupping them gently but without ever ceasing their ministrations on my erect peaks.

My flesh responds readily and he brings his hand down to feel my wetness. Now he is daring. He wants to touch me directly and tries to slip his hands under my panties, but I will not let him, not just yet. He has to tease me through the fabric first.

Just like my nipples, my tiny shaft wants to be caressed indirectly, gently scratched into submission. I moan and press my legs together, squeezing his hand in a soft embrace, holding him prisoner.

His thumb, at first gently discovering my warmth, quickly grows insistent on my swollen clitoris, rubbing forcefully along its length, crushing my still-clothed flesh. He catches the whole of my soaked sex with his hand, pushing at my entrance through the gusset of my panties. His fingertips desperately try to pierce through and directly touch my wetness. The palm of his hand massages my mound, grinding down on it, stopping short of my bud.

At the same time his tongue glides inside the cup of my bra, laboriously pushing the fabric down to uncover an engorged nipple. He takes it first between his lips, then his teeth, letting their sharp edge gently graze its stiffness while his tongue flicks over it at a dizzying speed.

I open my eyes. Of course, I am alone. I grab both my breasts, push them together and rub them in a slow kneading motion. I feel my skin growing hot under my hands, the warmth radiating through my body, right down to my throbbing sex.

If only he could see me like this, touch my skin so hot for him, taste my soaked, impatient flesh. He would soon grunt with desire for my fragrant bush and lick it in long strokes, wanting to taste all of me. Under his tongue he would feel my tiny shaft hard as steel, smooth and slick. Finally, he would find his way deep within me, discovering my silken tunnel, losing himself in its throbbing warmth.

But, in the meantime, my hand acts as a stand in. In the depths of my mind, the illusion is nevertheless complete. As usual, I bring myself to climax, pretending he is the one responsible for my pleasure. It is too soon, too quick, but I cannot hold back. Sweet bliss transports me and leaves me in peaceful slumber. I fantasise about falling asleep in his arms, our bodies both reeling from the frenzy of our coupling. Yet when I open my eyes I am alone, as always.

My thoughts are my own enemy, for each morning I awake with a growing hunger for him, a yearning that I fear might eventually become despair if my fantasy does not soon become reality. But I trust he will be mine. I have this certainty, the audacity and the determination of a woman in lust.

My plan is set. I am counting solely on the power of my desire to entangle him in my web. We are both alone in the office now. I know that in just a few minutes he will come over, stand behind me and look at my work over my shoulder.

So often, I have imagined the moment when I would take his hands and guide them over my engorged breasts. But today it will happen for real. I am so excited I can barely contain myself.

Finally, he approaches. He says those words he has repeated so often; I barely pay attention anymore. He stays silent for a few minutes, reading the figures on the screen. I look at him from the corner of my eye, happy to recognise the familiar profile, comforted and tenderly amused by the blond lock that softly curls over his right ear. His hand reaches forward to point something to my attention. This is the moment I have been waiting for.

Before he pulls back I gently take hold of his hand and bring it to my mouth. I kiss each of his fingertips in turn, then run my tongue all across the palm. I do not stop to see the look on his face: I have no need for it.

He does not pull away. Is he surprised? Aroused? Disgusted? I do not want to know. I immediately slip his hand in my cleavage and leave it there. The rest is up to him. He hesitates for a fraction of a second. Then his other hand snakes its way around my shoulders to join the first one. I extend my arms above my head, grab his neck and bring it down to mine. Our cheeks brush together and his mouth meets mine. Victory is near.

I let him discover my breasts. His fingertips are like spiders on my skin. I look down and watch them move under the thin fabric of my silk blouse. They glide downwards, slip under the minuscule cups of my bra and stop short of my nipples. My chest heaves uncontrollably, offering itself naughtily, but he goes no further just yet.

I am losing my focus; I do not know what to do. My carefully rehearsed plan has gone awry. I wanted to remain in control but suddenly I am quite happy to let him take the lead. I have stopped thinking; I just want to enjoy the feeling. I fear that this may be all I will ever get from him, and I want to be sure the memory of this moment stays with me forever.

He pulls away and suddenly I tremble at the thought that I might have failed. But his hands cupping my shoulders reassure me. He makes me stand and turn around to face him. His lips on mine are cool and moist, like a child's. Yet the arms around my waist are those of a man.

I dissolve in his embrace. His hold on me tightens briefly. His hips press against mine and already I feel his manhood growing turgid. My heart pounds just as hard as before, but now anticipation turns into certainty. His tongue invades my mouth and explores it furiously. I return his kisses just as passionately. My hands settle against the small of his back and I pull him closer to me still. I briefly caress the taut muscles, discovering them for the first time, after I had for so long tried in vain to imagine what they could feel like. They contract as he thrusts faintly, as do his buttocks under my straying hand.

He grabs my hair, loosening the bun I had crafted, and pulls it to make me tilt my head back. He finally lets go of my mouth and his lips trail along my jaw, my neck, my chest. Avidly, he tastes my skin, gnaws my jaw. I let him have his way. This is too good to interrupt. A frenzy seizes him and he becomes ravenous. Suddenly, I know I am no longer in control of anything, not even myself. I do not even want to be. I cannot go back now. I cannot stop him, no matter what.

His body now holds me against the desk. His hands rise to my chest and rip open my blouse to make way for his mouth. Grabbing my waist, he lifts me up and makes me sit on the desk. His mouth is furious, nibbling my earlobes, biting my neck, covering me with wet and warm kisses. His expert fingers are surveying my skin, wantonly caressing my neck and my shoulders before finally reaching my breasts.

My short skirt rides up my legs. The thick cashmere layer

114

slides up to expose the thin satin lining, the only thing now covering me. The heat of my thighs evaporates suddenly, making the cool air around me even more perceptible, leaving me feeling strangely exposed.

My legs part instinctively, letting my lover close. I feel my blouse glide down along the back of my arms and I shiver. Everything is happening so fast that I am surprised to see my bra falling to the floor.

My stiff nipples brush against the rough cotton of my lover's shirt. Between my breasts, his silk tie at first feels cool on my skin, but rapidly warms up and reflects the heat of my own body. I writhe greedily, now half-naked in his arms. Hungrily, he suckles my shoulder. At times I even feel his teeth grazing my skin. His hand finally comes up toward my chest. His fingertips aggressively trace its contours, caressing my skin, fondling its warm roundness, but without going anywhere near the erect peaks.

I try to pull back to give him better access. I want more than kisses now; I want him to touch me. I want him to tweak and pinch my nipples, to take them into his mouth and suck them hard. He holds me back. I hear him laugh softly, his mouth now nestled in the groove of my neck. He is still only teasing and I have to wait for him to decide what I am to do next. He holds me tight against him, rubbing his chest against mine to increase the pressure on my nipples. I whine loudly. Against the inside of my bare legs, the fabric of his trousers grates and excites me. I part them wider, bidding him to come closer.

Finally, he grabs my breasts with both hands, pushes them up together and holds them there. As I follow his gaze, I cannot help notice that he is admiring their roundness. His eyes gleam with lust and desire. To read such admiration, to see his fingers clutched around my pale globes, is a revelation. I am content.

He bends down and covers my breasts with long licks. His hands let go to settle on my knees and slowly snake up under my skirt. My back arches and pushes my chest towards his mouth. His lips seize my nipples and pull on them, sending bolts of excitement deep within my flesh.

He makes me recline on the desk. I obey, eager to abandon myself, to agree to anything he asks of me. I glance up at him and read desire, even stronger than before, in his eyes. He looks different now, not at all like the man who every day sits at the desk in front of mine. There is something about him I have never noticed before, something animal-like, and I am proud to have awakened this in him.

I surrender to this man I hardly know. The situation is so different from what I had anticipated that I wonder if I am once again imagining all this. Yet his hands on my legs are real, his firm caresses are not part of the fantasy in which I have so often indulged.

He parts my knees wider and briefly scratches the inside of my thighs. We hold each other's gaze. I cannot read what he is thinking, but I do know that he wants me. I squirm on the desk, my back arching again and my nipples pointing towards the ceiling in a blatant invitation. I am barely conscious of the folders falling to the floor, the papers flying in all directions. This is all of little importance to me. All my inhibitions have vanished. I know he will not refuse me, will not push me away now, but I take wicked satisfaction in taunting him.

My lover lowers himself on top of me, kisses me on the mouth first, then pulls back to lick my nipples. At first his tongue is like a butterfly hovering above them, barely touching them. Then it turns into a bird of prey, darting directly at its target to attack it fully.

He bathes my entire chest with hungry, long licks, from my armpits to the underswell of my breasts. I hear him groan with every breath. Against my crotch his member is now hard and impatient, pushing through the clothing that holds it prisoner. He takes a nipple in his mouth and sucks hard. It contracts further, elongating under the pull of his suction, which is so intense that I can feel it deep inside me.

Shock waves travel down my abdomen, collect between my legs and make me even wetter. His member gets harder and rubs against my swollen clitoris. The power line between my nipples and my sex gets overloaded. I am about to explode. But, just before I reach the point of no return, he suddenly stands, leaving me unfulfilled and wanting more. My wet breasts are covered in goosebumps, his saliva now turning cold and deliciously refreshing. But the fire raging within me is not quelled.

He rips off my panties and throws them aside. I want him to touch my swollen sex, to feel me inside and out. Yet he does not

116

seem in any hurry to discover more of me. He is in control, in charge. I have to obediently await his next command.

Someone has entered the room and is approaching. I can feel a presence behind me. My heart suddenly pounds with fear as arousal quickly turns to shame. I dare not turn around, dare not face anyone.

My lover looks at whoever is coming towards us. At first he looks stunned, as I am. Neither of us had expected this. I can read that in the expression on his face, the way his eyes open wide. I shudder at the notion of having someone finding me like this, yet I am unable to move away as shame glues me to the spot. I realise that everything was going too well to last, and that my fantasy is about to turn into a disaster. Just then my lover gives an amused smile. I do not know what to make of it, which worries me only the more. Forcefully, he grabs my shoulders to make me stand and turn around.

I do not know the man walking around the desk and coming towards me, but I've seen him before. And I remember my lover knows him; I have seen them together on occasion. What I cannot help but wonder about is to what extent they know one another, and what that could mean for me.

I raise my hands to my chest to cover myself, but my lover will not let me. He grabs my wrists and pulls them behind my back. Even as he releases his grip I do not move: once again I surrender to his wishes. I feel exposed, in more ways than one, but my shame only rekindles my arousal.

Without a word, the stranger approaches. His eyes are sombre. The dark stubble of his beard makes him look sinister. For a brief moment I dare look up and I catch an icy, greedy glare in his steel blue eyes. My instinct tells me his opinion matters little. What he is about to do worries me more.

The three of us remain silent and idle, as if our lack of a reaction is some sort of negotiation, an unspoken pact that we are agreeing to whatever happens next. Side by side, the two men look very different: my lover is fair and his hazel eyes show only lust and tender amusement, whereas in the dark stranger's glance I read more lubricity and even maliciousness. Yet I know their eagerness and their intentions are on a par.

The stranger takes off his jacket and loosens his tie. Behind me, I feel my lover's penis twitch against my buttocks. The stranger's move is casual but for my lover it is exciting, for me it is almost threatening. I already know I shall abide by these men's will. My lover will give me to him, share me with him, and there is nothing I can do about it; nothing I want to do about it. The thought fills me with anticipation, even apprehension, yet I will not walk out. I know this is far from what I had planned, yet this lack of control over the situation is much more exciting. I wanted to offer myself to my lover. Now I must see this through and agree to whatever he wants from me, even if that includes sharing me.

My lover sits on the edge of the desk and hoists me on to his lap. For a while I become a mere puppet in his arms, letting him move my body as he pleases. Setting his hands in the groove of my knees, he parts my legs, displaying my flesh for the benefit of the stranger. I am limp as a rag doll, offered for two men's pleasure.

Already my lover's fingers digging into my soft skin have heightened my arousal. My want is stronger than my will, and only these two men can fulfil my yearning. I have to let them take me, on their terms, or else I know I will be kept forever wondering what it could have been like, and slowly drive myself insane.

My lover is caressing my legs now, but staying clear of my sex. I can only guess that he wants his accomplice to be the first to touch me there. The stranger finally diverts his gaze to my flesh. I now stare blankly in front of me, unable to even look at myself. This man I do not know has me at his mercy. I know he is aroused already. Somehow, the notion is flattering, but also threatening.

Without any hesitation, any warning, his hand reaches forward to touch me. He sets his thumb, hard and rough, directly on my clitoris. He wiggles it forcefully but briefly. His touch is anything but loving, yet this assault reverberates through me and generates such pleasure that I cannot help but scream.

He continues torturing me until I come close to orgasm, but before I can feel the explosion I so desperately crave, he has already pulled away. He peers into my eyes. For a brief second I hold his gaze. I read such contempt, such disdain, that it frightens me.

Yet he knows that I want him to touch me again: that is the source of his power. Impassive, he attacks me again, this time plunging two of his fingers deep within me, stretching my flesh as much as it will. My wanton sex accepts the pain and turns it into pleasure. My lover has grabbed my breasts and is kneading them mercilessly. I writhe on his lap as his accomplice keeps torturing me.

I am close to orgasm, but I can tell that pleasuring me is not what my lovers want right now. They want to taunt me, to keep me at the height of excitement, to break me and reduce me to a wanton slave. And that is also what I want to be.

The men stare at one another without saying a word, as if they do not want me to understand their silent agreement. They have a bond, a relation, which I am not part of. I cannot even guess whether they will bring me or deny me the ultimate pleasure, but that matters little right now. I shall take pleasure out of satisfying them, for it is clear that they enjoy torturing me like this.

Although I am so weak with want that I can barely stand, my lover forces me to my feet. My skirt is bunched up around my waist, my hair is in complete disarray, but somehow finding myself in this obscene nakedness right in front of my desk does not appear so awkward. It feels naughty, at most. I glance around for a moment, almost surprised by my surroundings. I cannot even begin to imagine what I must look like from afar.

The men stand side by side as they undo their trousers. I dare not look down nor at them. I have seen what they look like: two identical figures clad in dark trousers and white cotton shirts, two men of the same height and build. One is the object of my affections, the other of my fears. Staring blankly in front of me, I await their command. My lover suddenly grabs my hair and forces me down on my knees. I do not try to resist. From now on they will not have to tell me what to do.

Obediently, I slip my hand in their underpants, one after the other, and release their swollen members. My lover's is long, with a slight bend in it. The hard shaft looks powerful; the purplish head is already seeping with expectation. The stranger's is shorter but thicker, more solid.

The stranger is the first to thrust towards my mouth. His move is unequivocal, and I have no desire to refuse him. The smell of him drives me wild. Despite my humiliating position, the scent of his arousal empowers me. I take pride from being at my men's feet, forced to pleasure them, unable to protest, like a good lover. This is much, much better than even my wildest dreams. I now long to taste them. I take the stranger's member in both hands and slide my lips over his engorged knob. I moan with delight. His knees start to tremble, his shins rubbing against my chest.

My fingers close around his shaft and I suckle him gently. I feel him seep in my mouth and I insert the tip of my tongue into the tiny hole to fish out every last drop. He is thrusting more powerfully now, wanting to penetrate my mouth. I let him, but only slightly. My clasped hands slide down along his shaft as I begin to milk him. My lips are still fastened on the swollen head, but I know he wants me to take him completely. His member pulses against my thumb and I feel he is near the point of no return. But he pulls back unexpectedly.

I look up at both men, eyes half shut, silently and obediently awaiting their next demand. The look in my lover's eyes is unmistakable. I open my mouth wide and engulf him readily. Digging my nails in his behind, I pull him towards me and hold him there. My lips form a tight circle around his shaft and my nose is buried in his thick curls. I suck hard and slowly pull away, letting the suction do the work. Under my hands his buttocks contract forcefully and I hear him curse.

Just like his accomplice, he draws back at the last minute. Both men thrust towards me in a silent bid to pleasure them both at the same time. They each grab my hair to pull it in the direction they please. I do not try to escape their hold. They thrust in to my mouth repeatedly, and I let them.

After a while, my lover relinquishes me to his accomplice and gets down on his knees. He positions himself behind me, between my parted legs. I moan loudly as he penetrates me, but I do not release my hold on the stranger.

My lover thrusts slowly, and I know he wants to make this last. His hand falls repeatedly on my behind, spanking me so hard that the shock waves make my breasts wobble underneath me. We move rhythmically. His jabs make my head bob as I try to concentrate on the man I must pleasure. Yet he is also holding back.

I cannot say how long we continue like this. I have lost all notion of time and space. I can no longer feel the carpet that only a few minutes ago so mercilessly grazed my bare knees. The position I find myself in, although initially humiliating, now seems completely natural.

Eventually, the stranger pushes my head away and grabs me

by the shoulders as my lover stops spanking me and pulls away. Together they pull me to my feet and bend me forward over my desk. Behind me, my lover pushes my legs apart whilst the stranger enters me. He thrusts so violently that I fear he will climax too soon. He draws back at the last minute, letting my lover take me once again. They change places like this all the time, and soon enough I can no longer recognise who is taking me at any given time. I cannot even recognise the hands that occasionally slip under my hips to torture my bud and heighten my excitement.

In front of me, I see nothing but an empty office. Deserted desks and cold, blank computer terminals mean absolutely nothing to me. What I see, although familiar, now seems foreign. I know where I am, what is happening to me, yet I am so detached from reality that my surroundings are totally unimportant.

My men thrust repeatedly, but never for very long, one of them constantly holding me parted so wide that my hips hurt. On the polished desk, the smooth skin of my breasts glides easily at first, but soon the heat within me creates a thin layer of sweat that creates friction, making the wood pull mercilessly on my stiff nipples. I discard the discomfort, concentrating solely on the sensations they afford me. Their assault is arousing, but not enough to satisfy me.

Yet they both take immense pleasure out of using me like this. I cannot see their faces, but I can hear their strangled cries. It is my only link with them, but it gives me immense satisfaction. I feel, strangely, that this is how they want it to be; they do not want me to see them, do not want me to know what they feel, how their faces look as pleasure roams through their bodies. I can tell they have finally obtained what they wanted.

This is enough to trigger my pleasure, as if my mind, controlling my body, finally agreed to let it run free and fill me, bringing on a sense of completion. This is so different from what I had originally planned. I could never have imagined this myself. Out of my control, my fantasy has evolved into something bigger than me, much more satisfying, simply because of its unpredictability, its absurdity.

I lie still on the desk as they pull away. I await their command to move, but soon silence tells me I am waiting in vain. By the time I turn around, they are already gone. Slowly, I get back on my feet. My chest and abdomen are moist with my own sweat and I cannot help shivering.

I stand alone in the office. All I hear is the whirring sound of the disk drive on my computer, which suddenly brings me back to reality. For a moment, I wonder if I have just dreamt the whole thing. My clothing is in disarray, my torn panties on the floor. I see the mass of papers strewn around my desk and it is enough to reassure me that I did not imagine it.

My wanton flesh is still reeling from the pleasure that just invaded it, craving more. But, for now, this is all it shall receive. This is how my men wanted it and I must wait for them to return, even if that means waiting for some other day. I accept that. I can wait and then my reward will only be the sweeter.

I straighten myself up as best I can. My blouse is ripped, but I can still fasten it. I slowly clean up the mess, gather all the papers and dump them on the corner of my desk. I feel lethargic, at times still shaken by my subsiding orgasm, slowly cooling down and recovering from the high the men brought me.

Before long, however, I hear voices behind me. The men have returned. They walk past me, go to my lover's desk, look at some files and leave. Their return has lasted less than a minute. They did not even look at me. I stand on the spot, paralysed with anticipation. It is impossible to tell, by looking at them, what has just happened. Their suits are impeccable, their ties properly fastened. In contrast, I am still standing in the same spot, half-naked and devastated.

My lover returns, this time by himself. He turns off his terminal, briefly nods his goodbye, and holds my gaze perhaps a fraction of a second longer than usually. I catch a brief flash, a mere twinkle. We understand each other. He knows I will be there again, waiting for him and the stranger to come and take me. He is counting on that. I want nothing better.

The Au-Pair

Claudia Francis

The Au-Pair

❧ ❧

*F*ive weeks in England had done nothing to ease Isabelle's homesickness. As she stood in the kitchen, ironing and folding the clothes of her six-year-old charge, Simon Empson, her thoughts turned, predictably, to her home town of St Guillaume, and the friends and family she had left behind.

Isabelle was beginning to regret ever having left her native France. She had hoped that au pairing would provide plenty of excitement and adventure, and a chance to sample a different culture, another way of life. But, instead, she found herself stranded in this oh-so-sleepy English village, where most people's idea of a good night out was a pint of lager shandy and a game of cribbage.

Back in St Guillaume, she had been used to a far livelier social life, visiting local bars and clubs with her girlfriends four or five times a week. She had made friends with next-door's teenage nanny, it was true, but the girl never wanted to venture further than the local pub, and simply wasn't in Isabelle's league when it came to letting her hair down.

Anyway, Isabelle could get by without female bonding. What she really missed was male company of the strong-jawed, hard-bodied, not-afraid-to-experiment variety. However, while her outgoing nature and curvaceous figure had ensured a steady stream of male admirers in her home town, here in Froxfield (population: 328) attractive, available men were disappointingly thin on the ground.

How long would it be, she wondered, before an English lover

walked into her life – not necessarily a true amour, just someone to share her thoughts with, someone to make her smile, show her the sights and sounds of England, and satisfy her darkest desires?

Not that Isabelle hadn't already made her presence felt. Yesterday, she had accompanied the Empsons to a lunchtime barbecue at the home of the village doctor. Wearing a long, white, Empire-line dress, her hair pulled back in an elegant chignon, her green eyes enhanced by a touch of mascara, she had entranced every male in the assembled company. Even her host, Doctor Dawson, had gently flirted with her, as he replenished her frozen margarita from the icy pitcher in his hand. And, while the old man droned on about his plans to retire to the south of France, Isabelle could see he was mesmerised by the two erect nipples pushing through the thin cotton of her dress.

And later, when the day turned cool and she started to return to the Empsons' car to retrieve her cotton wrap, Ben Barratt, sports master at the local primary school, had offered to accompany her. After they had exchanged the obligatory small talk, he'd hesitantly asked her if she would like to have dinner with him one evening next week. She had said that she'd like that very much. Despite his shyness, he was good-looking enough, with a well-muscled body and a slow, sexy smile – the kind who, decided Isabelle, put a woman's needs before his own when it came to the bedroom.

As her thoughts turned to sex, Isabelle's pubis idly grazed the cool metal frame of the ironing board, and she felt a delicious shiver spread through her loins. Safe in the knowledge that she was alone in the house – little Simon was at his prep school, her employers at their respective workplaces – she pulled open her short, checked cotton wrap-around skirt, exposing white satin panties, trimmed with delicate Breton lace.

With one slender forefinger, she began to stroke the swollen lips of her sex through her underwear. Within minutes, the thin fabric was saturated. Pulling the sodden gusset to one side, Isabelle fingered her bulging clitoris with long, practised strokes. Then, as she began to experience the familiar pulsing that signalled the onset of orgasm, she switched her attentions to her vagina, pushing two fingers in and out of her wet hole, while she continued to stimulate her clitoris with the heel of her hand. But just as she was beginning to lose herself in the sweet, fluttering sensation that seemed to fill every pore, the kitchen door was suddenly flung wide open.

'Have you seen my electronic organiser, Isabelle? I'm sure I left it on the kitchen table . . .' Councillor Empson strode into the room, his voice tailing off as he observed his red-cheeked *au pair* hastily rearranging her clothing.

As a prominent local businessman, who served on several parish committees, Duncan Empson was a highly respected member of the village community. What would his fellow councillors say if they knew he had such a wanton little minx in his employ? Isabelle tried to look innocent as she resumed her ironing, but he knew what she'd been up to – bringing herself off in his kitchen. Had she no self-control?

He knew he'd been right to choose the French girl. Of course, he'd persuaded his good lady wife that Isabelle's impressive qualifications and glowing references made her the best candidate for the job. But what had really convinced him of her suitability was the silky mane of chestnut hair, the full, high bosom, and the way her plump arse cheeks gently shifted in the flimsy muslin dress she'd worn for the interview.

Turning quickly to hide the growing bulge in his well-tailored trousers, Duncan mumbled that he'd probably left his organiser in the car after all, and left the room, closing the kitchen door behind him. It was about time someone took that girl in hand, he thought to himself, and he knew just the man for the job.

As she listened to her employer's Range Rover crunch down the long, gravel driveway, Isabelle wondered whether she'd lose her job for such a blatant misdemeanour. No, she decided on reflection, Mr Empson was a man of the world and, anyway, it was obvious from the way his eyes roamed her body that he wanted her. Yesterday, she had been busy at the kitchen sink and he had come up behind her, on the pretext of reaching for some fly spray on the shelf overhead. But he had lingered there just a moment too long, his body so close she caught a waft of his Paco Rabanne aftershave, and felt the gentle pressure of his crotch against her buttocks. And when Simon came running in to cadge an after-school snack, Duncan had hastily backed away.

Actually, mused Isabelle, the good Councillor wasn't bad looking for an older man. His tanned face, with its twinkling blue eyes, was remarkably unlined, and his body well-toned from twice-weekly visits to the gym. What's more, he had gone out of his way to make her feel at home – buying fresh flowers for her small, but bright, attic room, making a detour to the bakers for her favourite *pains au chocolat*, and treating her to a six-month membership at his well-equipped health club.

Not like that haughty bitch he was married to. The expensively-dressed, perfectly-coiffed Tilda Empson was clearly used to being the centre of attention. She was Duncan's second wife and, at thirty-four, some twenty years his junior. As a partner in an upmarket beauty salon in the market town of Bishop's Cross, some twelve miles away, she worked long hours and saw precious little of her family. And, when she was at home, she played lady of the manor, barking out instructions to the cleaner, the gardener, even her long-suffering husband. So far, Isabelle had managed to stay on the right side of Mrs Empson, but it was clear that her employer resented little Simon's obvious attachment to the new *au pair*.

Tilda was attractive enough in a well-groomed sort of way, Isabelle supposed, but she knew that her own voluptuous beauty was far superior. Allowing herself a small, smug smile at the thought of her own buxom breasts compared to Tilda's distinct lack of cleavage, Isabelle returned to her earlier task. Swiftly, she brought herself to a satisfying climax, and thus relieved, continued with her ironing.

It was 2 a.m., and the Empson house was in darkness. While Tilda snored gently, dreaming of the rather elegant young woman whose nails she had manicured earlier that day, her husband was standing over his sleeping *au pair*, planning how he was going to administer the punishment she so richly deserved.

Isabelle lay on her back before him, sound asleep, lips slightly parted, hair spread like a dark cloud across the creamy *broderie anglaise* pillow. It was a warm night and moonlight, seeping through the half-open window, illuminated Duncan's unclothed body and the engorged shaft that rose like a scimitar from the base of his belly.

Gently, he drew back the crisp cotton sheet that covered Isabelle's body, and gasped in awe at the naked body that greeted him. Her milky-white breasts – at least a C-cup, he thought lasciviously – were topped by two tawny nipples, that were already hardening as the night air caressed them. Beneath her perfect tits lay a gently rounded belly and, below that, a dark triangle of curly love-fleece nestled between smooth-skinned thighs. Duncan's hand strayed to his erect cock, the glans already glistening with fluid.

As he did so, Isabelle stirred and murmured a single word, 'Ben'. Then, to Duncan's surprise and delight, her right hand moved languorously down her body, and glanced across her breasts, before alighting on the secret space between her legs.

His eyes grew wide – not content with her earlier indecent display, the horny little mademoiselle was now poised to perform a floor show in her sleep! Giving a soft, low moan, Isabelle's hand went to work, her middle finger opening her slick labia and sliding back and forth across her clitoris. Already highly excited, Duncan reluctantly let go of his dick, afraid he was about to shoot his hot juices over her prone body. Then, as Isabelle's fingers began to probe her wet hole, her eyelids suddenly snapped open. Gazing up at Duncan, she made no attempt to cover her nakedness. Observing her employer's obvious state of arousal, her mouth formed a lazy smile.

'Monsieur Empson!' she exclaimed in mock horror. 'It's the middle of the night. Whatever are you doing in my bedroom with no clothes on?'

'I am here to reprimand you for that disgraceful incident in the kitchen earlier today,' replied Duncan, struggling to inject an angry tone into his voice. 'While you're in my home, you must practise a little self-restraint.'

'Oh, but sometimes I can't help myself, Monsieur Empson,' said Isabelle, squirming while she continued to stimulate herself. 'I am in a strange country, I have no boyfriend to take care of me, so I must take care of myself.'

'I can appreciate your frustration, but in the future you must come to me if you have any, er, extra requirements. I am your employer after all,' said Duncan. 'And now, my dear, you must accept your punishment.'

With that, he leant over the bed, and in one swift movement straddled her soft body. Bending his head, he began to trace slow, deliberate circles around her nipples with his tongue, till they rose up like two stiff bullets. At the same time, one strong knee prised her thighs apart, while his fingers stroked her pubis. Isabelle put up no resistance and, wriggling with excitement, she spread her legs even wider and guided Duncan's hand to her swollen clitoris.

Unable to believe his luck, he squeezed her slippery love bud between forefinger and thumb, while his tongue explored her eager mouth. The seduction had been remarkably easy, he thought to himself, and now here she was beneath him, wet and willing, while his wife slept on downstairs in blissful ignorance.

Aroused still further by the thought that Tilda might at any moment wake and discover his absence, Duncan took hold of his hard member and prepared to enter Isabelle. The feisty French girl, however, had other ideas. Shimmying free, she rolled Duncan on to his back and began to nuzzle the coarse dark hair that formed a line between his tanned pectorals. Slowly, her nose and lips traced a line down his toned stomach, till she was greeted by his throbbing prick. Taking the head in her mouth, she flicked her tongue across his glans, and was instantly rewarded by Duncan's appreciative grunt. Thus encouraged, Isabelle wrapped her lips around his shaft and began to suck on it greedily.

'That's it, my dear, you must work for your wages,' said Duncan cheekily through clenched teeth, as he watched the top of the *au pair*'s head bobbing up and down over his manhood, while her hair formed a glossy trail across his stomach. Engaged in this exquisite punishment, Isabelle remained oblivious to a small but distinct sound on the attic stairs. A few moments later, the bedroom door slowly opened, and a barefoot Tilda walked in silently.

After taking in the scene before her for a few seconds, she cleared her throat theatrically. 'Well, well, well,' she said in a loud, clear tone. 'My husband and the *au pair* . . . I knew it was only a matter of time. So exactly how long have you two been fucking each other?'

At the sound of Tilda's frosty voice, the startled pair immediately disengaged. Guiltily, Isabelle wiped away a tell-tale string of spittle from the corner of her mouth, and turned to Duncan for guidance.

'It's the first time, I swear,' stammered Duncan, pulling the sheet over their naked bodies. 'And anyway, we haven't actually fucked at all, as you so delicately put it.'

'Yes, but you were just about to, weren't you?' said Tilda

accusingly. 'Just a few minutes more and you would've been riding her – and I'd hate to interrupt anything.'

With that, Tilda loosened the sash of her toffee-coloured silk robe, shrugged it off her shoulders, and let it slide to the floor. Turning to reveal small, firm buttocks, she walked to the high-backed armchair that stood in the furthest corner of the room. Then, looking directly at Isabelle, she sank down into the velvet-covered seat and hooked a long, slim leg over each arm of the chair, displaying her neatly-trimmed bush. 'I am ready. You may continue,' she announced, with a small, tight smile.

Isabelle was bewildered. What was this strange game being played out before her? She was filled with apprehension, and yet was strangely excited at the same time. She had lasted a whole month without sexual intimacy, and wasn't about to let this extraordinary opportunity slip again.

Duncan was equally bemused. He had never considered Tilda sexually adventurous. Indeed, she always made love in a peculiarly businesslike fashion, in the same way she might administer a facial to one of her salon clients. Now here she was, urging him to fuck the *au pair* while she watched.

Needing no further encouragement, Duncan discarded the bedsheet and pushed Isabelle gently back on to the pillows.

'My wife is used to getting her own way,' he told Isabelle. 'We'd better do what she says.'

'Oui, oui,' whispered Isabelle. 'But first you must make me ready for you.'

With that, Duncan began to stroke her clitoris with the middle digit of his right hand, while his left hand reached under her buttocks to probe her vagina. 'Good girl,' he murmured encouragingly, as he felt her juices coat his fingers.

Turning her gaze to the corner of the room, Isabelle watched in disbelief as Tilda parted the silken folds of her labia, and began to strum her clitoris with long, leisurely strokes.

'I want to see you eat her,' commanded Tilda, who could scarcely contain her own growing excitement. For a woman like Tilda, power was undoubtedly the most potent aphrodisiac.

Obediently, Duncan positioned his head between Isabelle's moist thighs and began lapping at her love-button like an over-eager puppy. Isabelle's hips rose up to meet her lover's mouth, and she yelped in pleasure as he teased her vaginal entrance with the tip of his tongue. Grabbing two fistfuls of Duncan's hair, she pulled him deeper into her, till his tongue entered her body.

'*Mon dieu!*' she screamed, her breaths coming in short, shallow gasps.

'Quickly – mount her!' said Tilda in a strangulated voice. 'Fill her with your cock!'

A red-faced Duncan emerged from his *au pair*'s crotch and clambered on top of her.

'Yes, mon cheri,' breathed Isabelle, as she struggled to fight the pulsing waves that were threatening to drown her.

In one quick thrust, Duncan buried his cock deep inside her, and she felt the walls of her vagina grip him like a warm, friendly hand. Cupping her buttocks, he began to ride her, his ripe balls slapping against her with every movement.

'Faster,' screamed Tilda, as she bucked and writhed in her velvet throne. Straining over Duncan's shoulder, Isabelle watched as Tilda, her face and neck flushed with sexual arousal, probed her vagina with three fingers while her thumb jabbed at her clitoris. As the two women locked eyes for a moment, Isabelle felt a great tidal wave welling up inside her pelvis. Seconds later, a delicious contraction engulfed her body, then another and another, until she thought she could take no more. As the last waves of her orgasm died away, she heard Tilda begin to emit a series of shuddering breaths. 'It's coming, it's coming,' shrieked Tilda, as she too was overcome by an unbearably sweet climax.

The sound of his wife's noisy fulfilment was too much for Duncan. With the blood pounding in his ears, he felt a flood of white-hot fluid rush to the end of his penis. Scooping Isabelle's fleshy buttocks in both hands, he exploded inside her welcoming pussy in a series of violent bursts. As he collapsed on to her, his body drenched in sweat, Isabelle smiled a small, secret smile. Perhaps England wasn't going to be so bad after all.

The Demon Fiddler

Lilith Dupree

The Demon Fiddler

❦ ❧

Samantha had noticed the hot-eyed little Cajun peering at her through the ferns and vines of the courtyard while she drew, watching her at odd times as she moved about the hotel. His eyes, although barely visible through the foliage now, were bright and excited. He reminded her of a small feral animal hoping to be coaxed out of hiding to be petted and tickled. Would he bite and scratch like the little cat he reminded her of?

She'd heard him playing his fiddle during the day, and at a club where she and her boyfriend Erik had gone for dinner on their first night in New Orleans. He moved with practised skill, the fingers of one hand flying up and down the neck of his instrument while the other hand furiously plied his bow. The demon fiddler: that was the description that had popped into her head when she'd been stimulated by the electricity of his music and had felt those smouldering black eyes fixed unwaveringly on her own.

His fiddle was quiet now, but the eyes ... She glanced down at her page and there they were: hidden in the leaves and flowers she had drawn. And his hands were reaching out to part the foliage so he could come to her. She could feel her heart flutter and an electricity between her legs at the thought. Would those lightning-fast hands slow down to draw the music from her body?

'Allo, chère Samantha.'

The softly spoken words made her jump – they seemed to come from the drawing. Samantha jerked round to see Robie stepping from between the bougainvillea vines just as she had been imagining.

'Hello, Robie.' She was breathless, half frightened, half excited. What was it about this little man that made her instantly think of sex? He was a bit shorter than she, and slender, and a little pigeon-toed, but those eyes – and those magic hands – and that adorably cunning manner of looking at her from under his lashes. Yes, he was quite the little pleasure cat.

Robie had watched the pretty artist at work in the courtyard, and he had followed her down to the riverside where she sketched the people at the Café Du Monde and the stalls of the French market, but he didn't know that she had seen him there. Her hair gleamed so red in the sunlight, as bright as the bougainvillea through which he now peered. He loved that soft, white skin that came with red hair, and her beautiful green eyes. They made him think of a cat's eyes. He would have laughed if he had known that she thought of him as a little cat too. When he finally stepped out of his concealment to speak to her, she jumped and whirled on him, her cheeks paling, then blushing a petal pink, then falling back to their normal, fair shade.

Robie reached out a hand to lay it gently against the small of her back. 'Poor chère, did Robie frighten you?' He cocked his head on one side and looked at her with all the intensity of his desire.

Samantha couldn't speak for a moment, then, 'You just startled me, Robie.' His name came out barely a sigh; she found she almost needed to gasp for air. 'It's so hot out here. I'm all sweaty.' She laughed uncomfortably at the *non sequitur*.

She ran her hand down the moist column of her neck, then looked at it, wondering what to wipe it on. Robie reached out, laid his palm behind her hand and brought it up to his mouth. His tongue licked out, tasting the salt of her sweat on her fingers; she felt that fiery touch on her neck, and far deeper inside her.

All the while, he held her eyes with his, peering through the mop of wild curls that was his hair. Samantha wanted to run her fingers through those curls, wanted to move into his arms, to feel those lips on her neck, feel that tongue inside her. She shook herself free of the mesmerism of those dark eyes, gently but determinedly pulled her hand from his.

'I think I'll go and take a shower and lie down for a while.'

Samantha all but fled from the courtyard, abandoning her sketchbook and easel there beside him.

'Would you like Robie to help you?' The question and his gentle laughter followed her fleeing form up the stairs and along the balcony to her rooms.

Inside, she shut the door and leant against it to prevent herself from turning to accept the challenge of that question. Once, she had been a sleeping sensualist but, since Erik had awakened that side of her nature, she found it all too difficult to resist the temptations of fleshly pleasure. And she was sure that Robie knew more about fleshly pleasures than was absolutely good for her.

She tottered into her bedroom to undress. When she stood under the stream of water from the shower, feeling it caress her overheated skin, she had the sensation that, if she flung open the shower curtain, Robie would be standing there waiting to step in and join her. The desire she felt at that thought was almost disabling.

Her thighs trembled with the need to spread themselves and take him into her body. Her breasts were heavy with wanting his touch. Erik, her boyfriend, was only gone for a few days, and she was finding it almost impossible to remain faithful.

When she stepped out of the shower, she felt even more hot and uncomfortable than when she had stepped in. She was back in her bedroom and still wrapped in the towel when she heard a knock at the room's little balcony door.

'Who is it?' she called.

There was no answer, just a soft scratching sound on the panels.

Samantha stepped over to undo the bolt and open the door a crack. It was Robie, peering shyly at her through his lashes.

'Samantha, chère, Robie will help you with your fear if you will let him.'

She could hardly breathe, but she stepped back into the room, letting him follow her in. He closed the door behind him without looking, fumbling to slide the bolt home.

'Come here, chère. Robie will not hurt you.'

Samantha wanted to scream, to cry, to feel his hands on her body, to feel him inside her. She knew he would awaken feelings in her she had only dreamt of. She stood frozen while he reached out to pull the towel loose from her body.

He bent his head to kiss each of her breasts, then laid his hands at the sides of her waist. 'You will undress Robie, yes? Then it will not be so frightening for you.' His eyes asked her a question. He felt her need for him, but he also felt her tension.

She nodded and reached down to take the hem of his oversized jersey and pull it up over his head. Under it, he was slender and undeveloped, like a little boy, with the round tummy of a toddler. It made her feel strangely protective of him. She leant forward to place a gentle kiss on that tummy.

For such a sensual man to expose his almost androgynous body to a woman must be a difficult thing. She reached for the fastening of his jeans, wondering if what lay within them matched the rest of him. She undid the button, then slowly slid the zipper down. She spread the sides wide and slipped them down over his hips.

Robie bent to pull off his unlaced sneakers and slide the snug fitting legs of his jeans down over his feet. He stood there in his white cotton jockey shorts, waiting for her to remove them.

Samantha saw the bulge in the cotton between his legs and was relieved to see that it was not only there, but looked to be of a normal size. Her desire for him wasn't diminished by his unformed body – his sexuality came from something within him.

Then she looked up into his eyes. They burned and sparkled at her, and his lips were parted in anticipation. She smiled as she reached to slide his underpants down over his hips, then sighed as she saw that his penis was all that the little sensualist, or she herself, could desire.

Robie slipped his feet out of the shorts, then took her hand and led her over to the little bed. 'What can Robie show you, chère? What pleasures does your body want to learn?'

The question left her breathless. She didn't know, didn't know what to say . . . 'Everything, show me everything!' It was out before she could stop it.

Robie chuckled shyly at her, reaching to take her in his arms. 'Perhaps not everything at once, my Samantha.'

'Show me what gives you pleasure, Robie,' she told him.

He chuckled. 'To give you pleasure pleases Robie.' Then he was pressing her back against the bed.

She sat, then lay back, swinging her legs up on to the mattress.

Robie lay down on his side next her, slipping one leg over and between hers.

The feel of that weight and warmth of him between her thighs melted the last of her resistance. Robie gently caressed one breast with a hand, bending his lips to nuzzle at the nipple of her other breast, without ever looking away from her eyes.

When he felt the relaxation in her legs as her thighs fell apart, he moved up on to his knees between them. Samantha inhaled a shaking breath. She always liked the feeling of Erik's penis coming alive in her hands. She sat up, letting a leg dangle down on either side of the narrow bed.

'May I hold you Robie?'

He nodded, rising up on his knees and moving his hips forward for her. She slid one hand under the weight of his testicles, stroking his penis with the other. When she slid her finger under it to bring its tip to her lips for a gentle kiss, she felt him begin to stir.

She looked up into his eyes. The pupils were dilated. He helped her up on to her knees in front of him, then pulled her into his arms to put his lips on hers.

She felt his tongue slide between her lips but, instead of seeking out her tongue, it slid down between her teeth and her lower lip. He gripped the lip gently between his teeth and lips, laying it open so that he could run his tongue back and forth in the channel that was made.

It was such an odd sensation, but strangely pleasurable. Samantha felt herself responding to the stimulation of that gentle tongue, offering up her mouth, feeling the urge to moan catch in her throat.

Robie slid gently from her mouth. 'Do you want me now, Samantha?'

'Yes,' barely a sigh.

He lowered her gently back on to the mattress, waiting until her knees came up and spread themselves for him. He put a hand to the side of each of her thighs and caressed them, running his hand from her hip to her knee and back again. Then he bent his head to trail his lips and teeth across her abdomen.

His touches were so gentle, but they set her on fire. When she felt his moist lips and the edges of his teeth gliding across her abdomen, something inside her fluttered and her hips thrust themselves up at him. Robie smiled down at her, looking so impassioned yet so beneficent.

Then he moved one hand to slip between her legs, to the warm moistness inside her. 'You are ready for me?' He stroked in and out while he waited for her answer.

'Oh, God, Robie! You must know that I am,' she cried at him.

'Robie knows your body is ready for him, but is your mind ready, chère?'

She thought briefly, as well as she could with those gentle fingers stroking her into a frenzy. 'Yes, Robie. Yes, I really want this. I really want you, sweet Robie.' She was amazed at the rush of affection she felt for the little man. 'Please?'

He smiled happily at her, then held her hips as he slid himself into her. She gasped at the feel of him. He filled her up and held himself there for a moment, unmoving, until he felt the first reflex clasp of her body on him. Then he slid gently away and back again – the clasp came almost immediately this time – and out and in, and out and in.

Samantha was panting with the pleasure of those slow, deep strokes, looking up from half-closed eyes to see that Robie's face was contorted with his own pleasure. Then her hips began to rock to meet his, and his thrusts were no longer slow and gentle.

Their bodies surged together of their own volition and in their own rhythm, faster and faster, dragging Samantha and Robie along with them, up to the crest where her whole being swelled and throbbed with the feel of him. She felt him jerk inside her, savouring his last spasmodic thrusts before he slid away.

He supported himself above her with a hand on either side of her, his head hanging down and his breath coming in great whooping gasps. When he lifted his head to look into her eyes, she held out her arms to him. Robie fell into those arms, nuzzling his head into the crook between her neck and shoulder.

He turned his head to whisper in her ear, 'I love you, chère Samantha.'

'And I love you, Robie.'

They both knew that it wasn't the down-the-aisle kind of love, but the love of two sensualists who have found someone with whom to share their pleasures.

As Samantha drifted off to sleep, she marvelled that that simple sex act had moved her so deeply. Was it Robie, or was it that the two of them were just completely right for each other?

They dozed in the stuffy little room, sweat pouring from them. When Robie awoke and pushed himself up and away from her, the suction of their sweat-drenched bodies pulling apart made a kissing sound. They both giggled. Robie's eyes sparkled with his laughter.

'Come, chère, we will take the shower and be all clean and fresh for the evening.' He got up, drawing her after him.

She waited while he turned on the water and adjusted it to his preferences, then they both climbed in under its spray. Their nakedness did not feel sexual now.

Then Robie picked up the big sea sponge and lathered it with soap. They were facing each other as he reached out to gently rub the sponge over her breasts and chest with a circling motion. His eyes gleamed as her nipples came alive.

Robbie slid the sponge down to her abdomen, circling it playfully, lower and lower. When he slid it between her parting thighs, rubbing it gently back and forth, Samantha clutched at his slippery shoulders for support. She was whimpering at the pleasure of it, eyes closed, when he withdrew his hand and kissed her lightly on the lips.

'Now, chère, you wash Robie's back.' He handed her the sponge.

Washing his back was the last thing she wanted right then, but she began moving the sponge languidly around and around his back, then down to his buttocks and down between his legs.

He leaned forward at the hip, pressing his hands against the shower wall and sighing with pleasure at the sensation. Then Robie forced himself to turn around, offering his front for her ministrations. Samantha could see he was already beginning to harden.

She washed perfunctorily at his chest, then hurried down to his abdomen and slowed her hands to slide the rough sponge between his legs, massaging his penis and testicles as gently as she could. His rapid breathing told her he was ready to take her. She slid the sponge away and looked into his eyes.

'Turn your back,' he gasped, 'so Robie can wash you.'

She looked questioningly at him, but did as he asked. She felt the sponge swirling on her naked skin, then down her spine to her buttocks. She felt his arm slip around the front of her waist as she leaned forward and spread her legs for him. He slid the sponge slowly and firmly between her legs, swirling it gently round and round there.

Just when Samantha thought she would scream with the tension of it, the sponge dropped away to be replaced by his gently massaging fingers. 'Oh, please, Robie, please!' Her words were almost a shriek. Her chest was heaving and the tension in her neck was almost painful.

Then she felt him close on her and the hardness of him slid into her. She breathed a sigh of relief. Bracing her hands against the wall, she spread her legs further apart and tilted her pelvis forward to present herself more freely to him.

His arms circled her waist, holding her lightly as he thrust himself into her. Her breathing was coming more rapidly and she was rocking back to meet his thrusts as he slid his arms up over her chest, pulling her torso gently back against him.

His next thrust made her gasp anew, clutching him so hard to keep him there. 'Robie, my God, why does this feel so good?'

He slid away from her, then up and in, against the secret spot where her orgasms always seemed to originate. He was panting now with his exertion, but he answered her between his gasps, 'It is the angle, chère, it lets me reach the nest of your desire.'

Her body struggled to hold him inside, to maintain that precious, maddening sensation, while he pulled away, only to come back again, setting off a storm of reactions.

When they began to feel her contractions, he thrust still deeper into her, exciting the waves, stirring them to higher peaks which threatened to crush them both with their power. His last thrusts and spasmodic jerks within her were barely felt in the clutching of her body on him.

Her orgasm went on long after he had ceased to move, had become limp inside her. He supported her gently as she gasped out her pain and pleasure, waiting for the waves to release her from their buffeting.

When Samantha finally felt the last little phantom clenching of her body, she was too weak to stand. Robie lowered her gently to recline against the back of the tub. He washed first himself, then her, with the sponge, setting off renewed but weaker waves inside her. She whimpered with the near pain of it.

He knelt down to kiss her gently on the lips and to slip his arms around behind her, holding her and whispering sweet words into her ear in his soft Cajun dialect. When he felt her breathing deeply and the stiffening of her spine, he stood and bent to help her from the tub.

He wrapped a towel around her, drying her gently. Then wrapped and secured a towel around his own hips. He led her back into the bedroom, drew back the covers on the little bed and told her to lie down. Samantha dropped the towel then slipped between the sheets, turning on her side in exhaustion.

She heard Robie go out to the sitting room, then the hum of the air-conditioner. She was almost asleep when he slid into the bed opposite her.

Samantha awoke in the last of the twilight hour the French call 'l'heure bleue'. She whispered the words to herself. They seemed somehow appropriate here in what had once been home to a French planter, in New Orleans' French quarter, with this adorable little Cajun beside her.

They were facing each other on the pillow; his head was tilted down so that his forehead rested against her cheek and she could feel his hot breath on her collarbone. She ran her fingers through his curls, brushing them away from his face and drawing back to look at it. It was really quite a pretty face, small featured with a straight nose and wide mouth.

Robie looked so sweet and defenceless in his sleep. She kissed his cheek and stroked her hand down his side. His eyes opened and he smiled sleepily at her, rolling on to his back. She moved her hand to stroke his little round abdomen, bending her head to kiss the nipples on his unformed breasts.

Samantha found herself unable to stop kissing and stroking him, his purrs of pleasure were arousing an intense aggressiveness in her. She wondered if this was how a man felt when he was arousing a woman.

She stroked his breast with her hands while she nibbled kisses down his tummy to his manhood. She could feel the change in his breathing through her hands. She moved to kneel between his spread legs, sliding her hands down his torso to run her fingers through the thicket of curls that guarded his growing erection.

Bending over him, she lifted his testicles and penis up to meet her mouth. She closed her lips over the head of his penis, licking round it with her tongue. The she slid her mouth further along the shaft, closing her teeth gently over it and pulling away.

Just as her teeth reached the head, she plunged her mouth

back down the shaft, then scraped her teeth gently along it as she withdrew again. Robie was moaning her name and threshing his arms and legs with the painful pleasure of it.

When she pulled her mouth away and moved up on to her knees, his eyes focused on her in a question. Her eyes locked on his and she moved to kneel over his pelvis. Seeing his smile of realisation, she leaned forward to rest her cheek momentarily against his chest. His hand came up to stroke her cheek.

Then she moved upright and, spreading her thighs further, lowered herself on to him. Robie and Samantha gasped together at the release of being joined, then giggled shyly at their own mutual reaction. When she began to slide up and down his engorged member, her breaths came in pants and Robie flexed his knees to raise himself up for her.

Her body wanted to hold him inside. It was sheer torture to rise up and slide away from him, but returning to cover him again, thrusting him deeper inside and clutching him harder, made them both moan. Then their hips began to move in a faster rhythm, like the frenzy of his fiddling.

They started to laugh with the exhilaration of it, until the waves of sensation started. Their startled expressions said that the pleasure was only beginning; then they laughed, and they laughed, and the spasms came faster and harder, tossing them around like twigs, until the music slowed to just a tiny echo of itself and they were quiet again.

There was something about being the sexual aggressor that made Samantha reluctant to release her hold on the shaft that gave her so much pleasure. She wanted to keep Robie inside her just a little longer, even though he had spent himself. Just the feel of him there made her want him again.

Seeing the fierce look of passion on her face, Robie spoke. 'Come here, chère, lie beside Robie, and he will help you feel the pleasure again.'

She could barely breathe: the promise of more pleasure from this man excited her impossibly. Samantha stretched out beside him. They lay facing each other. He slid one of his legs between hers, bringing his thigh up to press against her throbbing sex. The he bowed his back to suckle at her breasts, licking the electrified nipples with his tongue.

The fire he started in her breasts rocketed down between her thighs and she felt her hips thrust forward against his leg, and her thighs clench as if they would pull him inside her. He pressed gently against her shoulder, rolling her over on to her back.

'Oh, Robie,' she breathed, 'what are you going to do now?' She knew it was too soon for him to have another erection, but she needed him inside her.

'Shhh, chère.' He stroked her cheek once again and looked lovingly and reassuringly into her eyes. Then, as he bent his head to kiss her, he moved on to his knees between her welcoming thighs.

The kiss went on far too long, his stroking, swirling tongue had her choking back the urge to scream with the feel of it. Samantha grabbed up fistfuls of the sheet, to grip it like a lifeline, while her hips thrust up at him.

Robie pulled away from her mouth and backed away to slip his slender fingers between her labia and slide them gently into her. She was so wet. She knew it. He gloried in it, sliding his tickling fingers around inside her then out, then in again to tickle and drive her wild with sensation.

'Robie,' she barely whimpered. Her hips were raised up, following those teasing fingers as they slid away from her. Then he thrust them back in, moving them in stronger circles inside her. Her hips began to rock against him as she panted out her ecstasy.

His hand followed her rhythm, stroking the spasms from her as he stroked the music from his fiddle. Samantha felt the ache in her back but she fought to maintain the waves of orgasm. She almost shrieked as she reached the peak of her excitement.

Then her thighs were shaking and her hips subsiding back on to the mattress. Yet Robie kept his fingers in her, stroking and swirling until the last little clench had spent itself. He pulled her knees up with his hands and bent his head to lick the moistness from inside her. Samantha whimpered as another series of faint contractions wracked her.

Then Robie raised his head to smile shyly at her. 'Would Samantha like to taste her pleasure?'

She was puzzled for a moment then, realizing what he was offering, nodded and held her arms out to him. He lay his body over hers, then put his mouth to hers, swirling his tongue still rich with her own fluids around her hungry mouth. No one had ever thought to share this with her: it was something she had only wondered about. If her body had not been so tired, the intimacy of it would have made her want him yet again.

Samantha wondered how long the little sensualist would be her playmate before he moved on. She hugged him to her.

He whispered in her ear, 'I love you, chère. You are a woman like I am a man. We will give each other much pleasure before we are done.'

She breathed a sigh of relief.

The next time Samantha opened her eyes, the room was chilled and she was alone. She felt a pang of loss. She had thought Robie would stay with her. Then she thought, how foolish: he has a life of his own: he can't be expected to let everything else drop for some hotel guest.

Just as she was laying a tearful head back on her pillow, she heard the balcony door to the sitting room open. At first she was frightened. Who could have a key? She wondered if Erik had returned early from his trip to Maryland. Then Robie was coming through the bedroom doorway carrying a tray and wearing a playful grin.

'Hello, my sleeping beauty. I have brought a wonderful supper for us to share.' He waited while she sat up in the bed, propping the pillow against its head for a back rest. He looked down at her goose-bumps and erect nipples. Smiling, he handed her the tray. 'Robie will go turn down the air-conditioner before his Samantha shivers herself into exhaustion.'

He had put on his street clothes. When he returned, he paused to pull off his sneakers and strip off his jeans and jersey. Samantha held the tray up until he had slid in beside her, wriggling up and next to her so that they were thigh to thigh. He slid one arm around her waist and held her to him. She settled the tray across their legs. His body was so warm, it felt very cosy there like that.

'What have you brought us, chère?' He laughed at her use of the endearment, and gave her a resounding kiss on the cheek. 'I have brought you one of New Orleans' greatest delicacies.' He whipped the cover off one of the dishes on the tray, and there were two giant sandwiches: rolls like big, oval hamburger buns, spilling olive salad and Italian cold cuts on to the plate.

'What is it, Robie?'

146

'These are muffeletta, chère. The rich, salty olives, the zesty salami, the creamy cheese, and all dressed with the good olive oil and the wine vinaigre.' He gave it all the Cajun French pronunciation. 'And, to drink: Robie's favourite.' He pulled two cans of cola from a bag which lay on the tray, opening first one can and then the other, to pour them into tall, ice-filled glasses.

Samantha laughed delightedly: he had described the sandwiches with such epicurean elegance, but his sweet tooth demanded cola to drink with them. What a delightful playmate. She wished now that she had had someone like Robie when she was growing up. He would have been so much fun, but she would have learnt far too much that it wasn't good for a young girl to know. She gave a throaty chuckle at the thought.

'What amuses my Samantha?' Robie asked. When she told him he smiled like a little boy, showing his dimples and blushing. 'Chère, you would not have liked Robie as a boy: very naughty, always in trouble.'

She gave him a kiss on the cheek before picking up one of the sandwiches. 'Sounds perfect to me.' She smiled at him over the top of her muffeletta as she took a huge bite. 'Mmmm, Robie! This is so good.'

Robie had picked up his own sandwich and answered her through a mouthful. 'They say the olives are an aphrodisiac.'

Samantha threw back her head and laughed. 'Do you really think we need one?'

He laughed with her, and then they settled down, leaning shoulder against shoulder, to eat their sandwiches. Samantha picked up her cola to take a sip.

Oh, it was perfect. Robie had been absolutely right about the combination of flavours, as she should have expected from the little sensualist. The next hours, the next days, promised to be the best she had ever spent. If only she could take the little pleasure cat home to be her pet forever!

A Predictable Kink

Xanthia Rhodes

A Predictable Kink

❖ ❖

'White or red?' he called through from the kitchen.

She rolled over languorously on the white fluffy rug, listening to him getting them both a glass of wine. There hadn't been time before. Her clothes were scattered over the room, tangled up with his: her formal black suit and her hair pins on top of his designer leather jeans. Her white silk shirt, she saw now, would have to be dry-cleaned because her lipstick had smudged when he pulled it over her head, in too much of a hurry to undo the buttons. A screwed up piece of paper was lodged under the chair, invisible except to someone lying on the floor. She smiled at the unusual perspective she was getting.

'White, then we won't have to let it breathe.'

'Wine should always be treated with respect.'

His kitchen was a masculine place, with black tiles above polished grey-green granite surfaces. The lighting was faultless: back-lit display cabinets held glasses and china that had been chosen for their shapes and textures and colours. His artist's eye never went off duty.

The wine was stored in what he jokingly called the 'cellar' – an electrically controlled, custom-made cupboard where the long-term investments lay entombed behind the short-term residents.

'Are you hungry? I'll fix some smoked salmon if you like. Or there's something here that needs to stay in the oven for about an hour. Shall I put that in?'

'Sounds great.'

151

She turned over and felt the long goat hair, harsh against her stomach and between her legs. She stretched and idly wondered if she should get up and find one of his shirts or a bath towel. She could see the open bathroom door through the tiny hallway. That too, was a haven of sophisticated living: gold taps reflecting their muted gleam on to navy and gold tiles.

'Don't you feel wicked, eating and drinking stark naked on a rug in the middle of the afternoon?' she asked. 'My colleagues are all still slaving at their desks, wrestling with contract law. I had to stay in the office till midnight last night to get the time off.'

'We have been getting too conventional,' he called back. 'People don't need to express their more bizarre fantasies only through sex.'

'But you've always been so careful before, in case the carpet should get spoiled.'

'The beauty of the room depends on utter cleanliness, and lack of clutter. I like to visualise it when I'm away. It brings a sense of order to my chaotic work life.'

One of his photographs, a misty moonlit view over the starkly wild Himalayas, dominated the modern, civilised furniture. He spent up to six months of the year on assignments that sometimes brought him into physical danger. He had nearly died on that one.

'Now, you can visualise me on the floor, naked and libidinous,' she said.

A glass-topped table stood on a reconstituted stone base that was a copy of a bench at a stately home.

'It's nice, isn't it?' she called.

'What's nice?'

'Knowing each other well enough to be uninhibited.'

'Like not feeling you have to pull in your stomach every time you change position?'

She could hear his chuckle, low and somehow dark and sultry, as he opened the fridge door. She could imagine him now: almost naked and more than desirable.

'Like feeling you can change position without being thought over-assertive or fussy. And not worrying that the other person will think you are kinky if you say what turns you on,' she replied.

'It takes a special kind of trust to admit to your real desires,' he agreed. 'Knowledge of intimate things gives people such power.'

She put her hand on her crotch and remembered the feel of his fingers, his tongue, merely minutes before.

Looking back on her sexual adventures with him always seemed like looking into a fantasy world. With the others, sex had often been a little sordid. But with him, strangely, even now they were able to act out their more esoteric needs, she seemed somehow cleansed after the experience.

'Who else would allow me to do the things I do with you? You positively like them!'

'Delete "like", replace "need",' she called back, laughing. 'Two kinks don't make a straight line, but they sure add up to a lot of fun.'

She rubbed herself luxuriantly over the rug, imagining his prick inside her, from the back, as he had taken her when she had first arrived, her bra and stockings still on.

He had undone her bra with his teeth and then cupped her breasts in his hands.

'This is the true meaning of uplift,' he had said, pulling her towards him and causing sparks of sheer desire to pulse through her. 'I expect this was how they invented the bra – some woman wanted to feel her man's hands on her at all times. Think of your bra like that in future, won't you? Every time you get up in the morning; every time you go to bed and I am not there; every time you move to reach for something in a filing cabinet and it pulls, it will be my hands, cupping you like I am now.'

He had thrust into her hard and fast until she was breathless, but he hadn't let her climax then. He had waited till he could hear from her cries that she was nearing a peak of delight. He gauged the moment with delicacy and withdrew, despite her moans of protest.

'Sit down, facing me, cross-legged. I want to see your desire and your arousal. You women have an easy time – you can tell immediately if a man is aroused.'

'Egotist,' she laughed, tipping her hips so he could see her clearly.

'I like to see your face when you want me,' he said, but he nuzzled between her legs and looked at other lips, not her mouth.

Later, his cock had felt strong and hard against her tongue, his balls had been tight from his excitement as she gently had held them in her silken well-manicured hands.

'I have an assignment in Florida,' he called through, amidst a clatter of cutlery and plates.

'How long this time?'

It was all a question of trust, she thought, as she brought herself out of her reverie and back to the present: the goat-hair rug and the sounds of a light snack being prepared.

'I'll be gone two weeks, maybe three.'

He stood at the door, a lovely, muscular man with unruly, longish hair and a huge erection peeping through her black crotchless panties. She had put them on him herself, as usual. The tiny, lace-frilled garments always made his bulge look even more exciting. They accentuated his extraordinary masculinity. His face was weather-beaten and lined from his unusual, hazardous way of life.

He often said she looked frail and ultra-feminine in his shirts. After the tough image she had to project at work, they emphasised and enhanced her intensely female sexuality.

'Nothing like leaving something to simmer for a while and then arriving to find it ready to eat. Delicious,' he said.

'I've simmered long enough. Come here,' she said, turning over to present her backside to him in invitation.

He sat on top of her and ran his hands down her back from her neck to his own groin. She could feel that he was ending each stroke with a curl of finger and palm around his own excitement.

She moaned slightly.

He turned her over with a rough impatience that left her breathless because it was so unexpected. The expression on his face was intense, totally focused and almost violent with passion. He ran the palms of his hands down from her breasts to her stomach, touching each square inch of skin as though it were a fragile negative that held a unique picture of a piece of the world.

He brought both hands to one of her breasts and held it with the gentle guiding movements of a potter about to craft a work of art.

He bent and grazed her nipple with his teeth. As she held his penis, he sat back and watched her, his breath coming quickly.

He moved up her body, sliding his manhood between her

breasts. She pushed them together to envelope it tightly and felt the velvety, cushioned tip touch her neck. He rubbed his hands over her nipples with immense speed and began to push against her. The goat hair caught in the crack of her bottom and she was desperate for stimulation between her legs. She tried to catch his prick in her mouth, but he held her hands in place and continued to push rhythmically.

'Please,' she implored.

'Please what?' He was smiling gently.

'You know what I want.'

'And you know me, too,' he whispered.

'Let's change positions, then.'

He let her go and they lay side by side, savouring the odours of each other's sexuality.

She held his thighs and adjusted her mouth so he was totally enveloped. She sighed as he slid his tongue around her clitoris and began to stimulate it with deliciously soft strokes.

She could feel her own lubrication, copious evidence of her lust. He licked her as though she were a delicious ice cream.

As if sensing her thoughts, he leant over and brought his wine glass to her crotch. He put the cold foot on her clitoris and she felt the marvellously smooth texture as he rolled the glass against her.

He poured a drop of liquid on the bud of her pleasure, and she jumped with surprise because it was so much colder than the glass. He swirled it around with his tongue, an exquisite contrast of temperature and textures.

'The only way to celebrate in style is with flawless goblets,' he said. 'Wine should be sipped and savoured from nothing but the best.'

His cock was pulsating in her mouth and she withdrew and sat up slightly, supported on her elbows, her breasts pouting upward as though bursting to be released from their tension.

He poured another droplet of wine on her and lapped at it. His jawline was beautifully smooth, as though sculpted by Michelangelo. She could so easily imagine him striding over the barren wastes of the world, places she would have been too afraid to visit, even if she were with him.

'Tilt yourself up a bit,' he said.

He moved round to face her, his head still near her crotch, and put a hand under her bottom.

This time the wine ran into her folds, shockingly cold, but welcome. He lapped it up with long, lascivious movements. His tongue felt hot.

He reached over and fumbled in the box that was never far away when they were alone together. He pulled out the dildo and pressed the switch. She felt her inner muscles tensing in anticipation. As he inserted it slowly, a feeling of peace invaded her body and soul.

She had bought the implement partly for fun, partly as an act of charity at a party with some girlfriends. She hadn't used it by herself. She hadn't needed to, after the way he left her feeling totally and completely fulfilled.

She had confessed to owning it one day, two glasses of wine into their orgy of sensual gratification, just before he set out for another ten days' assignment.

'Let me see it. Is it huge and pink – does it move by itself? Has it got strange knobs on?' He had laughed like a stand-up comedian at one of his own jokes, to encourage a sluggish audience.

'It is fully automatic,' she had said, trying to take the whole thing lightly, but knowing that, with him, her curiosity had been aroused. Why else had she confessed, if she did not want him to help her through her fantasies?

'My friends said it is better than the real thing. They giggled a lot and compared notes. In detail. I was intrigued, naturally.'

'And you haven't even tried it out?'

'I felt inhibited. I felt you might think it was a betrayal, a slight on your masculinity.'

He had begun to laugh.

'By that reasoning, I could be jealous of your own fingers, but I'm not. C'mon – let's see if it works. You wouldn't have bought it if you hadn't been curious.'

'That isn't totally true: I had to buy something. We were only there to help Suzanne get on her financial feet after her messy divorce. The sexual aspect was secondary. Besides, we all had a few glasses of wine and it was fun, a laugh.'

'You could have thrown it away and said nothing,' he had persisted, turning it on and laughing again as it pulsated slightly. He put it in his mouth and pretended to be convulsed in orgasmic pleasures. 'God, is that what I feel like to you?'

She had giggled.

The strange little object became the focus for several of their games: he held it inside her while she sucked him, or she would hold it while he sucked her breasts. She liked to rub it up and down his penis so the pulsations were passed to him. It was bigger than he was, but seeing the two together always excited her.

They always stopped before orgasm, each making the other wait. They had a pact: no climax until they were shaking with desire. The sight of his sweat-soaked pectoral muscles used to turn her on within seconds, but now she also liked the way he pleaded, and the way he made her grovel, wanting an end to the torment.

The exchange of clothing had been a later addition and came when he found the black panties she bought from the next sex aids party. He had insisted on wearing them with his penis and balls hanging out. He thought it was hilarious.

'They make you look huge – incredibly masculine,' she had said, over-awed by his potency.

'Not every couple would understand each other's strange little fantasies the way we do,' he had replied, smiling.

But that had been then. Now, the urgency of desire overcame her as she held the dildo tightly with both hands and moved it in and out gently. She flexed her legs and inner muscles around it. He moved up her body and kissed her mouth, taking his time, teasing her, refusing to give his tongue and enter her that way. She pushed her hips upwards as the intensity of the instrument's pulses fired her needs.

He watched her face carefully as he kissed her, her intensity mirrored in his own expression. He ran his tongue to her neck and up to her ear, the movements exquisitely gentle yet searingly hot in their effect. She felt she would explode soon. He brought his mouth to hers and pushed his tongue inside her, possessing her completely, then withdrawing with his usual teasing manner.

'Hold it for me,' she said decisively, but in reality she was pleading.

He smiled again, knowingly, understandingly, with compassion and excitement all at once. He held the dildo and kissed her clitoris at the same time so she climaxed in sudden sparks of fire. He pressed the button to stop its movement and lay beside her for a few moments as she rested.

He moved up her body and she ran her tongue down his neck,

his chest and to the centre of his stomach. She swirled it round his navel, pushing it inside with vigour.

Suddenly he was inside her mouth.

'That's right, deep. Now.'

It was how he liked it best and it made her feel secure this way because she could control her desires, and give him pleasure at the same time. She pressed the button on the dildo and the little instrument leapt into life. Her inner muscles contracted once more, this time with a feverish intensity. She rapped out her pleasures with sharp staccato cries from the back of her throat, muted by his hard manhood. She swirled her tongue around him, sucked the tip and then plunged herself deeply on the entire stem with rhythmic movements. He climaxed almost immediately, his body convulsed for a few seconds and then suddenly relaxed. He moved immediately to suckle at her nipples as she brought herself to a final, quiet, peak and rode on top for a delicious few moments. She prolonged the feeling as long as possible and then rolled down the other side.

'Very kinky,' he said, smiling, as she looked up at him. He kissed her brow. 'I always thought you were kinky – the moment I saw you in your black business suit surrounded by all those dull files and ledgers.'

'It takes two,' she replied happily.

He got up and walked through to the kitchen, his buttocks neat and tight.

Her head was almost under one of the upholstered leather chairs; she didn't remember moving so far across the room. She stretched across and fished out the screwed up paper, her lawyer's mentality irritated by the minor untidiness. She straightened it out and saw it came from his book of addresses and telephone numbers. The page for G. Her name began with G.

They phoned every evening if they didn't meet. Even when they were away from home they phoned, and had done for the past two years of their acquaintance.

She looked round the room, quickly moving into tidying mode. The smudged shirt annoyed her, but the warm memory of his ardour softened her. She rubbed the excess lipstick on her nipples. They were sore from his lust and each stroke brought back exquisite feelings. She began to dress. She put on her stockings and skirt and covered the smudge with the jacket.

'Can't you cut the trip short?' she called. 'I need you here, in case you hadn't noticed.'

The last time he had been away for over a week she had been so lonely and desperate she had been tempted to accept a one-night stand that was offered. She had eyed the dildo too, opened the box and fingered its length, but somehow, without him holding it, the allure just hadn't been there.

She hadn't given in, and the sex, when he had returned, had been out of this world.

'Maybe it's better because we don't meet so often – had you thought of that? Absence makes the heart grow fonder.'

She sat down and ran her fingers over the telephone receiver as though it were his limpness willing her to bring it to life.

She peered closer at the paper she still had, straining without her glasses, and saw that the only name on the destroyed and discarded page was hers: Gilly.

She sat rigid in the chair.

'What is the assignment?'

She willed herself to behave coolly and logically, in a lawyerly manner.

Had the afternoon been a last, farewell gesture? The frenzy of a man who knew he would never see his lover again because he was going to the States permanently? The last time was almost as poignant as the first, except that it was rare for people to know that it was positively the last time. That was usually the prerogative of the dominant person: the one who had fallen out of tune with the relationship first and who was determined to make the most of what was left.

'Some pop group wants a few specials. It will take days and days because none of them are photogenic. The music they make is first-grade stuff that hardly needs promoting, but the videos and stills are the problem.'

'And only you can work the miracles? Can't you send someone else?'

She began to shake with anger. With herself as much as with him. How could she have been so blind? She was a top lawyer – yes, not just some junior assistant solicitor who worked a sixteen-hour day for a pittance and some praise. She really had the talent and the ability and she had thought that, at last, she had found the lover to share her life, without getting jealous or competitive or demanding domestic commitments like marriage and babies.

'No. Apparently they like what I took of them. The transparencies are in my bag – I'll show you them when we've finished our wine.'

She put on her shoes and fixed the buckles with quivering fingers. She could smell his musk on her hair, the sweat of his exertions under her arms, in her groin. The two-faced bastard!

Or had he meant her to find it? Was this his insensitive but effective method of giving her a gentle hint?

She picked up his camera and wanted to hurl it through the window. Through the plate glass, it would fall three storeys, damaged beyond repair into the small garden below.

'He's a bit avant-garde,' her best friend had said, on meeting him.

'Not your usual – a little on the laid-back side, don't you think? Are you sure you can cope?' another friend had asked.

'I think he is the perfect foil for me – I have to be so ordinary and straightforward in my work, like an automaton. He is a way of rebelling vicariously. He gets to take the risks and live the exciting life I yearn for and would hate. I get to enjoy it second hand,' she had replied.

'And what does he get out of it?'

'He knows there is always a secure base to return to, with someone who totally understands him.'

It had sounded smug, but she had been so sure. So damned sure.

He returned from the kitchen and put his arm around her and the glass of cold Chardonnay to her lips. It tasted of hate and jealousy. She wanted to scream.

'The way I've taken their pictures, they look like gods. I'll show you. Those trannies are worth a bomb: more than a deposit on a garden flat in a better part of town.'

With her salary she could easily get a mortgage on a flat like that, but it would take two more years to get a reasonable deposit. She felt sick.

'Do you suppose,' she asked casually, extricating herself and sitting in the chair so he was excluded from her space, 'that what we see in one another is some kind of ego trip? I feel superior because you haven't got a steady job and you feel superior because you know you can get for one afternoon's work what I take a year to earn?'

'Opposites attract.'

He was smiling, unconcerned. Still nearly naked, he threw himself on to the sofa, one leg over the arm so that his limp penis seemed like an insult to her femininity. She rarely saw him in that state: by the time they had their clothes off he was erect every time, and on the occasions she had stayed the night they had been coupled up like two steam engines long before the alarm clock had rung, and then it had been time to rush into clothes for work.

She couldn't bear the thought of asking for her panties back. The very idea of putting them on when they were still warm from his body disgusted her. Previously it had been part of the excitement. She stared at his body, feeling downtrodden and used.

'I make my living pitting my wits against a lot of slightly bent businessmen,' she said. 'Usually, they aren't technically criminals but, morally speaking, they are. I don't like to be used or mocked.'

He adjusted his position, still at ease, happy and in control.

'I don't like the feeling – it isn't my idea of how a modern woman should feel. I thought feminism had banned such feelings for ever.'

He grinned and held up his glass. She felt cheated.

'That's what I love about you,' he said. 'Nobody's fool, but so wonderfully, unpredictably predictable when I get back from my wanderings.'

'Whereas you are predictably unpredictable,' she mused. The wine was, as usual, very good. 'Where did you find this brand? You haven't bought it before.'

'I was bored one evening in New Zealand two trips ago and you know I always like to make the most of any situation, so I sampled the local tipple.'

'I will admit that you know how to live, how to take your pleasures in whatever way you can, wherever you may be.'

She wanted to pour the entire ice-cold bottle over him.

'I never know what you are going to come up with next,' she went on. 'But I can be sure that you will surprise me. Totally.'

'You could come to Florida with me.'

His intonation was even, as though the matter were unimportant.

'I'm too involved in this fraud case.'

She was proud of the rapidity of her response: an amazingly cool, businesslike manner for turning down a fantasy.

His expression flickered.

Was it her imagination, or was he relieved?

'I knew you wouldn't want to come,' he said, evenly. 'But I wasn't expecting that excuse. Wow. You are unpredictably predictable, as I said.'

His expression was now wary.

'You don't even know when I'm going, so how do you know you can't come?'

He rose from the sofa, peeled off her panties and began to put on his clothes.

Men always looked undignified like that, she thought, but he managed to do it with grace, as though it were some ceremonial to celebrate the heights of human achievement.

'You really pride yourself on having style, don't you?' She could hear the bitterness creep into her voice.

He looked up, surprised, his eyes sombre with incipient hurt, but his composure infuriated her.

'You like to elevate each and every mundane action in life with a style that takes it into an art form,' she said spitefully. 'Even putting on your socks is a work of genius if you, the great artist of life, decrees that it should be so? Isn't that right?'

'Look, I don't know what this is all about, but I've clearly upset you in some way I can't even begin to understand. Are you saying it is the end? You want out?'

'Too damned right I do.'

God, she couldn't believe she had fallen into his manipulative little trap: he was the one giving her the push, cutting her out of his phone book without a word!

And now she was dumping him, no doubt just as he had hoped. It would suit his ego to make his lovers finish it, so he came out smelling of roses. Perhaps he had transferred her name to the page headed X, along with all the others!

She picked up his camera casually, as he turned to the window to pick up a shoe.

'Unpredictably predictable – that's what I said you would always be,' he said intensely. 'I have sometimes come back here after the most fantastic sex with you, and wondered how you would end it, if you did. Deep down I hoped you never would, but I couldn't help thinking you would meet some nice, ordinary lawyer who would always be there when you got back from work and didn't phone from the other side of the world.'

She slammed the door on his words, and dumped the camera, bag and trannies in the ornamental pond in the hallway.

He walked round the room, hunched with anger and frustration. He picked up her panties and threw them into the rubbish bin, along with her half-full glass of wine and the rest of the bottle.

For half an hour he sat immobile, after the fever of angry activity, staring into space.

He picked up the phone and punched in the numbers.

'Hi, John. Are you still looking for a flat? You are? Well, if we can square the lease with the landlord, you can have this one.'

He shifted position and put his foot on the coffee table.

'Yes, I know. I've decided to stay in the States. There are more opportunities there and I only stayed here for personal reasons.'

He walked round the room searching for a notebook. He read out the details of the outgoings and overheads.

'No, there's no chance I'll change my mind. There's no possibility she wants to move in with me, so there's no point in my staying. I wanted to make sure she really cared, was really ready for the commitment. So I gave her every get-out clause I could think of, expecting her to demolish my arguments. She didn't say a thing when I suggested that absence makes the heart grow fonder, that sort of crap; but within minutes she was finding difficulties I had never even imagined, and stormed out.'

He walked into the kitchen and began throwing out the porcelain mugs she had given him, the tea-towel she had brought from her flat, the bill for the meal they had had together two weeks previously.

'I feel so exposed. She knows all the odd little sexual fantasies I have, and responds just the way I like. I feel so totally, utterly, betrayed. I was so sure of her, I'd even taken the page out of my address book. What? Yes, I know, but it was just a boyishly romantic gesture when I was feeling pleased with life, because I knew – just knew she would be moving in with me.'

The Horse Warrior

Lisette Allen

The Horse Warrior

✦ ✦

North-West Frontier, India. May 1876.

'My poor Emily,' said Mrs Compton, 'you really have had a most fortunate escape. Another summer, and your complexion would have been quite ruined by this terrible climate.'

Emily, who was gazing out of the window, pretended not to hear her. Their carriage, which was little more than a covered bullock cart, was proceeding tortuously up the narrow, rock-strewn track, and the noise of the heavy wooden wheels all but drowned out speech. One of the bearers, who was walking alongside the horses, grinned at her, and she smiled back. He'd stripped to the waist, and the sight of his glossy, firmly muscled body made her pulse quicken secretly.

Mr Compton leaned forward from his wife's side and touched Emily's arm, making her jump in revulsion. 'A fortunate escape,' he repeated earnestly. 'You must be looking forward so much to your return to England, and civilisation.'

Emily turned slowly to face him. 'I do not wish to return to England,' she said. 'My home is here.'

Mr and Mrs Compton looked at each other with meaningful expressions. 'Nonsense,' said Mr Compton. He was a missionary, sent out here almost a year ago by the British Indian Evangelical Society, and he spoke to everyone in the same brisk tones. 'Emily, you are almost twenty, you know. Time for you to find a husband. You have no future here.'

Emily didn't reply. Instead, she turned to gaze out of the window again, remembering.

Last winter, in the bustling market at Peshawar, she had seen a horse warrior of the Afridi tribe striding arrogantly through the crowds of traders. He was proud and graceful, with lean, hawklike features, and piercing dark eyes. He didn't see her, but she never forgot him. She dreamed of him at night, of the things that a man like that would do to her. Her breasts tingled at the thought of his long fingers caressing them; and at the pit of her stomach the dark longing surged.

'A husband,' Mrs Compton was echoing happily. 'Some young curate, in a nice English village, Emily dear.'

Emily didn't listen any more.

This was their second day of travel from Peshawar, where she had lived for five years with her father, who was part of the British trade delegation to neighbouring Afghanistan. They were still in the foothills of the great mountain ranges, and the travelling was arduous. Emily gazed silently at the distant snowcapped peaks. The afternoon sun, warm for May, glinted on their sparkling tops, making them look like pinnacles of crystal against the azure sky.

By tomorrow, they would be traversing the flat Indian plains that encircled Lahore. From there, they would take the train to Bombay, then sail to England. She couldn't bear even to think about it.

Mr Compton was growing increasingly irritated at their slow progress. 'Dreadful,' he fumed, as they rocked slowly on their way. 'These Peshawar men are hopelessly inefficient. I was hoping to reach the next army post before dusk.'

Mrs Compton's plump face looked suddenly fearful. 'I've heard, Thomas, that the Afridi tribesmen sometimes prey on lone travellers after nightfall. Oh, I do wish you'd accepted Major Sullivan's offer of an escort.'

He patted her hand. 'The mountain tribesmen are cowards through and through. They would never dare to attack British citizens, in British territory. They prefer to skulk up in their hilltops, like the carrion they are.'

Mrs Compton, looking somewhat appeased, leaned forward to Emily and said in a confidential voice, 'My dear Emily. When you return to England, you must be discreet, you know, about the regrettable freedom that your foolish papa has allowed you in Peshawar. You must say nothing about the dreadful habits of the native people: the way they live, the things they make their women do.' She shuddered, but her pale little eyes behind the folds of pudgy flesh glittered with excitement.

Emily knew what the men of the hills did to their women. She'd learned Pashto many years ago, and the servant girls confided in her. Some months ago, when one of the girls was about to be married, Emily had come across her with her friends, being bathed and oiled. They'd explained to Emily that the unguent was to make the young bride's skin fragrant and smooth. 'It is also,' the sloe-eyed bride had whispered shyly, 'to ensure that my husband's formidable instrument of love will slip easily, sweetly inside me. He will worship me with his body. Oh, I cannot wait . . .'

Emily had envied her with all her heart. Her wandering thoughts were reclaimed by Mrs Compton, who was warming to her subject.

'The native people are animals – animals! Why, their women-folk claim to actually enjoy the men's disgusting attentions. You must forget everything you have ever seen, Emily, on your regrettable travels, or you will never, ever get a husband. It's bad enough that your skin is so brown, your body so thin. Any hint of scandal and your marriage prospects would be quite ruined. Isn't that so, Thomas?'

Mr Compton nodded solemnly. 'A good thing that you are so plain, Emily. At least it has saved you from the unwelcome attentions of the natives.'

Emily gazed at him. She was remembering how, on the first night that he and his wife had arrived to stay at her father's big house in the British enclave in Peshawar, he had paid two of the servant women to give him pleasure. Emily had been crossing the courtyard below when she'd seen him, up on the balcony. She'd backed into the shadows because she didn't want him to see her.

The missionary had been dressed in his clerical black suit, which was still dusty from travelling. He'd talked in a low, urgent voice to the two girls, and passed them money. Then, abruptly, he had unbuttoned his trousers. Emily saw that his pale penis was already rigid with excitement. He'd barked at one of the girls to take it in her mouth. She'd knelt obediently, her soft lips encircling the stiff little stem of his cock; he'd shuddered with pleasure, then reached to uncover the breasts of the other girl. Emily had watched dispassionately. His small penis had jerked and thrust a few times more; then he had gasped loudly, his hands pulling at the other girl's brown nipples, and was still.

Afterwards, the servant girls had discussed him with Emily, laughing scornfully over the man's pale, small phallus.

'My lover's is like the bough of a tree in comparison,' boasted one. 'And, oh, he pleasures me with it for hours. It is like riding to heaven, Mistress Emily.'

'My man's long tongue gives me more delight than that one's prick ever could,' said the other one, Nera, slyly.

His tongue? thought Emily. She had pondered over that, puzzled. Her imaginings had brought a warm blush to her cheeks.

That night, she had dreamed of the horse warrior. She dreamed that he came into her private chamber. He knelt beside her on her bed, and gently parted her thighs, pushing up her long white nightgown. She watched him without fear, marvelling at his beauty. Bending his head, still fully clothed, he began to lick at her belly, at the incredibly sensitive skin of her inner thighs. Then, without warning, his fleshy tongue darted out to probe the secret folds of her sex, running thrillingly through the plump pink creases, dancing over the tip of her hot little pleasure bud. Emily had cried out in shock and wonder as the dark melting sensations spiralled and spread. With increasing intensity, the stiffened tip of his tongue rasped slowly to and fro, spreading her legs wide, preparing her for unimaginable delights. And then, she woke, and he wasn't there at all, and tears of frustration had filled her eyes. She had had to ease her torment quickly with her fingers, rubbing hard at her swollen little mound. Her secret parts had been soaking with honeyed moisture.

The next day, she'd mentioned casually to Nera the serving girl that she'd once seen a horseman of the Afridi in Peshawar market-place. 'He moved so gracefully, yet with such strength,' Emily had said wistfully, describing him. 'His hair was black, and his features were proud and haughty, and his eyes glittered like a hawk's. His skin was pale, paler than the men of the Punjab. He wore a belt braided in blue and gold around his narrow waist.'

'Ah,' the girl had said with feeling, 'that would be the Lord

Karem. He is a prince of the Afridi, who come down from the snowcapped mountains when the weather is fair. My husband sometimes trades with him. He is wonderfully handsome, is he not? My loins melt with desire at the sight of him. They say he is a superbly endowed lover, with the strength of a wild stallion. Oh, I love my husband, mistress Emily, but what would I not give for one forbidden night in Karem's arms? To feel his mouth on my breasts, his mighty shaft plunging into me . . .'

Karem. Emily remembered that name, and often she muttered it aloud through her long, restless nights of dreaming.

The purple shadows were starting to lengthen over the coarse scrub that lined the track as the covered bullock cart moved laboriously on through the steep-sided valley. Emily was gazing out at a tumbling stream of melted snow that gushed from a rocky ravine, when suddenly the worn-out army horses that pulled the carriage ground to a halt again, accompanied by a cacophony of curses and creaking harnesses.

'What now, in heaven's name?' blustered Mr Compton. He opened the door and swung himself down, only to return a moment later. 'The harness has broken. I don't believe it. Such inefficiency, such hideous incompetence.'

Emily said, 'Do harness straps never break in England?'

He gave her a look of scarcely restrained impatience. His wife had gone pale with fear.

'Thomas. Will we be stranded here all night? There might be robbers, Thomas, marauders on horseback, coming down from the mountain passes . . .'

Her husband snorted. 'I'd like to see them try. Attack the subjects of her Imperial Majesty Queen Victoria, within the territory of the British Army? Don't be so foolish, Dorothea.'

Emily stepped out of the carriage. She lifted her face to the mountains, seeing how the glow of the sinking sun was tinting the pinnacled white peaks with rose. Somewhere a jackal howled – a lonely, defiant sound. She breathed in the clear air deeply, and her eyes sparkled with excitement.

Mr Compton was shouting at the confused servants, and Mrs Compton was anxiously wringing her plump hands, gazing with dismay at the ever-lengthening shadows that were creeping across the sides of the narrow, desolate valley. Suddenly she let out a low moan. 'Thomas,' she whispered. 'Oh, dear God. Thomas!'

Emily also turned to gaze at the rocky slopes that soared high, high above them. There was a cloud of dust, the sound of drumming hoofbeats; then she saw the horses clambering agilely down the crevasse by the tumbling stream. Their riders wore sleeveless jackets, and loose, white cotton breeches gathered into long leather boots. Afridi men. Her heart gave a great leap.

Dorothea Compton was trembling with fright. She grabbed Emily. 'Into the carriage. Oh, quickly. If they know that we are here – high-born English women – then there is no hope for us!'

Emily said calmly, 'They will have seen us already. The Afridi have eyes like hawks.'

But Mrs Compton, babbling almost incoherently now, dragged her inside the carriage and slammed the rickety wooden door. They heard the prancing of horses' hooves all around, heard the sharp, guttural Pashto of the horsemen and the shrill, despairing bark of Thomas Compton's voice. Mrs Compton was almost prostrate with fright.

'If they should take us, then you must do exactly what they say,' she moaned to Emily. 'Oh, my poor child. These heathen natives are mad with lust. They may command you to hold their beastly members, to stroke them, to satisfy their terrible animal desires. They may even make you take them in your mouth. Do exactly what they say, and we might yet escape with our lives!'

Emily looked at her with quiet scorn. 'If I am as plain as you say, then I am in no danger.'

'Oh, but you are English! You are a fair-skinned English memsahib – they will fight one another to defile you! Dear Emily, I would rather die than see this happen to you –'

The door was pulled open. Mrs Compton screamed. A man stood there. He was tall, wide-shouldered, with dark hair pulled back from his lean, hard-boned face. His clear grey eyes looked first at Mrs Compton, then at Emily. Emily saw the blue and gold braided belt at his waist, and felt her heart give a great, stunning leap of excitement. She remembered Nera's breathless voice: 'His name is Karem, lord of the Afridi . . .'

'Outside, *ferangi* women,' he said softly.

Mrs Compton stumbled out, whimpering. Emily followed. She saw that Mr Compton had his wrists bound, and was being guarded by two of the Afridi. The servants had all fled.

Mr Compton called out hoarsely, 'Pray. Pray for your life, Dorothea.'

The tall man with grey eyes turned to Emily. His sleeveless cotton jacket was open at the front; she could see the rippling play of tautly honed muscles beneath his silken brown skin. She felt her throat go strangely dry as he assessed her.

Then he looked back at Mrs Compton, and said, 'You travel, I believe, from Peshawar. Within your carriage you have something of value that was taken from my people. I must examine your belongings.'

Mrs Compton screamed, 'No! My jewels! You will not have them!'

He beckoned to two of his men to restrain her. 'I do not want your jewels,' he said.

He'd spoken English to them, in a husky, accented voice; Emily stepped forward and addressed him quietly in fluent Pashto.

'The object you require,' she said, 'is in the portmanteau on the floor of the carriage.'

He turned back to her. His dark eyebrows lifted, just a little, above his long, hawklike nose. 'You speak our language well. An unusual accomplishment for an Englishwoman.'

She met his gaze steadily, trying to control the thudding excitement of her heart, because he was just as beautiful as she remembered. She said, calmly, 'My father works for the British trade delegation to Afghanistan. I have spent much time with him, travelling between Peshawar and Kabul.'

'And now you are leaving?' His eyes rested briefly on the trunks strapped to the roof of the stricken carriage.

'So they tell me,' she said softly.

The portmanteau was brought out, and emptied at Karem's command. Within its recesses was a small leather case. One of the tribesmen opened it with care. It contained an exquisite little ivory jewellery box, inlaid with gems. Mr Compton, who had been watching in agitation, gave a cry of despair and lunged towards it.

'That is mine. Mine!'

The grey-eyed horseman Karem looked at him with contempt. 'It is not yours, Englishman. It is one of the treasures of the Moghul empire, stolen from the Afridi people by the British invaders.'

The Englishman sagged back in his bonds. 'How did they know?' he muttered. 'How did these devils know I had it?' With a last flurry of defiance, he called out, 'I know who you are. You are Karem, leader of the Afridi robbers. Karem, the thief of the mountains –'

Emily saw the dangerous gleam of anger in the horseman's eyes. 'I am Karem, lord of the Afridi,' he said. 'But it is not for strangers to defile my name.' He turned to his men. 'Bind his mouth.'

Mrs Compton began to sob wildly. 'Take our jewels,' she pleaded. 'Take the horses, take everything. Only leave the girl alone, I beg you! Her father is an important man – if she is harmed, you will have the British army to contend with!'

The man called Karem turned to Emily. 'What is she afraid of, *ferangi* woman?'

'She has heard,' replied Emily, 'that the people of your race treat English women badly.'

Mrs Compton, watching them talking, became almost hysterical. The more she struggled, the tighter the two men held her. 'Take me!' she cried. 'I know what you're plotting, you brute, but take me instead of her, I beg you!'

Emily watched as Karem walked slowly over to Mrs Compton. He moved with a careless, easy masculine grace that reminded her of her vivid dreams. A fresh pulse of excitement stirred at the base of her stomach.

He said to Dorothea Compton, in his husky English, 'I have recovered the precious treasure that you stole from my people. I want no more. Go and stand quietly beside your husband, woman. I assure you, we will soon be gone.'

'No! You will kill us if you don't get exactly what you want – I know, I've heard! Take me instead of the girl. I will sacrifice myself!' She'd managed to get one arm free, and with it she pulled frantically at her voluminous travelling cape.

Karem came back to Emily. He said in Pashto, 'I do not understand. Is this woman crazy?'

Emily said, 'Lord Karem. She is hoping that your men will force her to do their will. In fact, she will not rest in her protests unless they pleasure her.'

'How do you know this, *ferangi* woman?'

'I have seen her, with the native youths. Her husband does not find her attractive. When he is away, travelling, she pays the servants to come and give her pleasure.'

'This is the only way to calm her?'

Emily said, honestly, 'If your men disappoint her, she will cry rape anyway, to get her revenge. I saw her order a man to be beaten once, because he had refused her. She watched as the whip fell on his back, and took pleasure from his suffering. If your men give her what she wants, she will become quiet, and her lips will be sealed for ever.'

He nodded, his grey eyes resting all the time on her face. 'What does she enjoy, oh wise daughter of England?'

'Her delight is to take more than one man. Her desires are great, Lord Karem. Tell three of your men to offer themselves to her. But it must all be done well away from her husband's sight, so that she can openly revel in her pleasure.'

Karem spoke rapidly in Pashto to three of his men. Their faces betrayed little expression, save that of resignation. He told them to take Dorothea Compton a little way along the track, to where a tumbled heap of boulders offered some privacy. Dorothea pretended to struggle, for her husband's sake, but her pudgy face was blazing with excitement, and her little tongue was darting between her lips. Karem went with them, to point out the place; Emily followed. He turned, and looked at her questioningly.

'I want to see it,' she breathed.

A half-smile twisted his face. 'You take my breath away, *ferangi* woman. Why?'

'The woman is cruel, and has often humiliated the people of Peshawar, who are my friends. Now I wish to take pleasure in her humiliation.'

He shrugged, folding his arms across his chest so Emily could see how the breadth of his smooth chest narrowed down enticingly to his flat, hard stomach. 'Then we will watch together,' Karem said. 'But if the old woman is as lustful as you say, then this could take some time. Come and sit with me, in privacy.'

He climbed lithely to a wide, rocky ledge that was carved out beside the tumbling little brook. Emily scrambled after him, her long skirts trailing, her soft brown hair falling from its pins; but she didn't care. He took her arm to help her, and her heart jumped at his strong touch. From up here, she could see the high Afghan ranges soaring heavenwards, their crests vibrant with the fading light. Then she looked down quickly, because she could hear strange gasps and mutterings from below.

'You do not have to look,' Karem said.

'I want to look,' said Emily.

Down below, in a deep cleft in the rocks that was carpeted with springy sage, Dorothea Compton was pulling off her jacket, her bodice, her stays. Clad only in her dusty serge skirt, she triumphantly lifted her heavy breasts in her hands.

'Lick them,' Emily heard her command. 'You must take them, and taste them with your tongues.'

The men did not understand her language, but her gestures spoke for themselves. They did as she said, bending their shaggy heads to pull and lick at the woman's long, brown teats. She threw back her head in ecstasy.

'And you,' she gasped to the third man. 'Unfasten your breeches. Let me feel your cock. Oh, dear God . . .'

The man stood still as Dorothea scrabbled frantically at his groin and pulled out his long penis. It was already growing firm; her fingers caressed him with trembling rapture as the stout shaft swelled and hardened. She gripped it and began to rub the foreskin, muttering to herself in delight.

Emily and Karem's eyes met. Emily giggled, and sat down on a ledge of rock to watch in comfort. He sat beside her.

'She is rapacious,' he said. 'Are all your countrywomen like this?'

'Many of them, yes,' said Emily. 'They become cold towards their husbands and they wither inside. Until something like this happens.'

He nodded. 'They are like a dying fire, slumbering into oblivion until a fresh young wind causes the sparks to roar into life. In my country, we honour our women constantly with our bodies. We always remember that they are receptacles of love and passion.'

Emily felt a tremor run through her. She remembered Nera's words: 'They say he is a superbly endowed lover, with the strength of a stallion . . .'

Was he aroused by the things going on below them? She certainly was. Swallowing hard, she gazed again at Mrs Compton, who was caressing the man with fervour. Her victim was gritting his teeth, his dark eyes narrowed into blackness as his dusky cock leapt and throbbed within Dorothea's pudgy grasp.

Emily felt her own breasts aching hotly, felt a warning throb between her legs as her secret flesh swelled and moistened with need. Only Karem seemed unmoved as he leant back casually on one elbow, his long booted legs carelessly stretched before him.

Then he said, 'I am glad, *ferangi* woman, to have recovered my people's lost treasure – the jewelled ivory box. Word came to me from a trader that it would be leaving Peshawar for England, concealed in the missionary's carriage. Strange, that a humble trader should be so well informed.'

'Isn't it?' said Emily, rather faintly, because down below them the stalwart tribesman was beginning to spurt over Dorothea's frantic hand.

The other men watched hungrily as his lengthy dark penis leaped and spasmed with a life of its own. Emily could see how the man's balls bounced, fat and tight, beneath the thick root of his cock; she bit on her soft underlip, unable to drag her eyes away. Would a mighty weapon like that really fit inside the secret folds of a woman's tender sex? Wouldn't it hurt? She felt an almost unbearable throb of excitement between her thighs, was aware of the trickling, swollen hotness there beneath the dusty folds of her skirt. Her nipples ached almost unbearably. Taking a deep breath, she reached for Karem's hand, and placed it over her breast.

Instantly, her tingling nipples sprang out against the bodice of her gown, yearning for more. Gently Karem drew his palm over the taut crests, sending shivers of longing through her entire body. Then he drew her to him, and pressed his mouth against hers. The feel of his tongue, muscular and velvety as it thrust between her lips, made her feel faint with delight.

He drew away, and she gasped with disappointment. But then he said, 'Fair and wise daughter of England, I would honour you properly, in the way of my people. Do you wish it?'

'Oh, please,' said Emily.

With the utmost care, he unbuttoned her tight bodice and bent his head to kiss the rosy nubs of her nipples. As his long, skilful tongue teased each crest in turn with its hot wetness, she felt the tremors begin to rack her body. He fastened his mouth at last around one breast, sucking hard, drawing it deep into his mouth, and she felt the dark, forbidden pleasure pulling like cords at her stomach, felt the insistent ache between her thighs become an urgent demand. His hand was already on her calf, stroking the delicate stockinged skin above her little laced half-boot, sliding breathtakingly upwards.

With a regretful shudder, she pulled away. It was too soon. Her body would surely explode with the sweet, dark pleasure if he touched her now, at her very heart. Besides, she was ashamed of her wetness, her openness. She wanted him, too, to be consumed with need, just as she was.

Shyly, her cheeks rosy with warmth, she pulled herself up. 'Lord Karem. I too would honour you.'

His lean face blazed with passion as she reached for the blue and gold sash at his hips. Her hand brushed unwittingly against the muscular bulge of his genitals beneath his breeches, and she felt the renewed liquid throbbing of her vagina. Dry-throated with excitement, trying to control the trembling of her fingers, she carefully untied the braided sash and pulled down the loose folds of fabric at his waist. At last, she could touch his silken rod of flesh. It pulsed hotly against her hand; tenderly she eased it out, trembling as her fingers fluttered over his sublime manhood.

'Oh, Lord Karem,' she murmured. 'Truly, you are a prince among men.' Then she bent over his lap, and carefully took his shaft into her mouth.

The size, the strength of his dusky phallus took her breath away. And the taste: the hot, musky, virile scent of him intoxicated her. She was afraid of displeasing him; and yet she knew, from what she had heard on the streets of Peshawar, that this above all else was what men adored. Shyly she began to caress him, sliding her lips over the straining shaft, stroking with her little tongue round the bluntly swollen head, smiling inside as she heard him catch his breath and grip her shoulders hard. Daringly, she reached to cup the globes of his testicles, melting with delight as she felt their warm, velvety bulk.

He pulled himself suddenly out of her mouth. His penis glistened, angry and swollen, searching vainly for some enfolding orifice. Emily kept her head bowed.

'I displeased you, Lord Karem?' she whispered.

He put his hand under her chin to gently lift up her head, and she saw that his dark eyes were ablaze with passion.

'How could you displease me?' he said softly. 'Oh, most beautiful of women, you are everything that a man could wish. And I want to be the first to show you everything.'

Emily nodded, trusting him. Carefully, he laid her back on the mossy ground so her naked breasts were rosy in the setting sun. Then he pushed her heavy skirts up slowly, his strong hands stroking her slender thighs as if he were calming one of his horses, easing aside her undergarments of lace and cotton until at last the rosy lips of her pudenda, plump and glistening beneath their little mat of fur, were fully exposed to his gaze. Emily felt no shame now, only a deep, burning longing for the fulfilment that he was offering. He drew her stockinged thighs apart with his gentle hands, and knelt between them, his cock still jutting proudly from his groin, to run his long tongue between her labia. She cried out with joy and reached out to grasp at his strong shoulders as his tongue's tip danced in her moisture. This was what she had dreamed of.

'Karem,' she whispered. 'Please. I want you.'

He lifted his head. 'Soon, beautiful *ferangi* woman. Soon, I promise you your every desire.'

He moved himself up and over her. She gazed at his lovely dark cock thrusting towards her belly, and felt a moment's fear. It was so long, so thick. What would it be like to feel it moving inside her? Could such a mighty weapon really bring so much pleasure, as the servant girls had whispered? She flinched, very slightly, and he saw it and reached to toy with her nipples again, sending spasms of almost unbearable delight down to her groin. And then, she felt it: the hot, blunt head of his penis, tight at first, then sliding inexorably between the parted lips of her wet sex, filling her with wave after wave of delight, pleasuring her yearning flesh with such sweetness that she thought she would die of it. She wrapped her arms around him, running her fingers through his long dark hair. He kissed her mouth, her throat, her rosy nipples, and began to drive his penis even harder into her melting flesh. The pleasure gathered, peaked, exploded into waves of ecstasy as he tenderly continued to ravish her.

She clung to him desperately, as if she were drowning. He arched himself like a bow above her and drove into her, again and again, until she felt the leaping of his phallus spending itself deep inside her.

He drew himself up at last, facing the setting sun, and pulled her carefully into the crook of his arm. Emily leaned against his warm shoulder, her body still vibrant with pleasure. Down below, a disarrayed Mrs Compton was sprawled back against a rock, her legs lifted wide apart and her face beaming as the last of the tribesmen knelt before her and ravished her steadily. She was sighing noisily with bliss, her grey hair tumbling around her sweat-sheened face.

Emily looked up at Karem, and smiled. 'Your men have been good to her. She will, I think, be sorry to go back to her husband.'

He touched her cheek tenderly. 'She is a foolish woman, of no account. But what about you, most beautiful one? Do you go back to your husband?'

'They hope to find me one,' said Emily earnestly. 'But I am thin and plain, with lamentably straight hair. And my skin is too brown from the sun, my body too firm from riding and climbing in the hills. In England they like their women pale and plump, with curling golden hair.'

He touched her silky brown hair, which hung loose around her slender bare shoulders. 'Then your countrymen are fools. You wish to go back?'

'No. I love this country. I love the mountains, and the sky, and the fierce blizzards in winter, and the hot sun in summer. I love the people, and their language, and their customs. This is truly my home.'

'Then stay. Stay here with me.'

She looked up at him, as if searching for an answer. Below them Dorothea Compton, replete with pleasure, was getting up and dusting herself down. The tribesmen were loping with long-legged strides back towards their horses, their faces impassive. Emily and Karem both watched as the missionary's wife, hurriedly buttoning up her bodice and cramming her hat over her disordered hair, made her way hastily back to the carriage. Her husband, still bound and gagged, started to struggle wildly when he saw her. His wife began, with an expression of weary resignation, to unfasten him.

Karem's men, all mounted, were waiting for him further up the track. They were ready to leave. Karem helped Emily to her feet and held her hand, still waiting for her answer.

Instead of replying, Emily gazed down at the carriage, at the grazing horses, at the red-faced Mr Compton struggling to pull off the gag.

'I do hope they will be all right,' she said, almost to herself. 'It shouldn't take them too long to mend the harness, because the strap didn't actually break.'

Karem was watching her, his brows lifted in question.

'It just wasn't buckled properly, you see,' went on Emily. 'I loosened it myself, when we stopped for our lunch. I calculated that it would give way within the next hour, maybe two at the most – certainly before we left the mountains.'

Karem said slowly, with dawning understanding, 'You knew we would come?'

'Oh, yes. I knew you would want your jewelled box back.'

'So the message from the trader . . .'

'It came from me,' said Emily with shy pride. 'The trader, you see, is the husband of my good friend Nera. I knew that if I told Nera that the Comptons had the box, then she would tell her husband. And he, in turn, would ensure that the Lord Karem knew of its theft.'

He laughed. 'I don't think I can live without you, *ferangi* woman,' he said. 'Stay with me.'

'Oh, yes,' breathed Emily. 'I will.'

She walked at Karem's side towards the waiting horsemen, who were outlined high on the rocky path against the setting sun. Just at that moment, Mrs Compton, who was staring wistfully at the mounted Afridi while her husband struggled to fix the harness, caught sight of Emily.

'Emily!' she shrieked. 'Oh, my poor child. What have they done to you?'

Mr Compton too turned and saw her. 'Escape! You must escape, Emily!' he called out hoarsely.

Emily, her eyes sparkling with happiness, gazed at them and drew closer to Karem. 'I already have,' she called back.

Then, with Karem, she turned into the sunset. The waiting mountains, flame-tipped with orange and vermilion, soared into the darkening sky, welcoming her.

Complete Satisfaction

Fredrica Alleyn

Complete Satisfaction

❧ ☙

*E*mily was just about to step into the waiting black car when James spoke to her. Beneath her half-veil, carefully chosen to accentuate both her supposed grief and her dark, secretive beauty, her eyes widened in surprise. Widows were normally given privacy at the end of their husband's funeral service, even when the deceased had been seventy and the widow was twenty-nine.

'I need to talk to you about the will, Mrs Scott-Rawlings,' he said softly.

His voice was lovely, smooth and dark like her favourite chocolate, and Emily had always found him very attractive, when he'd dined at Briar House on business.

'I'd assumed it would be read back at the house, in front of the whole family,' she said, keeping her voice low and tremulous. Her training as an actress had stood her in good stead today.

He lowered his voice. 'The contents may take you a little by surprise. As solicitor and executor I felt it my duty to warn you, but I believe you'll manage very well,' he murmured.

Briefly she smelt the tangy scent of his aftershave, mingled with something else, something indefinably masculine. She turned quickly back to the car, although at a different time she would have watched him go, assessing the way he moved and carried himself. She'd always been drawn to tall, slim, athletic men.

It was a fifteen-minute drive back to Briar House, the large

Cornish manor house where she and Steven had lived for the past five years. She sat in the car alone because her stepchildren were in the second car, no doubt discussing the forthcoming reading of the will.

As the limousine moved slowly through the narrow winding lanes, Emily had time to think back over her marriage. Steven had met her at a time when her life had looked very bleak. After very early success in a television soap followed by a West End play she'd made the mistake of changing agents, and suddenly the work had dried up. The new, prestigious agency had bigger stars to worry about, and the public are always fickle. By the time they found a suitable vehicle for her talents she was no longer known, and at only twenty-four was considered old news. It wouldn't have been so bad if she'd had a family to help her through, or even a live-in lover, but she had no one. The lovers, like the work, had vanished as her popularity waned.

She'd met Steven at a dinner party held by a television producer. He'd been at the height of his fame then: not only a renowned historian but also a popular television personality with the knack of making even the driest facts come alive. His age meant nothing to Emily. He was still a physically attractive man, well built and with a shock of iron-grey hair, and she loved his intelligence and humour. Their courtship had been swift.

'At my age there's no time to waste,' he'd laughed when she'd asked him what his children would think about such a speedy engagement.

Because she admired him and knew that he could offer her an escape to a good life she became his third wife. He'd known that she didn't love him, she'd been totally honest about that, but he also knew that she liked him and would never let him down in public. His health wasn't good even then and he'd told her that he would understand if she looked elsewhere for sex. All he asked was her assurance that she'd never embarrass him, and she'd kept that promise. To the watchful public they'd remained an unlikely but devoted couple, and all her affairs had taken place in London, far away from their beautiful Cornish house and their watchful Cornish neighbours.

His two sons had viewed her arrival with dismay, but Charles, the younger by four years at thirty-six, had mellowed until slowly their careful surface friendship had flared into a burning passion, a passion that Emily had been terrified would show itself to Steven.

'Charles is lazy, selfish and a liar,' Steven had told Emily after she'd first met his sons. 'He's totally untrustworthy and when I go he'll get nothing, nothing at all. He knows that, which probably means he'll come round where you're concerned. After all, you're not going to take anything away from him, unlike Michael who would have inherited this house if I hadn't remarried.'

'I don't care whether he likes me or not,' Emily had replied.

But within a year she and Charles were lovers and every month they'd spent at least one night together in Charles's London flat. He hadn't been her only lover, but he was the only one she'd felt guilty about. Sometimes she hated herself for cheating on Steven with the only person he'd ever said he disliked, and his son at that.

At the memory of their most recent night together Emily squeezed her thighs together and clenched her pelvic muscles so that a shiver of sexual pleasure ran through her lower body. It had been an incredible night, they'd only slept for two hours in all, and when she'd returned to Briar House she could feel Charles's hands still on her breasts and his teeth on her nipples and inner thighs. Within a couple of days Steven's condition had taken a turn for the worse and she hadn't seen Charles since, but now she was free.

Only a few people had come back to the house after the funeral, which was a quiet family affair. The official remembrance service for friends from the academic and media world would come later. This meant that within an hour everyone except Emily, Charles, Michael and James Hogarth, the solicitor, had left.

'I take it you're here to read the will, James,' commented Charles who, Emily had noticed with some amusement, was having great trouble in striking the right tone for the occasion. His voice had veered from sorrowful to bluff and hearty in the past hour, and it still sounded too hearty when he spoke to James.

'I came to the funeral because your father and mine were close friends for over thirty years,' said James in the same sensual voice that had caught Emily's attention. 'With my father bedridden he naturally wanted us to be represented at the funeral service.'

'Yes of course, but there is to be a reading of the will, isn't there? And you are the family's solicitor.'

'Solicitor and executor,' said James, glancing over to where Emily was standing in the far corner of the room, her long-sleeved black dress following the liquid lines of her body to perfection.

Emily knew that he was looking at her, but she didn't return his glance. Instead she thought to herself how nice it would be to live with a man who spoke like that. The voice alone was almost sufficient to ensure a successful seduction, and she wondered idly what kind of a lover he was. Probably not all that good, she decided regretfully. Polite and careful no doubt, but very conventional. Somehow she imagined that was a necessity for anyone who felt his life could be fulfilled by working as a solicitor.

'Where shall we go, Emily?' asked Charles.

Emily turned to face him, moving slowly but elegantly and well aware of the effect she was having on him. 'Does it really matter?' she enquired softly, as though nothing mattered to her now that Steven was dead. This clearly infuriated Charles, who'd already trapped her in the kitchen pressing his body tightly up against her, even before the last of the mourners had left, and telling her that he wanted to take her there and then. Emily wouldn't have minded either but, having a more fitting sense of what was right for the occasion than Charles, she'd declined.

Michael looked both apprehensive and angry. 'Let's use father's study,' he said with an air of authority. 'I'm sure that's what he would have wanted.'

'I don't think your father would have cared if the will had been read in the kitchen,' said Emily, sweetly. 'He was never a man to stand on ceremony.'

'I think I know him better than you . . .' began Michael, but James was already walking towards the study and with indecent haste Michael hurried after him, followed more slowly by Charles and Emily.

'You're irresistible in black,' whispered Charles, touching her lightly in the centre of her back under the guise of ushering her through the door. 'Shall I stay on tonight?'

Emily shook her head. 'Not tonight, Charles. It wouldn't be right.'

'He's dead,' muttered Charles. 'Why should we worry about him any more?'

'Are you ready, Mrs Scott-Rawlings?' asked James Hogarth, politely. 'Perhaps you'd care to sit there, in the armchair. It must have been a long day for you.

Emily, who was beginning to feel like an actress auditioning for something by Jane Austen, nodded and gave him a sad half-smile worthy of any young, widowed heroine even Charles Dickens could have dreamt up. To her surprise, his eyes sparkled with amusement for a moment before he looked down at the papers on the desk.

'The will is very simple,' he told his attentive audience. 'Apart from some small bequests to staff and friends, which I don't need to bore you with, it reads as follows:

"To my beloved wife, Emily, I leave the rest of my estate, including Briar House and its contents, in gratitude for the six happiest years of my life. This, however, is on condition that she can convince James Hogarth, executor of the will, that she can manage to be the perfect hostess at Briar House by entertaining him there for a weekend and satisfying all his requests. Should she fail to do this, then both Briar House and the bulk of my fortune go to my eldest son, Michael. Should she succeed, then it is my wish that neither Michael nor Charles ever set foot in Briar House again."'

'What the hell does that all mean? It can't be legal,' declared Michael, furiously.

Emily was impressed that James Hogarth remained very calm. The extraordinary wording of the will and Michael's comment failed to cause any reaction at all, he merely glanced briefly at Emily and then spoke quietly to her furious stepson.

'It's perfectly legal,' he commented. 'I have no doubt your stepmother and I can easily come to some kind of arrangement that will fulfil the conditions set out by your father.'

'And if Emily fails, you'll contact me?' demanded Michael.

'Naturally. Mrs Scott-Rawlings, I'll telephone you tomorrow and we'll talk further. Right now I think it's time I took my leave of you. It must have been a very long and distressing day.'

'Yes,' murmured Emily, but her thoughts were miles away as she conjured up visions of how she might completely satisfy

James Hogarth, and with the blessing of her late husband. The prospect was deliciously exciting.

'Well, no doubt you consider it worth the six-year wait,' Michael snapped at her as he left.

'Has my beloved brother gone?' asked Charles, coming out of the dining room carrying a large glass of brandy.

'Yes,' murmured Emily.

'Good. What a strange condition the old man put in the will,' he continued. 'Still, it's nothing to worry about. Pleasing James Hogarth will be a piece of cake, and once that's done it's all yours and we're set up for life.'

He stood in front of her, pressed her back against the wall and lowered his mouth to hers. He smelt of brandy and cigarettes and, the moment his tongue invaded her mouth, Emily's legs went weak. She circled his neck with her arms as his hips thrust up against her.

'Let's go upstairs,' he muttered after a few seconds. 'I've been waiting all day for – '

'I think I should be going now,' said a calm voice from the study doorway.

Charles leapt backwards, spilling half of his brandy in the process, and Emily put her hands to her flushed cheeks.

'Mr Hogarth, I thought you'd gone,' she said feebly.

'I rather assumed that,' he replied.

She sensed that he was amused.

'I'll telephone you tomorrow morning. And if I might add a word of advice – ' he added as Charles walked away and Emily opened the front door for him.

'Yes?'

'I suggest that Charles doesn't stay with you tonight. I might find it a little difficult to consider you a suitable hostess and torchbearer for your late husband if I thought that...' He paused. 'I'm sure you get my drift?'

Emily nodded and, within five minutes of the solicitor leaving, Charles had gone too, protesting violently all the way to his car. But Emily had been adamant.

'We could lose everything,' she reminded him. 'I know we'd still have each other, but the house and the money would go to Michael.'

Charles had gone quite pale. 'No, you're absolutely right. We've waited five years, what's another week?'

190

She slept badly that night, troubled by the strange look of amusement in James Hogarth's eyes, but by the next morning she was feeling better and it was arranged that she would entertain James the following weekend, from the Friday to the Sunday.

'Is there anything you'd particularly like me to get in for you?' Emily asked.

'There's really no need, I'm easily pleased. Satisfying me shouldn't present a beautiful, experienced young woman like you with any problems,' replied James.

Emily's breathing had quickened with excitement.

'It could be worse,' said Charles, when she told him over the phone. 'After all, you're an actress. I don't suppose there's anything he could ask for that would shock you! Give him what he wants. I'll never ask you what it was, just as long as you send him away a happy man.'

Emily had every intention of doing exactly that.

The following Friday came round very quickly. Emily went through her wardrobe time and again, trying to decide what kind of an outfit the solicitor would consider suitable. She was his hostess, but also recently bereaved, and she had no idea whether or not he was aware of the fact that Steven had forbidden her to grieve.

'A waste of time, grief,' he'd told her only a few days before his death. 'Self-indulgent too. Remember the good times we had but move on. After all, we never had a conventional marriage.'

It was only at the very last moment that she managed to choose a black, crepe shirt-dress with a high Mandarin-style collar, large gold buttons, and a slim black belt that fastened with a gold clasp around her slender waist. The colour emphasised her bereavement, but the dress emphasised her perfect figure. 'Good compromise, Emily,' she told her reflection with satisfaction. 'Let's hope Mr Hogarth appreciates it.'

James arrived exactly five minutes late, and presented her with a bottle of wine and a large bouquet of flowers. However, he scarcely seemed to notice her dress, and she felt a distinct sense of pique after all the trouble she'd taken.

'I'll show you to your room,' she said with a smile. 'Then, once you've unpacked, we'll have a drink before dinner.'

'That sounds perfect,' he assured her.

Her stomach lurched at the sound of his voice.

After leading him upstairs, she preceded him into the large, main guest room where Steven had placed his closest friends. 'In the morning you'll see that there's a lovely view over the sea from here,' she remarked, drawing the curtains across the bow window.

'I rather like the view right now,' he said softly.

Emily turned and this time James made no pretence that he wasn't aware of the way she was dressed.

'Large buttons seem to cry out to be undone, don't they?' he murmured, taking a step towards her. 'This dress is wonderful, so demure and yet so erotic as well. That's how I see you, Emily, and the combination fascinates me. No wonder Steven was enchanted. Who could resist you, I wonder? Very few men I imagine, and certainly not a man like Charles.'

Emily's mouth was dry, but she had sufficient wit about her to widen her eyes in surprise. 'Charles? Why bring his name up?'

'Because I saw after the funeral how close the pair of you were, remember?'

'He was comforting me,' she said rather lamely.

James smiled. 'I hope I'm able to comfort you equally well during the weekend. It must be lonely here on your own, now Steven's dead.'

'Yes, a little, but I've been busy. I'll see you downstairs in a few minutes,' said Emily, hurriedly. She was very aware of James walking closely behind her to the door and then shutting it gently once she'd left the room.

Fifteen minutes later, James Hogarth joined her in the study and accepted a glass of dry sherry that had been Steven's favourite. Emily sat down opposite him and crossed her legs, well aware that they were one of her best assets.

'You must miss Steven very much,' he said politely.

Emily was tired of playing games. 'Of course I miss him, his physical presence here in the house, that is. But, as you probably know, we hadn't been man and wife in the true sense for the past two years. Although I was fond of him, grateful to him and admired him tremendously I wasn't "in love" with him. I'd never been in love with him. He knew that. This is like losing a dear friend. It leaves a gap, but it doesn't destroy you, and Steven wouldn't have expected it to destroy me.'

James nodded, a smile touching the corners of his mouth.

'That's very much the picture I got from your late husband the last time we met. Having such a beautiful young wife on his arm for public occasions meant a lot to him.'

'He saved me at a time when I was desperate. It was the least I could do,' said Emily. 'I wasn't a saint, but I was careful never to embarrass him.'

'Very thoughtful of you! Have you seen Charles since the funeral?'

'No,' replied Emily. 'You said it wouldn't be wise, and I agreed with that.'

'Good. What do you plan to do with Briar House, Emily?'

'Assuming that I satisfy you and inherit, I shall almost certainly sell,' said Emily. 'I don't want to spend my life in Cornwall, and it's far too large to keep as a weekend retreat.'

He moved towards her chair. 'I'll be sorry to see you go.'

Emily looked up into his dark-brown eyes and felt a tremor of excitement run through her. 'I have a feeling that you intend to test me out very thoroughly,' she said provocatively.

'It's my duty,' he said calmly. 'I owe it to your late husband.'

Emily swallowed hard. He was looking at her in a totally different way now and his breathing was rapid, making his excitement clear.

'It should be an interesting weekend,' she remarked, and at that moment the girl from the village came in to say that dinner was ready.

Conversation at dinner was more difficult than she'd expected. She tried to draw James out about his work, sport and even his short-lived marriage many years earlier, but suddenly he proved an expert at killing conversation. If nothing else, he was testing out her ability to keep the atmosphere convivial, and by the time they went into the drawing room for coffee she felt exhausted.

Settling back into a large winged chair, James smiled at her. 'Well done! I made that as difficult as I could. Let's hope you overcome the rest of the hurdles as easily.'

'At least I'm sure you'll like your room,' said Emily. 'It's beautiful. Everyone says so.'

'The problem is,' said James, slowly, 'I always have difficulty sleeping in a strange bed. I find a relaxing massage before I turn in helps a lot.'

'I'm sure that can be arranged,' said Emily calmly, but, inside, her stomach was tightening and she felt her nipples pressing against the thin slip that was all she was wearing beneath her dress.

James's invitation couldn't have been clearer, and the prospect of seeing him naked and relaxed while her fingers worked on his slim but muscular frame was intensely arousing. They each had a brandy and then Emily rose to her feet.

'I expect you'd like to go up now. Presumably you'd like to have a bath before the massage?'

He nodded, and without another word left the room, leaving Emily in a state of high anticipation. She wondered what Charles would make of all this. Although he'd told her that she should do anything James asked, she doubted if he'd expected the solicitor to make a move so early on in the weekend. It made her wonder what other demands lay in store during the next two days.

She gave him half an hour and then tapped on his bedroom door. On entering, she found him lying on top of the double bed wearing only a cotton bathrobe.

'Are you the masseuse, or do you provide a professional?' he enquired with a smile.

'I'm afraid there's only me,' she said, moving elegantly into the room.

'All the better,' he said, with a sigh of pleasure. 'Shall I lie face down?'

He sounded quite matter of fact, and Emily tried to match his tone despite the fact that her pulse was racing.

'If you would; and you'll have to take off the robe.'

He sat on the side of the bed, shrugged the garment off his shoulders, and then stood up to let it fall to the floor revealing his nakedness. Emily's throat constricted. He had an almost perfect body, and every muscle was clearly defined, despite the fact that he was slim. He already had an erection, and its size was very impressive.

'I like it best if my masseuse sits astride my back,' he murmured as he turned onto his face. 'You'll need to take off that dress though. I'd hate you to get it creased, or covered in oil.'

'How thoughtful,' remarked Emily, dryly.

She carefully unbuttoned the dress while James turned his head to watch her. Then, clad only in her slip and panties, she sat across his buttocks and smoothed her oiled hands over his lower back, pressing the muscles on either side of his spine upwards and outwards, fanning out until she was working between his shoulder blades, and his smooth golden skin started to unknot beneath her touch.

Sitting as she was, there was constant pressure on her vulva, and when James gave a gentle groan of pleasure she felt her internal muscles start to clench and the first stirrings of an orgasm quivered deep inside her. When she moved higher up his body to work on his neck she allowed herself to rock to and fro a little and the first tendrils of excitement grew into slithering coils that began to spread outwards, while all the time the knots of tension in James's body dissolved.

Emily's mouth was dry now and she squeezed her buttocks to hurry her moment of release, but suddenly James turned on his side and she was thrown off balance tumbling to the floor in a startled heap.

'I'm so sorry,' he apologised quickly. 'Didn't you hear me say that was fine?'

'No,' said Emily, her voice tight with frustration.

'Well, I feel wonderfully relaxed now. I'm sure I'll sleep like a log. You did that very well,' he added. For a brief moment she hated him for spoiling her pleasure at such a vital moment. Then she remembered that he was the one who had to be satisfied, not her, and she managed to smile at him.

'I hope you're right,' she said kindly. 'Sweet dreams.'

'You too, Emily,' he said softly as he pulled the duvet over his body and snuggled down for the night.

Although the morning was cool she only pulled on a cotton skirt and short-sleeved top because she knew how warm the long climb down to the pebbly cove made her, and that was where she wanted to go. Once there, she spent a long time gazing out over the water, lost in thought.

Half an hour later she heard the sound of footsteps on the pebbles and, looking round, saw James coming towards her. Dressed in fawn slacks and a dark green polo shirt he was very attractive, and again she felt her body tense with sexual desire, but she was beginning to wonder whether sex was going to be on the menu or not.

'How did you know I'd be here?' she called.

'I used to watch you and Steven here, from the clifftop, in the early days of your marriage.'

Emily's eyes widened in surprise. 'You did?'

James nodded. 'I was consumed with envy. You were so beautiful, and he already had fame and fortune. It didn't seem fair that he should have such a beautiful and loving wife as well.'

'I didn't love him,' Emily reminded him softly.

'I didn't know that then, although clearly he did. Didn't he mind?'

'No. He wanted a trophy wife, and that's what I was!'

'And you wanted what? His fame? His money? His body?'

'I wanted to be safe,' said Emily, flatly. 'I was broke, out of work and without any family or prospects. He gave me a chance to escape all that. I wouldn't have done it if I hadn't admired him and enjoyed his company, but since I did it seemed a fair bargain.'

'He was already unwell,' said James, slowly. 'I assume you did think that one day you'd inherit all this?'

'He told me I would, and yes that was an additional attraction, if you must know.'

'You were very honest with each other, weren't you?' said James, slowly. 'Until the arrival of Charles, that is.'

Emily stiffened. 'Charles?'

'Your husband knew,' he said, his voice suddenly cold.

Emily felt as though her heart had leapt into her throat and was threatening to choke her. 'How long had he known?'

'Right from the start. Charles had done it before, with his father's second wife. That's why Steven had no time for him. He got me to follow you in London and I saw you together. You weren't very discreet.'

'But he never said . . .'

'Who?' asked James, sharply. 'Your husband, or Charles?'

'Neither of them!' whispered Emily. 'But it was Steven I was talking about. Why didn't he say?'

'Would you, in the circumstances? He was waiting for you to be your usual honest self, but you weren't, and that's why he put in this clause. He knew that I could make you fail and ensure Briar House was never used to enable you and Charles to have a life together. He cared deeply for you Emily, but his hatred for Charles was implaccable. Nothing could alter that.'

'You can't make me fail the test,' said Emily. 'Surely you know there's nothing you can ask of me that I'll refuse to do.' She didn't have to act to sound sincere. She couldn't wait for the pair of them to make love, and his physical closeness was driving her insane.

'Of course I can,' he replied easily.

Emily felt her blood racing at the challenge. She simply couldn't imagine anything this man might ask her to do that wouldn't be a pleasure. She moved nearer to him and let her left hand rest gently on his right arm. 'Then ask it,' she murmured provocatively.

'Give up Charles and become my mistress,' he said calmly.

Emily stared at him. 'You can't ask that! That's not a weekend guest's request, that's blackmail. I only had to satisfy you for the weekend.'

'I think not. The will says you must satisfy all requests I make this weekend. Admittedly, if you went to court you might win, but somehow I don't think that would suit you or Charles.'

Emily was silent as she tried to make sense of what he was saying. She'd imagined so much erotic excitement, so many hours of sensual pleasure and as yet he hadn't even touched her, but he was asking her to become his mistress and relinquish Charles. The sense of his power acted as an aphrodisiac. She physically ached for him.

'How can I promise that when I don't know if we're sexually compatible?' Emily asked at last.

James grasped her hand. 'Perhaps we'd better find out,' he agreed, and began walking her along the beach.

'This isn't the way back,' she protested.

'It's where I want to go,' said James.

She realised he was heading for a cave.

Once inside, he sat down on a jutting piece of slate and looked at her with glittering brown eyes. 'Strip for me,' he said quietly.

She obeyed instantly, his calm voice adding to her excitement.

'Now come and sit on my lap,' murmured James.

She felt her naked buttocks brush against the soft fabric of his linen trousers. His erection could easily be felt through the material. Her left nipple was against his polo shirt. It quickly stiffened into a rigid peak when James lowered his mouth on to it and then nipped sharply at it so that a fierce surge of hot pleasure seared from her breast to between her naked thighs.

He rubbed her entire body with his hands, warming and arousing her at the same time, and then he stood up with her in his arms and laid her on the slate while he loomed over her, suddenly authoritative and threatening in the dim light.

She watched him remove his clothes, in a rush that betrayed his seething passion. And then he was lying on top of her, taking his weight on his elbows but allowing the pressure of his lower body to stimulate her belly and pubic mound; the tip of his erection nudged at her rapidly opening sex lips and then teased the head of her hard, swollen clitoris.

'Quickly,' she implored him, aching with the need to have him inside her.

He ignored her plea and continued to tease inside her outer sex lips with his glans, while his mouth nuzzled hungrily at her neck and breasts.

Outside the cave she could hear the sea crashing down on the pebbles, and as her whole body continued to tighten and throb with desire she longed for her orgasm to crash over her as well. But James was a consummate artist and he played with her body until she was sobbing with despair, using words she'd never have dreamt of using, as she thrust her hips upwards, quite frantic with the need for release.

Just when she thought she would go totally demented, he moved off her and she screamed at him in despair. He put a finger to her lips in a gesture of reassurance and then she felt his fingers replace the head of his penis and her slippery clitoris was being manipulated so skilfully that she felt her body swell and then burst as the liquid heat spread through her and her cry of gratitude was as wild and uninhibited as the call of the gulls outside.

Only then, when she had finally climaxed, did James enter her. He entered fiercely, like a man taking possession of a prize, and his thrusting was almost brutal. The fact that he could behave like this excited Emily still more, and when he climaxed she came again. Her second orgasm was so fierce it was almost painful.

When it was over they were both breathing heavily, and for several minutes neither of them spoke.

'Here, you'll catch cold,' said James finally, picking up Emily's clothes and handing them to her.

As she dressed he watched her closely, occasionally reaching out and touching her gently on the face or shoulders. She found that his tenderness after the violent passion only served to re-arouse her, but she was careful not to show it.

They went back to the house in silence. They then spent the day quietly, going through Steven's collection of books and watching videos of his television show, some of which Emily had never seen before.

'He looked like Charles, when he was younger,' she said, without thinking.

'Luckily he didn't behave like him,' retorted James.

That night he came to her room and they made love again. This time Emily was the aggressor, sitting astride his chest and teasing him by hanging her nipples in front of his face and then arching back when he moved to take them in his mouth. She tied his wrists to the bedposts and kept him waiting an hour for his release, so that when he finally came he shouted aloud during his spasms of pleasure, but they were the only sounds he made all night. He never spoke to her at all.

On the Sunday morning when she awoke, he was dressed and ready to leave, his overnight bag on the floor next to her bed. Emily stared at him.

'Why are you going now? The weekend isn't over.'

'Yes it is, Emily. All that's left is for you to decide whether or not you're going to keep Briar House.'

'But you haven't given me enough time to decide,' she protested. 'Today would have been even better than last night. There's so much more we can do.'

'I'm sure there is, but I understand the game you're playing and it isn't going to work. Of course you're irresistible, countless men can testify to that, including Steven and Charles, but you're also an actress. Passion is easy to simulate, especially when two people fit together as we do. The question is, are you willing to become my mistress and give up Charles?'

She hadn't expected such a direct confrontation. She'd imagined him to be too well mannered for that, but he'd caught her out and she had virtually no time to frame an answer that wouldn't commit her.

James laughed. 'Emily, don't rely on your dramatic skills, be honest for once. What do you want the most? Charles? Or Briar House?'

'Briar House means I have to be your mistress too,' said Emily. 'I've already given six years of my life to a man I didn't love to live here. It's different now. Michael can have Briar House. I'll have Charles.'

James nodded. 'Naturally I'm disappointed, but somehow it's what I expected. As soon as I'm gone you can ring him and tell him the news.'

'He won't want me without the money,' said Emily. 'You know that, don't you?'

James nodded. 'Oh yes, I know that.'

'And when he turns me down, you'll still make me leave, to start all over again, virtually penniless?' she asked, in what she couldn't help thinking was a rather good frail, wronged-young-woman-struggling-with-adversity kind of voice.

James was less impressed. 'It's your choice,' he reminded her.

'Suppose I give up Charles but don't want to be your mistress. What happens then?' asked Emily.

'That choice isn't yours. I made the demand, and I'm the man you have to satisfy. I never expected you to agree with what I asked. I simply wanted to find out what it was like to make love to you. Now I know. I'll never forget it, it was incredible. Better than I'd imagined,' he remarked, as he left.

She called him at the office the following morning. 'Do I have to sign anything, James?' she asked in a little-girl-lost voice.

'No,' said James with desire audible in his voice. 'If you've definitely decided that you can't satisfy my request, then Briar House passes to Michael and you inherit twenty thousand pounds. So, you're hardly penniless.'

'But I shan't see you again,' she said softly.

'It seems not,' said James. 'Emily, are you sure you couldn't . . .'

'I'm sorry, James. It was fantastic sex, but I'm not willing to become your mistress. It isn't as if you offered me marriage.'

'Once was enough for me, but I'd be faithful to you, I . . .'

'Goodbye, James,' said Emily with a secret delight, and then she hung up on him.

By the end of the day she'd packed all her personal belongings away and contacted a removal firm to take them to a London address on Friday.

Early on the Friday evening she picked up a small Chanel bag that Steven had bought her in Paris, then hurried out into the driveway. A car was parked there, waiting for her. Emily opened the passenger door and slid into the leather seat. Her cheeks were glowing pink with excitement, and when the driver bent over and kissed her their mouths remained locked together for what seemed like an eternity. Emily felt his fingers moving slowly up her silk-covered leg to draw circles on the soft flesh at the top of her thigh.

'Let's go, Michael,' she said in a husky voice. 'We've done it, and I want us to celebrate in comfort, in your London flat.'

'You were brilliant,' said Michael, admiringly. 'Father would never have left it to me if he'd known about us, and James will go mad when we return to Briar House together. He really wanted you, you know, that's why I knew he'd tell him about you and Charles, and father wanted him to have you too. He thought you were well suited.'

Oh, we are, thought Emily.

'You do love me, Emily, don't you?' asked Michael, anxiously, as they sped along to London. 'It isn't just for the house or the money?'

'You know I do,' said Emily. 'After all, I chose you rather than Charles.'

'But you knew you couldn't have the house and Charles . . .'

'I'll prove it to you later,' whispered Emily, running her fingers over his crotch and feeling the hardness there.

Michael sighed with contentment.

Emily put her head back and closed her eyes. It had all turned out very well. She'd spent the past six years working for this. She'd played off one brother against the other while keeping Steven happy, and now she had everything. The money, the house, a prospective doting husband, and what she knew would be a highly satisfactory love affair with James into the bargain. Drama school certainly hadn't been a waste of time.

All in all, Emily thought that things had worked out to her complete satisfaction.

Dictation

Madelaine Powell

Dictation

*S*ir,
 You asked for a detailed description of what happened in your office today. Please find below an outline of events for your consideration:

I entered the office this morning, as I have done for the past four weeks, dressed in a tight, black satin skirt, matching blouse, barely concealed suspender belt holding black nylons, and finished off with red, four-inch-heeled stiletto shoes. I had been conscious in the past that you were aware of me, but found it amusing that you decided not to react, your frustration showing in the way you averted your eyes. This of course made me more determined to attract your attention. Today, however, was different.

You had arrived a while before me: I, in fact, was my customary fifteen minutes late. I was aware of you watching me as I made my way to my desk which was placed outside the door to your office, in the outer room. Before undertaking any of my duties I decided to start the day in my usual way by purposely sitting down on my typing chair at just the angle whereby you could see the length of my leg as I crossed it over the other one. Reaching into my handbag, I took out my tube of bright-red lipstick and a hand mirror and, lips pouting, commenced redecorating my well-made-up face knowing all the time that you were watching my profile with fascination. I have made a habit of then pulling the hem of my skirt down, as it has by then moved up my legs and started to show the top of my

205

stockings; occasionally a glimpse of white thigh appears. I knew you had seen this and that it had had the desired effect, as you would cough and shift slightly in your large, leather-bound chair. I could only see the top half of you as the massive shape of the desk concealed the lower part of your body.

Having adjusted my skirt, I stood up to make your first cup of coffee of the day and, as always, I touched the second button of my blouse, the one that was pulling with the pressure of my breasts beneath it. It had become a habit because I was never sure that it had not come undone. Once, while bringing in a tray of coffees during a meeting, the button did in fact come undone and it pleased me to see the eyes of all the men present follow the line of my bra-clad breasts as I leant over the table to place the coffees in front of them. I had, that time, glanced down between your legs and seen the first obvious signs of the effect I had on you.

This morning, as customary, I stood with my back to you at the coffee percolator, very conscious of the fact that your eyes would be following the seam of my stockings from the four inches of my red shoes up to the hem of my short, tight skirt which left no question as to the shape of the buttocks and thighs it encased.

I turned round, holding the tray on which I had placed your china coffee cup, sugar bowl, jug of cream, and your favourite chocolate biscuits. With my shoes sinking into the thick-pile carpet, I walked towards you, hips swaying as one foot was placed carefully in front of the other. With a slight, coy smile, I placed the coffee tray on the front of your desk and then placed each item on the table, bending down slightly to reach the desired position. You glanced up and gave me your customary 'thank you', although this time I was aware that your glance held a certain confrontation that I was not used to. Suddenly I felt painfully aware of the shortness of my skirt and the tightness of my blouse, but chose to play on it rather than let it make me feel uncomfortable.

As I turned away to walk out again I stopped and, bending over from the waist, I picked up a piece of paper that had dropped off your desk. Feeling bold, I reached out to hand you the paper with as innocent a look as I could possibly conjure up, while a hint of victory was visible in my smile. It was wonderful how easily a man in such a powerful position could be brought down by a stockinged leg. I had always found myself unable to resist teasing: I was confident, in this particular situation, of my powers of control.

The usual course of events would be a few telephone calls, confirmation of the diary and then commencement of meetings. In the afternoon would be a session of dictation for maybe an hour, during which time I would sit in a high-backed chair, my legs crossed and my back straight as I took down your instructions in shorthand. From time to time I would swing the top leg up and down a little, the angle of my foot emphasising the slimness of my ankle and the height of my stiletto heel. Oh, how I revelled in the feeling of sexual power over someone who is so commanding in other ways.

However, as I have said before, today was different. Just as I reached the door to my office, I heard you suggest that I gather up my notepad and return. I was surprised as you are a man of habit and this went against your normal routine. Shrugging, I did as I was bid and nonchalantly returned. I was half-way across the room when, without looking up, you said 'Shut the door. I have something to sort out that needs a little privacy.' Unsuspecting, I turned insolently on my heel and pushed the heavy oak door closed. I was now enclosed in your room for the first time.

'Pull up your chair. No, not there – a little further away where I can see you.'

Surprised, I did as I was bid and placed my bottom neatly on the chair as usual, slowly crossing my legs as I flipped open the cover of my notebook. This was greeted with total silence.

'Eventually I glanced up, puzzled, my pen still poised to receive your dictation. My look was met with one that made my heart stop and my hand flew instinctively to my throat as I started to uncross my legs. 'Stay as you were,' was the reaction this received. I stopped, and this time saw that you made no effort to avert your eyes but instead deliberately inspected me, starting from the tip of my toe and continuing up my legs, along the length of my skirt, up the front of my blouse, pausing slightly at the second button, and then straight into my face. I blushed, this time averting my eyes.

'Feeling uncomfortable are we? Well maybe you have reason to. It's about time you were made clearly aware of who's boss around here.'

Rising from your chair, the leather creaking as you did so, you walked over to me. For the first time I became aware of your height and strong build. As you walked, you started to talk but I was barely listening.

'Well, what are you waiting for? Take this down. It is time my secretary learnt a lesson in office behaviour. I have been subjected too long to her complacent teasing, she is now going to learn what that results in. Don't stop writing until I say so.'

By this stage you were behind me, looking down over my shoulder, the heaving of my bosom now obvious under the tight silk of my blouse as my breathing became faster. Suddenly I felt you grab the hair in the nape of my neck forcing me to rise from the chair. I was then pushed forward over the front of your desk and within seconds found my skirt pulled up over my buttocks. Struggling slightly, I was then pinned firmly down as you leant over and picked up what could only have been a thin cane from under some papers. I gasped and put one arm behind me to try and cover my exposed buttocks.

'Take you hand away or I'll tie them!'

Neither wanting to encourage you by disobeying, or to allow you by not protecting myself, I left my hand lying by the side of my thigh. I was conscious of the back of my hand tickling the soft, downy hair at the top of my leg. My hairs had by then stood on end and my exposed skin had goose-pimples.

Sensing my total confusion at finding myself in such a humiliating and vulnerable position, you laughed scornfully, commenting, 'So we're not feeling quite so confident of our position, are we madam? By the time I finish with you, young lady, the best secretarial college in the country will commend your total, unquestioning dedication to your office duties. Which, in a few words, madam, is what ever I decide I want from you.'

With this ominous remark, you demonstrated your peculiar style of 'dictation' by landing me a stinging blow to my exposed buttocks, your target easily achievable from the carefully chosen angle from which you approached it. I wriggled to indicate that I would prefer not to have more of the same treatment.

'Well madam, not sure you want any more? Well maybe I'll let you think about it for a moment while I drink my coffee. Don't move. I find the view most enjoyable.'

As you reached for your coffee cup sitting a few inches from my face, I noticed for the first time what large fingers you had.

There was a slight pause as you walked silently over to my chair. As you sat down there was the sound of a slight squeak as it took your unaccustomed weight. I could just imagine your large legs planted solidly each side of the seat, the woollen material of your trousers pulled tight under the flies, which were things I had noticed before when you were sitting down. The startling thought of how well endowed you might be passed uninvited across my mind. I thought about the view I was presenting to you at that moment: you must have been studying the taut muscles in the backs of my stockinged legs stretched straight against the front of your desk; my heart-shaped bottom lifted a little above the top of the desk by the four-inch heels; and all I had to offer was framed neatly with the top and straps of the suspender belt and the wide, black band at the top of my stockings.

Starting to feel somewhat restless pressed down on the hard desktop, my only relief being the warm blotter pad on which my generous breasts were lying, I shifted my weight from one leg to another. Feeling a slight change in the atmosphere as your attention heightened, I did the same little movement again, managing to wriggle my bottom around at the same time.

'You cheeky madam, you're quite enjoying this really, aren't you! Well, maybe it's time I did your performance review. I am curious to find out whether your experience matches your enthusiasm. Stand up!'

Obeying your instructions, I stood and turned towards you, my tight skirt staying pulled up around my small waist. The buttons on my blouse, having given up their struggle to stay closed, revealed my tits in all their glory; my breasts were overflowing from my red bra, which was a favourite of mine as it always achieved the desired effect of lifting my bosoms up and out, as if they were sitting on a tray like two jugs of full cream milk.

With a look that took in every detail, you deliberately stood to your full height, putting down your delicate china coffee cup a little heavy-handedly on the small glass table beside you. The clatter rudely penetrated the silence of the thickly-carpeted room. You placed your hands on each hip and steadied yourself a few feet in front of me. I glanced down to see the signs of your appreciation, my eyes widening somewhat at the large, straight object pushing against your trouser leg.

'Kneel!' you commanded, pointing to a spot on the carpet just in front of you.

Tottering slightly on my high heels, I took a couple of steps towards you, noticing as I did a slight wrinkle in the ankle of my nylons. 'What sort of state will they be in after this?' I mused silently as I took my position in front of you.

Watching the bulge filling your trousers, now at my eyelevel, I saw you reach down and, with a determined motion, unzip your straining flies releasing the hardened heat of your cock. It flew to attention before me.

'Suck it!' you commanded.

Rather taken aback at the size of the problem facing me I hesitated for a moment, only to feel you grab the hair at the nape of my neck and push my head unrelentingly toward the glistening tip; it seemed to be nodding its approval as my lipsticked lips were pushed roughly against it. Being in no position to argue the point, I commenced to lick and suck you. I was fascinated more and more by the large balls that hung heavily on either side. I noticed that each time I tickled or sucked in a certain way they throbbed their appreciation, tightening and loosening like heavy venetian blinds.

Glancing around me as I worked, I saw the heavy legs of the conference table behind you and I pictured your management team at your weekly meeting, held promptly every Monday morning at 1100 hrs. 'I wonder if they all have the same equipment to play with,' I mused, imagining eight pairs of suit trousers unzipped, their contents spilling out under the table as they talked. 'It is a shame the table isn't glass,' I thought, imagining looking up at each of their faces as I took them in my mouth, one by one, each trying to hide the look of surprise and wonder as my tongue and fingers wriggled around their manhoods. I could just imagine their eyes getting wider and then glazing over as I worked on them, and then the redness in their faces flushing over them as their come spurted over my face. I could see them then shuffling papers as they tried to regain their outward composure. I could see their confusion and disbelief as they recognised the same reaction gradually working its way around the table, each not daring to interrupt the habitual mundanity of the meeting by bending down to look underneath.

Obviously, at this point you felt my attention drifting, for you suddenly thrust yourself further into my mouth, rudely forcing my concentration back to the work in hand (and mouth) and making me gag slightly as your size filled the back of my throat. Nearly at bursting point, you pulled away suddenly, making me fall on to all fours with my momentum. Looking up, my eyes travelling from straining cock to starched collar, I gulped as I saw your intention, signalled clearly in your expression.

Squealing, I was hauled up on to my feet by the hair; your hands deftly encircled my waist as you lifted me and plonked me squarely on to the aforementioned conference table. My bottom felt cold against the polished wood. As you pushed my legs wide apart, I saw my pussy come into view, indeed looking like a coiled cat, warmed by the fire of the preceding events. I saw your eyes fix on my exposed bosom, which was bursting out of its blouse and bouncing and quivering as I tried to hold myself up on each elbow. I watched as your cock aimed itself automatically at its target. Your large hands sank into the exposed skin of my thighs above the stockings as you pulled me roughly towards the edge of the table. Sliding towards you I fell backwards, which lifted my hips to a more accessible position. You lifted my legs up to your shoulders. Sliding your hands along my stockings, you tightened your hold on my calves, pulling them unceremoniously apart so that you could gain entry.

I watched and listened as you fucked me, your whole attention concentrated on the shaft that pumped in and out of me, filling me entirely. The force of your thrusts slapped against my bottom and my breasts bounced in unison. Raising my head, I looked down at my pussy: the rhythmic movement of your penis looking like the piston of a steam train as it raced along. With one final thrust your engine let off its stream of white smoke and you came to a shuddering halt with your head thrown back, hips pushed forwards, both hands still clutching my legs just above the ankle.

Letting my ankles come to rest on your shoulders, you tried to regain your breath. I was deafeningly aware of the throbbing and tingling of desire pulsating through me. I looked up at the stiletto heels of my shoes pointing toward each of your ears. Pulling away from me and letting my legs fall, you instructed me to stand up. Shakily obeying you, I straightened the seam of my stockings, aware of you watching my every movement. Having zipped up your trousers you made your way back to your desk and, sitting down with a satisfied air, you started to study a folder lying in front of you.

After a few seconds you said, 'Right, I now think we are ready to focus on the affairs in hand. Sit down on your chair and take some dictation!'

Wriggling my bottom to pull down my skirt to a relatively decent length, I hastily fastened the buttons of my blouse and pushed a strand of hair neatly behind my ear. Not taking my eyes off you, wondering what was to come next, I tiptoed across the carpet to my chair and stared at the top of your wide, intelligent head. We sat in silence for a few minutes which felt like hours. Then, glancing at the clock, you reminded me it was the customary time for tea and biscuits.

'We shall continue after our tea break. By the way, you have smudged your lipstick! I suggest you go to your desk and fix it.'

Fuming slightly, but still in a state of shock, I obediently laid down my pad and pencil and made my way slowly out of the office, feeling your eyes as they followed my progress.

'Leave the door open,' you called after me, 'and be quick with the tea. We have a lot more dictation to do before you leave this evening. Oh, and don't forget the biscuits, I fancy something sweet.'

Having carefully prepared myself and the tea tray, I made my way towards you across the vastness of your office. You glanced up as I placed the tray on one side of your desk and with a slight frown you enquired after the missing biscuits, your tone voicing your incredulity at my foolish disobedience.

'Oh, but I have brought you something sweet, just as you asked, sir,' I replied. 'Especially wrapped for our mutual enjoyment.'

You watched me curiously as I then walked around to your side of the desk where I slid one long, stockinged leg over your lap and lifted myself seductively on to the desk in front of you. Leaning back and lifting each foot to rest on either side of your chair, I pulled up my skirt. I saw you smile as I revealed a bourbon biscuit neatly cushioned in my pussy.

'I thought we could both enjoy something sweet, sir!' I said, taking the biscuit away to reveal the reddened button of my clitoris peeping between the furry hills of my pussy. Leaning on one hand, I slid my red-lacquered fingernails along the inside of my leg and, as you watched, tapped my fingers on my pussy just as you had watched me, a thousand times, tap the keys of my computer. I smiled to myself to think how you would always think of this moment when you watched or heard the buttons of my keyboard being pressed lightly and urgently as I transcribed your dictation of the day.

Continuing to tap away, I let my middle finger tap harder against my clitoris, sending tingles of want along my vagina. Starting to get excited, I could feel my clitoris begin to throb in time with the tapping fingers and my legs widened in want. Your eyes were now clamped securely on my pussy, displayed proudly before you. You shifted in your seat as your cock stretched upwards to see the view as well. The arm I was leaning on began aching slightly and I shifted position to place my hand on one of your broad shoulders for support. I could feel the tautened muscles leading to your neck underneath the pin-striped cloth, its texture and warmth feeling very similar to the blotting paper my bottom was at that moment placed on. The appropriateness of my fast-moistening pussy being presented on a blotter made me smile again, and I couldn't help giving a little giggle as I then lay back over your desk pulling your big, square head towards my awaiting clitoris.

Your hand slid down to your trouser front, and from your wriggling movements I could surmise that you were shifting the hardened cock as comfortably as possible in order to follow the direction I was pulling your head. I felt your breath brush over my stretched pussy and as the ache became urgent I groaned. Bringing my stiletto-clad feet up to your shoulders, I used my heels to pull you closer towards my throbbing pussy, its red-lipped mouth an open invitation to your lips to kiss it. You slipped your hands under my buttocks which rested comfortably in your large soft palms. You commenced licking me in a surprisingly gentle way. I let out a groan of pleasure and raised my head to watch you as you lapped at my pussy, the hill of which hid the end of your tongue as you worked on my clitoris. Your tongue's movements reminded me of your gold fountain pen as it scratched across the lined pad which normally lay open and ready before you on the blotter.

Grabbing handfuls of my bountiful bosom, I let my head fall back and played with my hardened nipples through the silk blouse. The electricity of my nipples sent shots of static into my blouse, which returned it to my nipples as they rubbed against each other. Straining to look along the length of my body, I watched your tongue work in as meticulous a manner as I was used to in your other routines. Very soon I could feel the results of your efforts as the inner rumblings of an orgasm start to work its way towards your flickering tongue. Wanting at that moment for the gaping hole of my vagina to be filled with another, larger tool, I tensed the muscles in my legs and bottom to raise my pussy, pushing it further into your mouth. Moulding the palms of your hands to fit my hardened buttocks, you encased my clitoris and sucked and licked, darting now and again to the edges of my gaping vagina, its rim hard with want.

You acknowledged the stiffening rush of my orgasm with a grunt of satisfaction. I arched my back in utter pleasure as the tingles burst like champagne bubbles into my clitoris and the mouth of my vagina. Revelling in the delicious sensation, my body remained stiff, balanced effortlessly in your hands. As the sensation subsided I relaxed my body, letting my legs fall wide apart and my bottom soften into your hands.

With my head back, dangling over the front of your desk, I noticed with a fascinated horror that the door to your office was wide open. As the clock on the wall also swayed into distorted view I realised it was nearly 11 a.m.: the time rostered for your weekly meeting with your line managers. Knowing that you were a stickler for timekeeping, it was a sure bet that someone would enter the outer office at any moment and, without there being anyone there to stop them, would pop their head around the very door frame I was staring at. I wondered which of the many possible heads would be first and how their startled faces would look upside down: the junior ones pasty from too much paper-pushing, the more senior ones carefully bronzed into an adequately affluent skin-tone by lunch-time use of the managers' sun lamp in the corporate gym. Their colour would soon change, I was sure, to a pinker hue, when confronted with their boss's secretary splayed over his desk with his head between her knees.

Noticing the time, you took hold of my wrinkled stockings around my slim ankles and swung them both to one side. You pulled me to my feet, telling me that I was a hussy and would be dealt with later. I straightened my clothing as you straightened the items on your desk and in your trousers. While I bent over to finish unwrinkling my stockings, the resounding slap of your hand on my bottom coincided with the click of the outer-office door. The sound of over-confident voices drowned my surprised squeal.

'Thank you, Madelaine. That will be all for now. Come in, gentlemen,' you said, stridently.

I strode shakily across the carpet and into my office. I stared intently at my barely used notepad in order to stop myself from laughing and to avoid meeting the oblivious gaze of the huddle of male managers now congregating around my desk.

Although this was a routine meeting and there was nothing contentious on the agenda I had handed out a couple of days before, I could feel that the atmosphere was slightly tense as they individually edged past my protruding bosom as I leant against the door frame to let them pass. One of the younger ones blushed slightly as his arm accidentally bumped against one breast, making it wobble like firm jelly under the silk blouse, challenging the straining button again. I knew that one of the handsome, somewhat cockier managers had noticed this, and hard as he tried he could not avoid his gaze resting on the hills of flesh as my long fingers fiddled with the offending button. I met his sideways glance for just a moment and then purposely turned and leant over my desk to place my notepad on it. As you will appreciate, this meant he then could not avoid bumping against the firmer, satin-covered flesh of my bottom as he squeezed through the confined space between me and the filing cabinet outside the door to your office. At that moment, from deep within your office, I heard you call my name. I stepped into the doorway.

You broke off from a conversation with one of your managers, and looking at me with quiet determination said, 'Madelaine, I would like a written report of this morning's proceedings on my desk by the end of this meeting. We will then review it over lunch. Thank you.' Without waiting for a reply you recommenced your previous conversation.

The sounds of chatter and laughter receded as everyone filed into your office, jostling to take their positions around the conference table. The partitioning door was closed by the last one to enter.

I sat in the quiet of my empty office and, thinking of the morning's events, began to gently tap the keys.

End of report.

Madelaine

Tumbling Scheherazade

Maria Lyonesse

Tumbling Scheherazade

❧ ❧

'*T*ell me your fantasies, Laura.'

His breath tickled my neck as he said it. But the words themselves sent a deeper shiver through me. A shiver that began in my throat, spiralled between my naked breasts and flared briefly between my thighs.

The afternoon sun had shifted since we'd begun our love-making some two hours before. Now a thick, dusty shaft of it fell through the crack in the shutters. It crept round until my moist pubis was bathed in light. I smiled and let my thighs roll open. The sun's warmth licked my slick vaginal lips. It penetrated deeply. It renewed the glow his eagerness had left in me.

'Won't,' I finally replied.

Sebastian grinned and wrapped his finger and thumb decisively around my wrist. He pinioned my arm back above my head. In such a position my breasts were thrust towards him. I felt that shiver again. I was dangerously and deliciously exposed to a man I'd only met the night before.

'Why not?' he demanded playfully.

'Can't have you knowing everything about me at once.'

I looked up at Sebastian. He wasn't in the least ruffled. In fact, he was enjoying the game. His smile wrinkled the corners of his eyes. I glanced down at his lithe body and then back at his face. The tiny lines on his tanned skin were the only giveaway that he was at least ten, maybe fifteen, years older than me.

'Why did you do it?' he asked. 'Why me?'

Why indeed? Ian and I had been in Saudi for six months now.

219

I was the dutiful wife, following her engineer husband wherever the latest big project might be. And I was bored. Here, in the overpaid foreign workers' so-called compounds outside Riyadh, hedonism was the rule. I'd already been tempted once or twice. Then, suddenly, there was Sebastian.

'Well?' he prompted.

I gazed along his supple body. I tried to look non-committal but I didn't feel it. There were dozens like Sebastian who regularly visited us. They jetted in every few months to advise the foreign professionals what to do with their outrageous tax-free salaries, then jetted on to do the same somewhere else.

So I told him, 'You were Mr Wrong at absolutely the right time. That's all you're going to get from me.'

'Scheherazade,' he whispered.

'What?'

'Don't you know the story? The one that binds all *The Arabian Nights* tales together.'

He still had my wrist pinned to the bed. Slowly he dipped his head and flicked his tongue against my nipple.

'There's this Sultan,' he continued between licks. 'Marries a new wife every night and beheads them in the morning so they can't cheat on him. Then he meets Scheherazade.'

My nipple was peaking towards him. Round and round went the tip of his warm, skilful tongue.

'She tells him stories,' Sebastian went on. 'Saves the punch line for the next night, though: he's got to know – he can't do away with her.'

'So?'

'So she's a clever woman. She's a tease. Doesn't give too much away. So you're my Scheherazade.'

He finally let go of my wrist and rolled away from me.

'OK then, tell me this instead. When did Ian last fuck you in this bed?'

Fuck. I tasted the word on my tongue and rolled it around luxuriously. It was so earthy, so honest, so here and now. I loved it. He obviously loved it, too. I could tell from the edge that crept into his voice he was getting horny again.

'Just before he went back to the oilfields, if you must know. I'm not simply another frustrated little ex-pat wife who's been without it for too long.'

'Mmm, now we're getting somewhere. So what are you, then?'

'Sebastian!'

I reached over and buried my hands in his hair. It was thick, springy hair – barely touched with grey – that tickled and resisted my palm as if alive.

'Stop asking questions.' I licked my lips ready to linger on that fiery, forbidden word again. 'Fuck me.'

'Persuade me.'

He smiled. I smiled back. I traced a forefinger along the curve of his tanned throat and down into the dark, silky hair that covered his upper chest. Just the right amount of hair – not sparse or boyish but not an overgrown thatch either. I loved the way it slipped between my probing fingers. I loved the prospect of grazing my nipples over it as I mounted him and jiggled my breasts against his chest. But not yet – not quite yet.

The line of dark hair trailed down across his stomach: an invitation to what lay beneath. Even at rest his cock was beautiful. The skin was smooth and perfect. How would it feel beneath my fingers: cooled by the afternoon breeze or warm and velvety?

I trailed my hand casually, letting the backs of my nails graze circles from his navel to his thighs. I never quite touched his cock. Sebastian gave a low moan of pleasure and frustration. Even untouched and after its exertions barely half an hour before, it began to swell.

I was entranced. Of its own accord, something that moments ago had seemed sleeping and vulnerable was now rolling upwards across his thigh. It lengthened and thickened. The veins gained definition. Finally it stood fully erect, stretching towards his navel. I wasn't yet sure what I felt about Sebastian himself, but one thing was certain: I was in love with his cock.

I wanted to show him how much. I wriggled down until my lips were level with the mouth of that fascinating organ. Sebastian had only just become my lover. I hadn't yet taken him in my mouth. I stroked the shaft lovingly first. It gave a little kick beneath my palm. I kissed the smoothness of his foreskin then dabbled the very tip of my tongue into that moist, puckering eye.

Sebastian gave another throaty moan.

'Laura, go on – suck me. I've already come twice. I'm not going to explode straight off. Please. Come on. Give me a long, slow suck.'

I opened my mouth wide and took in his warm bulbous glans. The blood rushing just beneath the skin tingled against my lips. I ran my tongue around and around. Sebastian's gasps urged me and aroused me at the same time. To have such power to turn a man on – that in itself was sexy.

I sucked until the swelling glans had pushed my jaw so far apart it ached. Then I rolled on to him fully and snuggled his shaft into my cleavage. I rolled my breasts experimentally against the coarser hairs on his thighs. Their rough texture against my nipples was exquisite. I shimmied against him. Glistening and ready, he left a moist trail all the way up to my throat. Then, like a predatory cat, I went on all fours above him.

Very, very slowly I stalked my way along my lover's body until we were level again. I lowered myself on to him, stroking the lips of my vagina up and down his promising erection. Still tender from his earlier, enthusiastic lovemaking, my labia felt all the more sensitive and ready to be filled. I reached down and enclosed his shaft in my hand. I glided the head up and down for a couple of strokes before I eased myself on to him.

Even though I knew how he felt inside me, I still gasped. His cock glided deep into my belly. The whole of my awareness was centred on that welcome penetration.

Sebastian reached up and cupped my breasts. His touch was so absolutely confident. He pinched both my nipples between thumb and forefinger – more roughly than before. I didn't feel quite in control. That hint of danger thrilled me. It sent little electric shocks straight to my clitoris. A delicious dilemma wracked me: to carry on and let his thrusting cock tip me over the honeyed edge of pleasure or to hang here offering him my breasts and seeing whether his rough stimulation could take me to an agonisingly slow orgasm.

Impatience slapped down my curiosity. Hungrily, I began to grind my pubis against his. I loved to ride a man. The angle of penetration was perfect. My clitoris rubbed against the base of his shaft; the firm head of his cock tickled exactly the right spot deep inside me. The whole length of my vagina felt on liquid fire with lust. And oh, what his brusque hands were doing to my breasts!

He moulded his palms around their outer curves and crushed them together more forcefully than the tightest basque. He pressed his fingertips into my flesh and jiggled them almost violently. Time and again he rolled and pinched my nipples hard. Then he drew me closer towards him and took my left breast in his mouth.

Sebastian moaned in obvious pleasure as he drew hard on my nipple. His frank appetite for my body turned me on even more. All the while, his hand was busy with my right nipple: rolling it, pulling it, pinching it vigorously.

Without interrupting my slow, grinding thrusts I wriggled my chest, trying to make him switch his attentions to the other side. He followed me. Now my right nipple was drawn deep into his mouth. I felt his teeth close on the very tip. That feeling, on the cusp of pain and pleasure, sent waves rippling through my stomach, thrills to meet the thrills from his rearing cock. I mewed and moaned for him to switch sides again. Frantically he began weaving from one yearning breast to the other. I wanted so much, too much, even. If only both nipples could feel that much luxury at once.

The familiar tickle began at the tops of my thighs. I slowed the rhythm of my hips, wanting to hold on to that delicious moment of pleasure for as long as possible. Slowly, very slowly, it blossomed into me. A warm flowering spread upwards and outwards from my clitoris as Sebastian bucked inside me and swelled even bigger as he came.

I collapsed against his chest, my nipples still raw and tingling with the excitement he'd given them.

'Tell me your fantasies,' he whispered against my neck.

This time, I did.

The box arrived at about eleven o'clock the next morning.

Dressed only in my Malaysian batik kimono, I was lazing on the bed after a late breakfast. I'd buried my face in the pillow, breathing deeply to catch the faint muskiness Sebastian had left behind. His scent tingled in my lungs. The pleasant rawness high in my vagina reminded me how real my lover was. My lover. I repeated the words as I lay on the bed and wriggled my body against the soft sheets, recalling how expertly Sebastian had caressed me. I felt truly wanton.

There was a knock at the door. Awkwardly I sprang up to sitting. A flush of embarrassment prickled my throat and upper chest. The Puerto Rican maid came in and handed me the box without saying anything.

'*Gracias*,' I murmured.

I locked the door and dropped the blinds when she'd gone.

I opened the box. There was no note. There didn't need to be. Inside were dozens of silk scarves. Their colours were rich, spicy, luxuriant. If you held them up to the light they were filmy. You could just about see through. If you dropped one it floated reluctantly to the floor as if the air were kissing it. If you drew one slowly over your inner forearm it felt like a lover's first touch: smooth and cool but confident it was going to be the start of something more. Like Sebastian's had been.

There was a tall Victorian dressing mirror in the corner. I'd sent for it as an extravagant gesture the first month Ian and I had been here. I stood before it and tugged at the belt on my kimono. The soft batik glided fluidly from my shoulders. It whispered over my body to the floor.

I took the first scarf from the box. It was a rich cerise colour. I drew it across my nipples. They were still smarting from their over-eager loving of the day before. This new touch tingled. They peaked into knots of excitement, curious to know more. I pulled out a second scarf. This one was flame orange. I knotted it end to end with the first one and criss-crossed the lengths of silk between my breasts and over my shoulders.

I pulled the material tight, cutting a little into my flesh. Under its pressure my breasts stood out high and proud. My nipples pouted with a 'come and get it' air. I was bound and defined but at the same time terribly exposed. I felt utterly whorish and I loved it.

Next I took three cool, aquamarine scarves and knotted them together. I wound them tight around my waist and hips. The sensation of being constricted focused the whole of my awareness on my womb – that most intensely female part of me. I felt its power.

The last scarf I pulled from the box was a vivid scarlet. I parted my thighs a little and snaked it between them. Backwards and forwards, the whispering silk brushed my labia. Just enough to fan a diffuse wave of sensuality throughout my lower body. Not enough to make me come. The promise of orgasm was all the more luscious for knowing I was saving myself for later.

For the moment I was content to smell the sweetness of my own arousal anointing the brilliant red scarf. I tied this one into my hair. Quickly I unwound the others from my body, bundled them into a shoulder bag and got ready to go out.

The maid who showed me into the villa was Oriental and demure. I caught a hint of amusement in her half-hidden smile, though, as she gestured I should follow her down the cool corridor into the enclosed gardens beyond. Like the rest of us foreign nationals in Saudi, she knew the score.

Sebastian was on the veranda with a young man whom I didn't recognise. He must have been mid-twenties, I suppose. He had a close-clipped, dark beard. Not many Westerners wore beards in this heat. I was curious. There was something about it – so very basic and obviously masculine.

'You haven't met Connor before, have you?' Sebastian began coolly. 'He's from Melbourne. The lease on this place is his. I just doss down here while I'm passing through.'

Passing through. No, I had no illusions about Sebastian.

'So what do you do for your tax-free readies?' I asked as I joined them at the table.

'I'm a doctor,' Connor replied. That was all he said but he grinned as he said it and the same amusement crinkled the corners of his eyes as I had seen in the maid's smile. Only, this time, more direct.

Sebastian offered me a plate of local delicacies: piquant but scarcely more than hors-d'oeuvres.

'Don't want to spoil your appetite,' he told me wryly.

I began to pick at the spicy balls of felafel. Connor made his excuses and wandered off between the fountains and flowering oleander bushes. I watched him closely as he walked, intrigued by the nonchalant rhythm of his hips. My own interest pulled me up sharply. At any time in my married life, prior to the last forty-eight hours, would I have looked at another man like that? Sebastian had done something to me.

I felt him take my plate. Tempting though the food was, I'd been eating it without really tasting.

Sebastian stood up and took my hand. A gentle but definite pressure on it made his next sentence less of a suggestion, more of a command.

'Main course,' he said simply.

The curtains in his bedroom were already drawn. The slight breeze licked and rippled them. The semi-darkness was rich with

spice tones; like anyone in the compounds, Sebastian could
afford to indulge his tastes.

As I was admiring a tall carving of a full-breasted African
nude, my lover came up behind me. He wrapped his arms
purposefully around my waist and buried his face in the curve
between my shoulder and my neck.

'Even your hair smells horny,' he said.

'Why do you think that is?'

His tongue began drawing little circles on the nape of my
neck. Every nerve down my spine tingled into life.

'I don't know,' he murmured. 'Tell me.'

'The scarf in my hair . . .'

'Where's it been?'

'Between my legs.'

'Where between your legs?'

'Right up against my pussy. Teasing me like a great red
tongue. Getting me ready for you.'

Sebastian moaned his appreciation. His hands moved up from
my waist and began to fondle my breasts. I felt his cock press
into the cleft of my arse.

'You did bring the rest of them, didn't you?' he asked.

'Yes, in that bag there. Why?'

'You'll see. Today is going to be your present, Laura. Let's not
spoil the surprise.'

'Presents get unwrapped.'

He chuckled against my throat. Slowly he let go of me and
moved round to the front.

'God, you're eager. Whatever am I going to do with you?'

He began to undo the buttons on my floaty Indian dress. It fell
to the floor as wispily as the scarves had done. My stiff lacy bra
obviously pleased him. He paused for a moment and admired
the way it pushed up and exaggerated the upper curves of my
breasts. He ran his fingertips lightly over my bare skin. Then he
slipped two fingers of each hand inside each cup and tweaked
my nipples. I reached round and unhooked my bra myself, keen
to let him fondle me more freely.

'Oh Laura, aren't you the impatient one,' he admonished, as
his lips brushed the tip of my right nipple.

His tongue and his breath were light and teasing on me. There
was none of the rough handling of the day before. But Sebastian
was so skilled a lover that I knew what he was doing and so did

. he. I dropped my head back and let him play my body as a virtuoso plays a violin.

He kissed his way down until his face rested against my pubic hair. Here he took a deep, appreciative breath, drinking in the musky scent of my arousal. Then, nipping the skin ever so lightly, he moved round to my left hip where my creamy lace panties were fastened with a tie.

He pulled the free end of the bow with his teeth. The material fell to one side leaving one buttock and half my pubic hair exposed. Then he tugged at the other side. I parted my thighs and let my panties fall to the floor.

Sebastian stood up from his kneeling position.

'On the bed,' he ordered.

I lay down. The sheets were cool against my tingling body and they had their own fresh scent. I closed my eyes and wriggled a little, enjoying their crispness against my skin. When I looked up Sebastian had up-ended the bag of silk scarves and was twisting a rich royal blue one in his hands.

'Sebastian, what . . .'

'Your turn,' he told me with a grin. 'Your turn to lie there and just concentrate on receiving pleasure.'

There was a mischievous hint in his voice. It intrigued me. Before I'd realised what he was doing, he'd knotted one end of the scarf round my ankle and tied the other end firmly to the foot of the bed. He grasped my other ankle and dragged it to the side. My thighs were parted to a distance verging on the uncomfortable. He tied this ankle likewise to the bed. I flexed my muscles experimentally. The knot was secure. Sebastian was no amateur at this.

'You've got a beautiful cunt,' he murmured. 'All sweet and slick. No hiding it away now.'

He chose another two scarves from the pile. I lay passively as he tied my wrists together and then looped the scarf round the head of the bed. My body was stretched out before him. The cooling breeze tickled the skin between my parted thighs.

Sebastian began to undo his shirt. I just lay there and looked up at him. The warm curve of his deltoid muscles, the firmness of his stomach: he was amazingly athletic for his age, or any age. He smiled as he saw me admiring his naked torso. Sebastian was a man who kept himself on peak form for sex, and he knew it.

The shirt was tossed aside. His thumb strayed to the waistband

of his jeans. He was wearing the sort that have a button fly. Pop
... pop ... pop: he undid them one by one, enjoying my
impatience as the soft fabric of his boxer shorts eased through
the gap.

The beginning of an erection was pushing against the material.
He slipped the boxers down over his lean thighs. My gaze leapt
to his cock. It was still only semi-erect but maybe that was the
fascination. What could I do to make it hard?

Sebastian dropped on to all fours on the bed. He crawled
towards me. Then he sank down between my wide open thighs
and began to tongue me with skill such as I had never felt before.

The sheer frustration of my spread-legged position was part of
it. I writhed and strained against the bonds, longing to squeeze
my thighs together and give my aching clitoris the release it
craved. I realised I was never going to come in that position. I
was at Sebastian's mercy. He could draw out this divine foreplay
as long as he wanted. I breathed a heretical prayer of thanks for
the joy of a truly experienced lover.

His tongue was warm and mobile, now skimming rapid circles
around my pouting clitoris, now easing itself between my moist,
swollen labia. It was more snakelike, more teasing than any
finger or any cock. Tiny shivers of pleasure darted over my mons
veneris and straining thighs. I knew they were the tingle that led
to orgasm but Sebastian just kept them tingling, always holding
me back.

Finally he raised himself up on to all fours again and covered
my willing body with his. I could feel his hot erection pressed
against my belly but he made no move to sheathe it deep in me.
Instead he gave me a rough, penetrating kiss. I was overwhelmed
by the taste of my own sex.

'Sebastian,' I gasped. 'Fuck me. Let me feel your gorgeous
cock. I'm so empty. Fill me.'

'Still impatient, Laura? You'll be filled up soon enough. Oh
yes.'

Still chuckling, he undid the red scarf in my hair.

'Close your eyes now,' he commanded. 'Good girls wait for
their surprise.'

I did as he told me. Sebastian tied the scarf in a blindfold. I
wondered how many times he'd done this before. I tried to open
my eyelids. With the dimness of his bedroom I really couldn't
see a thing.

There was a pause. I don't know how long. I heard a soft click like a door closing. Then an avid mouth engulfed my left nipple. The tongue flicked and circled just as it had done on my clitoris. I moaned and arched my back to meet him as far as I could under my restraints. The arousal that had plateaued out during his momentary absence began to soar again.

And then I felt something flicker against my right nipple. Too moist and yielding to be Sebastian's finger. My whole body stiffened. This couldn't be a trick. My breasts were being relished by two men at once.

I heard a low, familiar chuckle. Sebastian had realised that I had realised. This, my fantasy, breathed to him in the recklessness of afterglow. Only Sebastian would have dared!

The second man drew back a little and stroked his face over my breast. Springy hairs tantalised my skin. I thought back to the scene on the veranda. It had to be Connor.

I'd always longed to know what this would feel like. Two men worshipping my body at once. Two men aroused enough to forget about jealousy and possession and simply pleasure me. I relaxed against the mattress. Let my body go limp and surrendered to the waves of sensation as Connor's close-clipped beard brushed over the sensitive tips of my nipples and Sebastian's tongue flickered against my navel like a captive frog.

Someone undid the scarves around my wrists and ankles. But not my blindfold.

Two pairs of hands eased me on to all fours. One of the men was directly underneath me now. He reached up and stroked my breasts, cupping them and catching my nipples in a scissor action between thumb and forefinger. Whose fingers were they? Could they be the experienced hands of a man like Sebastian or the younger but equally deft hands of a surgeon? I wanted to know. I had no way of telling. There was something so deliciously wanton about it.

Then I felt two palms very firmly stroke my ass, pulling the cheeks apart. The delicate skin between them was stretched, tingling with the unfamiliar sensation. I tensed and waited. The bulbous tip of a cock – whose cock, I didn't know – nudged against my exposed perineum. Then with piston-like accuracy I was entered from behind.

He thrust into me, regular and rhythmic. The head of his cock drove against the elastic front wall of my vagina. There was no finesse or attempt to prolong the action. It was simple, animal fucking. It was pure, honest appetite.

I tried to tense my vaginal muscles, to hold and slow that relentless pounding. I was too wet with desire and his thrusts were too eager for it to be anything but a teasing token struggle. I still couldn't work out who it was.

If I could get my breasts to swing a little lower. If I could only brush them against the face of the man who was pinching and pleasuring them with his hands. Clean shaven or the ticklish sensation of a well-trimmed, springy beard? Then I'd know.

But whenever I tried to crouch lower either Sebastian or Connor would grasp my shoulders and pull or push to keep me firmly where I was. Eventually it became a constant struggle. The man beneath me turned his attention from my breasts and clasped my biceps, keeping me at arm's length. The fierce pressure of his fingertips stopped only just short of being painful. There was something undeniably wicked about the sensation of being restrained.

Then I felt the cock inside me swell even bigger. The man took one last almighty thrust and drove deep, deep into me, shuddering and gasping as he came. And still I really couldn't tell if it was Sebastian.

He slipped coolly out of me. My sex was glowing and pulsing with the hunger for an orgasm withheld. I wanted more.

I lowered my hips. My upper arms were still clasped by the man beneath me. I sat astride him, skimming my wet vaginal lips up and down his cock until that most sensitive part of me could tell he was stiff and ready. He was mine to ride to the orgasm that had been building up all afternoon.

His erection slipped easily into me. I snaked my pelvis and ground my clitoris against his shaft. I was intent only on my own pleasure now. Hands slipped round from behind me and began to fondle my breasts. Fingertips rolled my nipples like marbles and tweaked them to their own almost painful ecstasy. Then I felt a silk scarf drawn across them. The enforced sensitivity of my roughly treated skin made this new, soft sensation all the more explosive.

And I loved the feel of this cock inside me. It was so hard. Again I wondered: the virility of a younger man or the stamina of a more experienced one?

I sensed my orgasm was growing closer and I slowed the

rolling of my hips. I wanted to make this last. I spun it out until I felt my lover of the moment kick and shudder with his own explosive climax. A man coming inside you is such a voluptuous sensation. It tipped me over the edge. My orgasm plunged deep into my belly, achingly sweet like a warm knife of pleasure.

As I gasped, both sets of hands released me. I collapsed forwards into the arms of the man whose cock was still giving my vagina little aftershock kicks. I sought his mouth hungrily. The springy resistance of his beard met my lips.

Eventually I rolled aside on to the bed. My skin was damp and tingling. I revelled in the cool breeze caressing it again. Then I heard that click that might have been a door closing.

My blindfold was untied. I looked around. There was no one else in the room but Sebastian and he was grinning irrepressibly.

I lolled on the mattress and enjoyed the feeling of utter satisfaction permeating my body. I smiled back at Sebastian and thought yet again how lucky I'd been to find such an adventurous lover.

'Tell me your fantasies,' I insisted. 'Sebastian, I want to do something no other woman has done to you before. I want to turn you on more than you've ever been turned on in your life.'

'Think I'm going to give in that easily? Try a few. I'll tell you when you're getting close.'

'Scheherazade.' I returned the taunt.

I was looking forward to finding out, though.

Coming Home

Charlotte Lewis

Coming Home

❧ ❧

L izzie had taken the cottage for the whole of August.

'I need to write,' she'd told the petulant Tim, 'and that means being on my own. I'm sorry.'

That had been back in May, in London. He'd stomped around her flat waving holiday brochures and accusing her of selfishness, but she hadn't budged.

Now here she was, two weeks into her working holiday and loving it. She'd fallen into a natural daily regime of waking around seven and taking a walk along the craggy Cornish beach just two minutes from her cottage, then back for a skimpy breakfast before going into the room she'd set aside for writing: a lovely, light extension used by the owners as a study, and perfect for Lizzie's needs. Each day she worked through until five or six o'clock, occasionally getting up to make coffee or wander round the pretty little garden, mulling over the story-line or reworking a piece of dialogue in her head. In the evenings she'd take another walk, through the village and down to the beach, before returning to curl up with a book in the living room. At first she'd been worried about adapting to the solitude, but now she was relishing it. It was such a contrast to her busy life in London where she was always teaching during the day, socialising in the evenings, spending every hour of every week-end with the talkative Tim. She was beginning to wonder how she'd ever readjust to it.

It was the second Saturday of her stay, and she was struggling to write a steamy sex scene for her rather demure heroine when

235

she heard someone trying to let themselves into the cottage. She always bolted the front door, probably unnecessarily, she told herself, but it was an ingrained London habit. Several thoughts rushed into her head. Had the owners returned from Italy early? Was some opportunist local burglar unaware that the cottage was occupied? She leapt up from her desk and rushed to the front room. Easing the curtain to one side she saw a tall T-shirt clad man scratching his head and looking up at the bedroom windows. He then bent down beside an enormous rucksack.

'Hello. Anyone in?' came his voice through the letter box.

Lizzie thought she ought to see what he wanted, but she picked up a long cast iron poker from the fireside before she went to the door and opened it.

'Yes?' she said curtly, the late-afternoon sun dazzling her for a moment.

'Who are you?' asked the man, rather confrontationally she thought.

'No, you first,' she told him.

He held out his hand. 'Alex. Alex Parker.'

'Oh, are you related to . . .'

He smiled. 'I'm their son. I live here.' He peered over her shoulder into the house. 'At least, I did until I went to India.'

'They're away, I'm afraid. In Tuscany. I'm renting the house, you see.'

'Ah,' he said, running his hand through thick dark-blond locks. 'They didn't tell me. Maybe they tried. There's probably a letter waiting for me in a Bombay hotel.' He looked inquisitively at Lizzie, as though trying to calculate whether or not this stranger would even invite him into his own home for a cup of tea.

'Why don't you come in?' she asked. 'You'd probably like something to drink. It's so hot today.'

'You should try Hyderabad,' he said, heaving the rucksack over one shoulder and following her through to the kitchen.

'I did,' she told him, surreptitiously putting the poker down. 'Tea? Fruit juice?'

They talked politely over their ice-filled orange juices – mostly about India and other places they'd visited. Lizzie realised he was older than she'd first thought – late twenties, perhaps. But still living at home? That didn't quite fit.

There was a brief awkward silence while Alex seemed to be

taking in the familiarity of the room. He stretched all four limbs and looked disconcertingly at home on the old, wooden kitchen chair.

'So what do you do in London, um ... Sorry, I don't know your name.'

'Lizzie. I teach French. And you? When you're not travelling?'

'Oh, this and that. I trained to be an architect but couldn't settle to it, so took some time off to look at the world's beautiful buildings. Based myself here for the last year, but I've been away for most of it.'

Lizzie looked at the obviously travel-weary intruder and wondered what on earth she was supposed to do. Put him up? That certainly wasn't part of her agreement with the owners. Turf him out? She looked at her watch. It said 5.50. It wasn't too late for him to find a hotel or b. & b. They could call for a taxi.

As if reading her mind, Alex leapt up and headed for the phone. 'Do you mind if I ring a few guest houses?' he asked. Flicking through the directory, he stopped and looked over at Lizzie. 'Don't you get a bit fed up here? On your own?'

'I love the solitude,' she said pointedly. 'I'm writing a novel, you see. Well, trying to.'

Alex tapped out a number. Nice hands, Lizzie thought. But then everything about this person was rather appealing, particularly those deep blue eyes that contrasted perfectly with his tanned skin. As he turned to talk into the receiver, she caught herself admiring his straight, broad-shouldered back and narrow hips. A nicely rounded rear, highlighted by the tight faded jeans, protruded just enough below the T-shirt. Something in Lizzie stirred. She sat up straight in her chair and told herself to behave.

Alex put down the phone and shrugged his shoulders, then tapped out another number. He sat on a nearby chair as though settling in for a long haul. 'Do you have any rooms for this evening?' he asked again. 'No? OK, thanks.'

As he tried more numbers, Lizzie began to think perhaps she wouldn't object too strongly to putting him up for the night. Maybe, just maybe he'd be able to help ... She felt a little tense and decided a nice relaxing drink was called for.

'Gin and tonic?' she asked.

He put his hand over the receiver and smiled. 'Please.'

Lizzie felt his eyes on her as she poured the drinks and found herself nervously rearranging her long, dark hair then pulling down the skimpy cotton dress she liked to sit and work in – a short, sleeveless affair which, she was suddenly aware, clung tenaciously to her bra-less body. When she approached him with the drink, Alex didn't disguise the fact that he was taking in every inch of her.

'What a bummer,' he said, putting the phone down for the last time. 'Cornwall in August. I might have known.'

Lizzie was half-way through her large drink and beginning to feel its effects. 'I'm glad they're all full,' she told him, taking herself somewhat by surprise.

Alex raised his eyebrows at her, waiting for an explanation.

'I'd like you to stay here tonight.' What was she saying? 'I mean, this is your home, after all.'

He smiled. Did he know what she meant? She wasn't sure herself. All she knew was that she didn't want this interesting and attractive man to disappear. After all, he could be useful.

'That's very nice of you,' he told her, and asked if he might have a shower.

Lizzie told him to help himself. He picked up his rucksack then, as he passed her, gently squeezed her bare shoulder.

'Thanks,' he said.

When he appeared later in half-open shirt and jeans, hair slightly damp and a bottle of duty-free wine under his arm, Lizzie quietly caught her breath. He really was quite gorgeous. She threw together a light supper and, while they sat on opposite sides of the table in the gradually dimming light of the kitchen, she wondered if she was alone in feeling a certain electricity in the air. They talked about their lives – a little about their relationships – and what they hoped to do in the future. As the wine and food took effect the two strangers began to relax, and when their stretched legs suddenly touched beneath the table, neither of them moved. In the silence which followed, Lizzie looked down into her lap, knowing that Alex was staring at her.

'I'd like to see more of you,' he whispered.

She looked up at him and smiled. 'OK,' she said.

Emboldened by the drink and excited by the intimacy of the situation, she put down her glass and slowly removed her dress from one shoulder. Easing the soft cotton down her arm, she watched his gaze lower to the flesh gradually becoming exposed. Lizzie had always been happy with her breasts: they were neither too small nor too large, and were still pert. Now she was enjoying the act of revealing just one nipple to this appreciative man.

'Beautiful,' he told her, his eyes transfixed. Then he smiled. 'I'd love it if you touched yourself.'

Her hand obediently moved up to the soft warmth of her naked flesh and she allowed her fingertips to gently caress her breast, brushing occasionally against the nipple and causing it to tighten and become erect. Alex leaned across and pulled the dress off her other shoulder. His hands cupped her breasts and Lizzie found herself relishing his touch. He fondled her with his perfect tanned hands, then began gently squeezing her nipples with thumb and forefinger, creating delicious currents of pleasure in her breasts, between her legs. She wriggled in her chair and then let one of her bare feet inch slowly up the inside of his leg, coming to rest on the firm bulge in his jeans. As the sole of her foot slowly massaged him, Alex groaned almost inaudibly, closing his eyes so that he could concentrate on her caress.

One of his hands slid under the table and Lizzie could feel him undoing the buttons of his jeans. She soon felt the warmth of his firm, smooth cock beneath her foot and, as he leaned back in his chair, Lizzie ran her toes up and down the length of him, the ball of her foot occasionally applying pressure.

'Oh, wow,' he whispered, one hand now under the table and stroking her foot.

She heard his breathing quicken. When his hand urged her to push harder, she took her foot away and stood up. Her dress fell around her hips where it hung enticingly, revealing her navel and the top of her lace panties. Alex stood up and hurriedly removed the few remaining items from the table, then pulled Lizzie towards him. Their mouths met in a long, slow kiss and Lizzie was instantly aware of Alex's muscular chest against her breasts and the pressure of his erection through the flimsiness of her clothes. He eased the dress over her hips and it fell to the floor. Removing his lips from hers, his mouth then moved down, kissing first neck then breasts. His tongue flicked at one nipple then the other, then he sucked hungrily and urgently as his hands affectionately stroked the surrounding flesh. Leaning against the table, Lizzie began to feel dizzy with the pleasure this lovely man was giving her. She ran her hands through his soft, freshly washed hair and gasped at each new sensation.

239

Alex's kisses moved down her body as he lowered himself to a kneeling position. While his hands tenderly encircled her buttocks, Lizzie felt his mouth eagerly working on her through the lace of her panties. After gently pulling the material down, he let his tongue meander through the exposed bush of dark hairs before it began to lick tentatively at the sensitive little bud below. While Alex's lips and tongue gently played with her, his hands moved up again to her breasts, his fingertips tenderly squeezing the upright nipples. She began to feel little waves of intense pleasure working their way through her pussy as she slowly rocked herself in rhythm with his tongue, aware of the increasing dampness between her legs. When Alex pulled down her panties so that she could step out of them, Lizzie immediately opened her legs to allow him access to the aching area between them.

He lifted her on to the table and placed each of her legs on his shoulders. When his face disappeared into the space between them, Lizzie leaned back on outstretched arms and closed her eyes as his mouth worked expertly, sucking and licking and occasionally delving inside her. His head and her pussy rocked in unison as Lizzie cried out at the effect of his delicate touch. When she felt she couldn't hold back any longer, the beginnings of a climax threatening to bring this exquisite intimacy to an end, she pushed him away. For a while, she lay flat and breathless on the table.

Alex stood up and took off his clothes and, when Lizzie wrapped her legs around him, gently pulling his nakedness towards her, he slid effortlessly inside. Now huge, he filled her entirely. Rocking back and forth, he looked down at her passionately, taking in her face and body. She could feel his hands running up and down her thighs.

'God, you're lovely to fuck,' he told her and, as though turned on by his own words, he began to move a little faster. 'Lovely,' he repeated.

It felt good to have him inside her, gently probing from his standing position, intuitively changing his rhythm to match hers. He looked incredibly attractive as he towered over her in the semi-darkness of the candle-lit room, and the combination of sight and sensation made Lizzie oblivious to the hard wooden table beneath her. Alex bent down and they kissed hungrily, their tongues entwining excitedly through their breathlessness.

'Oh God,' she said as their movements became more rapid.

Through the damp and sensuous kisses, Lizzie let out a small appreciative cry as she reached a long, powerful climax, electric shivers passing through every limb, every organ. Turned on by her obvious pleasure, Alex swelled even more inside her. Within a moment she heard him groan as he came, and felt the little spasms as his orgasm subsided. While his body gradually relaxed, he kissed her face and shoulders.

'Beautiful,' he said, trying to recover his breath. 'Beautiful.'

'Yes,' she said, stroking his hair as she cradled his head in her arms.

They lay in their embrace, tenderly caressing each other, placing little kisses on warm, damp skin, until Lizzie became aware of the rock-hard table she lay on. She eased Alex up and they dressed in silence, the room now almost completely dark.

Lizzie lit another candle and began to make coffee. 'I like to be up very early,' she told him, determined not to let anything – not even this wonderful man – upset her established routine.

Alex looked at his watch. '10.40. I suppose I could always go to my aunt's place on the other side of the village,' he told her. 'I often stay there when . . .'

Lizzie turned and stared at him. 'You mean . . .'

Alex nodded sheepishly and they both laughed.

'Sorry,' he said.

When they kissed goodbye on her doorstep, she told him not to be sorry. Thanks to this unexpected visitor, she now knew exactly how to write that scene she'd been stuck on.

Luke and Julian

Rachel Carter

Luke and Julian

⁘ ⁘

'Of course, the thing about intercourse,' Anne had said as we sat back from our meal, 'is that we're all so uncomfortable about being close to each other.'

She had sipped her wine – an exquisite red that had sadly lost its taste for most of us after she'd emphasised how much it had cost her.

'Outside the bedroom, we need at least a metre of space around us at all times,' she'd continued.

Her boyfriend, Julian, had laughed at the time, along with the other guests. Except for me. I was flirting silently with Luke, who had run his toes up my thighs and was pressing them between my legs underneath the tablecloth.

I don't know what made me recall her words as I climbed the stairs to our apartment a few weeks later. It was early afternoon and I'd decided to work at home for the rest of the day. Getting the keys out as I reached our floor, I noticed the door was slightly ajar. Damn, I thought. One of us must have forgotten to lock up this morning.

I pushed against the door with my shoulder, slipping into the cool tranquility of my own home. But something wasn't right. I was aware of a tension, intangible, almost electric, hanging in the air. A rush of fear swept over me. Maybe we hadn't simply left the door open, maybe there were burglars. It was possible that there was a burglar standing within metres of me at that very moment. I tried not to breathe, straining for any sound. At that moment I noticed crumpled clothes scattered on the floor, a man's shoe overturned in the doorway to the bedroom. My thumping heart skipped a beat and I stood as quietly as possible. With adrenaline rushing through my body, the sounds around me amplified. My breathing, a slight creak from my throat as I swallowed, the crinkle of the plastic bag I held. And the sound of sighs. Soft, low, crooning sighs coming from the bedroom.

My heart and mind began to race as I tried to remember where Luke had said he'd be that day. But I couldn't focus – my attention was muddled by the loud thump of my heartbeat and the roar of my pulse inside my head. Then someone let out a low groan. It was Luke's voice. And it was that distinctive groan of ecstasy that so excites me. The familiar sound I love so much. Though seized by fear and panic, another feeling rippled through me – the exquisite pain of arousal. The groan grew louder. Then a series of low moans followed. I tried not to make a sound.

Moving slowly and carefully, I lowered my bag on to the sofa and placed my keys gently down on the coffee table. I moved silently towards the bedroom, very much aware of a delicious heat between my legs. I reached a hand out to steady myself and saw that I was shaking. Suddenly a sound brought me to a halt, mid-step, my heart pounding. There was that groan again, and a wave of sexual energy washed over me in response. But what had stopped me so completely was the other moaning. For there was another voice responding – a soft, low voice. A man's voice. Moaning in such sensuous, breathy tones that I could hardly contain my own sighs. A sound so sweet I almost cried.

I moved faster now, across to a point where the sunlight shone through the open doorway, reflecting on the dark, shiny leaves of the exotic palm beside me. Leaning over the plant, I could see clearly into the bedroom, through the crack between the door and the wall.

There was Luke, his firm, muscular body stretched out across the bed. His back was arched in a spasm of delight as he responded to his lover's attentions. And there, kneeling along-side the bed, was Julian, his lithe young body glistening with sweat, his head down, out of view behind Luke's raised leg.

I stood still, unable to move. Once again, Anne's voice came back to me.

'Anyway, it's not all it's cracked up to be,' she'd said.

Oh no? I remembered thinking, wanting to tell her that making love is just about the most incredible thing on this earth. But I'd refrained, as somehow I didn't think she was interested in my opinion. Her own opinion had dominated the whole evening, and it was clear that when she expressed her thoughts she expected only agreement, not argument. Instead, I'd smiled across at Luke, who shaped his lips into a kiss. Now I remembered that Julian, who usually looks so cool with his dark, neat hair and cute, boyish looks, was glaring at her, a furious blush rising on his cheeks.

'In fact I think it's totally overrated,' she had continued, oblivious to his distress.

The conversation had moved on at this point but, as the bottles had emptied, a guest, on being unceremoniously shoved outside by Anne for daring to smoke at the table, turned to her and asked her what her problem was. 'You're a retentive, stuck-up snob,' had been his words. At the time, I'd wondered why Julian bothered with her. I wondered how well they got along when they were alone. Clearly, sensuality played no part in their relationship.

Now they were closer, these two young stallions. Luke had pulled Julian up off the floor and was on top of him, facing him as he held him down, smothering his face and hair with kisses. They poised there for a moment, their sleek muscles intertwined, their bodies so full of strength and tension I could almost embrace it in the air. I watched, transfixed, as they moved together. I gazed at their grace, entranced by their taut muscles and satin skin. The burning in my own body gripped my senses. When finally they came, seized by ecstasy, crying out and thrusting themselves against each other, I staggered back against the wall, unable to trust myself to stand.

I stayed there for a long time, hoping they couldn't hear my heart thumping. Wanting to calm the trembling, I turned and stared blindly out the window, trying to focus my vision and my thoughts. I couldn't stop thinking of how magnificent they had looked together: two powerful bodies locked in passion. I stumbled, and knocked the palm beside me. The plant fell against the bedroom door, swinging it open. Startled, they raised their heads in sudden panic, and our eyes met.

I leant against the open door, my trembling arms folded against my body.

'You two are so sexy together,' I said.

With mischievous looks gleaming in their eyes, they laughed.

And they each held an arm out to me as I moved toward the bed.

'Come here, baby,' Luke said quietly, and smiled. 'We need you too.'

I moved closer. So far, Julian hadn't said a word. He was facing away from us, on the far side of the bed.

'Maybe you'd rather be alone,' I said, insecurity taking hold of me. I wasn't used to feeling anything but totally sure of myself, and I faltered, wondering what to do next.

'Yeah, right.' Luke reached out and, grabbing my clothes, pulled me towards him.

'Drink this,' Julian said, sitting back on his haunches as he filled three glasses. A red wine bottle stood by the bed. 'Hey, come on. I opened it with great care and attention. Especially for us.' He smiled.

I took the glass and raised it to them.

'To the sexiest men in the universe,' I proposed.

'And to us.' Julian tilted his head, his lips slightly parted and his hair falling to one side.

'Come on, angel, you know that's what I meant.' I lifted my jumper and slipped off my long skirt. Shoes got thrown against the wall, and my bra lay where it fell. I stretched myself out on my stomach, loving the freedom of being naked, loving the warmth of the two men beside me. 'And I have to say, I think you agree.'

'You don't wear underpants,' Julian said, looking at me.

'I love that about her,' said Luke, leaning over Julian's shoulder.

I smiled to myself: Julian could still be surprised by me and the things we did together. Was it because Anne held so few secrets, if any? I thought how horrified she'd be if she knew I went through each day with nothing on under my skirt. I remembered the last time I'd seen her. We'd tried to go shopping together, but the whole day had ended in disaster. I should have known.

'Why do you wear fuck-me shoes?' she'd asked acidly as we stepped out together.

'Why is everyone so afraid of erotica and sensuality in everyday life?' I'd retorted.

She'd had nothing to say to that. It wasn't that I'd wanted her to feel bad. I didn't. In fact, I really wished she could open up more. For her sake, of course, but I guess I thought mostly of Julian. He was such a great guy – why should he have to put up with her tight Victorian attitude?

Well, things had gone from bad to worse. By the end of the day I had been ready to take a break from her for a long time. We were sitting in a pub somewhere, trying to release the tension between us through a beer or two, when she had continued, 'And why do you wear that crap around your eyes?'

I couldn't help what had come out next. 'It's to ward off evil spirits,' I'd replied, glaring at her, 'but clearly it's not working.'

And with that I'd stomped out of the bar. In my high heels.

I glanced over at the boots I'd just thrown across the room. No, they weren't high, these ones, but the black patent leather and laces gave them a pretty good look, I thought.

And then I lost my focus. I thought of nothing as my head swirled with the air, the wine and the heat around me. A heat that was getting stronger, more heady, once again. Luke had lain down alongside me, and was caressing my buttocks and the small of my back. I parted my legs a little as he reached between them. Julian raised his head on his elbow, and traced a line over my shoulders as he watched.

Suddenly I pulled myself away and sat up on the pillow.

'No,' I said. 'Touch him. Touch his body the way you were touching it before. I want to stay here. And watch.' I held my wine glass close to my lips, swirling the wine around it and staring at them through the warped, reddened glass. I saw colour and I saw form, and I saw movement. Lowering the glass a little, I ran my tongue along the rim, back and forth, as I watched Luke's head begin to move up and down.

Julian lay back in ecstasy. He seemed to want to reach out to Luke, to run his hands through his hair, but he didn't make the move. No, this time I could see that he was thinking only of himself, at one with his body. Blissfully alone with the desire and the fire that swept over him, letting the sensation take over his body and his will. He moaned softly.

And I moaned too. His excitement was so powerful I could feel it in the air around me. I longed to touch him. To feel his limbs, so tense, and the heat of his skin. As I'd felt it so many times before. But somehow it seemed too much of an invasion to be a part of his pleasure this time. For, as the moment grew, something precious and intensely personal was happening, something only he could revel in. I leaned against the wall and watched his body. Swaying, gently rocking, and then at times jerking violently against Luke's head. At last, he moved around, Luke moving with him.

Quietly, I eased myself down until my body was alongside my lover's. I pressed myself up against Julian's back, aroused by the feel of my naked breasts against his wet skin. Still holding my drink, I raised his fingers and dipped them in the wine, before setting the glass down on the floor. I sucked a wet, dripping finger, moving it back and forward in my mouth. I gripped it tightly and ran my tongue around and around it, then I drew it slowly out. With my other hand, I caressed Julian's haunches, tensing with pleasure as I felt the velvet softness of his flesh against the firm, hard muscles of his buttocks. I parted them gently and pushed my wet finger into his hot, tight opening. He cried out as I moved it back and forward, each time a little deeper, and a little firmer, pressing against that special place that drove him wild.

Luke lay there quietly, softly moaning. Then he pulled himself up the bed and embraced both of us, holding me tightly against Julian, his nails digging into my back.

'Kiss me now,' he said, and we both raised our heads. We smothered him, kissing hard and wet, and with a fire that was growing ever stronger.

'Come here,' Luke whispered to me.

'No,' I replied. 'Just let me watch this time. Seeing you two together drives me wild.' I realised that my body was shaking. I could feel my hips sway in a movement I could hardly control. I became aware of my finger, still moving back and forth to the same rhythm, and I drew it out.

'Mmmm, babe, no!' Julian cried out. 'Keep it there, honey, keep it inside me.'

Luke took a long sip of his wine and I saw that his hand was trembling. Light drops of sweat dripped down over his moist lips, and I had a sudden sensation that I was looking at the very icon of my dreams. The god of lovemaking, perhaps. Julian must have been looking at him with the same thoughts, for he reached out to Luke and turned him around. I looked up to see the ripple of his muscles as he held Luke tight against his chest and, as I felt his back stiffen with tension, a throbbing sensation began to take hold of me. With a sudden, overwhelming rush the feeling tore through me, just as his whole body shuddered when he entered Luke. I moved my finger deeper, and with my other hand I reached down to touch myself. I closed my eyes, and the three of us became one as we rocked to the same rhythm. This was heaven, I knew. I held myself tightly, moving my fingers in that steady, flowing way that always made me feel so good. I felt the heat and strength of the man beside me, and pushed ever deeper inside him. As we rocked harder and faster, I let the depths of my mind open, allowing my most exciting, sexy thoughts to fill my head and take me over. Visions of Luke above me at the moment of climax with his body tense and glistening; the passion in Julian's rough embraces; the thrill of their cries in orgasm. And as we came together, we all cried out, to ourselves, to each other, to the passion and fire that enveloped us.

When the moment was over, we didn't move. We lay there, pressed tightly against each other, breathing as one. Minutes passed, and as our rapid breathing eased I became aware of the room once more, of the cool air that surrounded us and of the dappled light on the walls.

A thought sprang into my head and I couldn't help but say, in that knotted tone of voice Anne has, 'Outside the bedroom, we need at least a metre of space around us at all times.'

We moved even closer against each other.

Luke responded, quietly, 'But inside the bedroom . . . ah well, Anne, my darling, you'd be stunned to see how little space we need – and what pleasure we can find within it.'

Wednesday Afternoons

Roz Hart

Wednesday Afternoons

❖ ❖

Wednesday afternoon, ten past four. My weekly massage has been going on since three, and now it is nearly over. My skin is glowing and my muscles have forgotten the meaning of tension. I wriggle pleasurably as Janine's warm, oil-slick palms stroke firmly from the base of my spine up to my shoulder blades and back again.

'Lie there for a few minutes,' she says softly, slipping the fleecy towel over my body. 'No need to move till you're ready.'

In a little while I'll get up, put my robe on and help her fold the portable couch and pack its covering of thin futon mattress and pure cotton sheet. Meanwhile I do as I am bidden. I am almost asleep anyway; Janine's massage technique is soporific and erotic in about equal parts. Giving way to the first part is essential to the enjoyment, and as for the second ... Marcus has discovered Wednesdays are something to look forward to; straight after supper we'll retire upstairs with the rest of the wine and our own bottle of jasmine-scented oil.

But for the moment Marcus isn't here, and Janine's attentions have put my sexual appetite into overdrive. Lying there with half-closed eyes I breathe in the scents her oils have left hanging in the air: lavender and ylang-ylang today. She explained a few weeks ago about the properties of the different scents; I ask what effect these have.

'Lavender relaxes, ylang-ylang is said to build confidence and self-esteem,' she replies with her slow smile. 'It's also aphrodisiac,' she adds, turning away.

That explains a great deal.

I watch Janine move quietly around the room, gathering up tissues and bottles. Her mass of dark curls is neatly tied back, and the white tunic skims her knees and fits snugly over the discreet curves of her body; she looks every inch the caring professional. A couple of her fliers lie on the coffee table: ENJOY A RELAXING MASSAGE WITHOUT LEAVING THE HOUSE: JANINE PRITCHARD, MOBILE MASSEUSE, OFFERS ON-THE-SPOT SERVICE TO WOMEN.

Why only women? And why has it never occurred to me before? Marcus loves it when I smooth oil into his muscular back; he'd revel in the thorough, professional treatment Janine has just given me. I sit up. 'Don't you ever do men?'

'I used to, when I started out. I pretty soon stopped though.'

'Why?'

'Oh come on, Lia. Naked man, woman with couch and bottle of almond oil? And haven't you read the personal column of the local rag lately: "Call Greta for a sensuous Scandinavian experience brought to your door"?'

'I see what you mean.' Marcus always says I'm naive, but somehow I hadn't made the connection between Janine and Greta's Scandinavian experience.

Then again, it isn't surprising, when I think about the effect Janine's magic touch has just had on my libido. It doesn't help that the top button of her tunic is open; she bends over the coffee table to pick up the fliers and for a moment I have a perfect view of her full breasts. Not that I'm into that sort of thing, but . . .

'Besides,' she says, 'I prefer women's bodies.'

I lie down again as she straightens up; she turns her shapely back to me, standing perfectly still, taut and somehow expectant. I realise I am holding my breath, and let it out in a gust. I must be imagining things.

Janine moves away, gathering up the rest of her paraphernalia.

'I ought to get myself moving,' I say. 'Marcus will be home soon.'

I don't know why I said that; I'm not expecting him for at least an hour. I sit up and let the towel drop, swinging my legs over the edge of the couch. My clothes are at the other side of the room. I'm not usually self-conscious about being naked, but today I find I am carefully avoiding Janine's eyes. She picks up the pillow from the end of the couch and stands, clutching it to her, gazing at me.

'You've got a lovely body, you know, Lia.'

The room swims out of focus as it occurs to me that that glimpse of her tits wasn't accidental. My fingers dig into the padded edge of the couch and my thighs are quivering; I rub them together and watch Janine bend to zip her bag up. The top of her tunic falls open again.

'So have you,' I hear myself reply.

Our eyes lock together and the air between is suddenly charged. Neither of us speaks; there is no need for words. I suppose I always knew this would happen. I take the pillow back and lie down, kicking the towel to the floor. She takes the band out of her hair and shakes her curls free, then unbuttons her white tunic and peels it slowly over her arms. They are smooth and lightly tanned, like the rest of her body, including her full, pink-tipped breasts. The tunic drops to the floor. Now we are both completely naked. This is new territory for me. I am holding my breath again, unsure where to go from here.

I needn't have worried: Janine knows exactly what to do. She begins to massage my shoulders, her hands slipping a little further down with each movement. Usually she moves smoothly from chest to abdomen without touching my breasts; now she begins to stroke them, paying special attention to my tingling nipples. They harden under her feathery touch, and as she leans over to flick them with her tongue her own breasts fall forward and brush my arm.

I put out a tentative hand, and she gasps as I cup the yielding flesh. It feels strange to be touching another woman like this. She is soft where Marcus is hard, rounded and pliant where he is flat and firm. An electric surge of sensation courses through me as her teeth close gently around my nipple, and the strangeness dissolves into a pulsing wave of excitement.

Her skin is silky and supple under my quivering fingers. Suddenly I want nothing more than Janine's hands on my body, stroking my back, my breasts, my thighs, my secret places. She seems to read my mind.

'Turn on your stomach,' she says quietly, 'and part your legs a little.'

I do as she asks and give myself up to her hands. They move across me like warm liquid, over my back and hips, down the insides of my thighs and back again. As her fingers explore my sensitive crevices, I reach experimentally for hers. My hand meets damp, wiry hair, and ventures down into slippery satin folds of flesh. For a moment her hand stops stroking; then we are moving in unison. She is so wet that my fingers find their own way. I slip two inside her: it is alien territory, but so warm and smooth and pulsating. She tightens around me as I finger-fuck her; I feel her sway and steady herself against the edge of the couch.

Her hand is underneath me and my breath quickens as she homes in on my clit like a heat-seeking missile. I find hers with my thumb, and she flings her head back with a little moan.

The world goes into slow motion and everything is a blur of flickering hands, animal sounds and blistering, incandescent pleasure. As I tumble over the edge my ears fill with a low roar like a far-off aeroplane, or the purring engine of an expensive car. It is over too soon, in seconds probably; Janine slumps over me and for the first time our mouths meet in a delicate, exploratory kiss.

'Well, well, well. Now here's a sight for sore eyes.'

I freeze. Marcus. He isn't due home for ages. I sit up and look from him to Janine and back again. She picks up the towel and hands it to me, then looks at him blank-faced.

'I can explain,' I stammer.

'Explain? No need for that. I've often wondered how you spend your Wednesday afternoon. Had a kind of suspicion it might be something like this. I decided to come home early and check up – and what do you know, I'm right. Here you are, both of you, caught in the act.'

His tone is bland and amiable, but his face is hard to read; there is a hint of his familiar lazy smile on his mouth, but his eyes are hooded. I swallow hard and glance at Janine. She lifts her chin and sets her mouth in a line. My eyes take in her firm, proud breasts, and a frisson travels down my spine as my body remembers. Was it really just a few minutes ago?

Marcus is still speaking. 'I'm not absolutely sure if it counts as adultery, but whatever you call it, I reckon you've cheated on me.'

The words have an edge, and for a moment I am scared. We are good together, Marcus and I, in and out of bed. It means a lot to me to hold on to that.

'What are you going to do?' I ask nervously.

'Oh, I guess I'm entitled to exact a penance, don't you?'

Then I see the bulge in the front of his trousers. The bastard: he's turned on by what he saw! Janine is still standing beside me, completely naked and apparently quite unselfconscious.

'What sort of penance?' she asks. Her voice is quite expressionless, as if she has wiped it clean of emotion of any kind. Her glittering eyes tell a different story, and her hand on the couch beside mine is quivering, but whether with fear, anger or passion I can't tell.

Marcus takes a pace forward and lays his own hand on the edge of the couch. 'Oh, I expect I'll think of some suitable punishment,' he says, lingering over the last word. A few weeks ago he brought home a video which consisted mainly of girls in thongs being spanked by naked men. He got so excited that I've been expecting him to suggest that we have a go ourselves ever since. 'Not here, though,' he continues. 'Not nearly enough room. Upstairs, both of you. Quickly now!'

A wave of exhilaration sweeps over me; my libido, temporarily dormant after Janine's recent expert ministrations, blazes back to potent life. Spanking has never appealed in theory but, who knows? The practice could be fun. I slide off the couch, drop the towel on the floor and seize Janine's hand. 'Come on. Do as he says.'

We run along the hall hand in hand, with Marcus close behind. I feel a light slap on my butt and glance over my shoulder to see him pulling at his shirt buttons with one hand and tugging his belt with the other. He is smiling in a way I've never seen before. A thrill of erotic ferment shoots through me from knee to hip.

By the time we reach the bedroom Marcus is naked as well. He gathers up the duvet and flings it on to the floor. The bed is a king-size; and so is he: his cock stands out at a right angle, thick, rigid and a good seven inches long. I shiver with anticipation, feeling quite proud. He's an impressive specimen, this man of mine, whatever fate he has in store for us. He backs us up against the wall, and I steal a glance at Janine: her cheeks are pink and her eyes still have that glow.

'Right, Phase One.' He points at Janine. 'You, lie down,' he orders. 'On your back, knees up, legs spread wide.' He smiles, a dangerous glint shimmering in his eyes. 'Let me feast my eyes on you.'

Janine does as she is bidden, the corner of her mouth twitching as if it wants to smile. She parts her thighs slowly to reveal her sex, all pink petals and glistening channels. It feels odd, yet at the same time sensuous, to look at what my fingers explored only a few moments ago. I have never seen another woman's sex before.

Marcus folds his arms across his broad chest, his smile widening. 'That's beautiful. You look as if you're ready for the shagging of your life. Who knows, you may get lucky.' He half-closes his eyes and strokes the angle of his jaw. 'Now, babe, what shall I do about you? I saw a film once about a girl who cheated on her husband. She was stripped naked and displayed in the town square. Maybe I'll make you stand in the window and show your lovely tits to anyone who passes. But no – that doesn't take your friend into account. Not that I'm blaming her. I know what a seductive little vixen you are. I expect you led her on. Promised her a taste of paradise. In fact –' He puts his hands on my shoulders and propels me towards the bed. 'In fact, I think you should give her what you promised. Don't want her thinking this is an inhospitable household, do we?'

'What do you want me to do?'

'Go down on her. Get your head between her legs and suck her off.'

So it's not to be a spanking. Janine gasps, but says nothing. I look at the pink folds revealed by her open thighs, then back at Marcus. He gives me a little push.

'Get to it, babe. On your hands and knees, so I can look at your delectable arse.'

He folds his arms and I climb on the bed beside Janine. The undersheet is ivory silk; we bought it a month ago in a fit of extravagance. Both Marcus and I find it arousing. My skin shivers as it slides across the smooth fabric.

'Are you OK with this?' Janine mouths into my ear.

'If you are,' I murmur back.

'Oh, I'm fine. Perk of the job.'

My breasts brush her belly as I settle myself into position; she pinches my nipple and I gasp as it instantly hardens.

If fingering Janine felt strange, this is positively bizarre. I put out the tip of my tongue cautiously, experimentally, not knowing what to expect. When I go down on Marcus my mouth is immediately filled to capacity, his flesh hot, hard and throbbing.

Janine's clit is swollen and firm, but still small; it hardly extends past my lips.

As I flick and stroke with my tongue it swells even more and begins to quiver. She moves underneath me and lets out a little moan. She starts to writhe and to make feral sounds that raise my excitement level till only her hand on the back of my neck keeps my tongue at work on her. Her other hand reaches down for my breast; she pinches my nipple rhythmically, each nip activating the powerful erotic nerve-path leading to my crotch.

A whiff of *Eau Sauvage* drifts past me and the mattress dips a little. Marcus has moved in behind me. His cock probes between my legs and finds its way inside. My body moves up a couple of gears; I'm no longer sure who is fucking and sucking who. We move faster and faster and Janine's hips rotate and the low sounds leap out of her throat and become a long, drawn-out scream.

Her legs slide down the bed and I raise my head. Marcus slips out of me, panting hard, and I make to get off the bed.

'Oh no you don't, not yet!'

He pushes me aside and flips me on to my back. I open my legs, expecting him to move back inside me and finish what he started, but he bobs back on his heels and looks down at Janine. She is panting, a film of sweat on her skin, and she looks up at him. Her legs are still spread wide. Marcus strips the condom off, reaches for another from the bedside table and moves between her legs.

As he rolls the condom over his prick in a swift, skilful movement and thrusts into Janine's waiting channel, I don't feel jealous, just bereft. Then I'm hotter and hornier than ever as I watch his buttocks tighten and his cock slam in and out. Her eyes close, and she hooks her feet around his legs.

After a few moments he slows down and rolls off her, a grin spreading over his face. She sits up and hugs her knees, and meets his eyes squarely.

'I hope you enjoyed that,' she says, amused.

'Not as much as you did.'

'You flatter yourself. I prefer what Lia did.'

I suppress a smile as his cock begins to droop. He closes his hand around it and slides it up and down with a leisurely, almost lazy action, flipping the condom on to the mattress.

'Lia doesn't. Lia likes shagging. A good stiff cock inside her.

At least, I always thought she did.' He tightens his hand around the swelling shaft and begins to move it rhythmically. 'What do you say, babe?'

'I'm all for new experiences,' I hear myself reply.

'We've certainly had one of those today.' He grins. 'Good with her hands, is she? Yes, of course she is. They're the tools of her trade, after all.'

'I am, actually. Very good.'

She rocks forward on her knees and takes hold of his cock: it has regained its former glory and a bead of moisture glistens on the purplish, engorged tip.

'I thought you preferred women,' Marcus says.

'I do. But not exclusively.'

Marcus wraps his hand round Janine's. 'Tell you what: to show Lia she's forgiven for cheating on her man, I'll let you give her the benefit of these magic hands while I,' he wraps both hands round his cock and pulls the foreskin back, 'wank myself into orbit.'

I glance at Janine; she smiles a small, almost secretive smile.

'Lie back,' she says. 'Party time.'

The party has already been going on for twenty minutes, as far as I can tell. I'm hot and wet, and I'll have to summon up a few mind-numbing thoughts to stop myself coming in a fiery blaze the second she touches me. I pull a pillow behind my head so I can keep an eye on Marcus, then lie back and abandon myself to my fate.

I summon images of politics, football, even cleaning the oven to my aid; they are all useless. Janine's fingers slide in and out of me creating golden rivers of music, and then they home in on my clit with the rapid circular movements which she seems to know instinctively will launch me into the stratosphere. It's only a few seconds before the space rocket between my legs gathers itself for an earth-splitting take-off. Over and over again it explodes, flowing down my legs and up into my belly in sparks and spray and foaming fire. It goes on so long I almost miss Marcus's orgasm: I'm just beginning to subside when his back arcs off the bed and he lets out a mighty yell. Semen jets out of him and hits Janine on the arm, the next spurt splashes on my thigh and the rest forms a little puddle on his stomach. He lies, eyes closed and breath whistling for a few moments.

'Wow,' he says finally. 'Two's company, but three's a gala

occasion.' He raises himself on to one elbow and looks at me and then at Janine. 'This massage thing. Every Wednesday afternoon, is it?'

I nod and steal a glance at Janine; she is smiling. Marcus lies back languorously. 'Great. The office isn't too busy on a Wednesday. Maybe I'll make a habit of coming home early.'

In Pursuit of Knowledge

Saskia Walker

In Pursuit of Knowledge

❖ ❖

I watched the clock on my desk. The hand paused, then flicked forward suddenly, pacing over the clock face like an erratic heartbeat. My own heartbeat mirrored its mood, controlled, as it was, by the images in my mind. I was thinking about him. I was thinking about his skin. I could almost feel its touch on mine. His skin against my skin, both against my body, and inside.

My eyes focused on the long, smooth, jerking needle of time. Its movement began to twitch against my aching sex and I rode the ripple of sensation that climbed from there, stretching back in my chair.

Mercifully, it was not long until I would see him again. I closed out the familiar surroundings of the office, abandoning it for something more appealing. Barbara, the technical director, was humming to herself as she tidied her desk for the close of the day. I allowed her image to blur and fade, smiling to myself as his image settled in my mind. It was the picture that remained from that first time my eyes had touched on him across the space of the library. He was striking but contained, vigorous yet controlled. Delicious.

His long, dark hair fell loosely against the column of his neck and my eyes had climbed up, along the dramatic sweep of his hard jaw, across the angle of his cheekbones, and into the intent look of his amber-flecked green eyes. One long, firm finger gently stroked at his elegant mouth as he pored over his book. It seemed to brush the surface of my own lips, as it touched against his.

The space between us began to dissolve. I felt cool air rush across my tongue as my lips tingled and parted. I wanted him.

It had been three months since I had first spied him. I always went to the City Library on a Tuesday evening, reading for my part-time degree course; bringing alive my own world of literature and philosophy within that arena of grander ideas. I had always found the womb-like atmosphere both comforting, and stimulating. The atmosphere was steeped with a feast of ideas and images; the walls were heavy with mental nutrition, stimulation for life. I could visit the scenes in the books my spirit chose to enter. I could smell the heavy, pungent incense of Eastern love dens, sense the fragrance coursing through my body. Or taste the fruits of exotic lands, their juices flowing down my face and neck as I bit into their lush, tactile flesh. I would open books and gently draw their questions into my mind. Questions that I would strive and strive with until, finally, the release came and the answers would sparkle, and flood through me. Then, one day, I looked up, and I saw him.

He always sat in the same place, the third seat from the right at the long, heavy, polished wooden table set down the library's central aisle. When he rose to look for a book my eyes followed his long, lean frame. His legs were always encased in black jeans. Broken-in jeans, worn to the form of his body, outlining the angles and planes of his slim hips. He wore loose draped shirts that exposed his elegant collarbone to my eager eyes. The material flowed over his chest, as if it was my very hands touching his skin.

As the summer moved from gauzy sun-filled evenings to the humid dusk of late September, I gradually moved closer, abandoning my favourite desk in the shadowy corner of ancient history, to move out into the more exposed central corridor, where he sat.

'Is it a new man, Zoe?' Barbara had asked, when she noticed my increasing haste to leave the office. She gave a knowing smile and watched with amusement, occasionally commenting on my clothes or hair as I left the office; reminding me that she had noticed. She noticed too when I began to attend the library more frequently.

By chance I found out that he studied there three nights a week. One of the librarians had come to his seat to discuss the availability of a book he had requested. I lowered my head but lifted my attention when she began to flirt openly with him.

'I'll keep it under the desk for you then,' she offered.

Several curious readers had turned to observe the conversation, but her blatant simpering seemed to have little effect on him. He gave a cool, polite smile in response to her suggestive pout.

'Don't worry. If it's not here by Thursday, I'll be in again on Friday.'

His voice was quiet but resonant. I savoured its sound and tried not to show my amusement when he returned to his book, and dismissed the woman in doing so. My mind took the knowledge, and my timetable, my life rhythm, altered to meet his. The next night I moved closer still.

I sat facing him at the table, but some three spaces away, where I could best admire his profile over the lowered corner of my current text. He was so very intent. Would he be like this as a lover? In my mind's eye I replaced the rather grand surroundings of the library with a more intimate scene, where he arched over my naked body with similar intensity. My sex began to contract in response. I had shifted in my seat, my thighs crossing and uncrossing in an attempt to ease the raging desire I felt inside. He had glanced up. His eyes locked with mine. Electric. He returned to his book, but he also stepped outside himself. He was interested, curious. I could sense him taking my presence in. For nights it was enough to absorb the glorious knowledge of his awareness, and the feelings I got when his eyes lifted to trace a warm passage over my body.

Then I wanted to know more about him. I looked down at the book in his hand. I couldn't make out the title and on impulse I stood up. My body wavered when he glanced up to follow its passage, pleasure sweeping up beneath the touch of his gaze on my body. I circled the table, weaving in and out of the bookshelves. My fingers caressed the spines of the books as I passed, my eyes constantly drawn back to him, taking in the look of him from all angles. He glanced up occasionally to follow my passage, but my body told me he was really watching all the time. I stood in the aisle behind his seat. What was he reading? I wanted to see inside his mind while I touched his body. My fingers rested on the subtly ridged spine of a leather-bound book, but my eyes were still on him. He flexed his back and my hand closed on the book in response. I wanted to touch him instead. His head moved slightly, he was looking for me. I wanted to touch his hair. I slid one finger over the top of the book and drew it out. What was he reading? I imagined talking across a pillow to him, in between making love. My body was burning up with the idea of it.

I began to wonder if I could get near enough to see the books lying in front of him without succumbing to my desires. The deep throbbing emanating from inside was a demand so hot it was beginning to take control. I reminded myself to breathe. I began to move towards him again, my heart racing dramatically, as if to reach him before I did. When I got close he turned around towards me and I realised that the book I had been holding had slid from my hand and fallen on the floor. We both stared down at the book and then I dropped down to retrieve it, just as he leaned over.

'Thank you,' I heard myself say as I took the book from his hand.

We were inches apart, I could barely breathe.

'Any time,' he replied.

The ambiguity of his statement was reflected in the suggestive expression of his eyes. I took a deep breath and stood up. My body was tense with containment as I regained my footing and continued on my path. With his eyes on me like that I didn't think I could even try to see the books on his desk, but a title rose up to meet my eyes over his shoulder as I passed: *Anthropology and Understanding*. Another book beneath exposed only one word visible: *Behaviour*. As I got to the end of the table I tried to control my smile. Not philosophy, but even better: he was studying relationships, people, the body. I wanted him to study mine. As I sat down again he turned a page, but he wasn't looking at the words, he was looking at me.

The next night I rushed into the gloomy entrance hall of the library and bumped into somebody reading the notice boards.

'Sorry!' I said with a laugh, then paused and quietened when I saw that it was him.

He had been waiting to step out of the shadows, to catch me as I came in, I was sure of it. He put his hand on my arm to steady me and was looking at me with desire in his eyes, I could see it plainly. The hand on my arm may have been the only thing holding me up.

'My fault entirely,' he murmured. His hand stroked my arm gently before letting go; it was the touch of an intimate lover, stroking me on the inside as well. After a few moments he moved to hold the door open for me. As I passed, my body slowed and brushed against his. I couldn't decide which was more magnetic: the look in his eyes at that moment, or the mutual pull between our hips as they came so close together.

I sat down one seat away from him. It was so close that I couldn't risk staring, only glancing occasionally to reassure my eyes that he was there. My body already knew that he was. I was aware that he was observing me from under half-lowered eyelids. I dragged my eyes from the attractive outline of his hands to look at the book they held. He seemed to read my thoughts because he lifted the book, so that I could see the cover. I recognised it immediately. It was the biography of Anäis Nin – the queen of erotica – that lay on my own shelf, at home. My heart missed a beat. So, he wanted to know about women's desires, about women and sex. I wanted him to know me.

I lowered my book and stretched one arm out, flexing my shoulders and loosening my neck muscles with a sweeping curve of movement. He looked directly at me. His lips curled. I don't know who had smiled first. He put his book down and stretched back in the chair, giving me a look at the long, lean line of his torso as he moved. We began then to move in direct and immediate response to one another – the dance had truly begun.

The sound of Barbara snapping shut her briefcase called me back to the present moment. I returned from the landscape of memory and looked again at the clock. It was five. At last. I closed the file I had been working on, stood up and grabbed my things.

'The library again?' Barbara asked.

'Knowledge is power,' I replied flippantly.

She just laughed. 'When am I going to meet this mystery man of yours?' she asked, as we headed for the door.

'I haven't met him properly yet,' I replied.

Barbara shook her head, smiled and waved as she walked off towards her car. She was heading out of the city, I was going deeper into it. I would be at the library by half past five. He would already be there, and I planned to sit opposite him. I ran for the bus.

The humid skies began to open as I stepped off the crowded

bus. I hastened my speed but didn't escape the rain. When I got inside the huge mahogany doors I paused to catch my breath. Glancing down, I saw that the light cotton of my dress was splattered with rain drops. I pushed my damp hair back from my face and composed myself before going on. He sat back in his chair, staring blatantly at me as I walked towards him. I tried to appear as nonchalant as I could, but it was difficult because his bold stare told me he wanted me as much as I wanted him.

I focused my eyes on the seat I was heading for, my heart racing. In the corner of my vision I caught a barely perceptible movement and the chair I was aiming for suddenly shot out in front of me. I stopped, rooted to the spot. He must have pushed it out with his foot. The back of my neck prickled with sensation; his invitation was so clear that it scared me a little. I glanced at him: he was smiling, his eyes sparkling with amusement. I managed to get to the chair.

Before I sat down, I put my bag on the table. He was looking at my dress, through it, where the rain drops had clung to the plane of my breasts through the light material. I drew the book out of my bag and put it on the table: *The Gender Gap and How to Enjoy the Distance*. As I sat down, I caught his eye as he finished reading the book cover. He raised one eyebrow and his smile twitched and curled to one side. To my annoyance I felt myself blush.

I picked up the book and hurried through the pages, trying to focus on some words, but they eluded me as my eyes caught a movement opposite. He was reading from the Nin biography again, he was nearing the end and his fingers caressed the corner of the book in gentle, even strokes, back and forth. I watched the movement a while, each stroke going right down across my body, then deep inside me. I wanted him to touch me there.

When I re-focused I saw that he had been watching me as I stared at the book. My eyes traced the line of his hand where it rested against his face and then looked at his lips; my hand stealing up to touch my neck, where I wanted to feel his mouth on me. He watched the movements of my fingers and I felt compelled to lead his eyes with them, stroking down across the neckline of my dress, teasing the skin on my collarbone, my arm brushing across my hot, aching breasts. His gaze lingered there a moment and when he looked up again, there was an invitation in his eyes. A challenge. I met it.

I stood up, gently closing *The Gender Gap,* and went off to the twentieth-century literature shelves. The material of my dress swayed and rippled over my thighs as I moved, prickling at the alert skin there, a constant reminder of my body's state of arousal. I knew the book I wanted and thankfully a copy of it was there. It was Nin's: *The Four-Chambered Heart.* I leaned up against the shelves and looked down at the cover. I wondered if he had read it. The man in the story was not unlike him, with dark gypsy looks. The lovers met in the gloomy, moist hollow of a barge on the river. They were contained in the boat, as we were in this space in the library. The shifting water of their river was like the sweet rain that was lapping at the tall windows. My body rippled and moved away from its mooring at the shelf.

Was I brazen enough to carry it off? As I walked back I encouraged myself to carry on with the game, but I paused and grabbed another book to use as cover, in case my courage deserted me. I glanced down at the title: *Is Castration the Answer to Crime?* Oh god! I abandoned it. I would just have to rely on my courage.

Again he watched as I returned, his book half raised in front of him. I put Nin down on the table between us, taking a deliberate step forward in the game. His eyes rose from the cover to meet mine. The look was pure sex. He knew!

As I sat down we stared openly at each other, reciprocated desire cruising the airwaves back and forth across the table. The knowledge of it surged through me. I was so hot! I could barely open the book with my hands for wanting to touch him instead. He was flexing his shoulders rhythmically, as if poised for action. My whole body pulsed with need, the nerves beneath my skin danced in anticipation, the blood positively hummed in my veins.

My hips rocked instinctively forward, my sex reaching for contact against the hard surface of the chair. His eyes followed the movement of my body and then slowly lifted to meet mine. His look was so intense that I felt an urge to climb over the table and straddle him there and then. I closed my eyes, but his image was still imprinted against the warm red of my eyelids. A voice disturbed me from my trance and I opened my eyes. He was sitting as before, but had turned towards the main desk. The voice was on the loudspeaker.

'The library will be closing in ten minutes.'

273

I turned to the desk to see the librarian's mouth moving, to prove it to myself. Damn. Where had the time gone? His eyes were flickering with thought, he didn't want it to end yet either. A decision had to be made, should we step back or go forwards? The answer was there, we didn't need words to say it. He stood up. So did I.

He walked down one of the aisles, turning his head occasionally to see if I followed, and stopped in the gloom at the end of the aisle. His hand went up to the books, as if he was looking for something. I stopped about two feet away from him and did the same, the titles blurring in front of my eyes as my heart raced. His fingers slipped across to mine. I leapt at the touch and gasped as he grabbed my hand, pulling me over to him. His other hand climbed up my back, drawing me close. His mouth fell to mine. The kiss, the kiss, the long awaited kiss. As his lips parted I slid my tongue into his mouth, to meet with his, to make the vital connection. My body was trembling, so heavily aroused that I felt weak. The contact between us was so very good, I pressed closer against him, breathing in the musk of his skin, our bodies merging together in the deep physical embrace.

'This is crazy,' he murmured, as his mouth slid down against my neck. His voice was husky, heavy with desire.

'Yes,' I replied. Yes, yes, yes! I wanted to be set free, like all the words flying out from the pages of the books in the library. I wanted him to open the books and release me.

He pulled back and looked at me, his hand sliding along the neckline of my dress where I had led his eyes before, then it dropped to the outline of my breasts. I stroked my hands through his hair and let the heavy look of unleashed desire in his eyes weigh on me. My lips parted as his touch closed on my aching nipples, freeing a quiet moan. His body flexed in response and then he meshed his fingers with mine, turned down a narrow corridor and drew me along behind him. He reached out to try each door handle we passed until, finally, one opened. As the door clicked open he turned and looked at me with a question in his eyes.

'Are you sure about this?' he asked, his expression alert but controlled.

The amber-flecked green of his eyes flickered, awaiting my reply. God he was gorgeous! I felt myself opening up inside with an urgent demand: I was begging for him there. I smiled in reply, then pushed the door open and walked into a tiny room.

All that was visible was a clutter of equipment and a small window high up on the wall that let some dusky light fall over an old desk. He shut the door and stood in the corridor of mottled light that fell through the glazed panel. I leaned up against the desk to steady myself as he walked through the junction of light from the corridor and the window, and I felt his body close on me. The air seemed to be filled with the energy-force between our bodies, it positively hummed with anticipation.

He pulled me up against him, kissing me fiercely while his body pushed mine against the desk. My hands began to discover him, sliding over his shoulders and down his back, our arms entwining as they crossed paths in exploration. His body was slim and wiry, leanly coiled muscle covering his limbs and torso suggesting vitality, energy. His hips were hard, the dip of muscle that would drive him inside my body flexing beneath my hand. Perfection.

'I want you,' I murmured against his hair, as his mouth descended to my throat.

'That's good,' he said, and his hands moved down from my neck, to my shoulders and around my breasts, closing over them, dragging frantically at the material as they passed.

I hummed my approval and he pulled back, reached down, and lifted the loose material of my dress, sweeping it over my head. I felt the swish and sway of the fabric, the gentle tug over my breasts, and then the cool air moved around my body in its place.

'All I could do was look at you. You're so beautiful,' he whispered, as his hands traced the outline of my figure.

My breath seemed to be caught on the edge of his fingers, drawn along my skin in their wake, slowly, painfully.

'So are you,' I breathed in response. 'But we're here now, aren't we?'

I smiled and reached for his lips with my fingers. I felt him smile beneath their touch, then he pushed them away to reach for my breasts with his mouth. His warm breath travelled across my skin and I felt the gentle stirring of my nipple as his lips covered it. As his mouth enclosed me the touch of his urgent desire rose up from deep within him and soared through me, commuting through the channel at my breast and travelling from there, throughout my body. The touch was like torture. I wanted more.

I drew back, forcing him to rise up to me again, tugging at his shirt. He pulled at the buttons and I drew the rough linen off him, covering him instead with the warm strokes of my hands. He was lean and beautiful and I was going to have him. My palms rested over the hard, dark outline of his nipples, stroking him as I reached forward to take a taste of him, following a salty trail across his skin with my tongue. The musk of his skin was seeping into my own, intoxicating me. He moaned and flexed; I could feel the urgency of his desire beneath my touch and the power of it flowed through me.

He was angled towards me, his knee climbing against the desk, enclosing my hips with his thigh, the tension in his body building ever higher. His hands entwined in my hair as my hips rocked into his, absorbing the dense heat of his loins, savouring the feeling of a contained energy force. He was going to join us together with that force, soon. My teeth tugged gently at his erect nipple.

'Christ woman, I have to be inside you,' he said urgently, and his voice shot along that interior path that he wanted to travel.

I was so very wet with wanting! I leant back on the moonlit desk, resting on my elbows, and my shoes fell to the floor with a soft thud. The skin of my thighs fluttered and trembled as he climbed over them with stalking hands. His fingers lingered momentarily around the lace-edged tops of my stockings and then slowed their search in the heat that they met at the top of my thighs. One hand curved over the triangle of silk that lay between us and my body rose up into his palm, rocking my throbbing sex against him. He slipped a finger over the edge of the silk, then stripped it along the length of my legs, taking my breath with it. His fingers travelled back along my thighs and dipped down into the curve of my sex, like a tongue wanting to taste, opening me gently to his touch. I had to have more. The waiting was unbearable!

My hips pushed forward and my head fell back against the desk, my feet climbing up against the desk drawers for support. He jerked a drawer for me to brace against and as I found the foothold my legs fell open. He stroked the moist heat of my sex and then one finger ran against my jutting clitoris. Deep and heavy rhythms spread around his fingertip, then lunged and swayed up through my pelvis. He watched as the movements of his fingers reverberated up to my face and sounded through my body in the low moans that escaped me. It felt so good and he knew it did. He stroked his hands along the length of my body, then knelt down in front of me. I felt the cool air against my hot aching flesh and then his firm lips covered me. Ecstasy.

He gently sucked and then engulfed my clitoris with his mouth, moving rhythmically, spreading sensation wide and deep. In my mind I saw an image of a book falling open on the desk, pages beginning to stir in a gentle breeze. Sensation charged up across my body from his lips, my entire skin alive to his touch, each nerve ending turning in response to the questing tongue that reached inside. Words flew backwards and forwards as the breeze waved the pages. I wanted to read the words more closely. I wanted to write them.

'Now, now,' I whispered and pulled gently at his hair.

He stood up and stripped off his jeans. His penis stood erect in the ray of light from the window. The gleaming shaft arched itself from his body, charged with heat and power. I wanted the thrust and energy of it inside me and reached for him. He looked at me with passionate words in his eyes. Poetry.

He ran the thick strong line of his shaft along the damp lips of my sex, and rocked it there, pressing it hard between our bodies, sending wild shock waves through me. I was burning up with need, I could hear the whimper in my own breathing. My hands climbed up his arms in desperation, my body writhing beneath his. He pressed the swollen tip of his penis into the entrance of my sex flesh. I gasped, but he held the position, stretching his arms out either side of me on the desk. Then he slowly moved the engorged head of his penis into that oh so sensitive place, until I felt positively desperate – he was driving me insane with desire!

I pulled at his shoulders, my legs enfolding him, drawing him inside. He gave a low groan and thrust deep into me, pushing up against my moist aching sex with his beautiful sweet hardness. It felt so very, very good. For a moment, I couldn't even move. His hair fell around my face, and his mouth reached for mine, sharing with me the flavour of my own desire. His thrusts echoed through my body and my sex quivered and clenched in response. A quiet gasp escaped him when he felt that gentle embrace. Then he reached for it again and I reached for him, our bodies taking each other in the rhythm of the dance. He rode the rhythm, passing in and out of the shaft of light to meet, to meet me. Leading me, leading me back and forth. Moving with subtle precision, he timed our collisions so very perfectly until I felt as if I would come. Each and every time the head of his penis crushed against me, so very deep inside. Striding, striding, we were riding the rhythm together, chasing each other's thrusts, matching one for one.

A hot volcanic rock had lodged itself in my pelvis and smouldered there. It was getting ready to seep forth its hot lava, stirring, rising up, ready for release. My fingernails began to lock on to his back, ready to clasp him to me, before he was taken away. The words on the page faded in and out of focus, then began to blaze into white light. I felt his teeth sink into my shoulder as our tempo increased and we began to race for the prize. Racing for it, out of reach, but blistering, blistering on the horizon. Oh such sweet, sweet, torment.

Then, suddenly, the light in the corridor went out and we were plunged into a deeper concealment. Our movements paused and I became aware of the entwined partnership of our heavy, aroused breathing. His outline began to return to my sight, illuminated gently by the light that fell through the window.

'It looks as if we're locked in until morning,' he whispered.

The library was ours! My body began to stir and undulate against his, encouraging his vibrant rhythms to take hold of me again.

'Good,' I said. I wanted to keep him inside.

The Artist's Model

Rosie Stefani

The Artist's Model

❧ ❧

'I'm going to take these canvases down to the workshop to be framed. I'll be about twenty minutes, OK?' Nick strode purposefully out through the swing doors, clutching the paintings to his chest protectively.

Ruby shivered slightly as his theatrical exit sent a waft of cool air into the studio, making goose-pimples rise on her exposed skin. It felt pleasant, a soothing touch under the burning gaze of the eyes trained intently on her. She shuddered visibly, and the silk robe fell off her shoulders to create a confusion of fabric next to her smooth curves as she reclined dreamily on the dais. She made a beautiful picture; her pale skin contrasted sharply with her shoulder-length auburn hair and the rich tones of the silks around her.

Most of the students had drifted away after the first hour or so and only three now remained, working diligently on their sketches as they tried to capture the elegance of her naked form. She scanned the faces of the trio, searching for a sign of recognition or appreciation as their eyes flickered nervously back and forth.

Her attention was drawn to the tall, blond youth with the classic good looks. With a modesty that conflicted with the brazen display of her body, she cast her eyes down to the expanse of naked flesh laid bare for his observance. His piercing blue eyes followed hers, an act of intimacy that aroused desires in her that she knew were risky to entertain but impossible to deny. She longed to move, to open her legs wide and invite him

281

in, but she held her pose with a cool professionalism that belied the persistent ache in her pussy.

For a brief moment she wondered whether it was the intensity of the silence within the high airy room that was fuelling the lascivious thoughts that were racing through her mind. But any doubts were soon dispelled as warm sensations radiated from her belly to indulge her flights of fantasy. It intrigued her to read the students' expressions; it gave her pleasure to imagine the wicked thoughts they were having about her whilst they sat so calm and controlled. They appeared intent on producing a competent piece of work, but at the same time trying to suppress the desires her blatant nudity aroused in them.

She wanted to communicate with them and let them know that she revelled in their attentions, that it excited her to have them study every inch of her body in such intimate detail. And without Nick's authoritative presence she felt the urge rising within her to make some kind of gesture, an expression of her arousal.

They had all watched mesmerised at the beginning of the class as Nick had suggested positions for her. Almost thoughtlessly, he had roughly pulled open the robe to reveal her full, soft breasts, swaying enticingly with the impulsiveness of his actions. Nick had smiled knowingly at her as he noticed that her nipples were firm and erect: it would be a challenging task for the art students to capture the way they jutted out provocatively. At that moment she had felt as if everyone in the room had guessed that she had touched herself while waiting in the ante-room. Her arousal had been evident and she recalled how, in a fit of wickedness, she had pinched her hard little nubs firmly through the silk gown while she had waited for Nick to summon her. Her cheeks had reddened, not with embarrassment but with the flush of excitement that had washed over her. The obvious pleasure she had derived from her body was plain for all to see.

It had been a highly erotic moment: her breasts being crudely exposed; disrobing in front of strangers; having her arms and legs carefully positioned. She had tossed her auburn hair coquettishly to accentuate the confidence she had in her sensuality.

Through what seemed to be endless hours, Nick had taken long, considered pauses as he set up the composition. Fussing and adjusting her arms and thighs and the line of the silks against her breasts, it was as though he enjoyed taunting the students by drawing their attention directly to her sexuality.

Finally, to her great relief, he had turned her on to her side with her arm supporting her head and her left leg bent at the knee, exaggerating the V where her thighs crossed. A line of dark, wispy curls peeked out cheekily, the only clue as to what she concealed between the warm creamy flesh.

Having been manhandled with such little regard for her sensibilities had stirred hidden longings within her, and to her shame she had felt herself glow when Nick took the liberty of slapping her bottom cheekily to let her know that he was done. This public chastisement had warmed her sex and, as she recalled the earlier events, the memory simply served to increase the ache in her pussy. She had posed with subtlety and yet had let them know that she was excited by her public exposure, and wanted to excite them too.

The over-head lamp cast deep shadows over her lily-white skin and, despite her audacity, she felt thankful that the heavy blinds had been drawn, shielding her from the muggy evening light. It was as if the concentrated lighting directly above her dramatised her presence and the importance of her desires. Illuminated under the spotlight she was there purely to be worshipped and adored.

The second youth smiled at her, his attention lingering obscenely as he brushed the dark tousled hair from his eyes so as to view her charms with greater clarity. He had the cheeky confidence of youth, but instinct told her that his attitude was a bluff. She knew she could bewitch him with the faintest smile and have him attend to her every whim, such was his undisguised attraction to her. On the other hand, the girl sitting next to him, clad in denim and tight, white T-shirt, had maintained a cool, detached presence throughout the session. It was as though the erotic tension was either beyond her perception or of no interest to her at all.

Ruby felt a need to draw her companions closer to her, a longing to have some physical contact and have them take command of her lewdly exposed body. Her breath came in short gasps as she struggled to maintain her composure. She tried vainly to distract herself, gazing at the sketches and paintings hung irregularly on the walls, but they merely reminded her of Nick and his imminent return. But even this sobering thought did nothing to quell her mischievous intentions: quite the opposite, in fact, which shocked her. She had basked in the students' undivided attention as they had scrutinised every inch of her, but the idea of dogmatic Nick discovering her as she played with his students had been overwhelming. It made her feel so very, very naughty.

The blond youth caught her eye. It was a lingering look that could have had many meanings, but in her fevered state Ruby chose to read it as lust, pure and simple. Situations, it seemed, had a way of taking control of themselves, and she took the opportunity to push the proceedings along a little further.

'Having trouble?' she asked, with breathless innocence, at last breaking the tense atmosphere that had lingered ominously in the studio.

'Just a little,' he stuttered, the words coming almost too quickly.

'Would it help if you could touch what you were trying to draw?' Ruby continued. He didn't seem offended by her suggestion. The youth looked across at his companions for reassurance before he cleared his throat to reply. 'Yes. Yes, I think it would.'

The atmosphere in the room swung wildly, almost from second to second: the tangible relief that contact had been made was quickly replaced by trepidation, anxiety and doubt.

The blond youth placed his drawing board neatly on the floor and rose to his feet. Despite his casual, baggy clothing it was obvious that his body was young and beautifully toned. He thoughtfully brushed the creases from his jogging bottoms as he approached the dais. It was an innocently polite gesture that Ruby noted with a sweet smile that promised much. The fluid movement of the jersey fabric accentuated the obvious bulge at his groin; his arousal confirmed that her lascivious intentions were reciprocated. The young man blushed as he noticed her attention drift to his crotch. His cock moved and stiffened under the heat of her gaze. Ruby relished the power that she held over him. She nodded for him to kneel down on the floor beside the dais.

He obeyed in silence. Tentatively, he raised his hand to her cheek and lightly brushed her soft skin. The first touch was electric: having waited so long for some physical contact Ruby could hardly bear the thought that he might take his hand away.

Languorously, she closed her eyes, which felt heavy with the plethora of emotions that raged through her.

She savoured the sensations as slowly, with the delicate touch of an artist, he traced a line down to her red lips. Her deft little tongue snaked out to pull in his fingers. She sucked them into the velvety warmth of her mouth, running her tongue around and around as if she were circling the head of his cock. Ruby felt her sex moisten as a surge of energy passed between them; the relentless ache that she longed to ease grew as she sucked hungrily. The youth groaned long and deep before he abruptly withdrew his fingers. His inexperience dictated that he wished to sample as much of her as he could before the situation overwhelmed them.

Through half-open eyes she watched as the youth's nimble fingers found their way to her breasts. His touch was feather-light but inquisitive, and he soon found the dark outline of her nipples, which were pouting for attention. Ruby sighed and pushed herself forward, urging him on. His dexterity inflamed her desire to be used, to have her body explored and teased to the point of climax and beyond.

'Pinch it. Watch it grow,' she panted, cupping her breast with her free hand to offer it to him further. The blond youth glanced back at his friends, as though he were unsure whether to continue and needed their permission to do so. The tousled-haired lad gave an almost imperceptible nod of assent. The girl, however, sat entranced, as if she could neither believe what she was seeing, nor how it made her feel.

'Go on,' Ruby urged, conscious that precious time was being wasted and that Nick might waltz in at any moment. So, with a shaking hand he squeezed the hard nub between his thumb and forefinger and pulled it out firmly. He turned it subtly between his fingers before he let it slip from his grasp. His eyes widened, fascinated by the throb and twitch of the nipple. Then he repeated the action, turning the hard little stone and tweaking it with more confidence, trying to define the line between pleasure and discomfort.

Ruby watched his expression change as a profusion of sensations flowed to her hungry pussy with his every touch. She wanted to teach him more, to show him how her body responded to his hands and how good he made her feel.

A low moan seeped through her lips as he ran his nimble

fingers around the doughy flesh, making the circles narrower until he tickled the dark skin around the hardened tips. Her breath caught in her throat, as if she were choking on the pleasure of anticipation, until he took the entire swell of her breast in his hands. He squeezed gently at first, as if to test how firm and ripe she was, and then harder, until she squirmed.

'Lower, go lower,' she gasped.

The young man duly obliged as if he could sense her emotions simply through touching her hot skin. His hands lingered for a while, kneading her soft belly and tickling the curls that peeped out from where her legs crossed. Without a word of encouragement, she parted her thighs to reveal her sex, hot and moist. Instinctively, the youth dipped his head to take a closer look and, gasping with appreciation, breathed in the warm, musky aroma.

Ruby's heart thumped wildly as she realised what was about to happen between them, and that Nick would soon return to find them engrossed in each other. What if some other member of staff or a student stumbled upon their devilment? The repercussions didn't bear thinking about. It seemed wrong to want to be found in such a compromising position, but the idea just made her want to be more daring. There was nothing to lose now: they had made the first moves and clarified their intentions. Sexual gratification was paramount; if they were caught, then so be it.

Without a second thought, she used her free arm to pull his head forcefully into her hungry sex. He began to move his tongue in languorous strokes, delving between the fleshy folds to taste her sweat honey. Ruby felt almost delirious as he lapped softly at her pussy. At last she had his total attention, and that of the others. She was no longer merely the erotic subject in an art class: distant, alluring, and untouchable. Now she was the sole object of their desire. All she craved now was for the three of them to attend to her, to worship and pleasure her beautiful body. She basked, radiant in an atmosphere heavy with sexual urgency.

Ruby wriggled and squirmed as the youth pressed his warm mouth to her clit, sucking with his lips to draw it out. He tugged gently, caressing the tortured little bud with his tongue until he let it slip, blowing lightly on it to sharpen its responsiveness.

Ruby scanned the room, the thought of their discovery ever

present and arousing in the spacious studio. The presence of the other two willing students sent a wave of wicked thoughts through her and it took all of her strength to compose herself to speak.

'Would you like to learn more about the body?' she breathed, directing the question at the tousled young man who sat mesmerised by the erotic vision before him. Ruby knew that he would not refuse. Despite his wide-eyed eagerness he was in need of enlightenment when it came to sexually pleasing a woman, and Ruby wanted to show him how. Tilting her head flirtatiously, she beckoned him to her.

'Sit behind me,' she whispered, her voice fading as her body quivered with the attention being lavished so generously on her sex. For a moment the young man hesitated, his exaggerated self-confidence failing him now that he was about to become an active participant.

'Behind me, here,' Ruby insisted, turning to lie on her back with her elbows supporting her weight, a position that allowed her to spread her legs even wider.

The student approached cautiously, almost as if he were stalling for time. But Ruby had been driven beyond patience and she arched her back and thrust her pelvis forward, demanding his attention. It was an audacious display, but designed to show the callow youth that she knew exactly what she wanted and was determined to get it.

Almost immediately he reacted, as if awoken from a dream, and he straddled the dais behind Ruby's back. He gently cradled her between his strong thighs, letting his arms come to rest just beneath her rib cage. Despite his loss of bravado, she could tell that he longed to grope and paw at her crudely. His restraint showed that he was ready to wait until Ruby gave him her full consent to enjoy her body.

His hands were coarse, and dampened with perspiration that soon mingled with the beads of sweat that tingled on her skin. He appeared, and felt, harder than his companion: a fine stubble on his youthful face tickled her neck as he kissed, ravenously. She took his hands in hers and placed them on her breasts. He squeezed and manipulated the downy flesh. Ruby guided his strong masculine hands until the heaviness that had made her breasts swell and flush so outrageously eased a little.

The blond youth watched them from where he knelt, momentarily distracted from his task. Impatiently Ruby pushed herself up at him, urging him to continue pleasuring her. At last she had both young men where she wanted them. Only the girl still sat inactive nervously watching the proceedings. Ruby knew that it wouldn't be long before the performance would inspire her to join in.

'Watch him lick me,' she instructed, certain that the girl would be unable to resist watching another woman's sex being licked and relished by her friend. The youth obediently held Ruby's fleshy lips open, glancing at the others as he dipped his tongue in to taste the sticky moisture. As he delved deeper, his fingers wandered over her pussy. Her sensitised bud throbbed as he flicked at it to stimulate the centre of her sexual being. Such attention was unbearable and she bit her lip painfully in an effort to stave off her climax for as long as possible.

It was then that he took her by surprise. Forcefully, he pushed his hands under her firm buttocks to tease her tight anus with his fingers, lubricated with her copious, sticky nectar. With only a little extra pressure he invaded the little mouth that flexed and twitched indignantly as he went in further. It was divine torture as his finger probed deeper, and he swiftly returned his tongue to fill her completely. Maybe the youth wasn't as green as she had first thought him to be.

Ruby revelled in her obscenely sprawled body, her legs wide open and two young men playing with her in such a dangerous situation. Her heart beat a persistent rhythm, so loudly that she felt sure the three students could hear it echo around the studio. Ruby indulged in her fevered rapture. She knew that it was selfish of her, but all she cared about at that moment was her own gratification.

She could feel the lad behind her press his hard cock, still restrained by his clothing, into the small of her back. He was attempting to ease the pressure in his loins by moving against her and so Ruby pushed back on to him. Sensuously she matched his movements with a hypnotic rhythm, encouraging him to massage her luxuriant breasts as she did. It was as much as she was prepared to do for him for the time being.

Her sensitive nipples brushed against his coarse palms sending darts of delight along her taut nerves. The sensations combined with the heat radiating from her slick bud, so beautifully taunted by the other youth, sending her ever closer to her orgasm.

Despite all the divine pleasures being lavished on her she felt a pressure welling inside her that demanded more forceful attention. It was an unrelenting pressure, made all the more urgent by Nick's imminent return.

For the first time Ruby felt a flash of panic and a momentary loss of nerve. Yet, almost as soon as it began, it was tempered by her desire to reach her climax when, and only when, she was ready. If they were going to be caught then they may as well be found submitting totally to their desires and not trying hurriedly to cover themselves, with silly excuses and embarrassed faces.

In the haze of her indulgence Ruby hadn't paid the girl that much attention, but now she was ready for another pair of willing hands to help drive her beyond her sexual limits. She was therefore rather taken aback when she turned to face the girl: the little minx had unzipped her jeans and cheekily slid her hand into her white knickers. From the movements she made it was clear that she had crooked her finger and was leisurely caressing her hole as she watched them play. After the initial surprise Ruby smiled broadly, wallowing in the attentions of her male servants and excited that the girl had derived such a sexual thrill from watching her body being explored.

'I want to be fucked,' Ruby panted. The girl looked a little surprised that the command had been directed at her. However, Ruby knew that for all their youthful exuberance the boys would not be able to satisfy her. She didn't care whether it was a cock that fucked her or not, just as long as she was fucked.

The girl continued to touch herself, slowly and deliberately, her expression changing from confusion to mischief. Ruby felt driven to the point of distraction. She was in charge, she was the director of the proceedings. It was her sexual desires that were the most important for the moment. What was going on in this young girl's imagination?

'I want to be filled,' Ruby gasped desperately, momentarily fearful that the girl might not be as sweet as she appeared. Maybe she had other things in mind, Ruby fretted, as she noticed some of the more brutal objects lying around the studio that the girl could choose to fuck her with.

Then, slowly and with great composure, the girl emerged from her reverie and withdrew her hand from the comforting warmth of her pussy to reach into her bag. With a dramatic flourish she pulled out a long, slender can of hairspray. It was perfect, thought Ruby. Wide enough to stretch her, long enough to fill her and hard enough to satisfy her hunger. The bottom edge was rounded – ideal for sliding into the moist recess of her sex and Ruby nodded her appreciation. A fusion of relief and power washed over her now that she had all three students under her spell.

The girl glanced back at the door before she took her place between Ruby's splayed legs. The blonde youth shuffled to one side to let her in; he was reluctant to give up his position and Ruby could sense his disappointment. She held her hand out to pull him closer to her.

'I said that I wanted to be filled,' she said, 'and that means everywhere.'

It took a moment for the youth to fully comprehend what she meant, but when the realisation dawned on him it was with one swift movement that he freed his straining cock and offered it to her mouth. Her lips slid effortlessly around the taut, velvet-soft head and along his length, her tongue pulling it in as she licked and sucked wildly. At the same instant the girl brought the can between Ruby's legs. It brushed against her thighs and made her gasp sharply as the cold metal sent a chill through her, the shock increasing the pace at which her mouth fucked the erect cock.

The girl pressed the can against Ruby's glistening sex lips and watched avidly. It slid up with ease, almost as if Ruby was sucking it up inside her, just as she was doing with the youth's sweet little prick. Ruby struggled for breath as the coldness filled her; the girl was studiously increasing the pressure to force in the can until only the top of the cap was visible. Ruby arched and twisted madly, the cool metal soon absorbing the heat from the hot flesh that embraced it. The girl eased the can out with one long twisting movement and then, almost brutally, pushed it back up inside her. The next thrust combined with a further intrusion, as the girl impudently licked a finger and teased it into the tight, reddened mouth between her buttocks. Confidently she timed the thrusts so that the sensations doubled in intensity, and magnified Ruby's blissful agony.

Ruby's mind was flooded with erotic imagery; the thought that Nick might walk in at any point fuelling the urgency with which she gyrated her hips and thrust out her chest for the second young man to tug at her nipples. The rhythmic pumping increased in pace as the three students filled and pleasured her. Roughly, the blond youth took Ruby's head in his hands and pulled her full on to his cock so that it tickled the back of her throat. Events were now out of their control. They were, all four of them, slaves to their passion.

The way her body and desires had worked such magic on her three attendants, to the point where all they cared about was pleasure, was enough to push her to the very apex of her orgasm. She could barely control her beautifully tormented body. An overwhelming surge of heat in her belly spread to ignite every nerve ending that ran through her. The sensations ebbed and flowed until they reached a crescendo, and she felt as though she would scream with the intensity of the pleasure. She could hardly bear the ministrations of her companions, as every touch almost burnt her sensitised skin.

And then she heard footsteps. The slow, heavy thump of Nick's boots on the tiled corridor. She tried to ignore it. She hoped desperately that it was her imagination playing tricks on her. But the sound grew closer until the entangled quartet were distracted from their tasks and shot startled glances at each other. The double doors swung open with dramatic force . . .

'Nick. Oh, Nick.' Ruby's orgasm rioted through her sweat-drenched body as she fell back on to the bed. She smiled in a hazy glow of satisfaction, her desires sated after their energetic lovemaking. The sex had been passionate and frantic as Nick had insisted that she indulge herself totally and submit to her fantasies.

He lay down beside her and nestled his face at her neck, kissing her tenderly as he sighed. 'That was amazing, darling. I've never known you so daring, adventurous even.' He raised his hand and lovingly brushed the hair from her face before he continued. 'I can't wait until tomorrow. Just knowing that I'm the only one to enjoy the delights you have to offer, well, I don't know if I'll be able to keep my hands off you.' He laughed, almost as if he were unsure whether he actually meant it or not.

Ruby smiled as she returned his kisses, her body drained of energy and emotion but somehow eager for more.

'I hope that you're not nervous about standing in for Lucy tomorrow?' he asked. 'I mean, I wouldn't want you to do something that you weren't comfortable with, sweetheart. I didn't mean to pressure you.' Nick sounded concerned, but he had no need to be: Ruby was a determined and self-assured woman. After all, it was Nick who had encouraged her wild flights of fantasy: whether she shared them with him or not was another matter.

Ruby turned to look straight at him and gave a deliciously naughty smile. Being stripped naked in front of his class, having him position her with everyone watching and enjoying her beautiful body, as her breasts swelled and her excitement grew: why should that make her nervous? Turned on, aroused or insatiable were more appropriate words. Ruby felt the pressure return to her pussy and the desperate need for the ache to be eased.

'No. I'm not nervous any more,' she assured him. 'In fact I'm positively looking forward to it.'

BLACK LACE NEW BOOKS

Published in November

THE STRANGER
Portia Da Costa

When a confused and mysterious young man stumbles into the life of the recently widowed Claudia, he becomes the catalyst that reignites her sleeping sensuality. But is the wistful and angelic Paul really as innocent as he looks or is he an accomplished trickster with a dark and depraved agenda? As an erotic obsession flowers between Paul and Claudia, his true identity no longer seems to matter.

ISBN 0 352 33211 5

ELENA'S DESTINY
Lisette Allen

The gentle convent-bred Elena, awakened to the joys of forbidden passion by the masterful knight Aimery le Sabrenn, has been forcibly separated from him by war. Although he still captivates Elena with his powerful masculinity, Aimery is no longer hers. She must fight a desperate battle for his affections with two formidable opponents: a wanton young heiress and his scheming former mistress, Isobel. Dangerous games of love and lust are played out amidst the increasing tension of a merciless siege.

ISBN 0 352 33218 2

Published in December

LAKE OF LOST LOVE
Mercedes Kelly

Princess Angeline lives on a paradise island in the South Seas. She has a life of sensual fulfilment which she shares with her hedonistic friends. When her husband's gorgeous young manservant, Adam, is kidnapped and taken to nearby Monkey Island, Angeline sets about planning his rescue. Adam is being held captive by The Powerful One – a woman of superhuman desires – who is using him as her sex slave. Can Angeline confront this fearful female and return Adam to the Île de Paradis?

ISBN 0 352 33220 4

CONTEST OF WILLS
Louisa Francis

Sydney, Australia – the late 1870s. Vivacious young Melanie marries a man old enough to be her grandfather. On a trip to England, their journey is cut short by his sudden death. Melanie inherits his entire fortune unaware that her late husband has a grandson in England who is planning to contest the will. The louche and hedonistic Ric Lidell and his promiscuous half-sister travel to Sydney in a bid to get their hands on the money. Concealing his true identity from Melanie, Ric uses his satanic good looks to try and charm her. But other suitors have designs on the highly-sexed young widow. Who will win Melanie's heart and their way to her fortune?

ISBN 0 352 33223 9

SUGAR AND SPICE
A Black Lace short story anthology
£6.99

This is the long-awaited first collection of original Black Lace short stories. The book contains 20 unique and arousing tales guaranteed to excite. With contributions from female authors from Europe, Australia and America, this compendium provides a variety of settings and themes. Explicitly sexual and highly entertaining, *Sugar and Spice* is a kaleidoscope of female fantasy. Only the most erotic stories get into Black Lace anthologies.

ISBN 0 352 33227 1

To be published in January

UNHALLOWED RITES
Martine Marquand

Allegra Vitali is bored with life in her guardian's Venetian palazzo until the day sexual curiosity draws her to look at the depraved illustrations he keeps in his private chamber. She tries to deny her new passion for flesh by submitting to the life of a nun. The strange order of the Convent of Santa Agnetha provides new tests and new temptations, encouraging her to perform ritual acts with men and women who inhabit the strange, cloistered world.

ISBN 0 352 33222 0

BY ANY MEANS
Cheryl Mildenhall

Francesca, Veronique and Taran are partners in Falconer Associates, a London-based advertising agency. The three women are good friends and they're not averse to taking their pleasure with certain male employees. When they put in a bid to win a design account for Fast Track sportswear they are pitched against the notorious Oscar Rage who will stop at nothing to get what he wants. Despite Francesca's efforts to resist Oscar's arrogant charm, she finds him impossible to ignore.

ISBN 0 352 33221 1

If you would like a complete list of plot summaries of Black Lace titles, please fill out the questionnaire overleaf or send a stamped addressed envelope to:-

Black Lace, 332 Ladbroke Grove, London W10 5AH

BLACK LACE BACKLIST

All books are priced £4.99 unless another price is given.

BLUE HOTEL	Cherri Pickford ISBN 0 352 32858 4	☐
CASSANDRA'S CONFLICT	Fredrica Alleyn ISBN 0 352 32859 2	☐
THE CAPTIVE FLESH	Cleo Cordell ISBN 0 352 32872 X	☐
PLEASURE HUNT	Sophie Danson ISBN 0 352 32880 0	☐
OUTLANDIA	Georgia Angelis ISBN 0 352 32883 5	☐
BLACK ORCHID	Roxanne Carr ISBN 0 352 32888 6	☐
ODALISQUE	Fleur Reynolds ISBN 0 352 32887 8	☐
THE SENSES BEJEWELLED	Cleo Cordell ISBN 0 352 32904 1	☐
VIRTUOSO	Katrina Vincenzi ISBN 0 352 32907 6	☐
FIONA'S FATE	Fredrica Alleyn ISBN 0 352 32913 0	☐
HANDMAIDEN OF PALMYRA	Fleur Reynolds ISBN 0 352 32919 X	☐
THE SILKEN CAGE	Sophie Danson ISBN 0 352 32928 9	☐
THE GIFT OF SHAME	Sarah Hope-Walker ISBN 0 352 32935 1	☐
SUMMER OF ENLIGHTENMENT	Cheryl Mildenhall ISBN 0 352 32937 8	☐
A BOUQUET OF BLACK ORCHIDS	Roxanne Carr ISBN 0 352 32939 4	☐
JULIET RISING	Cleo Cordell ISBN 0 352 32938 6	☐

---------- ✂ ----------------------------

Please send me the books I have ticked above.

Name   ....

Address ....

....

....

.... Post Code   ....

Send to: Cash Sales, Black Lace Books, 332 Ladbroke Grove, London W10 5AH.

Please enclose a cheque or postal order, made payable to **Virgin Publishing Ltd**, to the value of the books you have ordered plus postage and packing costs as follows:

   UK and BFPO – £1.00 for the first book, 50p for each subsequent book.

   Overseas (including Republic of Ireland) – £2.00 for the first book, £1.00 each subsequent book.

If you would prefer to pay by VISA or ACCESS/ MASTERCARD, please write your card number and expiry date here:

....

Please allow up to 28 days for delivery.

Signature   ....

---------- ✂ ----------------------------

WE NEED YOUR HELP . . .
to plan the future of women's erotic fiction –

– and no stamp required!

Yours are the only opinions that matter.

Black Lace is the first series of books devoted to erotic fiction by women for women.

We intend to keep providing the best-written, sexiest books you can buy. And we'd appreciate your help and valued opinion of the books so far. Tell us what you want to read.

THE BLACK LACE QUESTIONNAIRE

SECTION ONE: ABOUT YOU

1.1 Sex (*we presume you are female, but so as not to discriminate*)
Are you?
      Male   ☐
      Female   ☐

1.2 Age
      under 21   ☐   21–30   ☐
      31–40   ☐   41–50   ☐
      51–60   ☐   over 60   ☐

1.3 At what age did you leave full-time education?
      still in education   ☐   16 or younger   ☐
      17–19   ☐   20 or older   ☐

1.4 Occupation _____

1.5 Annual household income
- under £10,000 ☐ £10–£20,000 ☐
- £20–£30,000 ☐ £30–£40,000 ☐
- over £40,000 ☐

1.6 We are perfectly happy for you to remain anonymous; but if you would like to receive information on other publications available, please insert your name and address

_____

_____

_____

_____

SECTION TWO: ABOUT BUYING BLACK LACE BOOKS

2.1 How did you acquire this copy of *Sugar and Spice*?
- I bought it myself ☐ My partner bought it ☐
- I borrowed/found it ☐

2.2 How did you find out about Black Lace books?
- I saw them in a shop ☐
- I saw them advertised in a magazine ☐
- I saw the London Underground posters ☐
- I read about them in _____
- Other _____

2.3 Please tick the following statements you agree with:
- I would be less embarrassed about buying Black Lace books if the cover pictures were less explicit ☐
- I think that in general the pictures on Black Lace books are about right ☐
- I think Black Lace cover pictures should be as explicit as possible ☐

2.4 Would you read a Black Lace book in a public place – on a train for instance?
- Yes ☐ No ☐

SECTION THREE: ABOUT THIS BLACK LACE BOOK

3.1 Do you think the sex content in this book is:
    Too much   ☐   About right   ☐
    Not enough   ☐

3.2 Do you think the writing style in this book is:
    Too unreal/escapist   ☐   About right   ☐
    Too down to earth   ☐

3.3 Do you think the story in this book is:
    Too complicated   ☐   About right   ☐
    Too boring/simple   ☐

3.4 Do you think the cover of this book is:
    Too explicit   ☐   About right   ☐
    Not explicit enough   ☐

Here's a space for any other comments:

SECTION FOUR: ABOUT OTHER BLACK LACE BOOKS

4.1 How many Black Lace books have you read?   ☐

4.2 If more than one, which one did you prefer?

4.3 Why?

SECTION FIVE: ABOUT YOUR IDEAL EROTIC NOVEL

We want to publish the books you want to read – so this is your chance to tell us exactly what your ideal erotic novel would be like.

5.1   Using a scale of 1 to 5 (1 = no interest at all, 5 = your ideal), please rate the following possible settings for an erotic novel:

Medieval/barbarian/sword 'n' sorcery ☐
Renaissance/Elizabethan/Restoration ☐
Victorian/Edwardian ☐
1920s & 1930s – the Jazz Age ☐
Present day ☐
Future/Science Fiction ☐

5.2   Using the same scale of 1 to 5, please rate the following themes you may find in an erotic novel:

Submissive male/dominant female ☐
Submissive female/dominant male ☐
Lesbianism ☐
Bondage/fetishism ☐
Romantic love ☐
Experimental sex e.g. anal/watersports/sex toys ☐
Gay male sex ☐
Group sex ☐

Using the same scale of 1 to 5, please rate the following styles in which an erotic novel could be written:

Realistic, down to earth, set in real life ☐
Escapist fantasy, but just about believable ☐
Completely unreal, impressionistic, dreamlike ☐

5.3   Would you prefer your ideal erotic novel to be written from the viewpoint of the main male characters or the main female characters?

Male ☐   Female ☐
Both ☐

5.4 What would your ideal Black Lace heroine be like? Tick as many as you like:

Dominant	☐	Glamorous	☐
Extroverted	☐	Contemporary	☐
Independent	☐	Bisexual	☐
Adventurous	☐	Naïve	☐
Intellectual	☐	Introverted	☐
Professional	☐	Kinky	☐
Submissive	☐	Anything else?	☐
Ordinary	☐	_____	

5.5 What would your ideal male lead character be like? Again, tick as many as you like:

Rugged	☐		
Athletic	☐	Caring	☐
Sophisticated	☐	Cruel	☐
Retiring	☐	Debonair	☐
Outdoor-type	☐	Naïve	☐
Executive-type	☐	Intellectual	☐
Ordinary	☐	Professional	☐
Kinky	☐	Romantic	☐
Hunky	☐		
Sexually dominant	☐	Anything else?	☐
Sexually submissive	☐	_____	

5.6 Is there one particular setting or subject matter that your ideal erotic novel would contain?

_____

SECTION SIX: LAST WORDS

6.1 What do you like best about Black Lace books?

_____

6.2 What do you most dislike about Black Lace books?

_____

6.3 In what way, if any, would you like to change Black Lace covers?

_____

6.4 Here's a space for any other comments:

_____

_____

_____

_____

_____

Thank you for completing this questionnaire. Now tear it out of the book – carefully! – put it in an envelope and send it to:

Black Lace
FREEPOST
London
W10 5BR

No stamp is required if you are resident in the U.K.